Praise for
HAPPILY EVER AFTERS

An Indie Next Pick

"*Happily Ever Afters* is the warm, nerdy, big-hearted rom-com of my dreams and I dare you to read it without grinning your face off." —BECKY ALBERTALLI, bestselling author of *Simon vs the Homo Sapiens Agenda*

"*Happily Ever Afters* is sweet, smart, and utterly charming. Following Tessa as she navigates friendship, romance, and family dynamics was an absolute joy." —BRANDY COLBERT, author of *The Voting Booth*

"*Happily Ever Afters* put a smile on my face from beginning to end. Elise Bryant's charmer of a debut is an unapologetic love letter to every Black and brown girl who's ever dared to imagine herself at the center of her favorite romance. My heart is full knowing young romance lovers will get to read about a heroine like Tessa." —ADRIANA HERRERA, author of *American Dreamer*

"This well-written, page-turning romance is packed with smart dialogue, powerful insights, and a lovable cast of characters. Highly recommended for all high school libraries." —*SLJ* (starred review)

D0963446

"Caught between pursuing a tale-worthy love and slowly losing herself, Tessa must learn to tell a story that's uniquely hers. Debut author Bryant creates a wholly genuine protagonist in Tessa; readers will surely root for her as she finds her voice."
—*PUBLISHERS WEEKLY* (starred review)

"Nimbly blends bubbly, will-they-won't-they teen romance with a frank look at issues ranging from impostor syndrome and identity to race and mental health. Bryant treats the tough stuff with nuance and compassion through conversations among a richly drawn cast of diverse and appealing characters."
—BOOKPAGE (starred review)

"A captivating, complicated, angsty, and beautiful love story of a teenage girl trying to grow into and embrace herself. For romantics of all ages, especially those who seldom see themselves in lead roles." —*KIRKUS REVIEWS*

"Bryant's debut will charm readers from the start. . . . While skillfully and realistically portraying Tessa's many challenges, Bryant never loses sight of the love story at the book's heart. Hand to fans of Jenny Han's *To All the Boys I've Loved Before* or Maurene Goo's *I Believe in a Thing Called Love*." —ALA *BOOKLIST*

HAPPILY *EVER* AFTERS

ELISE BRYANT

BALZER + BRAY
An Imprint of HarperCollins*Publishers*

Also by Elise Bryant
One True Loves

Balzer + Bray is an imprint of HarperCollins Publishers.

Happily Ever Afters
Copyright © 2021 by Elise Bryant
Interior emojis copyright © 2021 by Cosmic_Dreams / Shutterstock

ISBN 978-0-06-298284-1

Typography by Jessie Gang
21 22 23 24 25 PC/LSCH 10 9 8 7 6 5 4 3 2 1

First paperback edition, 2021

To Bryan,

"(God Must Have Spent) A Little More Time on You"

CHAPTER ONE

The doorbell rings, and I ignore it.

I'm right in the middle of writing an important scene. Tallulah and Thomas have found shelter from the rain, thanks to a conveniently located abandoned cabin, and they're standing face-to-face, so close there's an electric charge between the tips of their noses. And when he reaches up to pluck an eyelash off her cheek and tells her to make a wish, it's clear from the urgency of her sigh and the longing in her dark brown eyes that the only thing she's wishing for is him.

It's one of those swoony declaration-of-love moments, like something you see in those ancient movies they always play Sundays on TNT. But instead of that pale girl with the red hair, my protagonist has brown skin and a fro, and she's about to get her happily ever after.

Except she's not, because the Doorbell Ringer is still at it.

The only people who have come over in the weeks since

we've moved south to Long Beach have been crabby Mrs. Hutchinson from next door and two Mormon missionaries in starched white shirts and skinny ties.

I'm not going to stop the flow of words pouring out of me for them.

The doorbell rings again, though, followed by a swift knock that's barely audible over Miles's television blaring from the back of the house. My brother, the traitor, is on his second viewing of his Dream Zone DVD, and the person outside can probably hear it too, a sure sign that someone is home.

Enter the Dream Zone, the documentary detailing the roots and rise to stardom of the now very much defunct boy band, is the only reason we have a clunky player anymore, even though Mom went all Marie Kondo on the rest of the disks in the move. It's Miles's most precious possession. He treats the DVD and its accompanying booklet like some sort of sacred texts.

I tell myself that if it rings one more time, I'll get up. If it's really important—more important than Mrs. Hutchinson's concerns about the jacaranda tree between our houses or, you know, saving our souls—whoever's out there will try at least once more. I cross my fingers and wait one moment. And then another. But there's nothing except the nasal crooning blasting from the other room.

I'm in the clear.

Thomas blows the eyelash away, but his lips stay open, cradling the words that Tallulah has been longing to hear. And just when he's about to reveal what's written in his heart, he's interrupted by . . . a bubble.

A white bubble pops up on the side of my draft in Google Docs, followed by a few more in quick succession.

Why are you working on this one?

Collette needs another chapter

TESSA JOHNSON YOU PROMISED!

That kind of cliffhanger should be illegal don't make me report you

I know you're on here!!!!!!!! I can see your cursor

Caroline's cheese-face avatar accompanies each comment, a stark contrast to their stalker-y vibe, and a few seconds later, my phone starts buzzing.

So I guess no one wants me to write today . . . at least not what *I* want to write.

"Did you finish the chapter?" she asks as soon as I answer, skipping any sort of greeting, as usual.

I've known Caroline Tibayan since we were six, the only two brown girls in Ms. Brentwood's first grade class. When Jesse Fitzgerald told me I was ugly because I had skin the color of poo, Caroline hauled off and socked him in the nose. Lola, her grandmother, swatted her behind with one of her sandals when she got home that day, but Caroline still maintains that it was worth it. We've been best friends ever since.

"Monitoring my internet activity? Really? That's like something out of a Lifetime movie." I laugh. "Also, hi. That's usually how people start a conversation."

"Okay, yeah, hi. But can you blame me? You left off on such a cliffhanger, and then nothing for days? You're a monster!"

"And you're dramatic."

"Me, dramatic?" I can almost see her through the phone, crowded on her tiny twin bed in her tiny room, her long black hair splayed over the striped comforter. Lola took the second bedroom when she moved in with Caroline and her parents, so they converted the pantry into a space for Caroline. "You're the one who ended the chapter with Jasper standing outside Colette's window, professing his undying love, his purple hair freakin' ILLUMINATED in the soft glow of the streetlamp! TOTALLY unaware of the fact that Colette is macking on Jack in there at that very moment! C'mon! I need to know what happens now!"

"Sorry! I've been busy."

"With Tallulah?"

"Yep." Tallulah's the main character in my other work in progress—a swoony story about a mousy Black girl with a fluffy fro and Thomas, the hipster singer-songwriter with moody eyes and dark hair and deliciously broad shoulders, who moves to town and makes her his muse.

"Well, send me that one at least." She sighs as if it's a consolation prize. "And have they finally kissed yet? All the pining and googly eyes are getting to be a bit much. I need some action!

They're barely on base zero point five. Not going to lie, Colette is *so* much more interesting."

I smile and shake my head. "I can't help where the inspiration takes me, *Colette*."

"Your audience is waiting, *Tallulah*."

By my "audience," she means herself. She's my biggest fan . . . and my only fan. But I'm not complaining, because that's just the way I like it. I don't write for other people. I write for me and Caroline.

The stories have always come easy to me. My mom said I started writing stories down as early as kindergarten, but I was secretive even then, keeping whatever notebook I was working in safe under my pillow. The subject matter changed as I got older, the what-ifs transferring to what would happen if Harry ended up with Hermione instead? And then what would happen if Harry ended up with *me*? I felt embarrassed about the stories, but they also made me feel warm inside, and seen. It was empowering to create a world in which I was the center, the prize, the one desired.

Caroline talked her way into reading through one of my notebooks eventually. I expected her to laugh, but instead she praised me as a romantic genius and asked me to write her into a story too. (She always had a thing for Ron.) And she told me there was a word for what I was doing—fan fiction. That made me feel less embarrassed about my stories. At least I wasn't crazy or something. Other people were doing this too.

Soon I graduated from Harry and Ron to Edward and Jacob to members of our favorite boy band, Dream Zone. (Because *okay*, Miles likes Dream Zone because I liked Dream Zone. A long, LONG time ago. But I try to keep that shameful secret on the down low.)

I kept thinking the stories were something we would outgrow, like Dream Zone, but they never stopped. They just became about our relationships with my own made-up boys instead of someone else's. Like, fan fiction of our own lives. It wasn't like we could go to a bookstore and find many fluffy love stories with girls who looked like us in them.

Now that I've moved, I share my stories with Caroline through Google, instead of passing her my beat-up laptop at lunch. I act exasperated, but I'm also secretly happy she hasn't stopped asking. That, at least, this part of our relationship has stayed the same.

"Wait, what is that banging?" Caroline asks, "I don't think that's on my end."

I pull the phone away from my ear and listen. At first I think it's the fast drumbeat of Dream Zone's "Love Like Whoa." But no, that's a knock. A loud one. And it's followed by a faint but shrill "I know you're in there!"

The Doorbell Ringer is back, or maybe they never left. I *guess* I said I would answer on the third try. . . .

"Hey, Caroline, I gotta go."

"Okay, but tonight I better get—" The doorbell rings two

more times in quick succession, drowning out the rest of her demand.

Are you kidding me?

I sigh, close my laptop, and say a silent prayer that I won't lose the faint flicker of inspiration I was chasing, that Tallulah and Thomas's first kiss will wait. The *baby, baby, baby*s float in from Miles's TV as I maneuver around the boxes still littering what will eventually be the living room. He's singing along now, and he's turned it up even more—way past the fifteen volume limit that Mom has written on two Post-its next to the set.

The bell goes off again, just as I'm opening the door.

"Jesus Christ, have some patience!"

It comes out meaner than I planned, and my cheeks immediately redden when I see Mrs. Hutchinson there, reeling back like she's scared for her life. She clutches her pilled hunter-green coat around herself, even though it's a million degrees outside. "Sorry," I say, quieter. "Just . . . I was on my way."

I'm usually better at regulating my tone. I mean, I have to be. Because one note too loud, too aggressive, and I'm labeled as an angry Black girl forever. I can tell that's already what Mrs. Hutchinson thinks of me. But my apology seems to appease her enough for her stricken look to transform into her signature scowl.

"If you haven't memorized your address yet, you need to write it down." Her voice sounds like it's scraping the roof of her mouth, and she clenches her cheeks when she talks, as if she's passing something back from one side to the other. "I really shouldn't have to walk this over to you."

She holds out a pizza box and tries to push it into my arms, but I step back.

"I'm sorry, Mrs. Hutchinson, but that's not ours."

"Yes, it is." She says it like she's having to explain that the sky is blue.

"We didn't order anything," I insist, shaking my head.

"Yes, you did." She steps closer to me, so I can smell her stale, minty breath. Her slipper-clad feet are right on the door-jamb. "I called Domino's because the young man who delivered it was no help . . . basically threw it at me! They said it was ordered by someone named Johnson."

Her watery blue eyes drift to a sign hanging above the front door. My dad got it made by this lady who works in his office and operates an Etsy shop on the side. THE JOHNSON'S. He was so proud that I didn't have the heart to tell him the apostrophe was wrong.

"I don't know what to tell you, Mrs. Hutchinson. It's just me and my brother home, and neither of us—"

I'm interrupted by an explosion of laughter rising above the piano and synthesizer of Dream Zone's most popular ballad.

Miles's laugh is difficult to pin down. It's kind of like a sharp chord on the far right side of the piano, played by a little kid with no training but a lot of enthusiasm. It's also reminiscent of that squeal a car makes when someone slams hard on their brakes to narrowly avoid a collision. His laugh is equal parts joyful and jarring.

And right now, it's making Mrs. Hutchinson stretch her neck and step even closer, trying to figure out what's going on.

I know exactly what's going on.

We only have one landline in the house, tucked away in my parents' room, but I unplugged that this morning, like I usually do when I'm home alone watching Miles. The only other options are my phone or my computer, which can make calls when it's connected to WiFi. He could have gotten to either when I went to the bathroom a little while ago.

Mrs. Hutchinson's frown lines, which were already cavernous before, deepen further. "Now what exactly are you two trying to play here, young lady? What is this?"

"Uh, I—" Miles's gleeful laughs cut me off again, which makes her whole face turn red.

"Is this supposed to be funny?!" Her voice was already loud, but it's ear-piercing now. I try to scan the block to see if anyone is outside watching us, but she shifts her body into my view. "Is this the kind of reputation you want to get? Playing tricks on the neighbors? I can tell you right now, this . . . this . . . foolishness isn't taken too kindly around here!"

A reputation is actually the last thing that I want. But I can already see it now: her spreading around the neighborhood that we're trouble—if they can't already hear her hollering it now. Two weeks in, and already our chance to be normal is shot. I can feel my chest get tight and my breath start to speed up at the thought. My parents are going to be upset, and of course it'll be my fault. I'm supposed to be watching Miles, like I have been for most of the summer, while my parents settle in at their new jobs. I *was* watching him. But not close enough, apparently.

"Excuse me, Mrs. Hutchinson." A kind voice cuts through my spiraling thoughts. "Did my pizza accidentally get sent to your house?"

A guy steps up onto the porch, seemingly from nowhere. He looks around my age, with floppy golden hair that's overdue for a haircut, fair skin noticeably lacking the default SoCal tan, and big green eyes. His faded red Hawaiian shirt could be an ironic choice on someone else—one of those fake vintage pieces that they sell for a million dollars at Urban Outfitters— but matched with his cargo shorts, it's just . . . unfortunate.

Who is this guy?

Mrs. Hutchinson seems to recognize him, and his presence makes her bring her voice back down to a reasonable volume. "This isn't yours."

"Um, actually, I think it is?" Hawaiian Shirt's eyes flick to me, and then he tries it again. "It is mine. I'm sorry for the mix-up."

Mrs. Hutchinson considers both of us, moving that nonexistent thing between her cheeks again. Finally she smacks her thin lips together. "Well, whoever this belongs to owes me some money. The young man from Domino's told me I had to pay for it or he'd report me to the manager. Honestly! Like I'm some sort of criminal."

I turn to get my wallet from the entryway, but Hawaiian Shirt is faster than me, slipping a twenty into Mrs. Hutchinson's hand and taking the box out of her arms. She glares at me one last time before walking across the lawn back to her house, grumbling as she goes. Hawaiian Shirt stays planted on our porch, though.

"Thank you for that," I say quickly. "I'll pay you back—"

"It's okay." He cuts me off, waving his hand. "I just wanted to, I don't know, help? I saw what was happening across the street. And I know you're new, and Mrs. Hutchinson . . . she can be a lot. That's where I live, by the way. Across the street." Miles's maniacal giggles start again inside (because of course they do), and Hawaiian Shirt's eyebrows press together. "Is that . . . your brother?"

"Yeah, he did this." I nod too much. While my breathing is starting to slow down, I can feel my neck flaming, the familiar anxiety settling in. I want to shut the door and be done with this interaction, but the words keep coming out. "The Pizza Hut in Roseville—that's where we lived before—they literally started just hanging up whenever they saw our number on caller ID, which really sucked when we actually did want to order a pizza." I try to laugh, but it comes out hollow.

"Well, you should tell him to probably pick a different target for his prank next time." Hawaiian Shirt rubs the side of his face and looks at the ground. "Or, I don't know, maybe not do pranks at all?"

There's no judgment in his voice, but I feel the need to explain. "Thank you. And it's not like that . . . like what you think it is. I mean, it is, but it's different."

"Okay," Hawaiian Shirt says, cocking his head to the side in confusion. I can't blame him. I'm not making sense.

"It's just that . . . my brother. Miles. He has disabilities." The explanation is as familiar to me as breathing or blinking; I've said it so many times before. "This is one of the things he does . . . makes calls he shouldn't. I'm just glad he didn't prank call the cops again."

The thought of that makes me shudder, especially here in this new city where our neighbors don't know us, know Miles.

"Okay," Hawaiian Shirt says again, nodding his head now. He leans into the doorway, close enough to give me a whiff of the salty, melted cheese, and calls out, "Hello, Miles!"

Miles doesn't answer. But the crooning of Dream Zone stops, and I can hear the rustling of him moving around the room—probably arranging the remote just so and putting the DVD case in its specific place on the shelf. He's coming to survey the damage.

"Well, thank you. Again. And it won't happen again. Promise. Really, so sorry." I'm talking fast, trying to get this guy out of here before Miles makes his way to the door. It's not like I'm embarrassed by my brother. I'm not. But I don't want to deal with a whole big thing right now, especially because my heart's still racing from the scene with Mrs. Hutchinson.

I give him my best apologetic smile and try to shut the door, but he stops me with the pizza box. "I'm Sam."

"Um, okay." I blink at him, and he holds out his pizza-free hand to shake mine. Right, now it's my turn. "Tessa."

"Nice to meet you, Tessa," Hawaiian Shirt Sam says, shifting from one foot to the other. He clearly has something more to say, and I wish he'd just get on with it because I need to go.

"Uh . . . I talked to your mom a few days ago."

Of course he did. Mom talks to everyone and always ends up telling whoever it is too much information. The cashier at the Trader Joe's by our old house knew all about the emergency tonsillectomy I had when I was two, Dad's strained relationship with Grandma Edith, and my mom's dream to buy an Airstream trailer one day. I wonder what she told Hawaiian Shirt Sam. Apparently not my name. "Yeah?"

"Well, she was talking to my mom, and she said you were going to Chrysalis Academy. That you're, uh, a writer? I'm transferring there too. So yeah . . . that's pretty cool." He smiles, and only the right side of his mouth goes up, revealing a deep dimple. His eyes get all crinkly, little half-moons under his thick blond brows. It's a nice smile. Almost makes me forget the cargo shorts.

And okay, now I want to ask him more, like what conservatory he's in or if he knows what to expect tomorrow on our first day at the art school. Thoughts of the school have taken over my brain for the entire summer—that, and the fact that I'll be able to write every day and be around people who do what I do, but better. The whole thing is a thrilling, terrifying unknown for me at this point, and it would be nice to have someone to share it with. But I also hear Miles's footsteps now, shuffling toward the door. And I've already hit my peak tolerance for chaos today.

"Yeah, cool. So we'll see each other at school then. Sorry about the pizza. Bye!" I say it quickly and too loud, shutting the door on Hawaiian Shirt Sam's puzzled face. It slams closed, harder than I intended, just as Miles is walking up behind me, his ringing hearing aids announcing his presence.

My brother is three years older than me, but people usually don't assume that. He definitely looks younger. He's shorter than me, for one, but I think a lot of it is just the expression he carries on his face: wide, dark brown eyes, permanently dancing. And his full lips always hanging slightly open, upturned into a smirk, ready to say anything that will get a reaction. He's wearing his favorite Dream Zone shirt today, but it's all wrinkly. And his short, coarse hair needs to be brushed. I should have done a better job getting him ready this morning.

"That was a good one, wasn't it, Tessie?" Miles laughs, and I try to hold back my smile. It will only encourage him.

"No." I can't help but let out a little snort, though, as my nerves start to settle, and it sets him off into giggles of delight. "It wasn't funny at all," I say with more resolve. "I thought we all agreed that you were done with this now. New city, new start?"

He shrugs. "I was bored. Did you take a video of them?"

"*Why* would I have taken a video of them?"

"Because it was a good one," he says, and he begins to roll his head around, which he does whenever he's excited. It looks like someone doing yoga, trying to stretch out a stiff neck. I just shake my head.

"Wait." He grabs my arm, suddenly serious. "Where's the pizza?"

"He took it." I roll my eyes. "He paid for it, bud!"

"But I'm hungry. I ordered extra pepperon*iiiiiii*." The last syllable extends into a whine, and I can feel his mood about to shift, like how the air changes right before it rains.

"Let's get you some food," I say, wrapping my arm around his shaking shoulders and leading him toward the kitchen. "And maybe let's just keep this pizza business between me and you."

"C'mon, Tessie, but you know it was a good one."

CHAPTER TWO

My brother has disabilities.

We used to call it special needs before a teacher pointed out that his needs aren't special. They're just his.

"My brother has disabilities" is the canned answer I have ready to run off, whenever someone meets him for the first time, or he does something he's not supposed to (like ordering pizza for the neighbors), or I have to explain why he's not in college and still living at home even though he's nineteen. It's quick and to the point, so I don't have to spend too much time talking about it or talking in general.

I don't like to explain how the cord wrapped around his neck when he was born, leaving him without oxygen for too long, blue instead of brown.

And I hate listing all of his technical diagnoses. I always worry I'm going to say something wrong because it's not all clear-cut or what people expect. Athetoid cerebral palsy—that's the full name, but I rarely say all that. From what I understand, that's the center of everything. It's why his legs are stiff and uncoordinated, why his body moves without his control when he's really happy or really upset, and why he stumbles and rocks sometimes, like he's on a boat going over rough water.

Then there's cognitive impairment—I think that's the right term to describe why my older brother acts a lot like my younger brother, why I have to help him with his basic addition homework and weather his tantrums when things don't go the way he expects. OCD—but that might be unrelated. And vision and hearing loss—that explains the thick lenses on his glasses and expensive hearing aids that he somehow loses every few months. By the time I get to the end of the list, I'm a little lost too, ending it with an awkward "And . . . yeah." And then it usually leads to more questions or an invitation for people to tell me about how their cousin has cystic fibrosis or something, which is not even close to the same thing. And then something that I wanted to be done with has extended for a whole lot longer.

So I just tell people my brother has disabilities—and leave it at that.

Then I brace myself for one of the inevitable responses that I get every time. They're so familiar, I can recite them like the Pledge of Allegiance.

There's always the "Oh, what a gift to your family!" or "I'm sure he's taught you all so much." As if my brother is some prop for our own self-development. Yeah, growing up with him is hard. But his function in life isn't to teach us something. He's a human being, and this is *his* life, happening right now.

Anyway, people usually only say stuff like that when my brother is sitting quietly, rolling his head around and singing one of his favorite Dream Zone songs to himself. No one spews any of those inspirational Hallmark-card lines when he's running through the grocery aisles screaming because they don't have the brand of chocolate milk he likes, or flipping off the cars at the end of our cul-de-sac because they canceled his favorite show. No, they just avert their eyes or, worse, shake their heads disapprovingly at Mom. That's the second type of response.

But the third type of response, even worse than the look-on-the-bright-side mess that people try to dish out when they have no idea what they're talking about, is the pity-filled "I'm so sorry." Like we've suffered some tremendous loss. Like someone has died. I hate when people say that, because as difficult as life is with Miles sometimes, he's not dead. He's very much alive. And I don't like people insinuating that his life is somehow not enough, that I should be mourning the joyful, hilarious, and yeah, kinda annoying brother I was given. He is exactly who we want.

I gave my usual explanation today, and I was expecting one of the usual responses.

But Hawaiian Shirt Sam surprised me. He just said, "Hello."

Later, we're sitting down for family dinner.

Family dinner is not something that happens every night,

and that's why it's called family dinner instead of just, well, dinner.

The evenings are busy in our family. Dad works late a few nights a week at the shipping company where he's general manager, so he sometimes grabs drive-thru on the way home. And Miles always has so many appointments—with an occupational therapist, ENT, behavior specialist, psychiatrist, and whoever else he needs to see this week—so he and Mom end up snacking in waiting rooms or popping in a frozen pizza when they get home. Back in Roseville, I was left to my own devices for most dinners, so I usually ended up at Caroline's house, eating plates of rice and meat that Lola would constantly refill, insisting I was getting too skinny.

Things haven't changed much with the move. Everyone's still busy. I just eat a lot more cereal now.

"You should have seen his face," Miles says, shoveling a forkful of spaghetti in his mouth. Dad cuts up the noodles to make it easier for him. "He was so mad. He was flinging the pizza around and yelling about how he had to pay for it! Tessie should have recorded it, so we could put it on YouTube."

Miles told my parents as soon as they got home. He always does, out of guilt. But as usual, his contrition soon turned to pride, and even though it's hours later, he's still talking about his conquest.

"You didn't even see his face!" I say.

"Yes, I did. I was there the whole time. He was maaaaaad! Almost as mad as that old lady!" His head starts to roll, and his arms shoot back behind him, like a bird trying to take flight. I love how he shows his feelings with his whole body, no need for interpreting or second-guessing.

"Oh, okay," I say, giving him the side-eye, which sets off his laughter.

"Do you think I should check in with Audrey too? To make sure she's not upset with us? We had such a nice chat about you and her son going to Chrysalis last week, and now this," Mom says. Her thin eyebrows are pinched together, and she's looking past us in the direction of Hawaiian Shirt Sam's house across the street, as if she could send them an apology with her mind. "I already said I'm sorry to Mrs. Hutchinson about a thousand times, but lord knows that's going to take a while to smooth over. First the tree situation, and now this." Mom puts her hand up to her forehead and closes her eyes. "I just . . . I really wish you had been watching him better, Tessa."

And there it is.

"It wasn't that big of a deal, Mom. I handled it." I focus on pushing the spaghetti around on my plate so she can't see me roll my eyes.

"I know." Just like that, her voice is soft now, a switch flipped, and she reaches across the table to grab my hand. "You do a lot for us. I'm sorry if I don't say it enough."

My mom and I are nothing alike. She's all sharp angles, with pale, freckled skin and wavy blond hair that falls down perfectly on her shoulders as soon as she wakes up. I have hips and thighs that make me want to hide sometimes. And my tight curls look good eventually, but it's basically a part-time job to get them there. She talks to everyone and seems to thrive on these conversations, and most social interactions drain me. I'm perfectly content sitting in silence.

But one thing we have in common is that we obsess over everything we say, anxiously analyzing how our words might have been interpreted or affected someone. I can only imagine how exhausting this must be for her. I avoid talking to others simply because of it. I can see that now in her cloudy blue eyes, as she squeezes my hand one more time and gives me an apologetic smile.

"Maybe we should get rid of the house phone," she says. "One less thing for us all to worry about."

Dad, who has been studying emails on his phone for most of dinner, looks up. "We can't do that. What if there was an emergency?"

"I didn't use the house phone," Miles cackles. "I got Tessie's cell phone when she was pooping! She was pooping so long! Maybe you should just get your poop under control, Tessie."

I smack his arm, and he yelps in between giggles, trying to smack me back.

"Hey, hey," Dad warns, but there's a wide smile on his face. His phone's screen is dark now.

I jump up from the table and Miles follows, but I lap him and give him a noogie before pulling him into a hug, his laughter shaking both of us. Our golden brown skin doesn't match Mom's fair tone or Dad's deep brown, but we're the same.

My brother's disabilities are everything sometimes, but they're also nothing. Our relationship isn't remarkable or inspiring, like people expect. He's just my brother, and I'm just his sister. And my favorite memories with him—dressing up in my parents' clothes and pretending to be the new neighbors, walking down the street to get ice cream from Rite Aid—have nothing to do with what everyone else focuses on.

"So did you and Sam get to talk about Chrysalis?" Mom asks when we settle back down.

"Not really."

"He seems like such a nice boy," she continues. "And he's going to be a junior too! You guys could be buddies! Wouldn't that be great?"

"Yeah, I don't know." Don't get me wrong. Sam seems nice—really nice. The way he handled the pizza and treated Miles was different than what I'm used to and . . . intriguing. But I'm not sure he's the type I want to link up with on the first day. It's not like *I'm* judging him for his fashion choices, but the students at Chrysalis definitely will. Also, after seeing me as a flustered mess earlier, he's probably not so excited to hang out with me either.

"Why no enthusiasm? Are you still mad at me about the portfolio?" she asks.

"Is this about when you stole Tessie's diary?" Miles cuts in.

"Oh, here we go," Dad huffs with a weary look.

"It wasn't her diary!" Mom throws her hands up.

"It might as well have been." I had told myself I was over it, that I wasn't going to bring it up anymore, but the wound feels fresh all over again, and I'm reminded of her betrayal.

I'd heard about Chrysalis Academy long before my parents dropped the bomb on us that we would be leaving the place we'd lived our entire lives and moving six hours south to Long Beach, so my dad could take a more senior position within his company. The prestigious art school has produced a Disney Channel star, a violinist prodigy who was runner-up on *America's Got Talent*, and even a poet who was longlisted for the National Book Award.

So, when I found out where we would be going, I dreamed about Chrysalis a little bit, maybe as a way to cope with the fact that my life was going to be so dramatically changed. I imagined what it would be like to be one of Chrysalis's talented, special students. To meet other people who love what I love. And I made the mistake of talking about it at a family dinner one time. One time! But I never *actually* applied. I mean, I knew my love stories were not the kind of serious National Book Award–type writing they were looking for.

So, when I got my acceptance letter in the mail, I thought it was a joke. Or a clerical error.

I showed the letter to Mom, laughing about how bizarre this was, when her face broke into a knowing smile, and she spilled the beans. She could tell from what I'd said that I *really* wanted to go, so she filled out the application for me and then printed out some of my stories (my *private* stories!) as the writing samples. She had wanted to wait to tell me until I got in for sure, so I wouldn't get myself into a tizzy over it—one of her euphemisms for the anxiety I've had since I was in elementary school.

"I know I probably shouldn't have done it. But you wouldn't have gotten into Chrysalis if I hadn't. You would have self-rejected instead of taking the risk, and I just don't want you to let your worries have that kind of control," Mom says, reiterating the same defense she gave at the time. The same advice she's given me for years. "You're such a wonderful writer, Tessa. The world deserves to see that. And it all worked out in the end, right?"

I know I should feel good that I got accepted, and I do. Sort of. But Caroline's the only person I let read my stories. It makes my skin flame to think which of my romantic, silly stories Mom could have sent. She couldn't remember which she printed, and, like, I can't exactly go to the admissions director with that mortifying question. There was that especially bad one from a few years back that took place at a summer camp, where my brown-skinned, curly-haired protagonist had to choose between the hot guys who were, of course, inexplicably all in love with her. But surely Chrysalis wouldn't have accepted me if they had read *that*.

"Right?" Mom echoes again, looking at me hopefully. I just shrug.

"What time do you think we should leave tomorrow?" I ask, changing the subject, but before she can answer, we're interrupted by Miles standing up so forcefully that his chair falls to the floor.

"What time is it?" he asks. His eyes are blinking quickly and his arms are pulsing behind him.

Dad checks his phone. "Six fifteen."

"It started! I'm missing it!" He starts to cry, a high-pitched squeal, and runs from the room, toward the direction of the television set. "Stupid! So stupid!"

Mom stands up. "One of the Dream Zone members—Jonny, I think?—was going to be on *Access Hollywood* tonight. I should have remembered." She shakes her head, looking mad at herself. As if this is her fault. Sometimes I think it's easier for her to place blame on someone—herself, me, Dad—so she doesn't get mad at the universe.

"I'll go calm him down," she says, following after him, my question about tomorrow forgotten. I used to get mad at Mom for doing this—putting my brother first, dropping everything to help him—but I've learned to let it go. She's doing the best she can. We all are.

I pick up Miles's fallen chair and then help Dad clear the table.

CHAPTER THREE

I'm standing in front of my closet, trying to decide what to wear tomorrow, when Caroline calls again.

"I never got anything from you!"

"Yeah, didn't really have time for that." I fill her in on the scene from this afternoon, and she cackles. "Ah, I miss those pizzas! Someone should get that boy a reality show."

"Don't ever tell him that," I say with a snort.

"You're picking out your outfit now." A statement, not a question, because even miles apart, we know each other's actions like our own.

"Mm-hmm." I sit down on the floor in my closet, staring up at the options. After wearing uniforms at South High, I'm probably as excited about the possibilities of free dress at Chrysalis as I am about the creative writing classes.

"Well, you know what you have to wear."

And yeah, I know exactly what she's talking about. The rainbow dress.

It has a V-neck—not too low, but just enough—and a full skirt and vertical stripes in a pastel rainbow palette. I was on the fence about buying it from the little boutique in the Fountains shopping center, but Caroline convinced me. And it wasn't too hard—it did fit me perfectly, falling over my hips and highlighting my waist. But there's no way I'm wearing that dress.

Because, as I tell her now, "It's too much!" And she groans in frustration. "It is! You know it is, Caroline!" I say.

My general aesthetic is this: I don't want to stand out. Like, if someone does happen to notice me, I want them to nod and think, "That was a very subtle way of mixing patterns," or "The embroidered details on that Peter Pan collar are understated and cute." But I don't want to stand out. And a rainbow dress stands out. I know it's a lot of thought to put into what is essentially just protecting my skin from the elements and other people's eyes. I know that! But I think that the right outfit is important. It's a wish for the day! And my wish is that tomorrow goes EXACTLY. RIGHT.

All of a sudden, it feels hotter in my closet than it did a second ago. And somehow my fists are clenched? I try to take a deep breath, but there doesn't seem to be enough air.

"Uh, Tessa . . . ," Caroline says. "How are you feeling about tomorrow, buddy?"

I exhale and shake out my body. Of course it's not just

about the outfit. She knows how my brain works.

"Okay, I'm nervous." I sigh, as if that wasn't blindingly obvious. "Chrysalis is a big deal, you know? And I'm worried about not fitting in. I had a hard enough time at South High, and that was with, like . . . average, regular people. I don't have a chance with these cool, megatalented, sophisticated artists." I mean, these adjectives don't really apply to Hawaiian Shirt Sam, but I'm guessing he's going to be the outlier.

"Well, I don't know if my opinion matters as just a *regular*, but I think you'll be okay." I can hear the smile in her voice, letting me know it's only mock offense.

"You are the literal opposite of regular. You're a glittery, flying unicorn and a gift to this world that I treasure more than anything. But, like . . . you know what I mean."

"I do. South High is all shining-white football players and cheerleaders who look twenty-five and act like assholes, so it was easier to write it off when you weren't Miss Popularity there. Because who wants to hang out with them anyway? But if you're not accepted by these people, people you *actually* admire, then you're really a loser."

"Ha! Thanks!"

"What? I'm saying what you're thinking." I sigh. Because she is.

"But here's where I'll add," she continues, "that you will fit in. You belong there just like they all do, because you were accepted just like they were. Because you can write stories that are charming and heart-wrenching and unlike anyone else's. Don't doubt that, Tess."

"Thank you." Her little pep talk builds me up, but I also get another pang in my chest realizing I'll have to go through a first day of school without her. I remember the first day of fourth grade, when Caroline talked me down from a panic attack after I found out I would be in Mrs. Snyder's (aka Screaming Snyder's) class. And also, the first day of seventh grade, when Caroline didn't do any of the English summer homework because Lola was in and out of the hospital with her heart problem, and I spent all of lunch helping her speed-write an analysis of *The Outsiders*. We've always been each other's partners, a solid foundation that could weather anything.

"And maybe once you realize how great you are, you'll let someone besides me read your stuff."

"Yeah . . . sure." Though we both know I don't really mean it.

I did try posting a couple of my stories on WattPad once, at Caroline's urging, but one got three nasty comments and the other one, even worse, got nothing at all. That little dip of my toe into the pond of vulnerability was enough to turn me off completely. I'm excited about all the time I'll get to write at Chrysalis. I guess I can even sorta forgive my mom for sending my portfolio in because it got me there, and though I'll never admit it to her, she's right that I wouldn't ever have taken the leap. But I'm definitely not planning on sharing my work with my classmates. Even the thought of it makes me shudder.

"I mean, you'll have to show it to some people, won't you?" Caroline pushes on. "Like, at least your teacher. And probably even the other people in your class. That might be helpful, actually . . . they'll be able to help you a lot more than I can."

That last part stings. "Do you think I need help with my writing?"

"No, no! Of course not, Tessa! You're a brilliant, creative goddess, and your words are a gift to my life—"

"Be serious."

"Well, first of all, I am," she says, her voice full of patience. "And second of all . . . I just mean, you know, feedback is good for everyone. And sharing their work is what writers do, isn't it? That's the whole point of writing . . . right?"

"Right . . . ," I say, while my mind rushes to catch up.

Is the whole point of writing having other people read what you write? I've never really thought about it like that before, because I mostly write for my own enjoyment, but it makes sense, I guess. Why else would we have books? If that wasn't the point, writers would just keep their drafts saved on their computers, for their eyes only. And okay, I've thought about having a book with my name on it, but I realize, with a pang of embarrassment, that in my fantasies I jumped from sharing my stories with Caroline to being a celebrated, admired novelist totally detached from my readers, which . . . yeah, I guess is sort of stupid.

I don't know. Does that mean I'm not a real writer? Maybe

I'm just someone who writes silly things for fun. For the first time, I start to think about how my creative writing classes might actually work—because until now I've only considered, with excitement, the long, uninterrupted periods of time to write. Will we have to share our work with each other? Will my classmates be excited to do that? My stomach gets tight as the thoughts begin to spiral.

"Can we . . . can we go back to talking about my outfit?" That felt like too much to handle a moment ago, but it's definitely better than this.

"Sure, okay."

Caroline and I spend the next hour going over every possible outfit combo in my closet before finally settling on a suitable first-day outfit for me. My mind, thankfully, quiets down in the process. This is familiar. This is easy.

"Seriously, what would I do without you?"

"Wear jewel-toned sweater sets? Jeans with butterflies embroidered on the back pockets? Who knows?" She snorts. "I'm really doing a community service. Do you think I can put this on my college applications?"

"Yes, please do that. And hey, how are you feeling about your first day tomorrow?" I ask, and I feel a little embarrassed that I haven't done so already, too caught up in my own monumental change and anxiety.

"I don't know, fine?" she says. "It's just another day at South High. I'll be wearing some boring variation of the uniform and trying to keep my eyes open all day, as usual."

"Yeah, but it's our *first* first day without each other since, well . . . forever! Who are you going to sit with at lunch?" I know the question has been plaguing me. Just picturing lunch-time tomorrow makes the dull ache of missing Caroline flare up like a fresh cut.

She laughs. "I'm sure I'll find someone." And that makes me feel a little strange. First, because I wasn't joking, and second, because I'm definitely not feeling so cavalier. But we've always handled things differently. Maybe Caroline doesn't need me as much as I need her.

Eventually, after multiple promises to call Caroline as soon as I get home tomorrow (and also to send her the next chapter), I get off the phone, and then I pull my computer up on my lap, diving into Tallulah and Thomas's world of desire and romance again. Colette will have to wait.

I try not to think about anyone else's eyes on this story. These words are just for me.

Tallulah slipped into the coffee shop's open mic at exactly seven fifteen, the time Thomas had said he would be going on, not a minute sooner. Ever since their almost kiss was interrupted by the apparently unabandoned cabin's owner, Tallulah had been afraid to be alone with Thomas again. What if what had happened between them was all in her head? Tallulah didn't want to give that perfect memory a chance to be tarnished. She wanted to hold on to the delicate what-if forever.

So she showed up right on time, avoiding any chance of Thomas introducing her to his fellow musicians as a "buddy" or, worse, ordering a mocha from the hot, blond, sophisticated barista who was probably, most likely, in love with him too.

Tallulah found a place in the back of the shop, just in case she had to rush out in embarrassment, and watched as Thomas took his place at the front of the room. The twinkle lights cast an ethereal glow over his tousled black hair. Tallulah watched as he tuned his guitar, his slim fingers working with intention, and she imagined what it would feel like to have those same fingers on the small of her back or stroking the side of her face. The thought made her cheeks flush and her heart beat faster. Thomas looked ready to begin, but then he stopped and searched around the room, eyes squinted. Tallulah wondered, with anxiety, who he could be looking for—the blond barista? But she didn't have to wonder for long, because when his eyes fell on her, a wide smile spread across his face. "For you," he mouthed.

Thomas's eyes didn't leave Tallulah as he played his first song, and then his second and third. Even though the room was full of people, Tallulah felt like it was just the two of them. All of her worries melted away, because it was so clear from his words, his gaze, the music that flowed between them, that the moment in the rain had been real. This beautiful boy saw her—wanted her—like she wanted him.

After his final song, Thomas ignored the cheers and attempted conversation of everyone else, and strode straight up to Tallulah, enveloping her in a hug. She took his hand and led him outside, the night brightened by a full moon.

"I didn't know . . . that you felt that way." Tallulah sighed. "The

other day . . . I thought it might just be me."

"Don't you see?" Thomas said, wrapping his arms around her. "Ever since I moved here . . . it's always been you. It always will be you, Tallulah."

Then he pressed his soft lips against hers.

CHAPTER FOUR

I wake up at five a.m. On purpose.

It's not because I'm a morning person. I'm not. And it's not the excitement or anxiety I feel about the first day of school.

It's because I have to do my hair.

I've spent the past sixteen years figuring out how to do my hair. With a white mom, it didn't come natural, but she did a better job than most. She never sent me out of the house with frizzy messes that would make old Black ladies at the grocery store purse their lips and shake their heads. No, she studied my aunties and my granny when we would visit them in Georgia, taking notes and asking questions as if she was working on her thesis. And she learned how to sculpt my hair into perfectly conditioned puffballs and braids laid straight and even on my scalp.

When I started sixth grade, I begged Mom to let me press my hair. She resisted. She never let me relax it growing up, even though all my cousins did and my granny suggested it a few times. The chemicals didn't feel right to her, and "Your hair is beautiful just the way it is," she always used to tell me. But I wanted my hair straight. Straight and *smooth*—like Meghan Markle. Of course, I didn't know who the heck Meghan Markle was back then, but when I saw all the frenzied royal wedding coverage a couple years later, it was the first thing I thought. *That.* That *is what I was going for.*

I never really got it, though. Mom eventually gave in and took me to the shop every two weeks to get my hair freshly pressed. And she even let me use the relaxers that burned my scalp but made it possible for me to stretch out my appointments even further. But I never quite achieved the Meghan Markle dream. I always had bangs that frizzed every time I sweated and ends that broke off and refused to grow.

I pull the satin cap off my head and survey what I'm working with this morning. My hair is short now. Just a couple inches. And it's not straight anymore. It's curls that are wild and infuriating and exhilarating and magical, all at the same time.

After studying natural hair accounts on Instagram and watching beautiful curly-haired girls on YouTube for months, I finally did the Big Chop in June—cutting off all my processed hair and leaving an inch of my natural pattern, the promise of something new. I felt less scared knowing that I was going to a new place, that I would be starting over at Chrysalis, where people wouldn't know the difference and *notice* or, even worse, *comment.*

I thought it would be more convenient. I could jump into the pool when I wanted to and I didn't have to worry about the rain. But I wasn't suddenly overwhelmed with pool party invites, and it doesn't rain much around here anyway.

And I thought it would be easier. I could just wash it and go. But a wash-and-go, I've learned, does not involve simply washing and then going. It's washing and conditioning (sometimes deep conditioning), detangling and conditioning again, smoothing and rubbing, oiling and gelling. It's a process. A ritual. It's the reason why I'm up at five a.m.

I've tried doing my wash-and-go at night, like the natural hair influencers on YouTube suggest, but when I go to bed with my hair wet, I wake up with a troll doll situation going on— hair flat on the sides and exploding on the top. And it never looks right when I dry it with a diffuser . . . it gets all poofy on the back of my head like a poodle. So I planned to wake up early enough to let it air-dry this morning, to ensure I could have the perfect Day One hair on the first day of school. And today is going to go exactly according to plan.

I wash my hair first and then condition, finger detangling as I go. It's hard to maneuver around the tiny shower in the bathroom that Miles and I share. Every minute, an elbow or a knee seems to collide into the many bottles lining the edge, knocking them on my toes and making me curse.

After I'm finally done, I step out of the shower, place a towel over my shoulders, and then divide my hair into four sections so I can start raking in my current rotation of creams and conditioners. I have to handle each section differently, delicately, because while most of my hair is 4A, the very top is more 4C, and the right side is definitely 3B. They each have their own specific hand movements and saturation of products to get the curls all uniform.

Like I said, it's a process.

Someone bangs on the bathroom door, making me jump and drop the tub of cream styler that smells like roses on the orange shag rug. I scoop it up frantically like it's my child—that stuff is too expensive to waste.

"Tessie, let me in! I have to goooooo!" Miles's muffled voice comes through the door, and he bangs on it some more.

"Not right now. Use Mom and Dad's!" If I step out now, he'll be in here for who knows how long, and then I'll be all off schedule. Usually I would just let him in. But not today.

"But I really have to go! Please!!!!"

"No," I say firmly, and he squeals and screams as he runs off to the other bathroom in the house. I feel guilty because he's going to wake Mom and Dad up and I may have triggered a tantrum, but I so rarely do what's best for me. *I'll apologize at breakfast, and it's just today,* I tell myself. Because today, like my hair, will be perfect.

After patting my hair dry, I go back to my room, text Caroline a string of emojis to say good morning, and put on the outfit we finally decided on last night: an off-white lace shift dress with a medallion pattern, tiny gold hoop earrings, and pointy tan mules.

The dress will contrast with my skin, making it glow when I sit outside for lunch, and the golden highlights in my hair will shine like a halo in the SoCal sunshine. And a boy, maybe one who caught my eye in the hallway earlier, will see me sitting there, sun goddess incarnate, and come over to talk. And on our first date, he'll bring me roses the same exact shade of cream as my dress, because the image of me from that day is still singing in his brain. And it will until our wedding day, years later, after I've published my first book and he's put out his first solo album (he's a musician, of course), and yeah . . . that's good. I'm gonna type that up later.

I can hear raised voices through the closed door—Miles's yelps and Dad's stern directives and Mom's placating coos—but I don't go out to see what it is. I plant myself on the bed, letting my hair dry and reviewing my schedule for the millionth time. I don't want to get sucked into whatever crisis is happening and mess up my chances for a good day.

My schedule sends a thrill through my chest, just like it did the first time I saw it. I have all the usual classes I would have had at South High: American Lit Honors, Spanish 3, US History, precalc, and physics. But all of the boring academic classes are done before lunch at Chrysalis, leaving the afternoon hours for our conservatory classes. I'm taking four classes in the creative writing conservatory: a genre study of magical realism on Tuesdays, Book Club on Wednesdays, and the school's literary magazine, *Wings*, on Thursdays. But what I'm most excited about is the class that will bookend my week, the Art of the Novel, every Monday and Friday.

They usually don't let new students into the class, the creative writing director told me when I went to tour the school. But I wrote an email to the instructor—and celebrated fantasy author—Lorelei McKinney, pleading my case by telling her I was working on not one but two novels currently. It was scary, writing a successful author and acting like what I do is even anything comparable to that. But I had to try. When I got my schedule and saw that I'd been admitted, I screamed so loud that Mom came to check on me. I'm still in shock that I'll get to do something I love so much, something I usually do *for fun*, as part of *school*. It almost makes me forgive Mom for invading my privacy and submitting my work.

At seven forty-five, I finally leave my room. My hair isn't fully dry, but it's as dry as it's going to get, and after I picked it out a little bit, it actually looks really nice.

Dad's already left for work, and Miles is in the family room, eating a bowl of cereal with his eyes glued to Dream Zone. They're performing "Together Tonight," his favorite song. Usually I get Miles his breakfast so Mom can finish getting ready. But she's in the kitchen all dressed in her business casual and has already done my job. Except she's doing this thing where she picks things up and then puts them down in another spot in the corner, moving piles around instead of really tidying anything. It usually means something is wrong.

She lets out a sigh, so loud I can hear it across the room, and finally pauses her restless hands, pressing them together into a steeple. Her eyes zero in on me.

"Why didn't you just let Miles into the bathroom this morning?" she asks, the accusation clear in her question. "He said you weren't in the shower."

My stomach sinks, guilty, but then I puff my chest up with more confidence than I actually feel. "I was doing my hair. There are two bathrooms in this house." I brush past her to grab a yogurt out of the fridge, but I make sure to avoid her eyes.

"Yeah, and he had an accident on the way to the other bathroom. It's all the way on the other side of the house." All the craziness I heard this morning makes sense, and my chest feels tight, thinking about the extra work it probably made for my parents, how upset Miles must have been. Mom shakes her head and then goes back to moving things around on the counter.

"We need to work together here," she says as a carton of milk goes next to the sink, then over to the island, then eventually into the fridge.

"I know," I say, looking down. "I'm sorry."

"I just don't understand why you couldn't have let him in," she continues. "It would have bothered you for maybe a minute. We could have avoided all this."

That makes me bristle. It's like she expects me to be able to anticipate every problem. Can't she see that it's my first day of school too?

"I said I'm sorry. How was I supposed to know he would

41

have an accident? He hasn't had one in months!"

Her eyes flicker to the family room, checking if Miles is paying attention, but his music continues on. "Watch it," she warns.

Anger builds in my chest, hard like a rock, but I hold in my words and eat my yogurt instead. Fighting with Mom this morning doesn't fit into the plan. I can feel her presence a few feet away—pacing, tidying—but I hold my body stiffly, refusing to look up. The yogurt is tasteless and feels heavy going down my throat.

When I finally walk past her to throw my trash away, though, she grabs my hand, and her eyes are soft again. "I'm sorry, Tessa. I'm just tired. There's so much going on with this move. . . ."

The fury that was building inside me suddenly deflates, and I squeeze her hand. "I know."

It's our usual pattern: picking and poking and then apologizing. Tension and then release.

"This transition is really hard for him," she continues, her eyes watery. "I think that's why he's acting out, and these old habits are showing up again. We have to be patient with him . . . and with each other."

This transition is really hard for me too, I want to say. But I nod instead.

"We should leave soon, shouldn't we?" I say, letting go of her hand. "Are you going to take Miles first?"

Luckily, the high school in our neighborhood, Bixby

Knolls, has a program for students eighteen to twenty-two that's perfect for Miles, so he won't have to go far. But Chrysalis Academy is across town, closer to the ocean. School doesn't start until eight thirty, but we'll need to get going soon if I'm going to get there on time.

Mom's giving me a confused look, though, as if this doesn't make sense.

"I thought I told you," she says, shaking her head. "I'm going to sit in on Miles's class for the first period today. He's really agitated about it, and I want to help him settle in."

"How am I going to get to school?" I have my license, but no car. And it's not like I can just walk the seven miles to Chrysalis.

"Sam from across the street is going to drive you. He offered last night when I went over to talk to Audrey. He seems like such a nice boy. Is that okay?"

I want to say that it isn't. But then I think about Miles all alone at his new school. He hasn't had an accident in a long time, so he must have a lot of feelings going on. Change can be so hard for him, even if he doesn't always show it in conventional ways. I know Mom going with him is the right decision. Of course it is.

So I just force my lips into a smile and nod my head. "Sure."

CHAPTER FIVE

Hawaiian Shirt Sam is wearing another Hawaiian shirt, if you can believe that, though it's light blue this time. It must be, like, his thing. Only today, he has a corduroy blazer over it and khakis that are too loose, making him look like a kooky college professor. And he must be burning up, because September is still very much summer in southern California. Even this early, the sun is already peeking out.

I cross the street to his white Tudor-style house, trying to avoid the last of the season's slimy purple jacaranda flowers on the ground so my shoes don't get dirty. He waves at me, and there's that same half smile on his face. "Hey, carpool buddy!"

I wave back and try to swallow some of the irritation I feel at Mom for putting me in this situation. I had a plan for this morning, and my stomach aches now that it's all changing. She was going to drive me to school but drop me off half a block away, so no one would *know* that my mom dropped me off. I would walk up to my fresh start at Chrysalis, unencumbered by any history. Just me. A new girl in the creative writing conservatory with a perfect wash-and-go and a perfect outfit.

But now I'll be arriving with Hawaiian Shirt Sam, and I can't exactly ask him to drop me off down the block. And look, it's not like I'm shallow or anything. *I'm not.* But with his dorky fashion sense and hair that falls down without any kind of style—and *oh*, I just realized that he's wearing bright-white dad sneakers too, but like how a dad would, if that makes sense. With all that going on, Hawaiian Shirt Sam is going to attract attention. And I hate attention.

"I was just going to come over and get you," he says, swinging a leather messenger bag over his shoulder. At least it's not a rolling backpack. "Having a good morning?"

I shrug. "It's okay."

"Well, it's about to get a lot better." He practically skips over to his silver Honda Civic. "Man, I'm so excited. Aren't you?"

I shrug again. "Yep."

I'm planning on saying as little as possible on the drive over to Chrysalis, allowing myself to stew in my bad mood, so I can hopefully get it out of my system. But that intention goes out the window when I open the passenger door.

"Oh my god, what the heck is that?" The scent that wafts out of the car is so thick, I can almost see it moving through the air, curlicues and clouds, like a cartoon. It's nutty and sweet and makes me feel warm inside, like I got a big hug. My bad mood instantly evaporates.

He laughs and reaches into the backseat to produce a muffin tin, as if he's just pulled it out of the oven, the delicious smell getting even stronger. The muffins are studded with plump raspberries and covered with a crumble that seems to sparkle. My mouth waters just looking at them.

"Do you usually keep baked goods in the backseat of your car?"

He rubs the side of his face, suddenly self-conscious. "I don't know. Yeah? I left them in here to cool this morning."

"Okay, you need to explain that," I say, laughing.

"Baking is my thing. Like writing is your thing."

"So you're in the culinary arts program?" I ask, sliding into the passenger seat. He nods, offering me a muffin. I scoop up one of the warm pastries gladly and eye the other ones that he covers and places on the backseat again. "I saw on the website that Chrysalis just added that this year. Is that why you're transferring this year as a junior?"

"Yeah, I've wanted to go to Chrysalis for years because . . . I don't know, well, because. So when I saw they were creating the program this year, it seemed like fate or something. I still can't believe I'll get to do what I love for school credit."

He gets a wistful look on his face as he starts the car and pulls out of the driveway. "I feel that," I say, nodding my head.

"And I know people probably don't consider cooking an

art," he adds hurriedly. "It's not respected like dance or theater or painting or whatever, and I mean, it's not like my muffins will hang in galleries. But I think we belong at the school just as much as everyone else."

It's almost like he's rehearsing a defense that he knows he'll have to deliver today, justifying his place at Chrysalis. So I guess I'm not the only one who's worrying they won't belong.

I try to smile reassuringly. "Of course."

And then I take a bite of his muffin.

I thought the smell was special, but tasting it transports me to a whole other world—somewhere divine and holy and elevated. The taste awakens every one of my taste buds, as if they had been sleeping until this moment. It makes me feel safe, cozy. It reminds me of being little and crawling into my parents' bed in the early hours of the morning when Dad would leave before the sun for work.

A car honks behind us, waking me out of my baked-goods trance, and Hawaiian Shirt Sam quickly turns his head back to the road and accelerates. He was watching me.

"Whoa," I breathe, and he beams, his right dimple so deep I get the sudden urge to stick my finger into it.

"This is art," I declare, making him smile even more. "You are a magician of butter and sugar. This belongs in a museum."

"Brown butter," he corrects.

"What?"

"I browned the butter before adding it to the batter. It's like this, uh, process? That involves slowly cooking the butter after it melts," he explains. He rubs the side of his face as he talks, faster as he continues. "The water cooks out, and then the milk in the butter caramelizes, you see, until it turns solid, into these brown little gems that sink to the bottom. That's the nutty flavor you probably picked up on. It makes it really fragrant too. And the whole thing looks beautiful—going from bright yellow to this dark amber color. It feels a little bit like magic, getting it just right. You have to watch it carefully, because about two seconds after it's perfect, the butter burns. And burned-butter muffins wouldn't taste good at all."

The explanation seems to transform him. Instead of the awkward, geeky guy in Hawaiian shirts and dad shoes, he seems like a master of his craft. Could I speak about my writing in the same way? Probably not.

"See? You're an artist." It's clear that's true about him, but I don't know if I could say it about myself. "So why do you cool them in the back of your car?" I ask. "Is that some sort of special technique?"

"Yes, it's an ancient baking secret. It's been passed down in my family for generations." His face is serious, but when I raise an eyebrow, a laugh breaks through. "No, it's just that I wake up every morning at five to bake, and my mom asked me to stop keeping all my creations in the house. They were all going to her hips or whatever."

"Well, I *guess* I can make the sacrifice and be your taste tester. If I have to."

We spend the rest of the ride to Chrysalis alternating

between me gobbling up muffins (I take two more) and him explaining why each bite tastes so good. I almost forget about where we're going and my anxiety and irritation from before. I even start dreaming about a love interest for a new story I want to begin—a shy but charming baker who creates dishes based on the curly-haired girl he's falling for. He wouldn't look like Hawaiian Shirt Sam, though, because Hawaiian Shirt Sam is not one of those swoon-worthy guys who carry a romance novel.

When we pull into the Chrysalis parking lot, I'm snapped back into reality, the first-day jitters looming before me again.

Chrysalis isn't a traditional school building. It's a newer school, and it's not like there are empty lots sitting around in a city as cramped as Long Beach. Most of the campus is a converted bank building, five stories tall, modern and sleek. They also got ownership of an ancient brown craftsman house that's next door, a huge wraparound porch and wide green lawn surrounding it. Oh, and a few blocks in the distance, the ocean! I'll never get tired of seeing the ocean just hanging out there like it's no big deal. In Roseville, we would have to fight traffic and stay overnight somewhere to see the water, but I guess it's going to be my everyday view now.

Students swarm around both buildings, and already I can see they're different from the masses of South High: a couple in matching black lipstick and cat ears, girls with tight buns and swaths of gray and pink tied around them, a guy in knee-high shiny maroon boots. It's thrilling.

I'm about to get out of the car when Hawaiian Shirt Sam stops me. "Wait."

"Yeah?" Is he going to want to walk in together? My hesitation from this morning creeps back in.

"There's, uh . . . there's some white stuff on the back of your head. Like some hair stuff or something?" He rubs his neck and winces. "It's just . . . I know you probably would want someone to tell you . . . so you're not embarrassed."

My whole face turns red as I feel around the curls on the back of my head. Sometimes the cream I use doesn't get all the way worked in, especially if my hair is not completely dry yet. So much for the perfect wash-and-go.

"Did I get it?" I ask, turning so he can check. I'm equal parts grateful and mortified. But at least it's just Hawaiian Shirt Sam and not some cute guy in one of my classes. I would have curled up and died then.

"Not quite."

"Can you, like, help me? Um, show me where it is?" Desperate times.

"Okay, uh . . ." He lightly takes hold of my wrist. My heart speeds up. "I'm gonna move your hand to where it is. Don't worry, I won't touch your hair. I know that's not kosher."

That makes me giggle a little bit, breaking the tension. He moves my hand to the spot on my head. "There."

I quickly work in the product some more, making sure to not lose the definition of my curls.

"Did I get it?"

"Yes. All good."

I turn back around, and then I'm face-to-face with him, closer than I expected. I should be worried about how huge my pores look this close, or how he can see the cluster of zits on my chin. Those are the types of thoughts that usually spiral in my head when I get close to a boy. But instead I'm distracted. His eyes are the same exact shade of green as Thad's, who used to be my favorite member of Dream Zone growing up. And there's a sprinkling of dark freckles under his eyes, so precise they look like they're drawn on. He smells like butter and sugar.

"Well, here we go," he says.

"Yep." I snap out of it. "I better get going. It's late. I have to find my first class." I jump out of the passenger side quickly, brushing muffin crumbs off my dress. "Thanks for the ride!" I call back to him. "Meet you here after school?" I basically sprint away, not even waiting for Hawaiian Shirt Sam's answer.

I guess I can just call him Sam now.

CHAPTER SIX

Turns out that academic classes are pretty much the same at Chrysalis as they would be at any other school, with the exception of my US history teacher, Mr. Gaines, trying to rap along his syllabus to the *Hamilton* soundtrack. It takes immense physical restraint not to roll my eyes.

The difference is the students, though. They're nothing like the boring pod people I was surrounded by at South High (with the exception of Caroline, of course). I find myself getting distracted by everyone sitting around me, trying to figure out if the hippie-looking girl in a long floral skirt, with hair full of dry shampoo, is in the visual arts conservatory, or maybe instrumental music. The guy vlogging all of precalc until Ms. Hernandez makes him turn off his phone has to be in film and television.

Another thing that keeps grabbing my attention is just how diverse the school is compared to Roseville. The area got a little more swirl from when Caroline and I first met, but at South High, there was always at least one period in which I was the only the brown face. I am painfully familiar with being asked to speak for the delegation of all Black people in too many history-class discussions, with English teachers who barely spoke to me all year telling me with confidence, "You'll like this one!" once we got to the one short story by James Baldwin.

At Chrysalis, though, I don't exchange any knowing glances with the other brown people in the room because there are so many of them, in so many different shades. And though each teacher allows us to sit wherever we want, there isn't the natural segregation that I always noticed, people sitting with people who looked like them, where they felt comfortable. When this happened, I always felt like I didn't belong anywhere, white or Black or somewhere else. I always felt like I had to perform what each group expected me to be as a Black girl, so it was easier to just not try with anyone.

But apparently no one at Chrysalis has been informed of the rules. People seem to flock to those who share their passions instead: a group of girls doing scales in the corner before American lit begins, a pair in matching Slytherin robes looking like they're on their way to their first day at Hogwarts. It's amazing what a different setting six hours and a few freeways can bring. Here, maybe I can fit in with anyone.

When it comes to lunchtime, though, a lot of that "It's a Small World" kumbaya positivity disappears, and I'm in the bathroom, panicking like usual.

Caroline and I always sat alone. We had our own little corner outside the D building, where the Wi-Fi was strong and we could pass the laptop back and forth in peace. Every once in a while, one of Caroline's other friends from Yearbook would join us, Glory McCulloch or Brandon Briceño, but I liked it better when it was just us.

Caroline isn't here to save me today.

I'm looking in the mirror, trying to calm my nerves and will myself to leave (because eating alone in the bathroom is a whole other level of pathetic that I'm not willing to reach yet), when a girl walks in.

I try not to stare, but she looks like a model. With dewy deep bronze skin, high cheekbones, and a perfect little mole under her right eye that looks like it was drawn on just so, this girl must be used to stares. She's gorgeous. Plus her outfit is aspiration-worthy. She's wearing high-waisted, wide-legged black-and-white polka-dot pants and a sleeveless chambray button-up tied in a knot at her waist. There are gold bangles up and down her thin arms, and matching gold wire woven through her long locs. A scarf, in bright shades of pink and orange and green, is tied over the top of her head, a complicated bow in the front like a crown. Her outfit makes me want to take a picture and start my own street-style (or bathroom-style) IG account, if that wouldn't be so creepy. Of course, she catches me looking in the mirror.

"I love your hair," she says, her bubble-gum-pink painted

lips stretching into a wide smile. "Is that a twist-out or a wash-and-go?"

"A wash-and-go," I say, smiling back.

"Man, I could never get my wash-and-gos to look like that." She nods approvingly.

I'm about to say thank you, but that may seem snobby, like I know my hair is great and I have a big ego or something. And then I'm about to compliment her hair, but I'm worried it won't sound genuine, coming right after what she said, and I don't want her to think I'm a faker. I need to figure out the perfect thing to say to segue this little interaction into a lunch invitation, because this girl is the stylish, sophisticated friend of my dreams. But then her nose wrinkles and her eyebrows press together, and I realize I've been smiling for too long and not saying anything. And I can feel how awkward I'm making it, but I just keep smiling, paralyzed.

This is why I only have one friend. I can't even respond to a routine compliment without spiraling into a panic.

"Well, see you around," she says finally, giving me a sorta half wave before leaving, and I put my head in my hands and begin obsessing about what a complete social disaster I am.

But her voice interrupts my thoughts. "Uhhh, sis? I don't mean to, like, offend you if this is some kinda performance art thing, but you don't seem like the type."

"What?" I turn around to face her, and see her eyes bugged out as if she's watching a car wreck.

"It looks like you got a visit from that bitch Auntie Flo," she says, gesturing toward the mirror, and I follow her eyes to see my worst nightmare: a dark red stain spread on my off-white lace dress, just below my butt.

Those stomachaches I've been feeling all morning haven't been because of anxiety.

"Oh my god. Oh no no no." My neck gets hot and my chest feels heavy as I wonder how long I've been walking around like that, and I start to reexamine every interaction I've had today to determine if they were laughing at me without me even realizing. Before I can stop it, my eyes start to burn and then I'm crying. Freaking crying! Having a full-on meltdown in front of this model-looking girl who probably already thinks I'm a nutjob.

"What am I going to do?" I croak, staring at the floor as it starts to spin. I can't call my mom. She already went in late today for Miles, so it's not like she can leave early. I don't have any other clothes. Should I have been carrying extra clothes? Apparently so, if I'm going to have accidents like a freakin' toddler. I'll just have to stay in this bathroom forever.

"Uh, you good?" the girl asks, and I look up to see her hand hesitantly reaching in my direction.

"No." My breaths are coming in short and fast, and now my whole body feels like it's burning. I want to curl up and be done.

"Okay, it's okay—just, breathe. Breeeeathe." She comes up

and pulls me into a tight hug, her right hand rubbing my back in wide circles. "It's okay. You're okay."

And I don't know what kind of magic she's wielding. But one moment I'm teetering on the edge of a full-blown panic attack, and the next I'm believing her words like it's the gospel. I'll be okay.

We part, and I gape at her, amazed.

"Now, what are we going to do with you?" she asks, tapping her chin as she considers me. "Oooh! I got this." She quickly unties the scarf on her head and whips it off, revealing a halo of frizz at the top of her locs.

"I couldn't get in for a retwist this weekend, so I was tryin' to hide this mess." She scratches her scalp. "But desperate times and all."

A look of concentration on her face, she shakes the scarf out wide and then pulls it around the back of my hips, tying it in the front just under my belly button. She adjusts it a couple of times, making the bow look like a little flower, and then spins me around toward the mirror.

She presses her lips together, satisfied, and snaps a finger. "There you go, girl. Work!"

With the exception of my tearstained face, I look pretty okay. The bright colors of the scarf contrast well with my lace dress, and my outfit looks put together, intentional.

"Thank you," I say, quiet and unsure.

"No thanks needed." She shakes her head. "You would

have done the same for me."

I wouldn't. I know that. The conversation would have been too awkward. "Yeah . . ."

She digs in her purse and pulls out a tampon. "Now go take care of business, and then we can go get some food."

"Oh, you don't have to sit with me . . . ," I start. My computer is fully charged. I can probably just eat in the bathroom after all, and get some more words in for Caroline's Colette story.

"Girl, after all we been through? You trying to ditch me already?" She laughs. "Plus, you got my favorite scarf. I gotta make sure you don't try and jack it."

CHAPTER SEVEN

It turns out my own personal supermodel stylist savior is named Lenore Bennett.

"It's kinda an old-lady name. I was named after my grandma, so yeah—but I guess even she was a little baby Lenore at one point. All little ol' ladies gotta start somewhere. And eventually all these Novas and Khaleesis are gonna be grandmas too . . . whoa."

I quickly pick up on her habit of talking fast, jumping from one topic to the next like her brain is playing hopscotch. And it's about as hard to keep up with her conversation-wise as it is to keep up with her physically. I trail after her fast pace as she leads me outside and across the lawn, weaving around groups of other students as we go. Eventually we reach the porch of the old brown house, where she stops in front of a lanky guy sitting in a rocking chair, his black leather bag sitting in an identical one next to him.

I recognize him from Mr. Gaines's history class earlier today. His outfit caught my eye right away: a white and baby-blue seersucker suit, bright against his tan skin, with a buttoned blazer and shorts that hit midway on his thighs. His shiny black hair is tucked under a straw boater hat. On anyone else, it would look silly, but confidence wafts off him, heavy and thick, his own personal fog machine. Of course Lenore is friends with this guy.

He must notice our arrival, because he pulls his bag off the other chair, but his eyes don't move off the sketch pad in front of him, where he's drawing an angular figure in a dress made of flowers.

"This is Theo," Lenore says.

"My name is not Theo," he says, his voice stern. "That is just a nickname that Lenore has been unsuccessfully attempting to make happen for the past two years. But it has never happened. My name is Theodore Lim."

"And like I've told *you* many times," she says, rolling her eyes, "you don't get to decide what I, your best friend, call you. *Theo*, this is our new friend, Tessa."

I reach out to shake his hand, but he doesn't see it because he's still concentrated on his sketch.

"Only friend."

"Excuse me?" I don't understand *how* he's trying to make fun of me, but my defenses immediately go up.

"Lenore is my only friend. I just want you to get an accurate picture of our relationship. This is a by-default type situation."

His right hand, holding the pencil, continues to move vigorously across the paper, but he gives a slight wave with his left hand. "Hello, Tessa."

I'm about to just walk away because I don't need to be where I'm not wanted, and this snarky little artist obviously doesn't want me here.

But then Lenore laughs and leans in close to his face, snapping her fingers. "Earth to Theo! There are some humans here attempting to interact with you. She's gonna think you a douchebag!" He brushes her away like a fly, adding some detail to the bottom of the skirt.

"He always gets like this when he's in the zone. Like, testy is the nice way to put it, but asshole-y is probably a little more accurate," she says to me, a hand cupped over her mouth as if he can't hear her. "It's my job to pull him out of it, or his goddamn hand will fall off before graduation."

She reaches over and snatches the boater hat off his head, placing it on her own.

"Hey!" he yells, finally putting his pencil down and looking up at us. His eyes are dark and shiny, like polished obsidian, and he has the kind of perfect eyebrows that make me immediately self-conscious of my own.

"It looks better with my outfit," Lenore says, posing.

Theodore looks her over appraisingly before finally nodding his head in agreement, "Yes, I suppose it does."

"No offense, but you low-key had some Christopher Robin vibes going on there. Or like one of those old-timey, creepy ghost boys in movies about haunted houses? They look all sweet and normal until, like, their faces rip apart and maggots come out or something. . . . I'm really doing you a favor."

"I was worried it was too much." His voice is softer now, and he glances down at his outfit. It makes me like him more. "Is it too much?"

"You look great," I say, and he gives me a slow smile.

"Thank you, Tessa. *You* can have Lenore's rocking chair."

I hesitate, but Lenore does a dramatic bow thing as she gestures to the chair, before leaning against the railing surrounding the porch. "It's all yours."

"So what conservatory are you both in?" I feel a little silly after the question comes out, because it's not like Theodore is sitting here sketching but is also a prodigy violin player.

"Visual arts," Theodore says, his hand moving quickly again, adding a crown of leaves to the beautiful girl on his page. "I dabble in painting when I'm feeling a little masochistic, but my focus is primarily illustration."

"On paper, I'm in the visual arts conservatory too. Drawing, photography, watercolor, printmaking—I do it all," Lenore says. "But I've taken classes in the film department before, and also digital media. This year I'm invading the production and design department too, because my pockets are getting real empty from too many trips to Jo-Ann's this summer, and those guys get as much fabric as they want."

"You make clothes?" I ask, amazed again at how cool this girl is.

"Yep! Made these pants from a tablecloth Grandma Lenore was gonna throw out." She laughs and poses with her hands on her hips and her shoulders rolled forward, like she's modeling for an invisible camera. "Aren't they perfect?" she says, and I nod in agreement.

"I didn't know you could take classes in multiple conservatories."

"You can when you're as talented as me!" she calls, snapping her fingers above her head.

"Oh yeah, of course. I'm sorry," I say quickly. "I didn't mean to, uh, question whether or not you were talented enough or anything."

I can feel my neck burning red. But she laughs again, and nudges my toes with one of her perfect lemon-yellow slides.

"Girl, chill. Do *you* want to try other conservatories too? They usually let anyone try it if you can state your case. What conservatory are you in, anyway?"

"Oh . . . I just write." I look down at my hands, so I won't see the look of boredom, or worse, *fake* interest on her face.

"Nah, don't say you *just write*," she says, imitating my mumbly tone. "You won't ever catch Theo here saying he just draws." He wags a finger with his left hand while his right hand continues to work. "You *write*. Period. And you must be pretty fucking good at it to get in here, especially as a transfer. So own it, sis!"

I shrug and let myself smile a little bit. She's being nice, and I appreciate it. But she might say different if she knew I wrote romances.

Lenore, luckily, picks up on my vibe and switches gears. "Okay, so the writers usually sit over there," she says, pointing to a spot on the other side of the porch, covered by a large tree. I see some of the hard-core Harry Potter fans from earlier, but there's also a cluster of girls in novelty prints and Peter Pan collars, lots of people wearing various shades of faded black, and at least two fedoras that I can count. "Shady, less glare on their laptops. And I think they like sitting there because it has the best view of the place. Lots of material for their next novels."

"Is there, like, assigned seating or something?"

"No, of course not. But people like to be with their people, you feel me? And most of all, people like to feel like their people are better than all the other people. It's, like, the human condition or whatever." Lenore speaks with her hands, like she's giving a TED talk. "We don't have cheerleaders or football players here, yeah, but there's a hierarchy like anywhere else."

"Yeah, the dancers? Totally cheerleaders," Theodore cuts in. His pencil is down now. This topic interests him.

"Mmm-hmm, the way they prance around in their spandex and leotards—they don't need to be wearing that shit all day! They just want to show off their nonexistent booties and, like, ribs or whatever." Lenore points to a crowd of girls and a few guys sitting on the steps of the bank building. "That's them over there."

"And the jocks here? The musical theater kids," Theodore continues. "Everything always has to revolve around them, and they expect us to care about their next big show like little towns in Texas care about football. I don't even need to show you where they are."

He doesn't. There's a huge group singing "Seasons of Love" a cappella on the far side of the lawn.

Theodore continues to give me the lay of the land with Lenore's quick commentary, pointing to each group as he goes along. The production and design kids mostly hang out inside. ("They can't be exposed to sunlight, or they will, like, burst into flames.") The new culinary arts students are wild cards. ("But I wouldn't mind me a hot chef boyfriend.") The visual arts kids flock wherever light is good and the inspiration takes them, and they're the cool, artsy ones. ("Of course.") And the instrumental music and creative writing kids are the nerds, apparently. ("No offense, but, like, the writers all started bringing typewriters last year. Like, it was a trend. You can't tell me there's a reason to lug around that obsolete technology! With that and the tubas, they probably all got scoliosis.")

I follow Theodore's finger around the campus, fighting the urge to take notes, but I miss what he's saying about the film department because I'm distracted by another group that he hasn't labeled yet. The musical theater kids may be acting all extra to get everyone's attention, but this group does it effortlessly. There are four of them sitting in the very middle of the lawn, center stage. One guy is impossibly tall and freckled, with flaming red hair. His whole body shakes with laughter, and even though I'm too far to hear it, it's contagious. I want to be right there, laughing along. Lounging next to him on a spread-out flannel shirt is another white guy with a backward snapback covering shaggy golden hair, and there's a girl with them too. She has dyed gray hair, milky skin, and dark lipstick. She's wearing an oversized denim jacket over a black dress so short I can almost see the curve of her butt cheeks.

They look perfect. They look like the cast of a CW show posing on the cover of *Entertainment Weekly*.

And the centerpiece of it all is the gorgeous specimen standing in the middle of them, talking and gesturing animatedly, like he's delivering one of Shakespeare's sonnets or Ali Wong's comedy sets. His friends orbit around him, marveling at him just like I find myself doing now.

The boy has dark eyes that I can see sparkle even from here, olive skin, and tousled chocolate hair, short on the sides and long, loose curls on the top. As he speaks, it falls in his face, and he brushes it back in a way that makes my stomach do backflips. He has broad shoulders that hold his crisp white T-shirt with a round, stretched-out neck like a hanger over his skinny frame. His legs are long and lean—like, remarkably so—and this is only highlighted by his tight, faded black jeans and brown leather shoes with no socks.

He's straight out of the story I'm currently working on, the Tallulah one. Thomas, the unbelievably cool singer-songwriter, come to life—walking out of my words and into my life, ready to make me his muse. It takes all of my strength not to run over there and profess my love right now. I want to whip out my laptop and record every detail.

"Who are they?" I ask, subtly gesturing toward the group with my chin. I hope I sound casual even as my heart rate speeds up in anticipation.

"Oh, *them*," Theodore responds, rolling his eyes.

"More theater kids?"

"No . . . well, actually I think Grayson may be in the theater department, but he's strictly the highbrow stuff, no musicals," Lenore says, talking loud and blatantly staring at the group. I wish she would turn around. "Those are the founders' kids."

"What does that mean?"

"Their parents are super rich and donated all the money to start the school ten years ago, just so their precious prodigies could go here one day," Theodore explains, his face full of disdain. "So they, by default, think they're the shit even though their talent is remedial, at best."

"Theo's just bitter because Poppy—that's the girl—beat him out for a featured gallery in the winter gala freshman *and* sophomore year," Lenore laughs.

"And I *deserve* to be bitter. . . . Poppy's work would make more sense as the stock photos in frames at West Elm," Theodore scoffs, returning to his sketch pad again. "I mean, how many gouache beach landscapes does the world need? Really."

"She looks cool. . . . I mean, I like her hair," I say feebly.

"Oh, don't let her looks fool you," he mutters. "Her exterior may be manic pixie dream girl, but inside she's all Regina George."

"*Anyway,*" Lenore goes on, "Poppy is in visual arts.

67

Rhys—the ginger—is in film, I think, and the guy in the middle is Nico. He's in creative writing, like you. None of the rules we just explained to you apply to those kids. Money and status trump conservatory when it comes to social groups here, and they've got that to spare. They basically run this place."

Nico is in creative writing, like me. I try to steal another quick glance at him, but when I look up, my view is blocked by Sam, lumbering across the lawn to our group. His corduroy jacket is tied around his waist now, and he's carrying a lunch box. My neck starts to feel warm, worrying about what my new friends will think of him.

"Hi, Tessa!" he calls as he walks up.

"Oh, is this your boyfriend?" Lenore asks, shimmying her shoulders.

Sam turns scarlet, and I'm already shaking my head.

"No. *No.* Not at all. We're just friends." I'm talking too fast. "Neighbors, really. We just met."

Theodore looks up at that and arches one perfect eyebrow.

"Oh," Lenore says with a smug smile, "Well, Tessa's neighbor, I like your shoes. You should join us."

"Yeah, okay. Thanks. Thank you," Sam says, nodding too much and awkwardly crossing his arms and leaning against the railing. "Tessa, you, uh, changed your outfit?"

"Yep." I look past him, not wanting to relive that mortifying recent memory, and I make direct eye contact with Nico across the lawn. He grins right at me, bright as the sun, and winks. Winks!

"How's your day going?" Sam asks, somewhere back on Earth.

I can feel the smile on my face, so big it hurts.

"Better."

Tallulah thought back to the day she had first met Thomas. Or maybe "met" isn't the right word, because they didn't actually speak. Saw. No, that's not right either. Connected.

Tallulah was walking down the halls of Roosevelt High, talking to her best friend, Collette, when something—the universe, divine intervention—told her to stop. Pay attention. This is important.

She looked up, and the sea of students parted to reveal a perfect specimen of a boy standing in the middle of the hallway. He was tall and thin but still had a powerful presence, like he had stepped off a runway somewhere. His dark hair tumbled over his eyes, almost masking the alluring energy of his warm gaze. He was wearing a faded shirt for a band she didn't recognize, jeans that hugged his body perfectly, and loosely laced black boots. He was new here. He had to be. Tallulah would have noticed him before today if he wasn't. This boy was not someone who goes overlooked and underappreciated.

Collette pulled Tallulah along to their English class, repeating a question that she must have missed. She could tell from Collete's tone that her friend was irritated, but she didn't care. Her mind swirled with thoughts of the boy, and also, surprisingly: "I will know him and I will love him." Tallulah was as sure of it as of the sun's rising and setting.

And then he winked at her, but it was more than a wink. It was a sign, a promise, that he felt the same way.

CHAPTER EIGHT

Writing has always come easy to me. I mean, yeah, I've gotten writer's block before, and there are nights when it takes me a whole hour to write a sentence the way it's supposed to be. But I've always known that the words are there—have *always* been there—floating in the air above my head, waiting for me to snatch them down and arrange them just right.

So, with everything I've worried about today and everything that's gone wrong, I'm not anxious about the actual writing. I've been looking forward to it, actually—the beacon at the end of this weird, exhausting, not-perfect day. At least I'll have time to write. I can catch up with my characters, find the peace that's always waiting for me on my laptop screen, and send Caroline a new chapter tonight. Maybe two.

At the end of lunch, I follow Sam, Theodore, and Lenore back into the main building for conservatory classes. But Sam and Theodore wave goodbye at the second and third floors, and by the time I reach the fifth floor with the frenzied tide of students, I realize I have no idea where I'm going.

"Oh, that's back at the house," Lenore says, glancing quickly at my schedule where it says BB instead of a room number next to Art of the Novel. "Everyone calls it the Bungalow.

"See you later, girl," she calls with a sympathetic smile before flitting off to her class.

I turn around and fight my way back down the crowded staircase. It takes a while, a fish swimming upstream, and my heart is beating fast when I finally reach the ground floor again and the final bell rings. I'm late.

I run across the now-empty lawn, trying to ignore my rising panic, and scramble up the steps of the brown house I was sitting on the porch of not too long ago. I can't believe I wasted so much time, that I didn't check my schedule. I studied it like a sacred text all week. How did I miss that?

I open the bright yellow door of the old house, the Bungalow, and it lets out a loud creak that's jarring in the silent room. Where is everyone?

"Hello?" My whisper sounds like a yell and each footstep a thud. I walk past what would be a living room in any normal house, three couches arranged with no coffee table in the middle.

I walk around a staircase in the middle of the house and through an empty kitchen. I'm just about to give up and go ask someone in the office for help when I hear the faint tinkle of laughter and voices coming from a door, slightly ajar, that I missed before. A basement. I didn't even know houses in Southern California had basements. I open the door hesitantly, revealing a set of narrow stairs, and the voices get louder.

You're okay, I tell myself. I take a deep breath and then make my way down the stairs.

The first thing I notice is the books. It's impossible not to. Every inch of wall space in the large room, floor to ceiling, is covered with full shelves. And more random stacks populate every corner, table surface, and even a few spots on the stairs. The beautiful sight of so many books makes my heart soar. I want to run around, stroking the spines and singing like Belle.

But the second thing I notice is the eyes—ten pairs of eyes, to be exact—staring at me. There are tables and chairs and even some beanbags around the room, but everyone is sitting in a circle in the middle. And they're all silent, pursed lips and assessing eyes, as if I've interrupted some secret meeting.

"Art of the Novel?" I ask, my voice small.

"Yes, dear," says the woman at the far end of the circle, who I know is Lorelei McKinney. "I'll excuse the tardy today because I know you're new to us, but don't make it a habit."

Ms. McKinney looks different from the pictures I pulled up when Googling her online. Her blond hair is darker, tinged with gray, and her acne scars are more apparent without Photoshop. I don't know why I expected her to dress like a carnival fortune-teller or something—scarves and hippie-dippie skirts—but she's just wearing faded jeans, a plain blue shirt, and Converse. Nothing about her says "Published author of a successful adult fantasy series, beloved by a small but dedicated fanbase." But I guess there's not much money in that market for people other than the Game of Thrones guy. Otherwise, why would she be here in a basement surrounded by teenagers? Regardless, though, I'm excited to learn from her, and my neck is burning red thinking that I've already given a bad impression.

"Mmm-hmm. I'm sorry. Won't happen again." There's no room for me in the tight circle, so I sit in another chair off to the side, trying to keep my head down. But to my horror, she doesn't continue. Instead she keeps looking at me.

"You're Tessa, right? Please join the class." She gestures to a couple of the students, and they move their chairs apart, making room for me.

I squeeze between one of the fedora guys I saw at lunch and a girl with the cover of *Pride and Prejudice* on her shirt, adjusting the scarf around my waist as I sit down. Ms. McKinney nods before finally continuing.

"As I said, for this upper division course, the structure of the class will be fairly loose. We might begin the period with brief lessons on topics of interest, maybe some questions if they come up, but you will have most of the time to yourselves to write. Because that is truly what will get your novels completed."

I feel my shoulders relax a bit. That I can do.

"At the end of the day, we will come together and work-shop the writing of one student. We will be going through your names alphabetically, so there's no argument about who gets to share. And no one dominates the time by sharing every day."

She shoots a good-natured look at Fedora, and everyone in the room, except me, laughs knowingly.

What was that? Workshop?

"And, of course, you will also submit whatever you're working on to me weekly, so I can offer you feedback. I promise that the rumors aren't true. I'm not in the least bit mean." She looks around the circle and smirks. "If your writing is good, that is."

The rest of the class laughs again, but I can feel my heart beating fast again, my chest heavy. *Stop it, anxiety,* I want to say. *Haven't I already been through enough today?*

But my mind starts to spiral, thinking about what she just said. Caroline was right. Of course she was. I am going to have to share my writing with everyone in this class. They're going to be able to read it and tell me how much they hate it, in person, not hidden behind a computer screen, but right here to my face. And then I'm going to have to submit it to this published author, who will rip it apart with even more skill, who will realize what a fake I am, and that I write nothing more than silly kissing scenes and trope-y plots.

Somehow, in all of my fantasies about this school, I never once considered actually sharing my writing with other people. Not until Caroline broached the topic last night. I realize now, looking around at all these people who aren't at all shocked, just how stupid that was.

How did I not see this coming?

Ms. McKinney is going on now about the winter gala and how someone will be chosen to read there or something, but

I can't focus on her words. My mind is a mess and her voice is both too quiet and too loud at the same time, like I'm listening from underwater.

The sound of the basement door opening and footsteps down the stairs pulls me out of it, and I look up to see an angel. I blink a few times, rub my eyes that were embarrassingly starting to water, but he's still there.

Thomas. No, *Nico*. The gorgeous writer I spotted at lunch.

"Hello, Nico," Ms. McKinney says. "I was just discussing how I will select the lucky reader for the gala. Join us."

I should be mad that he didn't get the stern tardy warning like me, but instead I'm impressed.

He drags a chair across the hardwood floor, and nods at Fedora, who quickly scoots to the side. And then, just like that, Nico is sitting next to me, so close that I can smell his intoxicating scent of boy soap and sweat and grass. He smiles at me, revealing shiny white teeth behind his full lips. He could model for Crest. He could model for *anything*.

"Hey," he says, sticking out his chin in a way that's effortlessly cool.

I let out a sound that's a mix between a mumble and a squeak, but thankfully Ms. McKinney starts talking, hopefully masking my mortification.

There's some more information about the gala, then something about format and maybe grading? But the words continue to float past me until she claps her hands. "Okay, well, that's enough of me jabbering. You can get started now, and we'll skip the workshop today, give you a chance to find your inspiration. Feel free to go where you're comfortable."

Nico and I both stand up at the same time, but I scurry over to a beanbag in the corner, avoiding eye contact. I pull my laptop out of my bag and open up the Colette story. Here. This is something I can do now. Caroline will be asking for it tonight, and now that Tallulah and Thomas have finally kissed, I can let that story rest for a bit. But I can't stop my thoughts from creeping back to what Ms. McKinney said about sharing our work. I could never read a page of this book, or my Tallulah one, to this class. And *definitely* not to Nico. The class would roll their eyes. They would laugh at me. Nico would never see me as a true artist, like he surely is.

Taking a deep breath, though, I try to push the worries away. Because that's not happening now. I can figure it out when it comes time.

Last place I left off, after the mix-up with one guy outside her window and another one in her room, Colette was meeting Jasper at the park in their neighborhood. It was late, a cold November night, and they were huddled together at the top of the slide, Jasper's thick peacoat keeping them both warm. This is an important moment. Jasper knows about Jack now, and he's demanding that Colette finally choose. I thought up about half of the dialogue in the shower this morning.

But with my hands ready on the keys, two hours to write in front of me . . . nothing.

No words come.

I look up, and everyone else around me is writing. Fedora is tapping away at a keyboard attached to his iPad. *Pride and Prejudice* is scribbling in a spiral notebook. Nico, of course, looks perfect hunched over his Moleskine, loose brown curls cascading over his face.

I have to write.

Colette clutches Jasper's hand against her chest.

I hit delete. That's not right. Too bow-chicka-wow-wow. They've only kissed once. And "clutches" makes it sound like some old-fashioned novel where people have fainting couches or something.

I try again.

Colette holds Jasper's hand against her cheek.

Okay, maybe, but then says what? What does she decide?

Backspace again. Backspace freaking backspace. Colette says nothing, does nothing. Because my mind is blank. Nothing.

I'm suddenly aware of how loud it sounds when I'm tapping the keys, and now that I'm not typing anything, do the others notice the silence? Can they tell I'm not being productive like them?

And then there's the fact that I don't type like I'm supposed to, the way the others use all of their fingers over the QWERTY keyboard. I never learned, and I can hunt and peck pretty quick now—it would only slow me down to change it up at this point. Not that it even matters. Nothing is coming out anyway. Can they tell?

"I think I'm going to try writing in my notebook," I whisper to no one in particular, and only Ms. McKinney looks up, giving me a small smile, like she's humoring me or something. She probably knows I don't belong here. She was probably laughing when she read my pleading emails after reviewing whatever my mom put in my portfolio. She was probably just being nice when she let me into the class, her act of charity for the semester.

I want to shrink myself.

I want to disappear.

With my notebook and my favorite felt-tip pen, still the words don't come. I look over the loose outline I wrote for the story, and it inspires nothing. Finally, paranoid that everyone, especially Nico, can tell that I'm not writing, I begin to write "I don't know" in my notebook.

Over and over again.

I don't know I don't know I don't know.

I furrow my eyebrows occasionally, tap my chin like I'm thinking, and keep going until however long it takes for the class to end. Hours.

My words are always there. They wake me up, yelling for attention, in the middle of the night. They whisper in my ear during boring classes.

My words are the reason I somehow tricked this school into admitting me.

But now there's nothing.

My words are gone.

CHAPTER NINE

I barely speak to Sam the whole drive home, brushing off all his first-day questions with one-word answers. The corners of my eyes burn with tears, but I push them away. I try to keep my mind clear, so it's open for whatever flicker of an idea comes my way. I try to dream up the next scene in my head, because sometimes the inspiration is stubborn like that, only coming to me when I'm not in front of my computer screen.

But it's no use.

Nothing.

I throw a "Thank you" to Sam over my shoulder, trying not to feel bad about how puzzled he seems, and then power walk across the street to my house. Chrysalis gets out later in the day, almost five, but still—it's surprising that everyone is there, gathered in the kitchen, when I walk inside. It smells like pizza, and I don't ask if it was ordered specifically for this household.

"There's our writer girl!" Dad calls, a huge smile on his face when he sees me. He was hunched over a slice at the counter, his phone open to work emails next to him, but he comes over to me and pulls me into a tight hug, kissing the top of my head.

I wish he wouldn't call me that.

"Tessie, there's pizza!" Miles yells from the table. He sits at the table alone, and Mom is mobile with her meal, taking quick bites while she puts the dishes away.

"I see. Thanks, bud." I run my hands across his coarse hair as I walk past him to grab a slice. I know I should ask him about his day—how he adjusted to the new routine, if he liked his new one-on-one aide. But my mind is just too full. I keep my backpack on and make my way toward my room.

"Now hold on," Mom says. "We want to hear about Chrysalis!"

If I were able to have any sort of honest conversation with them, I would tell them how I'm apparently broken. How I wasted all the time I was supposed to use to write today. How I might not even belong there in the first place.

I shrug. "It was good."

"Good, okay. . . ." She's wiping her soapy hands on a dish towel, ready to hunker down. "And where did that scarf come from? I don't think I've seen that before."

I had almost forgotten about the first half of the day, even though it felt like the end of the world at the time. I feel like my life will forever be measured in PLW (Pre Loss of Words) and

ALW (After Loss of Words) time.

"I got it from a friend."

Dad is studying his phone again, and Miles is humming a Dream Zone song to himself. But Mom is zeroed in on me. Of course she is, *now*, when I don't want it at all.

"Well, your hair looks really beautiful today," she says, trying a different tactic. "You know, I was looking at a copy of *Essence* when we were waiting for Miles's ENT last week, and there was this really cute style—Bantu ties? No, Bantu knots! We should try it. You would look so cute."

"Um, thanks, okay." I need to get to my room before I fall apart. "I've got stuff to do. Can I go?"

Her eyebrows furrow. And I know we're going to have a big discussion now, which is the last thing I want to do.

"Mom, chinga tu madre," Miles says.

"WHAT?" Mom yelps, eyes bugging out.

"Justin, my new friend in my life skills class, said that. Is it bad?" His laughter is bouncing around the room, and his head starts to roll around. He knows that it's bad, and he's ecstatic—he got a reaction.

"Oh my god . . ."

Saved by the brother. I take the opportunity to escape into my room.

After I change my clothes and fall down on my bed, I feel the tears start to come again. I try to take a few bites of the pizza to distract my brain, because crying isn't going to help anything, but it feels like cardboard in my mouth. I can't eat. I can't cry.

I need to write.

I pull my laptop out of my bag and open up Google Docs. Because maybe it was just being in class with everyone around me. My anxiety just got the best of me—it's happened before. But now that I'm back on my bed, the safe space where I've written so many of my stories, the words will come. They have to.

I stare at the blinking, taunting cursor for ten minutes before Caroline calls.

"Helllooooooo!" she chirps, playful and happy. The opposite of how I'm feeling.

"Hi."

"So how did it go? Did they marvel at your overwhelming genius? Do you have a book deal already? Do you have my next Colette chapter?"

I ignore all of her questions except the last one. "No, sorry. It was more of a warm-up, getting-to-know-you day, you know? The teacher gave us a specific prompt to write about."

That's obviously a lie. And I know it sucks to be lying to my best friend, who would probably be nothing but supportive if I told her the truth. But I don't want to tell her that the one thing I have, the one thing that makes me even a little bit special, may be gone.

"Bummer. But there's always tomorrow, right?"

"Right, and get this," I say, changing the subject. "My mom didn't take me to school today like she promised . . . of course. She arranged for the boy across the street to take me instead."

"The Hawaiian shirt guy? With the pizza?"

"Yeah."

"But you said he was a big ol' nerd, right?"

"Well, yeah . . . but I guess he's not that bad, actually. He was very nice."

"Is he Dungeons and Dragons nerdy? Or, like, those glasses that turn into sunglasses when he goes outside nerdy?"

"Is there, like, a spectrum or something? Have you made charts?"

"Hmmm, no, I guess not. But I can!" She laughs. It's loud in the background, clanging pans and slammed cabinets. I know it's Lola making one of her delicious dinners, right outside Caroline's pantry/bedroom door. I can almost see her floral apron and gray-streaked hair, and it makes me feel a twinge of homesickness, missing dinner with the Tibayan family.

"Okay, now, get this," Caroline continues. "They put me in AP Lit."

"What?"

"Right?"

She starts laughing, and I join in because we both know that while Caroline is a prolific reader, her taste skews more toward my stories and the romance novels she sneaks out of Lola's room, not the works of dead white guys. She barely passed tenth grade

English with a C because of her refusal to read anything but the SparkNotes for *Brave New World* and *Animal Farm*.

"But that's awesome! I bet your dad will be happy, and it's not like you aren't as smart as any of those AP kids."

"Yeah, I know! Smarter, probably, because *I* don't waste my time reading something 'important' when I could be reading something interesting."

I laugh, even though my chest feels tight thinking about Art of the Novel and knowing what side of that divide my silly stories are on. "Are you going to transfer out?"

"Well . . . I was. But then the counseling office was too busy. So then I went to class and Brandon was there. Brandon Briceño—do you remember him? From Yearbook?"

"Uh-huh, yeah."

"So he was there, and we got paired together to read this William Blake poem about a chimney sweep, or whatever. And he read the whole thing like Bert from *Mary Poppins*, which I'm pretty sure is super offensive because of the look the teacher gave us, but I'm not really sure what the poem was about because I was laughing so hard."

She's laughing again now, and I try to join in.

"Anyway, yeah, I guess it probably doesn't make sense now. You had to be there."

And I wasn't.

"Who did you sit with at lunch?" I ask.

"Oh, Brandon! And he brought a couple more of his

friends, Michael Giles and Olivia Roswell. Did you ever meet them? They're really nice."

"Yeah? That's awesome."

"I think I'm actually going to meet up with them tomorrow after school. They always go to Denny's on Tuesdays, and they invited me. Not going to lie, that place is super basic . . . but I don't know, it might be fun."

"Yeah, yeah, definitely."

I know I should be happy that Caroline had a good first day. She's my best friend, and it's not like I want her to be lonely or unhappy. But it sort of makes me feel like maybe I've been holding her back all these years. Maybe *she* wasn't okay with our solo lunches, passing my laptop back and forth. Maybe she was just waiting for me to get out of the way so she could have an exciting social life.

My eyes start to water again, and I let them this time.

There's a knock in the background, and then the sounds of Caroline and Lola speaking Tagalog to each other.

"Listen, I gotta go now," she says quickly. "But I still want to hear all about your day! And send me a chapter tonight."

"Uh-huh." That's not going to happen.

When we hang up, I shove my computer under the bed and do my US history homework instead.

~~When Thomas kissed her, Tallulah felt happy.~~
~~Cheery? Delighted?~~

~~Beatific.~~ Tallulah needed to throw away her thesaurus.

~~Tallulah felt like there were fireworks banging in her chest.~~ Banging? Really?

~~Tallulah felt like a new woman.~~

~~Tallulah felt nothing.~~

CHAPTER TEN

I don't write on the second day of Art of the Novel. Or the third. Or even the fourth.

And the thing is, it's not just in Art of the Novel where I'm frozen. I don't write outside of that class either. At first I hold out hope that maybe I just can't write with people next to me. So I try my bed, the backyard, and the sunny spot on the couch that was becoming my favorite, but still nothing comes.

I decide to seek out inspiration. I reread *Anna and the French Kiss* and *The Sun Is Also a Star* and *Simon vs. The Homo Sapiens Agenda* and basically everything by the queen, Sarah Dessen. I scroll through my favorite Twilight fan fiction (Jacob and Bella). I read and then watch *To All the Boys I've Loved Before*. I binge those ancient movies with the red-haired girl, which are definitely a racist, sexist mess but also kinda good.

Most of those stories don't have protagonists who look like

me. But that's nothing new. I usually have no problem mentally superimposing myself onto white-girl love interests.

But still, nada.

I don't have Art of the Novel every day, though, so my week is only bookended with the demoralizing reminder that I'm a fraud. With all of my other conservatory classes, I can almost forget that I'm not actually earning my place here. I can almost feel like I belong.

For a creative writing program, I can surprisingly get away with not doing a whole lot of writing. My genre study of magical realism meets on Tuesdays, and that just turns out to be a chance for Ms. Becker, who studied abroad in Colombia way long ago, to talk about how much she loves Gabriel García Márquez. Wednesday is Book Club, and my group chooses to read and study *The Hate U Give* (and they don't even stare at me meaningfully after making the choice). And then Thursday I work on the school's lit mag, *Wings*. When they asked for volunteers to copyedit, I quickly signed myself up—not that there was much competition. Everyone else wanted to write.

I should be relieved, right? I should be thrilled that no one has noticed I'm not doing the one thing I'm supposed to be doing here.

But I don't want to spend my time at Chrysalis tricking people. I want to be *actually* writing in class instead of just pretending to. Instead, left with no choice as the due date arrives, I send Ms. McKinney old chapters of my Tallulah story and cross my fingers they weren't in the portfolio Mom originally sent. When I get her first feedback, little bubbles on the side of the document just like the ones from Caroline, I scroll through them slowly, my heart racing like a monster may jump out at any moment. They're okay at first: "Nice!" and "Love this description!" But then I see "Repetitive" and a longer comment that starts with "Not sure if this is realistic," and I stop reading. It's all too overwhelming.

The reality of my situation follows me around like a dark cloud. When I'm driving with Sam, eating lunch with my new friends, walking the hallways that should bring me joy—it's always there. *You shouldn't be here. You shouldn't be here.* I'm terrified at every moment that someone will find out my secret. They'll realize my admission was a mistake and send me to the regular high school where I belong.

One Tuesday evening, Dad is working late and Mom has to drive to Huntington Beach to run some errand, so I'm on Miles duty. The home phone is unplugged, and we're watching old Dream Zone interviews on my laptop (at least I can find some use for it).

"Do you think a place can bring on something terrible?" I ask Miles, interrupting Thad's monologue about his favorite foods. Miles scoots back to lean against the wall. "Or does it reveal flaws that have always been there, and it's just, like, sparking the inevitable? Like, maybe this was always going to happen and I really should be thanking this place instead of resenting it for showing me so clearly that I should just get out now."

"I know exactly what you mean," he says, his voice steady, and that makes me spring up.

"You do?" *I* don't even know what I mean.

"Yeah, that's how I felt the first week at Bixby High when I went to the vending machine and they had Sierra Mist instead of Sprite."

I laugh. And then he laughs because he made me laugh. I pull him into a hug, and his short hair scratches my chin. "Glad you can relate, bud."

Then his whole body goes still, which it never is, and when I look down at his face, he's looking at me with bright, clear eyes.

"You'll figure it out."

"How are you so sure? Let me tell you, it's not looking promising."

"Because you have to. You've got this." He wriggles out of my hug and shrugs, like it's just as simple as that.

And I want it to be. I have to figure it out because I can't disappoint my parents. Because I don't want to leave this school that feels like the right place for me (you know, outside of the whole being-an-artistic-fraud thing). And I can't let down Caroline by not sharing new chapters with her. It's our thing, and the long distance is already pushing us apart.

Writing is what I do, and who even am I anymore if I don't write?

CHAPTER ELEVEN

It only takes me a few more days to realize that I actually don't got this. Like, at all.

I need help. I need Caroline.

Telling Caroline should have been the obvious next step when all of this started a few weeks ago. Except every conversation we've had starts with a new story about Brandon and his friends. About new inside jokes and hanging out after school at diners and meeting up at the mall. About his hand that accidentally brushes hers in AP Lit and a full analysis of what that means.

I really am happy for her, but it's hard not to feel left out of her new life. Talking through my chapters was always our common ground, and now I don't even have that to offer anymore. I've found myself avoiding her calls. And I hate that. She's my best friend, and if anyone would be supportive—it's her.

So, on Thursday night when my phone rings, another Art

of the Novel class looming before me tomorrow, I decide that it's finally time.

"Are you okay?" she yells as soon as I pick up. "You left me on read all day! *And* I left you a voicemail last night. You know I never leave voicemails."

"Yeah . . . I've just been busy, uh, writing." The lie just slips out, without me even trying.

"Oh, thank god! Not going to lie, you had me worried there. I thought maybe you died or something. Like, maybe nerd boy across the street kidnapped you and chopped you up into pieces and put you in a cake or something."

I laugh. "Naturally . . . so, um, any new updates with Brandon? What comes after the traditional inconclusive brushing of the hands?"

"Oh, shut up! You're one to talk, with the turtle pace of Tallulah and Thomas. You, more than anyone, know that the thrilling, ambiguous early days of a courtship is the shit."

"Courtship, huh?" I ask with a smile.

"It's moving in that direction, yeah," she says, and I can hear the smile in her voice. "And for the record, what comes next is him asking me to study with him alone after school, which he definitely. Did. Today!"

She lets out a little squeal of excitement, and I squeal right along with her.

"But anyway, you've been writing! That's good! But why haven't you sent me anything?" she continues. "It's been for-*ev*-er!"

My stomach feels sick with the anxiety, but this isn't going to go away. And if I don't say something now, I'll just lose my nerve.

"I can't write anymore." I blurt it out before I can stop myself or tell another lie.

"What?" she yelps. I can picture her in my mind, sitting up suddenly on her bed. "Like, today? Girl, that's probably for the best. It's okay to take a break! Though I wish you would share what you've been working on with me. . . ."

"No, like, I'm not writing at all." The words hurt coming out. I'd give anything to go back to talking about Brandon now, but I have to keep going. "Not since the first day of school."

"Wait, huh? But you said—"

"I was lying. I . . . I'm—I'm so sorry, Caroline. I shouldn't have waited this long to tell you." I take a deep breath, willing myself to go on. "I kept thinking I would get past this block, and then it wouldn't matter." I can feel tears pooling at the sides of my eyes, and I blink them away. "But I can't write anything, Caroline. I sit at my computer and just . . . stare at it."

Saying it out loud makes it feel real, permanent. And the admission of it all is overwhelming. It sits on my chest like a heavy weight while I wait for Caroline's response.

"Oh, wow . . . but are you sure?"

"Of course I'm sure!" I don't mean to yell that, but all the anxiety and fear (and maybe a little bit of annoyance too) mix together and pop off like a chemical reaction. I take a deep breath and try again, calmer. "This isn't something I would just not be sure about. It's serious to me."

"I know, I know," she says quickly. "It's . . . I'm surprised. You've always been able to write. It's . . . you."

Her words hit me like an arrow to a target—because they echo the fear that's been whispering in my brain for the past few weeks:

Writing is you.

And if you don't have writing, then who are you?

How do you fit into your new school, your family . . . this friendship?

The tears I was holding back flow freely now.

"Writing is my whole identity, you know? It's the one thing I have. The one thing I'm good at it. Like, that makes me special?" Once I start, the words rush out, escaping in between choked sobs. "And writing is the only reason I'm at that school. And I just love the place so much. I feel like I belong and I don't stand out because of how I look, because no one even cares about how I look, how I look is nothing compared to the people who wear, like, tails and Slytherin robes, or whatever. But I don't really belong, right? I'm not a writer, not now—maybe I never was? Maybe I never was! And I can't fully relax there because I'm constantly terrified that people are going to figure out that letting me in was a mistake. That I'm an imposter! I mean, I feel like Harry in *Deathly Hallows*. I know we're trying to lay off the Harry Potter talk—but when his wand breaks when they're leaving Godric's Hollow? And he feels, like, empty and scared because he's supposed to freaking defeat the Dark Lord! Except he has no wand!

And, like, I'm supposed to be this great writer, writing a novel is like my Voldemort and . . . I don't even know where I'm going with this—god, I'm just as bad as the people who wear robes to school . . . BUT AT LEAST THEY CAN WRITE!"

My face is wet, and I'm breathing too fast. Caroline is silent.

"Hello?"

"I'm sorry," she says. "I . . . I don't know what to say."

I hear a door open, and her dad says something in Tagalog. His voice sounds stern, and I can picture the scrunched-up face he makes when he's mad.

"I'm sorry. I'm really, really sorry, Tess. But I have to go. Talk later?"

I know it's not her fault. This happened all the time when I lived close by. Her dad would make her get off the phone, and whatever—we would see each other the next day.

But I just confessed everything to her. I revealed my deepest fears, and I need her help. She's my best friend. Don't I deserve more than a "Talk later?"

I've worried Caroline would lose interest in our friendship once she found out I wasn't writing anymore. I'm already not there physically: I can't eat lunch with her. I can't hang out in her little pantry room, laughing over the silly covers of Lola's romance novels. But I guess she has Brandon for all of that now, which . . . can I blame her? He's there. I'm not.

I've been so worried that my words disappearing would also mean my friend disappearing.

I think I was right.

CHAPTER TWELVE

I wake up to five missed calls and double the number of texts from Caroline.

Answer your phone!

I love you call me back

Are you asleep? How are you asleep??

We need to talk asap. I have an idea. Call me as soon as you wake up!

I CAN FIX YOUR WAND HARRY!!

I'm not even fully conscious yet, but I can feel a smile stretch across my face.

"I know how to get your groove back!" she screams into the phone as soon as she picks up. I have to pull it back and turn down the volume.

"Like Stella?" It's one of Lola's favorites.

"Yeah, but your writing groove, not like your sex groove. Though I suppose a sex groove could be involved."

"Caroline, what are you even talking about?"

I can hear her flop down on her bed. "Sorry, I didn't get a lot of sleep last night because I was figuring out how to fix your life . . . hold up. I'm gonna switch to FaceTime, so you can get the full effect."

The phone beeps, I press the screen, and then there's Caroline. Tan skin, shiny black hair pulled up into a messy topknot, and these elf pajamas that her mom bought for the whole family last Christmas. She even got me a pair, which made me cry. Caroline's sitting in the tiny room I know like the back of my hand—with books and dirty clothes cluttering the floor, and the tattered Dream Zone poster that she never took down. And all the bad feelings that I had last night disappear because she's still Caroline, my Caroline.

"Are you ready for this?" she asks, her tone probably way more serious than the situation requires.

I wipe away the goobers from my eyes and stifle a yawn. "Uh . . . maybe?"

She props up the phone on something, maybe a pillow, and throws her hands out, like she's projecting something on a marquee. "Operation"—she pauses and waggles her eyebrows for dramatic effect—"Tessa's One True Love Story!"

I look away from her excited face, trying to shoo away the disappointment.

"I already know I have to write love stories again," I say, keeping my tone lighter than I feel. "I mean, thank you. I appreciate you trying. But putting the word 'operation' in front

97

of it isn't going to magically make it happen."

"No, you're not getting it," she says patiently. "We are going to create your real-life love story, so you can start writing love stories again."

That stumps me. "What?"

"Listen, you've been getting even more Yellow Wallpaper since you moved to Long Beach. . . ."

"I don't know what that means."

"Well, okay, I only do *kind of* because Brandon and I were writing notes when the class discussed it. It's a short story. And basically it's like this: You've been cooped up. You're not socializing—"

"Hey, I have friends! Sam—and Lenore and Theodore!"

She raises an eyebrow. "Their names rhyme? They sound made up."

"Well, they're not! They're real friends." *Yeah, that's very convincing.*

"Okay, okay," she concedes, putting a hand up. "But I've been thinking about it all night, and no wonder you're not writing. You need to get out. You need to find inspiration. You need to find love!" She sings the last word, drawing it out like it's some power ballad.

Now I raise my eyebrow at her. "Find love?"

"Yes, love! How can you write about love if you don't have love? If you've never had a boyfriend, you know, never have *experienced* things. If my blossoming romance with Brandon has taught me anything—"

"Hey, I've experienced things," I say, cutting her off.

"Daniel doesn't count."

"And why not?"

I met Daniel at a young writers' camp at Sacramento State the summer between eighth grade and freshman year. He wrote these really interesting contemporary fantasies with fairies set in San Francisco. We bonded over the cheese fries in the dining hall and snuck away to kiss behind the aquatic center on the last day of camp—my *first* kiss. We texted the rest of summer and the first few weeks of ninth grade, but it eventually ended. He lived in a different city, and he got tired of a girlfriend on his phone and found a real one.

Okay, maybe a little bit of what Caroline is saying is right.

"From your descriptions, you guys kissed like how cousins kiss, all closed mouth and boring," she says, making me forget whatever I was thinking about her being right.

"You kiss your cousins?" I wrinkle my nose.

"Ugh, you know what I mean."

"I really don't," I say, cocking my head to the side and smirking. "I don't know if I should be taking advice from a cousin kisser."

She huffs in exasperation but then joins in with my giggles. God, I miss her so much.

"Okay, but back to my point," she continues. "Actually, this proves my point! Do you remember how much you wrote when all that was going on with Daniel? You were prolific! I could barely keep up!"

It's true. I wrote more that summer than I ever have. "Yeah, okay . . ."

"Now imagine if that was love! Passionate, all-encompassing, noncousin love!"

"I need you to stop with the cousin stuff. We kissed normal!"

"We need to find you a lover," she says, not missing a beat. "You need to experience love, so you can write about it again. And I'm talking making out in the rain, sneaking out of the house, getting busy in the car because you can't stand to wait any longer. All of that stuff!"

"All of those things have happened in my stories. . . ."

"Exactly. Where do you think I got the examples from? But the well is dry, Tess. That's why you can't write! I'm sure of it! And you just need something real to draw from, so you can start writing again. What do they say . . . write what you know? You need to know more, so you can write more!"

I let myself dream for a moment. My own happily ever after doesn't sound so bad. It sounds exciting even, and maybe that would be enough to conquer the other fear blocking me. That's what happens in all of the great love stories, right? The girl gets the guy, and then everything else sort of falls into place.

I think back to my writing spree when I fell in, well, *like* with Daniel. How frantically, urgently I wrote, even when my wrists started to get carpal tunnel. I would give anything to feel like that again.

"So, say I agree to this . . . ," I start.

"Yessss!" She does a little wiggle of excitement.

"Say I agree to this," I say louder, shaking my head. "How do you intend to do anything from Roseville? Is this gonna be a Cyrano-type situation?"

"I don't know what that is. But I am currently drafting a list of situations, moments, and circumstances that will lead you to your happily ever after."

"That's so vague. What does that even mean?"

"Actually I like that. New name!" She stretches out her hands again, all over-the-top. "Operation Tessa's Happily Ever After!"

"Still vague."

"And as far as candidates go," she continues, ignoring me, "maybe *Sam*, yeah? I've noticed you mentioning him a lot."

"No!" Caroline's eyes bug before narrowing suspiciously.

"No, no, no," I add quickly, probably too insistent. Caroline's eyebrow is arched and I can tell she's about to probe further, so I keep going. "There's this other guy, actually. His name is Nico. He's in my novel class. And he's so gorgeous . . . it's like a little scary? He looks like Thomas from my story."

"WHAT!" Caroline jumps up so abruptly that she knocks the phone over. Picking it up quickly, she shouts, "Nico! Why didn't you tell me about *Nico*? This is perfect! And he's a brooding, skinny white guy. Why am I not surprised?"

"Hey! Why do you say it like that? I don't only like white guys! Daniel—"

But she cuts me off before I can remind her that Daniel was

Black. "Chill, I'm just messing with you. You're allowed to like white guys, Tessa. Now, let's get back to your hot writer suitor."

"Not suitor—*acquaintance*!" Even that is probably an exaggeration. What do I call someone who I stare at longingly from afar? Who probably doesn't even know I exist?

"Okay, but awesome," Caroline continues, undeterred. "Every love story starts somewhere. This is even better. I only said Sam because I thought maybe you liked him, which would totally be okay if you did. But to tell you the truth, I'm kinda glad that you don't, because we don't need your first boyfriend having a Hawaiian shirt addiction."

"Yeah, yeah," I say, but it makes me feel sort of guilty, because his shirts really aren't that bad when you get used to them.

"So, Tessa and Nico. I like the sound of that. Now I might need to reformulate my plan with this new development. . . ."

"Mmm-hmm," I say, nodding my head seriously and pretending to take notes. Her annoyed face makes me burst into giggles.

"Yeah, you laugh now, but you just watch. Boom, I'm going to make you and Nico fall in love, and then, bam, you're going to start writing again." She punches her fist out to accentuate her points.

"This all sounds very violent."

"Not at all," she says, and grabs a sheet of paper off the floor "So, are you ready to hear what I have so far? Prepare yourself."

I laugh and shake my head. "Sure."

"Okay, first, you gotta be clumsy. Clumsiness is a classic romance heroine characteristic. Spill a drink on him, fall down some steps, get hit by a car—preferably his, and at a low speed—and he's going to be alllll yours." She looks up and sees my wide eyes, but then apparently decides to keep going. "And I know it doesn't rain there much, but it's essential that you and Nico get caught in the rain together. So keep an eye on the weather report. And we need to orchestrate a one-bed situation somehow. Do you have any leads on that?"

She looks up again, face still completely sincere. How long did it take her to come up with this shtick?

"Yeah, and maybe we can get stuck in an elevator too," I snort.

Caroline's eyes light up at that. "Yes! I saw when I was doing my research last night that there was one on your campus! And you could just, like, push the emergency button when he's not looking or something. It's like a guaranteed nonstop trip to love town from there!"

I blink a few times, waiting for her to finally laugh, maybe do some finger guns, and exclaim, "I got you!" But her face remains earnest and open. This isn't a joke. This is her real plan.

"Caroline." I start slowly, carefully. "You don't . . . you can't seriously think this will work. I mean, did you just stay up watching a bunch of romantic comedies and write down all the tropes you could find?"

"No," she says, sounding offended. "I left out a makeover 'cause you already look good."

I groan, but I can't help but smile. "Okay, but, seriously . . ."

"Seriously." She cuts me off. "I know it seems a little crazy, but I really think this might work for you, Tessa. I mean, even if you and Nico don't fall in love—which, trust me, I think you will, if even half of the things I have planned happen—it will give you some new ideas. And it'll be something fun for us to do together . . . like old times."

That thought warms me up, and I try unsuccessfully to hold in a smile. Caroline's face cracks wide open into a wild grin. She has me, and she knows it.

I let out a deep sigh for show, but we both know what I'm going to say next.

"Fine."

"Yay! I'm so excited! So, SO excited!" She drops the phone again, trying to clap and hold it at the same time.

"But you're going to have to think of a better name. Operation Tessa's Happily Ever After sounds like a Disney Channel original movie or something."

She rolls her eyes. "Okay, we'll call it . . . How Tessa Got Her Groove Back."

"Apparently," I say, imitating her eye roll, "I've never had a groove in the first place."

She tries again. "To All the Love Stories I've Loved Before?"

"That doesn't even make sense."

"Okay, well, we can think of a name later, but this is going to work, Tessa, I know it. I can help you create *your* love story. I mean, I learned from the best. *You.*"

I don't know how much faith I have in this plan. I still think it's a long shot that Caroline could help me fall in love from four hundred miles away, let alone with *Nico*. And it's even more unlikely that this will fix my probably permanent writer's block.

But I nod my head along with her anyway, throwing in a few suggestions and vetoing things that are a little too ridiculous (I will *not* get hit by a car). And by the end of the phone call, we have a list that I agree to follow faithfully. Why? Because this makes it clear that she cares, when I thought she might be slipping away. Maybe this is just what we need to tie us together again, despite the distance and all the changes. Caroline has always been my best friend, and she still is. SHE STILL IS! Only a best friend would come up with a plan as ridiculous as this.

Tessa's Happily Ever After

(That's the name we're sticking to. Get used to it!)

1. Get stuck in an elevator
2. Spill something on him or fall in his general direction—CLUMSINESS IS KEY
3. Find out a secret about him that no one else knows
4. Go to a party together and have a moment
5. Even better: a co-ed sleepover. Where there is conveniently only one bed

6. Get caught in the rain together—going forward, MUST stop carrying umbrellas
7. Dance of ROMANCE. Are there any dances coming up? Need to research.
8. Make him jealous—love triangle possibilities?
9. Fall asleep at the same time, somewhere cute, but you first so he can SEE you
10. Ride a Ferris wheel together
11. Big dramatic speech declaring your love, with signs

CHAPTER THIRTEEN

It's a couple hours later, and I'm in the passenger seat of Sam's car on the way to Chrysalis.

"What's wrong?" he asks.

"Nothing," I say quickly, even though I know that's not believable at all. Our drives have come to be filled with long stories about the exploits of his over-the-top bubbe in New York and giggles over something funny that Miles said the night before, plus lots of delicious treats. It's easy with him. But today I'm silently staring out the window, trying to slow down the thoughts that are spiraling in my mind.

"If it's nothing, then why have you been looking like . . . I don't know, Eeyore? . . . all morning?" he presses.

"I have not."

"Yeah, you have. You might as well have a rain cloud hanging over your head. Did something happen?"

"No. I just have a lot on my mind."

Caroline's crazy plan to fix everything made sense earlier, but now, as I'm heading to school, it's starting to seem more and more ridiculous. Getting stuck in an elevator with Nico isn't going to do anything about the fact that that Johnson is next on Ms. McKinney's alphabetical list. Unless, of course, we're trapped there for all of Art of the Novel.

"You'll go on Friday," she reminded me last class. "I can't wait for you to share what you've been working on."

There was a kind smile on her face, as if she was delivering good news. I tried to match it, but my face probably looked plastic.

There's no way that I can share my silly Tallulah and Thomas chapters, the ones I've been passing off to Ms. Mc-Kinney as new work, with the class. So far, people have shared scenes with characters having long and important conversations about life and fantasy stories with magical systems that I can hardly wrap my mind around. I can just see them rolling their eyes and hiding their laughs if I were to read about Tallulah pining over Thomas. Especially with Nico *right there*, Thomas in the flesh.

What am I going to do?

"Okay, nothing's wrong. Sure. But if something was wrong . . . would another donut help?"

"No." They are lavender flavored and have a lemon glaze, with candied peel on the top, and I had to fight the urge to lick my fingers after finishing my first. I crack a smile. "But I'll take one anyway."

"Well, I hope your day goes up from here," Sam says as we pull into the Chrysalis parking lot.

"I doubt it," I sigh, and okay, I guess I get the Eeyore comparison. "But thank you anyway."

Cutting the ignition, Sam puffs out his chest and does this weird little waddle thing in his seat. "Oh bother, I think this is something that a nice pot of honey could take care of." He makes a dopey face and then moves side to side again.

I blink. And then blink again before erupting into giggles. "What *was* that?"

"Winnie the Pooh, of course," he laughs, his cheeks flushing. "You know, because, like, Eeyore . . . they're friends?"

I fall forward, my sides aching from laughing. "Oh my god. Please don't ever do that again. Especially not in public, or I'll be forced to deny this friendship ever existed."

"Hey, it got you to smile!" He points at me and winks, exuding major dad-joke energy. "See you at lunch?"

We get out, and I smile at him over the top of the car. "Yeah. See you later."

A call comes from a few spaces over in the lot.

"Hey, Whiner!"

I look around, confused. But then I follow Sam's gaze to a black Audi parked across from us. And getting out of it are Nico, Poppy, Grayson, and Rhys. The founders' kids, the CW cast.

I get the sudden urge to run away. My conversation with Caroline this morning is surely written all over my face.

Acquaintance? What was I talking about? Nico and I aren't acquaintances! The crazy stalker vibes are wafting off me, and he's going to pick up on them and then this plan will be dead in the water before it even begins. Plus, Sam is wearing those cargo pants that zip off at the knee, you know, to, like, make shorts? Why they even make these I have no idea. Do people find themselves in situations often where they have to quickly change the length of their pants? I like Sam a lot, but these pants don't belong anywhere in my love story.

There's no time to escape, though. The four of them are heading right for us.

"Hey, Whiner!" Nico says again. I don't get it. Is Whiner, like, Sam's nickname or something?

Sam looks like he's just going to keep walking, but Nico comes up and does one of those slap-back things that guys always do. They are polar opposites of each other: Nico is slim and intimidatingly tall, while Sam is eye-to-eye with me and has a soft belly that pushes against the bottom buttons on his shirt. Sam has relaxed shoulders and an easygoing demeanor, and Nico's posture is sharp, like he's standing at attention.

I'm struck again by how much Nico is like Thomas. No wonder I gave his name so readily to Caroline when she brought up Sam.

"Sam Whiner!" Rhys, the ginger, says. So it's Sam's last name. Whiner is probably really Weiner. I feel kind of silly for not knowing that already, after weeks of drives and lunches together. "So you finally got in. Third time's a charm?"

Something changes in Sam with that. His face, which was just doing a goofy impersonation to make me laugh a few moments ago, gets hard and tight. "Yeah."

"Did you make it into the theater conservatory?" Grayson asks, a smirk on his face. "We all know you can turn on those waterworks, huh, Weiner?"

Grayson draws out "Weiner" in a high-pitched tone. I decide immediately that I don't like him—if only for the way that Sam's jaw tenses as he looks away. Plus, Grayson also has a fuzzy hope of a mustache littering the top of his lip that only a douchebag would think looks good.

"Oh, but you must be in the new culinary arts conservatory, right, Sam?" Poppy asks. This is the first time I've seen her up close, not just from me sneakily spying on them during lunch. Her skin is poreless, but not because she's wearing a whole bunch of makeup—because it's actually that flawless, like one of those girls who model for Glossier.

"Yeah, I am," Sam says.

"And I'm sure your famous mommy joining the board didn't have anything to do with that," Grayson says under his breath. Famous mommy? I don't know what that means. But I do know that I want to punch Grayson in the face. Nico, I notice, doesn't join in when Rhys and Poppy laugh along with Grayson.

"Sam's really good at what he does. He made this," I say, holding up my half-eaten donut. Probably not the defense Sam was looking for, but he sends a secret smile my way.

"Tessa, right?" Nico's looking right at me, and then everything else kind of slips away. All I can think about is that his eyes are like pools of chocolate. I want to step closer, so I can dive into them. I want to trace the path of his collarbone that's peeking, just barely, out of the top of his button-up.

But instead I say, "Mmmmm."

"We have Art of the Novel together?"

I'm suddenly only capable of single syllables. "Yep."

"We better get going, babe. You know Mr. Garcia has it out for you with the tardies." Poppy puts her arm around Nico's waist, and he sticks his hand in her back pocket. They fit together.

Of course they're together. I don't know how I missed it in all of my lunchtime stalking. Guys like Nico like girls like Poppy. I'm going to have to find someone else for Caroline's plan. Or maybe just forget about it altogether.

"Bye, Tessa. Bye, Weiner."

By the time I finally croak out, "Uh, yeah, bye!" they've already sauntered off too far to hear me. Sam looks at me, his eyebrows pressed together, a clear question there. But I ask one before he can. "Are you okay? What was that?"

He rubs the side of his face and shakes his head, and he gives me a sad smile. "I'll see you later, Tessa."

At lunch I don't let him slip away so easily, though.

"Okay, are you ready to tell me what's going on?"

We're sitting in what has become our regular spot on the

porch of the Bungalow. Three rocking chairs and a stool that Lenore swiped from a group of creative writers last week. I'm fighting the urge to look up at Nico and his group, sure I'll see all the relationship signs I missed before with him and Poppy.

Sam's perched on the stool, writing in a notebook that I know contains his recipes. He shrugs. "It's nothing. Really."

"It isn't nothing," I insist.

He looks up at me with a smirk. "I don't know . . . maybe I just caught your bad mood from earlier." Touché.

"Y'all better tell us what's going on instead of carrying on like we can't hear you," Lenore cuts in. She's wearing another magazine-worthy outfit today: a black leather beret, Doc Martens, and a sleeveless black dress with gold-embroidered bugs.

Sam lets out an exaggerated sigh but then nods, giving me permission, and I quickly fill Lenore in on the weirdness of this morning, knowing she'll be able to get the details out of him. I need to know Sam's history with Nico. Okay, yeah, he *may* have a girlfriend, but this hasn't been verified just yet. And Nico wasn't, like, mean to Sam or anything—not like Grayson and Poppy. Sam might have an in.

"Ooohh, so Sammy boy knows the founders' kids," Lenore chirps. "How come you didn't tell us about your bougie friends?"

"They aren't my friends," Sam says. He closes his recipe book, looking exasperated. "Look, I went to middle school with them, and our parents knew each other . . . but we weren't friends then, and we aren't now. In eighth grade, they all auditioned for Chrysalis and got in, and I didn't. . . . I think they made that pretty obvious."

"What other conservatories did you try out for?" Lenore asks.

"Film . . . and creative writing." He looks at me. "But I wasn't very good at either. They weren't my things . . . I just wanted to come here instead of Bixby High."

"So, no acting?" I don't want to mention what Grayson said about the crying, but I also want to know what he meant. Thankfully Sam gets the message without me having to say more.

He sighs again. Maybe I'm pushing this too much. "That's . . . it's just an old stupid joke. I don't know why they keep bringing it up. I was on this show when I was in sixth grade. . . ."

"Oh, wow, so you're, like, a child star?" Lenore interrupts.

"No. No, no. It was a baking show. Like one of those competitions on Food Network? I got sent home, and I cried. It was stupid."

"Nah, real men cry," Lenore says, getting up to pat his back. I quickly nod in agreement.

"It wouldn't have been that bad, except Rhys recorded it and, like, put it up on YouTube—it was black and white with all these effects, like falling leaves and a fake storm. It was stupid. But I don't know . . . maybe it started his interest in film, so it was, like, valuable or something." He gives us a sarcastic smile.

"And what did that asshole mean about your mommy—

mom getting you into the school?" I ask. "That's not true, right? I mean, he obviously hasn't tried your chocolate-chip cookies."

That finally makes Sam's dimple appear, for the first time since the encounter this morning. But then his face clouds over again, and he looks down at his hands, picking at the side of his nail.

"My mom did join the board this year . . . but that's not the reason I got in. I had to audition, same as anyone."

"But who's your mom? He said she was famous?"

"My mom's Audrey Weiner." He forces the words out, like they taste bad. "I just . . . I don't like people to know or, like, think of me differently."

The name sounds familiar, but I can't quite place it.

Luckily, Theodore does it for me. He was deep into his sketch, but that makes him look up. "Your mother is celebrity chef and four-time James Beard Award winner Audrey Weiner?"

Just like that, her face snaps into place: dark curly bob, signature red lips. I can see her saying her catchphrase, paired with a snapping finger, at the end of every recipe. "And there you go!" She's everywhere—her own show on Food Network, appearances on talk shows, restaurants. Like the female Guy Fieri, but less irritating.

"Damn, Sam! How come you didn't tell us you were rich? My mom watches her holiday specials!" Lenore side-eyes me. "And you guys are neighbors. Are you rich too, girl?"

"No, I mean . . . we're comfortable," I sputter. "But, like . . .

I don't know. This isn't about me!" I look at Sam, who's still studying his fingers. "How come you didn't tell me your mom was Audrey Weiner?"

Why has he told me all about his bubbe's last three boyfriends and her year-long grudge with a personal shopper in Saks, but not this? I replay all of our conversations in the car, searching for times his mom could have come up.

He shrugs. "Your mom met her. Figured she told you. And is it really important anyway?"

"Not at all," I say. "It's not like all of a sudden I want to cozy up to you because you have a famous mom." That makes Sam's cheeks turn red. "But it's just a lot to not mention. That, and then all the drama with the founders' kids. That's the kind of thing you tell your friends."

"Other people's opinions of me aren't really my business. And I think that situation says more about them than it does about me. So I've let it go." And then he shrugs. Like that kind of perspective and confidence is no big deal. I wish it was so easy for me.

"Whoa!" Lenore shouts. "Drop! That! Knowledge! Samuel!"

I'm reminded of the conversation we had in his car on the first day. It's like a filter has been removed, and this whole other side of him is being revealed again. I've assumed a lot about Sam because of the bad hair and the dorky clothes, and I feel like a jerk. I hate when people do that to me—because of my skin color, because of my awkwardness. Maybe I need to let Sam be whoever he is, zip-off cargo pants, Hawaiian shirts, dad shoes, and all.

"Mmm-hmm, okay, but can she, like, introduce me to Alton Brown?" Lenore says, pursing her lips. "I'm interested."

"Disgusting, Lenore," Theodore says. Then, pausing, "But also, I suppose I wouldn't turn him down, with ten years and a little disillusionment under my belt."

I laugh so much that I almost forget what's coming for me next period.

CHAPTER FOURTEEN

I have it all worked out.

Ms. McKinney usually starts the workshop in the last thirty minutes of class, which seems like too much time to me. But we always somehow go over—with some readers going on and on, making allusions to Beckett and Vonnegut in an attempt to show off their literary knowledge, and some writers trying to justify every last thing that was criticized in their work. It may be my day to share, but I don't plan on being in class to participate in the circle of creative torture. No, I'm going to find an excuse to leave forty minutes before class ends, disappear until the final bell, and then deal with whatever consequences when I get back. It's not like they'll sit around waiting for me. Those real writers will be jumping over each other, probably, to take my place.

I've never been one to ditch class (and does this *really* count?), but I'll do whatever I have to.

See, I don't deserve to be here.

When I first figured that out, realized my lack of words was my new normal, it was a gaping wound. This thing that I've loved for so long wasn't mine anymore, and someone might as well have chopped off my arm or something.

But the pain is dulling. And now that Caroline and I have a plan, however silly it may be, all I feel is overwhelming resolve that I'm definitely, *definitely* going to keep Ms. McKinney and Nico and all these real writers from finding out what I've been hiding. Because I may not deserve to be here now, but I'm going to fix that soon.

So I stare studiously at my computer screen, I type my name and my address about a million times, and I even grab a book off the shelf—*A Clockwork Orange?*—to look like I'm using it for a reference or something. But when the clock hits go time, I close my computer and quietly walk up to Ms. McKinney.

"Miss, can I go to the restroom?"

She looks past me to the clock on the wall, and her eyebrows press together.

"Can you wait until class is over? It's almost time to begin workshop."

"It's kind of . . . uh, an emergency."

She clutches her hands together and looks me right in the eyes. "Are you sure? You seemed fine just a minute ago. It appeared you were typing a great deal."

Her eyes are pale blue, almost clear, and it feels like they're seeing right through me. I almost confess right then, taken with her magical teacher powers, but then I look past her and see Nico. He's looking up from his Moleskine and watching our interaction.

Nope. I gotta leave.

"I'm having, like . . . stomach problems." I clutch my waist and wince to really sell it. "I need to go to the restroom. Now."

That seems to do it. "Okay, well, do you want to leave your copies here, so we can pass them out while you're gone?" she asks, but I'm already fleeing.

"When I get back," I call over my shoulder.

I run up the stairs like someone's chasing me, and as soon as I reach the top, the tightness in my chest releases. Yeah, I basically just said I had to poop in front of the most gorgeous guy in the world, but whatever. It was necessary.

I'm good. For today.

Except, while I definitely had a plan for getting out of class, I didn't really figure out what I was going to do after that. My stuff's down there, including my phone. And I can't go walking around campus—one of the administrators or the security guard would stop me, and then I'd have to explain that to Ms. McKinney too.

I go to the restroom on the main floor of the Bungalow, to feel a little less like a liar, but then I end up in the kitchen, out of sight from the basement door, and lean against the counter. The worry kicks in immediately. Should I be counting the minutes to make sure I don't go down too early? But I guess I'll hear the people come up when class is done. Unless Ms. McKinney sends someone sooner. Would she tell them why I was gone? Like, am I going to get a reputation as Diarrhea Girl or something? Is that worse than being known as a nonwriter?

My pulse is rising and my neck is hot again, and I must jump three feet when I hear the squeak on the hardwood floor announcing someone's arrival in the kitchen.

"Whoa, sorry, didn't mean to scare you."

I don't want to look up, knowing who that voice belongs to. But of course I do anyway, taking in his full lips and shiny brown curls. He has tight black pants on, brown boots, and a navy polka-dot button-up with the short sleeves rolled up. It takes all my willpower not to visibly swoon.

"Uh, hi."

"Hey. Ms. McKinney sent me up to find you, but you seem . . . better?"

"Oh yeah, I'm fine, totally fine." Then I remember I'm supposed to be selling it, so I add, "Now. Now I'm fine. I just needed some air." *Not because I was pooping!* I want to scream, mortified, but I just press my lips together so I don't seem even more unhinged.

He smiles, and I notice that his eyes look a little sleepy when he does, heavy lidded under the weight of his dark eyelashes. They're so thick, the kind of thick girls go to expensive monthly appointments in order to achieve.

"Yeah, I get it," he says, leaning on the counter. "Ms.

McKinney can be kind of a know-it-all sometimes. I need air too. And my dad says her books aren't very good anyway . . . never made the list."

He laughs, and I find myself joining in, even though I don't really agree with what he's saying.

"And those people in there." He shakes his head. "Those workshops are torture."

"Right?" Though I obviously don't think they're torture for the same reason.

"But you . . ." He reaches one of his brown boots across the kitchen floor and taps the tip of my hot-pink ballet flat. I feel it pulse through my whole body in an instant, like an electric shock. "You probably are going to blow them away. Your writing's probably real deep . . . real *soulful*. I can tell."

I fight the urge to raise my lip. *Probably just a poor choice of words.* Instead I laugh, and I hope it doesn't sound as manic as I feel. "Well, I don't know about that."

"Nah, I'm sure of it," he says, nodding his head and smiling at me. One of his loose curls falls into his face, and he pushes it back.

"So, are you dating Weiner?" he asks. "I noticed you always drive together."

My breath catches in my throat. He *noticed me.*

And not just that. He's looked at me enough to notice *patterns.*

"No, we're neighbors," I say quickly. "He lives across the street. That's why he drives me."

"Ah, okay," he says, and then he just stares at me. It's silent. But it's not, like, an awkward kind of silence that I know well. It's heavy. And *meaningful*.

"Nicoooooo, are you in here?" A chirpy singsong voice calls from the front of the house, and I jump, startled. That would be embarrassing enough, but even worse, I trip over the rug in front of the sink and fall forward.

"Oooop!"

I fully expect to land flat on my face, but strong arms catch me, and suddenly I'm looking up into Nico's brown eyes.

"Oh my god. I'm so sorry. I'm so . . . *clumsy*." The words make me freeze. Clumsy. *CLUMSINESS IS KEY*. Number two on our list! I didn't even do it on purpose, but it worked. It really worked! I am being held in Nico's warm embrace. Only a few inches from his soft lips. If I wanted to, I could probably . . .

"Tessa?"

"What is wrong with her?"

Poppy's face falls into my sight, and I jerk up quickly, detaching myself from Nico. Her gray hair is half up in a top-knot, and she's wearing a white crop top, showing a slice of her porcelain skin.

"I'm fine. Sorry . . . I'm fine. Just tripped. Didn't see that rug, is all."

"Uh, okay. That was weird," she says, looking me up and down. Then she turns back to Nico. "Let's goooo, baby. I thought we were going to meet outside five minutes ago."

So maybe *that's* why he came to look for me.

"Yeah, I was just talking to Tessa here." Her turns to me again, eyes full of concern. "Are you sure you're okay?"

"Yeah, yeah." I can feel my cheeks turning pink.

"Well, come on." Poppy grabs his arm. "I only have so much time before Ms. Vaughn notices I'm gone."

She puts her tongue between her teeth as she speaks, one of those mannerisms some girls have mysteriously mastered that are a mixture of both sexy and cute. I wonder if it's genuine or affected. And it makes me both hate her and want to practice it later in the mirror.

It seems to do something to Nico, anyway, and he snaps to her side like a magnet, nuzzling the top of her hair. I look away, not wanting to seem like a creeper.

"See you later," he says, giving me a half wave. And then they walk out, arms wrapped around each other, probably going to their special spot to make out.

When I finally go back downstairs after the bell, Ms. Mc-Kinney is deep in conversation with Fedora (who's actually not wearing a fedora today, but I never figured out his real name). I grab my bag and sprint back up the stairs before she notices I'm there.

CHAPTER FIFTEEN

I'm staring out Sam's passenger-side window at the cotton candy skies, waiting for Caroline's responses to my ecstatic texts about the successful first move with Nico.

That's when I see him.

"Oh, no."

"Hey, isn't that your brother?"

I want to tell him no. I want to tell him to keep driving, to take us away from this street, somewhere else. Anywhere Miles isn't sitting on the corner, screaming at passing cars, and crying so hard snot drips down his face.

I close my eyes, my chest getting tight as the panic sets in. "Yes."

Miles's scream is unique to Miles, just like his laugh. It shakes my bones. And it's so loud now that we can hear it through the car doors, over the music.

How is this happening? Where is Mom? Did I forget I was supposed to watch Miles?

I notice Mom's car in the driveway, though, and then our front door hanging wide open. Did something happen to Mom? Is she hurt? All the worst-case scenarios play like a horror movie in my head.

But then I see her, standing on Mrs. Hutchinson's front steps, face frozen in disbelief. And then, like a switch flips, she jumps into action, sprinting over to Miles.

We pull into Sam's driveway, and I start gathering my stuff, frantic.

"I—I'm so sorry. This is so—"

"Don't be sorry." He cuts me off, putting his hand on my arm and giving it a light squeeze. His green eyes are soft. "You have nothing to be sorry for. Your brother has nothing to be sorry for."

"Thank you."

"Can I . . . I don't know, help in any way?" he asks.

I'm getting out of the car now, my heart beating fast. Mom's already made it to him, and I can see her talking in his ear, rubbing his back. But his shrieks still echo across the street.

"No, we've got it. But thank you."

This happened all the time at our old house. Miles always runs when he's most upset, like he can escape whatever is causing him trouble. Usually it wasn't a problem. The neighbors knew him, and they'd just let us handle our family business. They wouldn't even come outside unless we asked for their help.

But one time, the Wachowskis' cousin was house-sitting for them, and I guess it scared her, Miles out there screaming and crying. I was supposed to be watching him, but I went to Caroline's house down the street real quick to grab a book she was letting me borrow. Miles didn't want to come. Dream Zone was doing, like, a Where Are They Now? special on some cable channel, and I knew I would be gone for just a second.

Then the stupid cousin called the cops. And there's no tragic ending here. I want to make that clear, because that's where my mind goes first too. But the officers didn't lay a finger on Miles. They were nice and patient with him, even. I mean, we lived in a pretty tight-knit neighborhood and all of the neighbors came out to vouch for our family (except for the stupid cousin). Though I know even that doesn't make a difference most of the time.

But none of our new neighbors in Long Beach really know us yet, except for Mrs. Hutchison, who's standing on her porch looking irritated. And Sam—he's at least going inside. The Hwangs, the old couple that lives next to him, though, are standing at their door now, staring at Miles. And I can see the curtains moving on the Agrawals' window too. They may be hesitant to come outside and gawk, but that doesn't mean they'll be too hesitant to call the police.

We need to get him inside.

"She wanted to talk about the tree again. I was just next door," Mom says quickly when I get there, like she owes me an explanation.

"Fuck you!" Miles screams, his anger directed at a BMW turning the corner. The windows are tinted, but I can imagine the wide eyes of the person driving it. "Fuck you! Fuck everything!"

"Miles, honey, what happened?" Mom asks. Her arms are wrapped tightly around him, and she's speaking softly in his ear.

"My DVD . . . ," he moans. His body rocks back and forth, and his hearing aids ring. His glasses are gone, probably discarded on our lawn. "It broke! It broke! Fuck everything! EVERYTHING!"

We don't need him to explain which DVD it is. And it's easy to think it's a little thing—inconsequential, stupid. A DVD broke, whatever. But to him, it's a big deal. You can see it in his eyes. He looks as if he's in physical pain.

It actually pains me too, to see him like this, to know that there's nothing I, or anyone, can do to make him feel better. It's like the earthquakes that appear out of nowhere and make the floor roll and rock a few times per year. Everyone outside California thinks they're a huge deal, terrifying, but when you've grown up here, they're just something that happens, a normal part of life. Miles's tantrums are our family's earthquakes. We just need to get him somewhere safe and ride it through.

"Oh, honey, I'm so sorry," Mom says, rubbing his back. "Maybe we can fix it." He must know that's a lie, because he screams even louder. "Or we can find another one."

"NO!" Miles yells, throwing her off him. "NO, NO, NO! I want that one! THAT ONE! FUCK EVERYTHING!"

"Okay, Miles, now I want you to take a deep breath. Breathe in, breathe out." Mom stands up to do it with him, modeling the breathing with exaggerated movement, but it's doing nothing. Miles shrieks again. A blond lady walking with her daughter a few houses down grabs her little girl tightly by the shoulder and turns her around.

"Mom, maybe we should just—"

"Miles, would it help to meditate?" she says, ignoring me. "We need you to be calm, so we can talk about this. I have the meditation app on my phone."

"FUCK EVERYTHING!"

She scrolls to the meditation app, like she doesn't hear him, and starts playing this guided meditation, as loud as her phone speakers will go.

"Let's calm your body, Miles. It's okay, honey."

I look around again, and another neighbor whose name I don't know—a red-haired woman wearing an apron—is standing on her porch staring. We are officially a scene.

"Mom, I have headphones," I whisper to her. "Can he put in headphones?"

Mom turns to me, and her blue eyes are cold.

"Are we embarrassing you, Tessa?" she asks. It sounds like a challenge.

"I'm not! It's just . . . I don't want . . ." I can't finish a sentence. I'm not embarrassed by *my brother*. It's not like this is his default setting—he's upset. But I don't want to be the center of any kind of attention at all, and this situation is bringing on all of it. Is that so wrong? Who likes to have their new neighbors standing outside and shaking their heads? Who likes to have all eyes on them in this way?

"The neighbors . . . ," I finally say, feebly.

"He is your brother, and he is sad. That's what you should be worried about right now. Not what the neighbors think." She sighs heavily, like I'm some nuisance. "God, Tessa, I can't believe you. I really wish—"

But she doesn't finish the sentence, interrupted by another one of Miles's wails.

I really wish you weren't such a disappointment? I really wish I only had Miles to deal with and not you too?

I don't want to know the end of that sentence.

Miles continues to cry and Mom continues to instruct his breathing. And I stare at the street, trying not to cry, because that will only make Miles more upset. It will only make a bigger scene.

A dark gray truck slows, and I'm ready for someone else to stare at us, to shake their head. But the truck stops at the corner and throws its hazards on, and I realize with relief that I know this truck. It's Dad. He's dressed nicely for work—a baby-blue button-up, dress shoes, and slacks—but he strides over to us and gets down on the ground next to Miles.

"It's okay, my boy," he murmurs. "Let's go home."

He scoops Miles up with his strong arms, carrying his nineteen-year-old body like a baby's. My tears come now.

I keep my head down—avoiding the neighbors' eyes, avoiding Mom's—as we walk home together, all four Johnsons.

CHAPTER SIXTEEN

I stay inside all weekend. And when I say inside, I mean inside my room. I want to avoid the windows, just in case the neighbors are out there, staring at our house and having whispered conversations about what to do about the new, disruptive family.

And I want to avoid Mom. I'm still pissed at her for somehow turning Miles's tantrum on the corner into something I was doing wrong. And there's also a little part of me that's afraid she's right.

Usually on Sunday mornings, I watch Miles when Dad plays golf and Mom goes on a Costco run, but everyone stays home this Sunday. We don't talk about it.

Caroline and I also haven't talked since Friday. When I looked at my phone again, it was full of *I told you so*'s about Nico and strategizing about the next steps—and also hints at something else big with a string of mysterious smirking and confetti emojis. But when I tell her what happened with Miles, she switches to hearts instead and then gives me my space. She's been witness to enough Johnson-family lawn meltdowns to get that I need a couple days to lie in my bed and read my favorite Sarah Dessen book for the millionth time and wallow.

By Sunday night, though, I'm sufficiently wallowed and ready to get back to business. She answers after the first ring.

"Okay, okay," she says quickly, as if we're midconversation. "Friday's action was really promising. I should have known that clumsiness would do it. Classic! But we can't get complacent. We need to follow that up strong. I really think it's going to be the elevator. . . ."

It feels so good to laugh again. "Oh yeah?"

"Wait, but first, how's Miles?"

"He's good. He was good about an hour later, but it's taking the rest of us a little bit longer. You know . . ."

"I do. I'm sorry."

"It's fine. It's life." I don't want to talk about my family right now. "But girl, I don't know how I'm going to, like, lure him to an elevator. . . ."

"You're still not trusting my genius?" she scoffs. "Anyway, I found Nico on Instagram—"

"What? I didn't even tell you his last name."

"Well, *that* wasn't hard to find. And then I just typed Nico Lucchese in, and, boom, I got it . . . nicothesedays." But then her tone shifts. "Except listen, you didn't tell me that he had a girlfriend. . . ."

I know she's waiting for me to explain, but I stay silent, holding on to this plan for one more moment. Before she tells me that she's over it, it's too impossible, and gets mad at me for wasting her precious time that she could be spending with Brandon and her new friends.

"Tess?"

"Okay, I know, I know. But I just found out Friday. *After* we talked. And I'm not really sure how serious they are even. . . ." She's definitely done now.

"It's kind of important information for me to have if I'm going to be setting you up with your soulmate. How can I make an effective plan if I don't know all of the possible obstacles?"

"Wait, what? You're not out?"

"No, of course not!" she says, as if I just suggested something crazy. "I mean, at first it felt a little skeevy, you know, trying to take away some other girl's boyfriend. But then I looked at her page."

"You did?"

"First of all, her name: Poppyyyy. With four Ys. Ew."

"Uh, is that really so bad?"

"Alone, no. But then she has one of those pictures. You know the ones: his hand is outstretched, holding hers, and she's looking back at him with this cool smile, like aren't we just having the best day together and I'm so happy you're taking this spontaneous photo. Even though you know she made him do it and probably did, like, fifty-five takes. There are a million other pictures just like it on IG, with other girls and their

Instagram boyfriends. It's clear he's just a prop to her."

"Okay, I don't know if I'd say—"

"And he's only posted one photo with her in the past two months. Did you see it?"

I put her on speaker, so I can open the app and find his account. I surprisingly hadn't looked him up yet—terrified that a rogue finger would like something on accident and cement me as a psycho stalker . . . which I guess I might be now.

"Do you see the caption?" she asks again.

"'Love you?'" I ask, confused. "Why do you want me to see this?"

"Not love you. L-U-V and the letter U."

"Maybe it's just faster to write?"

"He's in the creative writing conservatory with you, right? And it's literally three more characters! No. No, no, no . . . there are cracks forming in their relationship. It's built on shaky ground—basically falling apart. This is a perfect moment for you to ease on in there." I can't see Caroline, but I can picture her crazy eyes. Usually they're reserved for when she's been grounded too long or when I make one of her characters do something she doesn't approve of, like die off or choose the wrong guy.

"Hey, what's your big news that you were hinting at?" I ask, hoping she'll slow her roll.

"Yes, that! Well, I've been wanting to tell you since Friday because of course there's no one else I want to talk to about this. . . ."

She draws out the last word, waiting for me to attack her with questions.

"Do you want a drum roll or something. Spit it out already!"

"BRANDON ASKED ME OUT!"

I simultaneously feel like fireworks are exploding around me and also like someone punched me in the stomach. It's confusing. "What?"

"Yeah, on Friday, during AP Lit," she says, talking a mile a minute. "We were paired up again, and we were reading this poem. It was called 'To Caroline,' can you believe that? I don't really get what it was about, but Brandon was reading it to me, and I got what he meant by it. You know what I mean? And after he was done, he took my hand under the table and asked me out. But he did it in rhyme, like the poem. 'Please, Caroline, know that I'm true. I want to go on a date with you.'"

"Wow."

"Isn't that, like, perfect? It's like something out of one of your books!"

I shake my head, snapping myself out of it. "That's amazing, Caroline! I'm so happy for you."

"Anyway, we went out last night, and it was just everything, Tessa. Really."

My mind races to catch up with what she's telling me. Caroline is smart, beautiful, and funny. Any guy would be lucky to have her. But somehow this isn't making sense. For years we've dreamed of exactly this—whispering about our ideal boyfriends during sleepovers, countless games of MASH—and now it's finally happening . . . when we are hundreds of miles away from each other. I was supposed to be involved, to be *there*.

Finally I mumble, "But . . . how did you get your parents to agree?" Caroline's dad is super protective. Like, he watched her walk down the street to my house kinda protective. I'm pretty sure he's told her she can't date until she's forty.

"Him and Mom were out themselves—to see that new Tom Hanks movie. I encouraged it, told them they needed a little date night to, like, reignite the spark or whatever."

She spends the next thirty minutes describing every last detail of their date: how he took her out to get fro-yo at the Westfield Galleria, how he wore a green sweater because he remembered that was her favorite color, how he tried to end the night with a chaste kiss on her cheek before she grabbed his face and "To tell you the truth, basically rocked his world."

I do my very best to to say "Ahhhh!" at all the right parts and tell her how perfect it all sounds. That's how I feel, genuinely, but it's like half of myself is having to remind the other half of that. I don't know why this isn't coming easier.

"This is our year, Tessa. I know it. I have my first boy-friend, and you're . . ." There's a long pause. We both feel it. "Well, you're going to kill it with your writing *and* find your happily ever after. Amazing things are going to happen for us."

I wish I could believe her. But the rest of our call is devoted to analyzing Brandon's swoony follow-up texts and discussing what she'll do tomorrow morning at school, all part of Caroline's very real love story, and I feel silly bringing up my hypothetical love story at all.

"You look pretty," Mom says when I walk into the kitchen Monday morning.

In between reading and wallowing, I used some of my free time this weekend to study YouTube tutorials on twist-outs, and I'm pretty happy with how it turned out. And I'm wearing one of my favorite skirts—it's tight at the waist but goes out full, with a forest-green floral print. I paired it with gold flats and an eyelet sleeveless top.

But I don't want to talk to my mom about it.

"Thanks."

"Do you want a ride today? I have a later shift, and I'd love to see Chrysalis again. . . . Maybe we could talk?" She pushes the laptop in front of her to the side, and I can see that she has a tab opened to eBay. I've heard her and Dad having panicked discussions about it all weekend—they haven't been able to find a copy of *Enter the Dream Zone* anywhere, probably because Miles is their only remaining fan.

"No, that's okay," I say, grabbing a yogurt from the fridge. "Sam can drive me."

Miles walks into the kitchen. He's still in his pajamas even though it's getting late, but Mom doesn't rush to him immediately, which is . . . different. Instead she keeps trying to catch my eye.

"Are you sure, Tessa?" she says. "I think it might be good for us. To have that time."

I shrug. "I don't want to ditch Sam." Ignoring her searching face, I make my way over to Miles. "Do you want me to help you pick out something to wear? I think slippers may be against dress code."

He smiles real wide. "You're not the boss of me. And these look better than what you have on!"

"Oh yeah, who made you Mr. Fashion Police, bud?"

"One day you're in and the next day you're out!" He's trying to do some accent I can't place, but it just dissolves into mischievous giggles. "And you're out, Tessie!"

"Wait, Project Runway?" I laugh. "Is that still on?"

He smiles even bigger, pleased that I got it. "I watched reruns yesterday! I watched it alllll day! That's how come I know that you're out!"

"Tessa . . . ," Mom cuts in. But the doorbell interrupts her, and I happily flee to answer it.

I'm confused, though, when it's Sam standing there, two plastic Tupperware containers in his arms. "Wait, am I late? I'm sorry. I don't even know what time it is. . . ."

"No. No—it's just . . . does your brother, uh, does Miles like Oreos?"

"Um . . . yeah?"

His shoulders drop as he lets out a large exhale. "Okay, good. I should have checked. But I just . . . I don't know, didn't. So, uh, I made him these cookies-and-cream donuts." He opens the larger container, revealing perfectly iced donuts with crumbled Oreos on top. "I know they're not exactly a healthy breakfast, but he can always save them for later. And, um, this is chocolate ice cream I made with Oreos and chocolate chips. It actually should go in the freezer pretty quick."

I know I should say something, but I'm speechless. Sam's cheeks turn pink, and he looks down and starts rubbing the side of his face.

"Maybe I shouldn't have. I mean, maybe it wasn't my place—"

"No! Not at all! Just . . . why?"

"He just seemed so upset on Friday, and that DVD, it's not available anywhere online. Did you know that? Well, yeah, I'm sure you guys do." He's talking fast again, but still not looking at me. "And I just wanted to help, and this is the only way I know—"

"Sam Weiner, is that you?" He's interrupted by Mom barreling in from the kitchen, which forces him to raise his head and make eye contact.

"Hi, Mrs. Johnson. These are for you. Well, for Miles."

"Oh my goodness! Aren't you just the sweetest?" Mom beams, and Miles comes running to the door, hearing his name.

"Donuts!" Miles shouts. He does a little dance in excitement. I look at Sam, and he's just smiling. And not the fake smile that people do when they're uncomfortable, but the real kind. I'm smiling the real kind too.

CHAPTER SEVENTEEN

I spend the rest of the day worrying about seeing Ms. McKinney again. She's for sure not going to just forget that I ditched the end of her class, and it's not like I can fake more stomach issues. I have to think of something else to say—some other reason she should skip me and move on to the next person on her alphabetical list.

But it all ends up being for nothing, because she's not in Art of the Novel anyway. We have a sub—some guy in his early twenties, who spends most of the class ignoring us and typing on his laptop.

I was also worried that Nico would ignore me today, that he'd pretend our moment in the kitchen was nothing. Because, you know, to him it probably was. He caught me in his arms . . . and then he snuck off to go make out with his perfect and beautiful and definitely experienced girlfriend. One guess which of those interactions was more memorable.

But no, he makes a point of pulling up a beanbag right next to mine. And I mean *right* next to me, so close I can see his adorable scratchy handwriting in his Moleskine (though I make sure I hide my computer screen). We don't really talk much, but the space between our legs is charged, like the pulse coming off an electric fence. And at one point, he readjusts his legs, and his jeans brush against my bare knee.

That little touch is enough to carry me home on a cloud, a whole gospel choir up there with me, hyping me up and singing hallelujah.

When Sam pulls onto our street, luckily Miles isn't on the corner again, but my mom's blue CR-V is in the driveway, which makes my stomach feel sick just the same. I don't want to walk into whatever serious talk she has planned.

"Can I come over?" I blurt out as soon as we take our seat belts off.

He stares at me for a second, blinking too fast, and I'm worried that I'm going to get turned down.

"Of course, yeah. Come on down!" He does a cringe-worthy impersonation of a game-show host, pointing to his house. I laugh and gratefully follow him up the steps.

Sam's house stands out on our block. Most houses are craftsman or Spanish style, like my own, but Sam's house is a white Tudor with rounded windows and a dark, pointy roof. With its out-of-control rosebushes, cobblestone path, and round tower-looking thingy in the front, the house looks like it was pulled out of a fairy tale and plopped down on our street.

But the inside isn't from another time. Sam unlocks the door and reveals a living room with bright teal walls and a gray couch filled with pillows in different shades of yellow, plus off-white lamps with beaded shades. There's a marble-and-gold coffee table in front of it, stacked high with issues of *Food & Wine* and *Bon Appétit*, and the back wall is filled with pictures, like a gallery wall was started and then took on a mind of its own. There's a good mix of art and family photos, Thiebaud's *Cakes* next to a blown-up shot of little Sam missing his two front teeth.

"I was just planning on trying out this recipe, if that's okay," Sam says, throwing his backpack down on a shiny brass table on the side of the room. "Ever since I started Chrysalis, I've been flooded with ideas. There's almost not enough time in the day to get through all of them. I'm sure it's the same for you. You can write if you want to."

"Oh yeah, a lot's going on in there," I say quickly. "But I'm just going to let them, uh, simmer for now." *Very convincing.*

I turn back to the pictures, so I don't have to make eye contact with him. In all the family pictures, it's just him and his mom. The two of them standing in front of a brand-new restaurant, posing with Mickey at Disneyland, Sam in a chef's hat with his mom proudly gazing behind him.

"So it's only the two of you."

"Mmm-hmm, I don't have a dad."

My neck burns. "I'm sorry."

But he just laughs. "Oh, you don't have to be sorry. I never had one. Well, I guess technically I did, but he was just some guy who donated, his, um . . . materials. Probably so he could pay for college or something. Mom had me on her own, but not in a sad kinda way. Just because she was getting older and didn't want to wait around anymore."

"Wow, she sounds awesome."

"She is. And, uh, she's not going to be home until late tonight. So it'll just be me and you." He does that fast blinking thing again and then quickly turns, almost knocking over one of the beaded lamps. "Whoops," he mumbles, steadying it, and then speed-walks into the next room.

I follow close behind him. I don't know why he's acting so weird, but I guess I did just invite myself over to his house—maybe he wasn't feeling like company. I know I have to prepare myself for social interaction sometimes.

The kitchen is obviously the creation of a chef—or two chefs, that is. There's a double oven, two dishwashers, open shelving with jadeite bowls and plates on display and two KitchenAid stand mixers, one butter yellow and the other hot pink. Sam immediately seems at home when he walks into the room. He starts pulling mixing bowls and measuring cups out of the cabinets.

"Um, can I tell you something?" I ask.

"Yeah?"

"I almost watched the video that you told us about on Friday like a million times this weekend." It's true. I had it queued up and everything, thinking it might make me feel better about my failure to write and the scene my family had caused in front of the neighbors. Misery loves company, or whatever. And also, I was just curious. Of course, I don't tell Sam all that.

"You did?" His busy hands steady.

"Yeah, almost, but I felt like I was betraying you, you know? So I have a solution."

"What's that?" His eyes lock on mine.

"We should watch it together."

He barks out a laugh. "Why would I ever want to do that?"

"Okay, hear me out. It might be good for you, you know? To face your fears and your biggest embarrassment. It might confirm for you how far you've come since then, right?"

"Also, you just really want to watch it?" he asks with a sly smile, his dimple showing.

"Also, I just really want to watch it." I shrug and smile back at him, and he laughs again, the sound warm and comforting. That laugh makes me feel like I've accomplished something.

I pull out my laptop and slide it over to him, and he types in the keywords "weiner cries over cake" with surprising speed, like he's done this a million times before. And then we're watching little Sam stand in front of a panel of judges: two chefs I don't recognize and a woman who played the older sister on a sitcom Miles and I used to watch.

Sam has a short, spiky haircut and particularly rosy cheeks, and he's looking at them anxiously, waiting for their feedback on a three-tier chocolate cake sitting on a pedestal. And their feedback is brutal. The actress says the lavender in the cake tasted like her grandma, and one of the other judges attacks his natural instincts as a chef, choosing such "unfortunate flavor pairings." You think they'd be nicer to a kid, but they rip him apart.

When they finally tell him he's being sent home, little Sam's face crumples. I want to reach into the screen and give him a hug. The video shifts into black and white then, with dramatic piano music playing in the background and dead leaves floating across the screen, and the crying gets louder, a female voice now.

"That's when Rhys's edits start," Sam says, shutting my laptop.

"What a jerk," I say, shaking my head. "And of course you cried! I mean, there's nothing wrong with that. Those judges were mean to you." I reach out and touch his arm, but when he startles, I pull back.

"They weren't," he says quickly. "They were right. I just didn't know how to take feedback then." He turns to the cabinets and continues getting out more supplies. "That cake had chocolate, lavender, five-spice, and pistachios. It was gross. I was trying to do too much, and they were honest with me like they should have been. I'm grateful for the experience. . . . You can't learn without critique."

I don't know if I agree with that, as the possibility of critique is keeping me from even producing anything *to be* critiqued. But I nod anyway.

Happy with all the tools he has out, Sam turns to the fridge and the pantry and begins getting out his ingredients: heavy cream, sugar, eggs, a long bean-looking thing. I watch him as he measures everything, leaving ingredients in the measuring cups instead of immediately pouring them into a bowl. He meticulously cuts the bean and scrapes out a dark paste, making the whole room smell like vanilla. The whole time his face is calm, his movements steady. He is entirely in his element, and he looks . . . different.

"What are you making?"

"Ice cream." He smiles proudly, and then his eyes cloud over. "Sorry, this must be really boring for you."

"Not at all."

"It's just . . . I had this idea last week. I was looking at one of those travel magazines in the doctor's office—you know the ones that no one *actually* reads? And there was this little blurb about something called ísbíltúr."

The last word he says sounds like something out of *The Lord of the Rings*. "What?"

"Ísbíltúr. It's, uh, this thing in Iceland. It means something like 'ice cream road trip.'"

"I like the sound of that."

He laughs. "Right? It's this tradition, or something like that, where the family takes a long drive to get ice cream, and then when they get the ice cream, they take a long drive to enjoy it." He's talking fast, excited, and his hands continue to work, pouring ingredients into a saucepan. "So I was thinking it might be a good idea for a food truck. Or maybe even a restaurant? The sitting area could be these classic cars, but like with tables and chairs. And there could be videos of the open road projected on the walls. And we could serve all kinds of ice cream—sundaes and ice cream sandwiches and dipped cones."

He looks up at me, suddenly self-conscious. "Anyway, I don't know . . . it could be cool. And I've just been working on some ice cream flavors this week . . . just for fun."

"I love it," I say, and his deep dimple reappears.

"And oh, you gotta try this." He runs to the fridge, reenergized, and pulls out a glass bowl with a cloth over it. He dips a spoon into the bowl and then puts it up to my mouth. He's really close, so close I can feel the heat of his body and smell his signature butter-and-sugar scent, and I get this overwhelming urge to get even closer. But if I did, I would basically be under his arm, so I push that thought out of my brain and just taste whatever's on the spoon.

"Mmmmmm," I murmur, involuntarily. It's delicious. "What is this . . . Lucky Charms?"

"Cereal milk." He beams. "I've been steeping it all day. I just hope the flavor shows up after the custard has been frozen."

I don't know if it's seeing him so passionate about his work—the way I used to be about my writing—or the way he's allowed himself to be vulnerable with me by showing that video. Or it might even be because we're standing so close together now. But it's like something unlatches within my brain. I take a deep breath.

"Okay, I have a confession for you," I say. "It actually

isn't the same for me. You know what you were talking about before?"

"What?" He's blinking at me again.

My defenses shoot up. It felt safe in the moment to share this with Sam, but maybe I should take it back. Maybe this wasn't the right move after all. But I'm filled with this over-whelming desire to get a baseline check from someone I trust. And I know I can trust Sam.

"I'm not, like, filled with ideas since I started Chrysalis," I admit. "I actually haven't written anything."

He steps back from me, leaning against the counter. "At all?"

"No. Nothing at all, not since the first day. I've been com-pletely blank." It feels so strange to say it out loud, but it also releases something tight in my chest to have it out there with someone else.

He rubs the side of his face and nods his head, taking it in. I expected myself to feel embarrassed, but there's nothing judgmental in his expression. "Why do you think that is?" he asks finally.

"Well, it started in my Art of the Novel class. . . ." Every-thing about that first day pours out easily. I tell him all about the workshop that happens every day at the end of class, how we're all supposed to just share our writing and listen to others tear it apart. I tell him how I lied and ditched the end of class Friday.

"So you're scared to share your work?"

"Terrified. It's, like, my biggest fear."

He looks surprised. "Really? Your biggest?"

"What—you don't think that's valid or something?"

"No, no, of course it is," he says, putting his hands up. "I'm just surprised. I mean, most peoples' biggest fears are . . . I don't know, home invasions and, like, dolls that come alive or something."

I laugh, and he looks satisfied with himself.

"And most people at Chrysalis go there because they want to share their work," he continues. "Being an artist means other people consuming your art and, uh, having opinions about it. Not that you're not an artist. I mean, of course you are. I'm just surprised, is all. So many of the people there are, like, knocking over each other to get a chance to be the center of attention."

Maybe I'm not an artist, I want to say, but I just look down at the tiled floor.

"Okay, so what are you going to do to get your words back?" He's giving me his full attention now, the cereal milk cast aside. "You know, when I am having a hard time thinking of new recipes, I go to restaurants, read cookbooks . . . I don't know, anything to get inspiration."

"I tried that already. I've read every story I could think of, but still . . . nothing."

"Okay, well, why don't you think about what your readers want? Some chefs do, like, special tastings to try out new menus and get feedback—oh, but I guess you've never had readers. . . ."

"I have readers!" I say defensively. "Or . . . a reader."

"You do?"

"My best friend, Caroline, from back home. She reads everything I write—or, well, *used to* write. And actually, we kinda came up with a whole crazy plan to fix this. . . ."

"You did?" he says. "Well, why didn't you lead with that? What's the plan?"

I shrug, my cheeks turning pink. "I don't really want to say just yet. You know, it might be bad luck before I'm a little further along." And also, I have enough self-awareness to realize it's the kind of ridiculous thing you can only talk about with your *best* friend. I trust Sam, but we're not there yet.

He nods, as if that actually makes sense. "Of course. Well, the problem has been identified. You have a course of action. Seems like you're on your way to writing again."

I hope so. I just need to figure out what's next.

Caroline, of course, has strong opinions.

"We need to strategize about number eight," she says when we're on the phone Thursday night, all business.

"Make him jealous?" I laugh. "Yeah, I don't think that'll be happening. I don't just have other guys hanging out, waiting to be part of a love triangle. That's the whole point of this."

"What about Sam?"

I almost fall off my bed.

"Are you kidding me?"

"Hey, if he's up for it! You guys are friends, yeah? A love

triangle really gets things moving—you could just fake it to make Nico feel some type of way. That's a classic love story maneuver."

"Absolutely not."

"Who's in charge here?" Caroline starts, ready to go off on a rant, but my mom knocks and opens my door. I hate when she does that. What's the point of knocking if you're just going to open it anyway?

"Hold on, Caroline." I give my mom a look. "Do you need something?"

"I just wanted to see if you're up for talking. It's been almost a week. . . ."

She's been trying to have a sit-down with me since Friday, and I've been avoiding it. I'm finally feeling okay, *hopeful*, and I don't want to ruin my good mood.

"I'm busy."

"Maybe you could call Caroline back?" she suggests, stepping into my room. "I'm sure she wouldn't mind."

"I really can't. It's important."

Her face changes at that, matching my cold stare. "Okay."

She closes my door, and I can hear her walking fast down the hall.

"You good?" Caroline asks.

"Yeah."

"Okay, now hear me out. What if you, Sam, and Nico end up in the elevator together, and—"

"Caroline!" Before I can explain to her just how crazy that

152

is, though, there's another knock on my door. And then, softly, "Tessa?"

It's my dad. He never opens the door without asking.

"Hey, I have to go."

"All right, but text me later what action you plan to take tomorrow! It is essential you get one in before the weekend."

"Um, okay." And then, to Dad, "Come in."

He opens the door hesitantly and only steps in when I nod for him to. He's still wearing his work clothes: a striped polo and gray dress pants. He must have just gotten home, even though dinner was hours ago.

I used to get mad at Dad for working so late, always being on his phone, but I have to remind myself it's for a good reason. He's taking care of us—trying to give Miles and me the childhood he didn't have. It's the same with the move. I was so mad at first, but how can I stay mad at him for doing something good for our family? When it all shakes out, he puts us first. And he's the bridge between Mom and me.

"Can we talk, baby girl?"

I sigh, knowing what's coming. I gesture toward the spot next to me on my bed. "Yeah. What does she want you to tell me?"

He eases himself down next to me. I can feel the bed sink a little bit underneath his weight. My dad's a big man. It's the first thing you notice about him, all the muscle and height. He has to shop in a special section of the store.

I remember Mom told me once that when they first brought

Miles home, he couldn't cry—the main thing babies are supposed to do. Dad used to stay up with him all night, so Mom could get some sleep. And he watched his every breath, trying to make sure he was comfortable, or just alive, I guess. At first it surprised me, imagining my dad's huge hands doing delicate, precise tasks like changing Miles's feeding tubes or feeling for air under his tiny nose. But it actually sums him up pretty well: both strong and soft.

He takes my hands into one of his huge ones now.

"She feels bad for what she said to you on Friday," he says, looking toward the door. His voice is honey, smooth and sweet—just like the crooners on those Motown albums he and Mom listen to when they're cleaning Saturday mornings. His voice sands down some of my sharpness, as I realize with irritation that she's probably out there listening.

"You didn't do anything wrong. The situation was just . . . tense. We understand how you were probably feeling, that happening in our new neighborhood and all. And that's okay—to feel that way."

"Are you sure this is coming from her too?" I ask, giving him the side-eye.

"Y-yes," he says, and we both know I don't believe him. "Yes." He tries again, more firmly this time. "Your mother knows you love your brother. She's just constantly protecting him from people with not-so-good intentions and advocating for him at school. Sometimes I think that just boils over and pops off in the wrong direction. Does that make sense?"

"Usually in my direction," I mumble to myself, but he doesn't acknowledge it. That would be parent treason.

"You didn't do anything wrong," he repeats. "And your mom is sorry. She wants to tell you that if you'll let her."

I nod. "I'll talk to her." He gives me the side-eye now. "I will! For real!"

He leans forward and kisses the top of my head, his hands squeezing my cheeks. "We've actually been thinking about getting a respite worker to help with Miles . . . just a few hours throughout the week, to help your mother. She needs to get out more and build a life here too, outside of you two. And this way, there won't be as much on your plate. I know we ask a lot of you, especially this summer, keeping an eye on him. . . ."

"No!"

He shoots me a look. I don't know why that idea bothers me so much, but it puts me instinctively on the defensive, like how moms throw their right arms out over the passenger seat when they know they're going to brake suddenly. It feels wrong to have anyone else helping with Miles. It's my job. I'm his sister. And I love being with him—getting him breakfast in the morning, hanging out with him when Mom and Dad are out—even if it's hard sometimes.

"I don't mind," I say quickly, quieter. "I like helping with Miles. Unless Mom doesn't think I do a good job or something."

155

"It's not that at all, baby girl," he says, pulling me into a hug. "You love your brother and always do right by him—we know that. We just want you to be able to enjoy your life too. Be a teenager, you know what I mean?" He pauses, considering that. "But not too much of a teenager."

I laugh. "I can do both. My social life isn't that busy."

"Good," he says, laughing too. "Well, good if you're happy with that."

"I am."

"Then your old man is happy with that. I'm in no rush to have any boys up in here."

If only he knew what Caroline and I were planning.

Dad stands up from my bed, the springs underneath loudly squeaking.

"And you'll try to talk to your mom?" he asks, standing at the door. "You guys are on the same side here."

"I will. I know."

Because no matter how mad Mom and I get at each other, we have that fierce, unifying tie between us: our love for Miles. We always find our way back to each other for him.

CHAPTER EIGHTEEN

The next day at lunch, I find my eyes drifting to Nico and his friends, like he's the sun and I'm defenseless against his gravitational pull. I mean, it's hard not to when they sit in the middle of the lawn, center stage. With our happily ever after plan floating in my mind—and Caroline's texts this morning, reminding me again that it's time for my next move—it's hard not to imagine myself sitting there with all of them.

Except Poppy, that is. I guess Poppy wouldn't be there anymore. And she certainly wouldn't be knee to knee with Nico like she is now, their upper bodies pressed together tightly, his hands circling her waist. . . .

"Tessa, is that okay with you?"

"No, yeah—what?" I realize that Lenore, Sam, and Theodore are all looking at me. I must have missed something.

"Theo—" Sam starts.

"Theodore."

"Sorry, Theodore asked if I could help him carry some can-vases to his car after school," Sam continues. "But it means I'll be a few minutes later to drive home. Is that okay?"

"Yeah, sure, of course." I take a bite of my sandwich and try to ground myself back in reality.

"What are you staring at?" Lenore asks, giving me the side-eye. My cheeks redden as she jerks her head around, trying to retrace my gaze, and then she stops on Nico's group and starts nodding knowingly.

"Ahhhh, someone's got it for one of those—" I jump up and cover her mouth, knocking over my Coke. But it's no use, Theodore and Sam are already looking in their direction.

"No, no, it's nothing," I say quickly, but even I can tell how unconvincing I sound. "I was just trying to figure out what to do about this poem I'm editing for *Wings*. It's, uh, too long, and yeah . . ."

I don't even bother to finish that excuse. "I'm gonna go get some napkins."

Lenore is giggling, and Theodore mutters, "What an unin-teresting crush." But Sam has a strange look on his face—there's this crease between his eyebrows and his jaw is tight. I smile at him and then escape over to the student store for napkins, try-ing to hide the blush that's spread to my neck now. I must look like a tomato.

On the way there, though, I can't help but steal another glance at the group on the lawn. Nico has his hands on both of

Poppy's cheeks, and he's just staring at her face, the heart-eyes emoji incarnate.

She's probably used to being held like that, being looked at like that. It's foreign to me, though. No boy has ever seen me in that way, because I'm not a girl like Poppy.

It's not as if I don't think I'm pretty. When I look in the mirror, I generally like what I see. I don't wish I had straight hair or lighter skin. It's just that, to most guys, my kind of pretty isn't the same as Poppy's kind of pretty—even with the gray hair. I'm an acquired taste, and Poppy is, like, pizza. Pizza doesn't have to worry if people are just ordering it to look cool or complete some type of image. No one goes through a pizza phase. Pizza is universal.

Nico runs his hands through her hair as he kisses her deeply, and I wonder what it feels like.

I wonder what it feels like to be a girl like her.

She probably isn't paralyzed with fear when it comes to being critiqued on her work. She probably doesn't care at all about what people think about her or her art. And why would she? She loves and is loved back. She is wanted.

All at once, I know what I need to do.

I try to play it low-key when class starts, sitting on the stairs so maybe Ms. McKinney will forget I exist. I've turned in some pages. Yes, it was old chapters again. But at least I turned something in. Maybe that'll be enough to keep her attention off me until I get my real inspiration back.

To my surprise, Nico follows me to the stairs like it's no big deal, tapping my foot with his as some sort of greeting and giving me a line about how the inspiration is strong here. I try to do this cute little laugh, but then it catches in my throat and I start coughing, loud and phlegmy, like someone who smokes a pack a day. Nico starts patting my back and says, "You okay there, turbo?" which makes me cough even more. And soon everyone in the room is staring at me, including Ms. McKinney, whose eyes narrow in my direction. So playing it low-key isn't in the cards. And also maybe Nico and I are friends?

My coughs finally, thankfully, stop, and that's when I smell him. Not in like a gross BO way. I can just smell him because he's that close—his signature scent of boy soap and sweat and grass that I've memorized and could recognize with my eyes closed at this point. And it makes my heart rate speed up. I want to move in closer, so I can inhale him and maybe even stick my finger through that tiny curl that's sitting there at the base of his neck—and wow, yeah, I realize how creepy I'm sounding.

Focus, Tessa.

I pull up our list again on my computer, looking very studious and writerly in case Ms. McKinney is watching, and weigh my options. It's not raining and there are no Ferris wheels nearby. No matter how much Caroline insists, I'm not luring him into an elevator. And I think if I started grilling him on secrets that no one else knows right now, he'd (rightfully) think I was a weirdo, and I'd lose whatever ground I have gained.

Yeah, I think I'll opt for number two again, since it worked so well last time.

I unscrew the cap on my water bottle and take a sip—just in case he's watching me as much as I'm watching him. I put the bottle down on the step I'm sitting on, but precariously close to the edge. And when I go to pretend to type something profound on my laptop, I whip my elbow around, just overtaken with the inspiration. The water bottle tips over off the step, soaking my legs and his hair and shirt.

He yelps, jumping up, and I stand up too, making my best shocked and mortified face.

"Oh my god, I'm so sorry. Oh my god." Did I spill too much water? Is he going to be mad?

"Uh, it's good. I'm okay," he says, wringing his shirt out. I try not to gawk at the peek of his hard stomach, the sprinkle of dark hair down by the top of his jeans.

"God, there I go again! I'm such a klutz. Can I help? I can go get napkins."

"Uh, yeah—"

He's interrupted by Ms. McKinney coming up to the stairs, glaring at us sternly. "What's going on here?"

"Sorry, Ms. McKinney," I say. "It's my fault. I spilled my water bottle."

"Okay," she says, shaking her head. "Well, just go upstairs and get cleaned up, and bring some paper towels for this mess."

Nico and I start up the stairs, but her voice stops me. "And Tessa, get your materials ready for workshop when you return.

I'm sorry you missed your turn last week."

I don't turn to see the knowing look I'm sure is on her face.

We go up into the kitchen on the main floor of the Bungalow, and Nico takes the roll of paper towels off the holder. He wipes his neck once but then focuses on his Moleskine, delicately patting the cover and the edges.

"Again, I'm so, so sorry," I say, standing there awkwardly next to him. I want to offer to help again—the idea of patting him down sounds very nice. But I'm worried I'll reveal my crazy infatuation with just my voice.

"Don't worry about it," he says, holding up his notebook. "This is okay, and that's all that matters." He smiles at me, all cheese face and sleepy eyes, and it melts me a little bit.

"Here, you have some water on your legs too. That was a big-ass water bottle." He gets on his knees, paper towel in hands, and begins to dry off my right leg, starting at my ankle and then moving all the way up to just above my knee, where my pink floral print shirtdress ends. If I thought I was melting before, I'm the Wicked Witch of the West now—a big old green screaming puddle on the ground. Melted. Dead.

Thank you, Caroline.

I hope he can't feel my legs shaking. I'm glad I shaved them this morning. I hope I smell good. And is it just me, or is he taking longer than he needs to? It feels like something, but maybe I'm just being desperate, set off by the slightest touch.

He stands up and throws the paper towels in the trash, giving me that perfect smile again.

"So you're going to share today? I'm excited to read your work."

That makes my chest tighten. Back to reality. I look down at the ground and shake my head.

"What?" he asks. "You nervous?"

"No . . . no. I mean yeah—I am. It's just . . ."

"The work's not ready yet?" he prompts, and when I look up at him, his brown eyes are full of understanding.

"Yeah, that's it."

"I get it," he says. "They expect us to be these little factories here, just churning out art because they say so. And that's not always how it works, right?"

I nod quickly. "Right, right. We need more time." It feels good to have him validate this. Maybe I'm not the only one who's gone through a dry spell.

"Exactly. I mean, Jack Kerouac wrote *On the Road* in three weeks, but it took J. D. Salinger like ten years to write *The Catcher in the Rye*, and that book is way short. Sometimes the inspiration is there, and sometimes it's not. But you can't force it. It's not a light switch or something."

Well, okay, what's happening with me feels different, because I'm definitely not working on some classic novel. And I've never read anything by Kerouac, but I'm pretty sure I'm not on his level either. I'm freezing up just trying to write a basic, uncomplicated romance novel, which doesn't feel the same at all, but I just nod my head some more. "Yeah, yeah, definitely."

"See, I get you, Tessa," he says, tapping my foot with his again. If this is becoming our thing, I love it. "You're different from all those posers down there."

I let the compliment fill me up, even though I don't deserve it.

We make our way back downstairs, and when we get there, the class is already sitting in a circle, waiting for us. I feel a strong urge to flee, but that's impossible now without making a scene. I wish I could shrink. I wish I could become a little tiny speck, so I would only take up the space I deserve.

My neck feels hot and itchy, and when I reach up to touch it, I feel the hives. They only appear when I'm really, really anxious. I hope they're not as flaming red as they feel.

"Tessa?" Ms. McKinney says from the head of the circle. "Do you have your copies ready to pass around?"

"I . . . uh—"

I scramble for an excuse, to explain why the only thing I could pass around would be blank pages, but luckily Nico saves me.

"Ms. McKinney? Tessa's water bottle spilled on her computer." I turn to him wide-eyed, because we both know the water didn't go anywhere near my laptop. He raises his eyebrows, as if to say, *Go with it.* "Would it be all right if I go instead? Just for today."

Ms. McKinney doesn't look happy about it, but she nods and waves her hand. "All right, go ahead, Nico. But Tessa, I want to speak with you after class about your . . . technology issues."

I quickly nod and sit down, savoring my relief, no matter how temporary it may be.

Nico sits next to me. "So, this is what I have so far of my first chapter," he says, looking around the circle. And he doesn't talk us through his process or try to explain away any criticism that we may have before starting. He just opens his Moleskine and begins to read, his voice full of confidence. Like he's doing us a favor—and maybe he is. I wish I could be like him. Or just *with* him.

His scene is a dream sequence, and I'm amazed at how talented he is—the beauty of his words. I'm also distracted by the beauty of his face, though—how his full lips cradle each word, how he pushes the loose curls that fall into his eyes out of the way, like it's no big deal and not something that makes my stomach do somersaults. To be honest, I actually don't understand much of the chapter. It's full of dark mirrors and trees with eyes and other trippy images that I'm sure mean something else. But that's how I know that it's probably very good.

When he's done, he leans back in his chair and takes the criticism and compliments he receives like they're no big deal. Even when Ms. McKinney tells him he needs to revise most of it, he just nods and smiles. It makes me swoon.

After class is over, I grab my stuff quickly, hoping I can walk out with Nico and keep whatever was happening upstairs going, but Ms. McKinney stops me.

"Tessa—a word."

She gestures to the chair next to her but waits for everyone else to leave before speaking. There goes my chance of talking to Nico more.

"Tessa, I just wanted to speak with you a bit about what I've noticed in the past couple of weeks," she starts.

I decide to play dumb. "What's that?"

Her lips press together, and she stares at me for a beat before saying, "I've noticed how you're avoiding participating in the workshop. And it's not just sharing your own work, though you've definitely avoided that very effectively." She blinks at me, and my neck burns. I haven't fooled her at all. "I've also noticed that you don't participate when other people share their work by giving meaningful critique—or, well, any critique at all. We can learn just as much as writers by engaging with the work of our peers."

I look down at my hands and begin to scratch the side of my thumb. "I'm sorry."

"You don't have to be sorry," she says. "It's perfectly okay to be intimidated by the workshop setting. Especially when it's your first time. It can be difficult, I know. In grad school, I used to throw up before I had to present my work. My friends thought it was hilarious."

I smile, imagining a younger Ms. McKinney getting the nervous pukes before a critique. So I'm not the only one.

"But actually, that's not the main reason why I wanted to

pull you aside," she continues, the warmth in her voice suddenly gone. My stomach drops. "I make it a point to review the portfolios of all the students admitted to my Art of the Novel class. To check for strengths, style, and areas of growth that I can help them with. And when you began sending me chapters from the new novel you're working on in this class, I couldn't help but notice some . . . *similarities* with the chapters of another manuscript in your portfolio."

She gives me a hard look, and it's clear. *She knows.*

"As you know, and you've probably seen from my comments on your draft, you're expected to submit new material in your classes here at Chrysalis. This is an extremely selective program, and we can only work with young writers who are able to push themselves and work hard." She shakes her head. "I must say, I'm really surprised. I was expecting something different from the girl who sent such passionate emails asking to be admitted into this class. I expected more from you."

I can feel wetness forming in the corners of my eyes. *I expected more from myself too,* I want to tell her. *I'm working on it. I have a plan.*

But I stay quiet. Somehow I know Ms. McKinney wouldn't find my plan very encouraging.

She's looking at me, waiting for me to say something, but all I can muster is a strained smile. I don't know how much I can tell her. It seems better just to keep it all in.

"Well, producing new work is nonnegotiable," she continues. "Do you need any help from me? I'd be willing to work with you one-on-one. And I know you're working on some-thing . . . I've seen you wrestling with it in class. I'd love to help you develop that."

Ms. McKinney has a kind smile, and I appreciate her pre-senting me with a hand up, a chance for things to be a little easier. But how would that smile change if I told her I don't have *anything* for her to develop—that anything I've been "wrestling" with is pretend. That they made a huge mistake and I don't really belong here. Would she tell the principal? Would I be sent away to a different school?

"Yeah, yeah, I'll—uh—maybe I'll do that," I mumble, but I can tell from the way her face shutters that I'm not con-vincing her.

"Okay. I hope to get something new soon. Tonight, even," she says, her voice stern now. "And I just want to remind you that you'll have to share your pages in the workshop at least once by the end of the semester to pass the class. I'm willing to excuse you for your past submissions, but I won't be so lenient going forward."

Pass the class? I thought I was doing enough to get the low-est possible passing grade, a C minus. So now on top of losing my ability to write, I'll lose my halfway decent GPA too? This is a mess.

"Yes, Ms. McKinney," I say, and then take my opportunity to escape.

When I reach the top of the stairs, I have my phone out, ready to text Caroline. Because I'm realizing that this plan is stupid. No little moment with Nico is going to fix what's obviously wrong with me, and maybe I should just get out now before I, like, ruin my chance at college or something. I'm so anxious and flustered that I almost miss Nico sitting on the old floral couch.

"Hey," he says, standing up. "I was waiting for you."

"For me?" I just about float up to the ceiling.

"Yeah." He laughs. "I'm having this thing at my house tomorrow. A party—I guess you could say. And I wanted to invite you."

"Me? Oh, wow, yeah. Yeah!" I know I'm sounding kinda crazy, but I can't stop it. My insides are doing a little dance. "I have to see if I have any plans, but I probably don't have any plans."

"So you'll come?"

Why do his words get to come out all flawlessly Times New Roman, and mine are, like, Wingdings?

"Yes." He smiles, and it's perfect.

"But what about Poppy?" It comes out before I can really think about how ridiculous it makes me sound. *He's asking you to come to his party, not proposing, Tessa!*

Nico's eyebrows press together, but luckily he keeps the smile on his face. And doesn't run away. "Poppy will be there. We're, um . . . together. Sometimes. We're kind of on-again, off-again, I guess?"

That's news I didn't get from analyzing his IG with Caroline or watching him at lunch. Good news. *And which one are you right now?* I want to scream. But instead I just mumble. "Oh, cool, cool."

Abort mission! my brain is shouting. *Get out of this conversation while you still have an invitation!*

"Okay, so . . ." He reaches forward and I think he's about to take my hand (and then I'm definitely going to faint). But instead he takes my phone and types something quickly.

"There, I just texted the address to myself, so you'll have my number too." He winks at me. WINKS! AT! ME! "Call me if you get lost."

CHAPTER NINETEEN

I walk to Sam's car after school, filled with *Nico gave me his number* energy. He's not there yet because he's probably still helping Theodore, so I sit down on the curb and start texting Caroline about all the new developments—the spilled water, the wiping of the leg, the party invite. She interrupts my texts by calling me, and we both squeal in excitement. I don't even care who might be looking.

"I'm a genius."

"You are a genius. You should write a book!"

"No, *you* should write a book. You *will* write a book when this is all said and done! Just make sure to thank me in the acknowledgments. And I'm talking a whole page—don't give me some throwaway sentence."

"Pages! I'll devote pages to thanking your genius if this all works out."

"I mean, I had my money on a little elevator hostage situation today, but the spilled water . . . classic."

"I guess so."

"And it led right into number four. Maybe even number five!"

"We both know there's no way my dad will let me sleep over at some guy's house. And that one-bed thing only happens in romance novels. I was just humoring you by letting you put that stuff on the list."

"Yeah, okay. But now, the winking, let's talk about the winking. Can you get on FaceTime right now? I want to see what kind of wink it was—like a sexy *come hither* wink or a subtle *do I have something in my eye or do I like you* wink, you know, with plausible deniability."

"You want me to demonstrate?"

"Of course."

A pair of zip-off cargo pants appears in front of me, and I look up to see Sam standing there. There's a dusting of flour on his cheeks and arms.

"Hey, I have to go," I tell Caroline, waving at Sam. He gives me a big one-dimpled smile as he unlocks the car.

"But we need to talk strategy! This is big. This could be a real turning point! His girlfriend is going to be there, so we need to figure out how you'll circumvent her. I started reading this book for AP Lit, *Lady Chatterley's Lover* . . . well, I'm mostly reading the SparkNotes, but—"

I slide into the passenger seat, holding up my hand and

making a face that says *I'm sorry* as he starts the car. "Caroline?" he mouths, and I nod.

"We can talk tonight," I say.

"Okay, but you need to try and get trapped in a closet with Nico. Write that down somewhere! It's important."

I laugh and roll my eyes. "Oh my god. Bye."

"Call me before six! I—"

I hang up before hearing the rest.

"Sorry about that," I say, looking over at Sam, but his face is different now. His jaw is tight as he stares straight ahead at the road.

"You okay?" I ask. "More drama with Giancarlo today?"

Giancarlo is the guy who shares Sam's station in their classroom kitchen, and Sam's been complaining lately about his messiness and lack of adherence to mise en place, whatever that means.

"What was she talking about—getting trapped in a closet with Nico?" he says, still not looking at me.

"You could hear that?"

"Yeah, your volume is up really loud."

"Oh." I can feel my cheeks turn pink. "It's, um . . . Nico invited me to a party at his house this weekend. Do you want to come? You can if you want to."

"I'm good," he says, shaking his head. "But what does that have to do with going into a closet with Nico?"

I cough a few times and fan myself. All of a sudden it feels really hot in here. "Can I roll this window down?"

"Sure."

I can feel him sneak a glance at me quickly before turning his attention back to the road. He laughs, but it sounds exasperated. "Are you really not going to explain that?"

I sigh. "Okay, okay! But you have to promise not to make fun of me."

"Uh . . . all right."

I clear my throat. And then clear my throat again. "Can we turn the air on too?"

"Tessa!"

"Okay! It's just . . . I, well—you know I have a plan with Caroline."

"Yes."

"Yeah, it's been really good for us. It's like we're back to the way we used to be, before I moved."

"And . . . ?"

Man, he's really going to make me say this out loud.

"And," I continue. "Well, our plan. It's kind of . . . unconventional. That's why I didn't tell you too much about it before. To help me get my groo—my writing back . . . uh, well, *Caroline* thinks that if I make my life into one of the love stories I typically write, that maybe that'll help me start writing again. It will, like, fill up the well."

"And Nico is the guy in this love story?" His voice is quiet.

"Yeah, and I know you guys have sort of a history," I say quickly. "But he's not a jerk like Grayson or anything, right? He's actually really nice."

We stop at a red light, and Sam turns his whole body to face me. "But Nico has a girlfriend. Poppy. How can you make a love story . . . or *whatever* with him if he's already with someone else?"

The question makes me feel a little bit icky, but I shake it off. Like Nico just told me, they're on-again, off-again. I haven't done anything *wrong*. And I'm not planning to.

"Well, Nico might not always be with Poppy. They break up a lot." Okay, I don't know *that*. But "I'm not going to make him do anything he doesn't want to."

His eyes narrow. "Do you hear how that sounds?"

"Whatever." Luckily the light turns green, and he has to turn his attention back to the road. This is why I didn't want to tell him—tell *anyone* other than Caroline. He's making me feel silly, and yeah, I recognize the plan is a little silly. But why can't he just go along with it or just, like, laugh it off? That's what friends are supposed to do. Why does he have to be all judgy?

We continue the rest of the ride in silence, but I'm boiling as I get more and more self-conscious, which makes me more and more irritated.

"You said to look for inspiration," I say finally as he's turning into our neighborhood. "I write romance. This is inspiration."

He rubs the side of his face. "This wasn't what I meant."

"Well, I think this is going to work. It's already working."

"You've written something?" He says it like a challenge.

"No. But something is happening with me and him. I could feel it today, and I'm going to see it through."

When we pull into his driveway, he turns off the car, but then he doesn't move. He just sits there, staring at his hands. I don't understand why he even cares. Maybe Nico was more involved in the bullying when he was in middle school than I thought?

"I thought it was your anxiety," he eventually says, his voice low but harsh. "Like we talked about Monday? I thought you were nervous to share your work, and that's why you weren't writing. How will going after Nico change that? It seems like it's dealing with the problem on a . . . I don't know. Shallow level."

Shallow. That word stings. Maybe because I'm worried it's true.

"I mean, yeah, I'm still nervous. But this will help me to write something that I'm proud of. Something real. I was thinking about all the old stuff I used to write, and I really didn't know what I was talking about. And you have to write what you know. That's probably what made me freeze up in the first place."

There—that feels better, getting it all out.

But then Sam laughs. And again, it's not in a nice way. I can feel my neck burn red.

"Listen, I don't really want to talk about it anymore," I say, opening my door with more force than I need.

"Fine," he spits out. "Then we won't." And he opens the car door and walks away.

CHAPTER TWENTY

I spend most of Saturday morning scrolling natural hair Instagram accounts, trying to find the perfect style for tonight. It's a good distraction from worrying about what Sam said and whether or not he's right.

I finally find a style I like with a few diagonal braids in the front and a low poof in the back, and I think my hair might be long enough to do it. But it also means I'll have to ask for help. No matter how many times I practiced on my American Girl doll growing up, I can't French braid. I can barely even regular braid.

I find Mom in the living room under a blanket, even though it's not cold, watching some city of the Real Housewives—they all look the same to me. I extend my phone like an olive branch.

"Can you do this for me?"

Mom stares at me for a second, looking stunned, but then she smiles, bigger than I've seen her do in a long time. She takes my phone and studies the picture, nodding her head.

"Yes, of course, sweetie."

We get out a pointy comb and a Denman brush, and I sit between her legs as she puts tight braids on my scalp, just like my granny and aunties taught her to do, like she did when I was small.

I tell her about the party tonight and give vague answers to her questions about school this week—leaving out all details of the love story plan because I don't want a repeat of whatever happened with Sam earlier. We don't talk about Miles's tantrum on the corner, but I feel like I hear her anyway, through the way she rubs mint almond oil on my scalp and how she gingerly finger-combs through tangles.

When she's done, we go to the bathroom and admire her work in the mirror. It's exactly what I wanted, and my head starts spinning, dreaming about what could happen tonight with my hair looking perfect like this.

"You look beautiful," she says, and her eyes get all crinkly on the sides. They're a different color, but the same as mine.

"Thank you."

She turns me around and gives me a hug, tight and warm.

"I'm sorry."

"I know. Me too."

And just like that, there's peace between us again.

I could feel Lenore's side-eye through her text messages when I explained that Nico had invited me to a party at his house, and I wanted her to come with me. But she agreed to borrow her parents' minivan anyway, and she shows up at my house at seven, wearing a skirt made of iridescent feathers, a black military-style jacket, and her locs pulled up into a huge bun. There's a garment bag trailing behind her and a blush-pink plastic Caboodle under her arm.

"Oh, wow! I had one of those when I was in college," Mom says.

"Are you getting Tessie ready for a date?" Miles asks.

"Better not be," Dad says, giving Lenore his perfected stern face.

"Oh, don't you worry, Mr. Johnson," Lenore says. "I am only escorting Tessa on a night of good, clean fun, to a party in which there promises to be an acceptable ratio of girls to boys. And I will get her home at whatever time you deem an appropriate curfew."

They all smile and give us our privacy at that. She's a pro.

Lenore adds delicate gold cuffs to the braids my mom did for me and applies black eyeliner in a perfect wing—like how you see it done in magazines but can never actually do in real life. I was going to wear this simple chambray shift dress, but Lenore opens up her garment bag to reveal another dress that she found at a thrift store. It's navy blue, with sheer long sleeves cuffed at the wrists and glittery silver constellations embroidered on it.

I hesitate before putting it on. "Is it too much?"

"Oh, girl," Lenore says, wrapping her arms around my

shoulders. "You've got to learn the subtle art of not giving a fuck. I can teach you. That's basically *my* conservatory."

And she's right. I put it on, and I feel good. I still feel like myself, but . . . elevated. I feel like myself if I didn't have all the worries—the constant barrage of voices in my head telling me that I don't belong, that I need to shrink and be quieter. And that's how I want to feel tonight.

"You're like my fairy godmother," I say, smiling at her in the mirror.

Her nose wrinkles. "I'm not your fairy godmother, Tessa. I'm your friend." She looks me straight in the eye, sending me about a thousand words with an arched eyebrow. But before I even have a chance to apologize or word-vomit up just how much she means to me, she waves her hand and smiles. "And that's why you're going to do this for me one day when I find myself someone worthy. But not anytime soon, because the boys at this school are crusty, and I have taste. No offense."

I laugh, relieved. "None taken. And I am ready and waiting to be your wing woman." I give her a salute. "So, Theodore is going to meet us there?"

"Yeah, he was already planning on going with his secret boyfriend."

"Is he—he's not out to . . . everyone yet?"

That makes Lenore giggle so much that she falls forward, her giant bun flopping around. "No! Of course he is! Did you see the faux fur capelet he wore Wednesday?" She gives me an exaggerated side-eye. "No, he just never really brings him around to lunch or anything, so I started calling him that. Says lunchtime is his work time, or whatever, so he doesn't have time for his boo then. That boy. Seriously . . ."

I hug my parents goodbye, watch one video that Miles wants to show me (he's found most of the Dream Zone footage on YouTube, thank god), and then Lenore and I are off. When I open the door, though, I'm shocked to see Sam in the dim evening light, walking across our lawn. And he looks just as shocked to see me.

"Sammy boy!" Lenore shouts, her arms out. "You coming with?"

He shakes his head, looking down at the paper box in his hands and then looking back up at me. "Wow, Tessa—you . . . you look really pretty. You guys, uh, both do."

Lenore's head whips between the two of us, but luckily she just smirks and says nothing.

"I just wanted to say that I'm sorry. For yesterday. I'm not . . . it wasn't . . ." He's rubbing the side of his face, which I'm starting to notice he does a lot when he's processing things. "I don't know—it just wasn't what I expected, but I shouldn't have reacted that way. It wasn't my place to judge, and I should have respected your ideas and your choices more. And Nico . . . Nico would be lucky to have you."

"Thank you, Sam," I say with a small smile, embarrassed that he's talking about my secret plan so openly. I hope my parents aren't listening in.

"And I—uh, I made you cookies," he says, presenting the

box in his hands. "They're a re-creation of the Milk Bar's corn-flake marshmallow cookies—have you heard of them? Except they're a little different. I added peanut butter chips." I take the cookies from him, my hand brushing his.

"Anyway . . . yeah. I hope you two have a good night." He holds my gaze, something there that I can't read, but then he turns away and gives us a small wave. My cheeks flush as I watch him walk away.

CHAPTER TWENTY-ONE

I spend the whole drive explaining to Lenore my writer's block and Caroline's plan and Sam's reaction. I'm a little hesitant to share it all with her, but there's really no sweeping it under the rug after that interaction with Sam. And I figure, if anyone is going to get behind this plan, it's Lenore.

Luckily, I'm right.

"Girl, get it! I'm so in," she says, holding a cookie with one hand and snapping her fingers with the other. Her knees balance the wheel, and I have to fight every instinct not to lunge over and steady it. "Plus, him and Poppy break up allllll the time! They're, like, *super* messy. It's been like that for years. 'Bout time he moved on!"

I resist my urge to do a happy dance at that new information.

"Damn, these cookies are good!" she shouts, taking a bite so big we swerve into the other lane.

"Sam's very good at what he does."

"Shit, you've got it good with Sammy boy across the street, just bringing you gourmet treats every day." She shakes her head and the minivan shakes with her. I try to discreetly hold on to the passenger door. "I thought for sure you and him had something going on, and then all this . . . plot twist!"

"Me and Sam? God, why does everyone think that?"

Lenore raises her eyebrows.

"I mean, he's a good friend, and I like him a lot . . . but not like that. He's not really my type, you know, looks and all." I bite my bottom lip. "Does that make me a jerk to say?"

She shrugs. "Everyone is someone's cup of tea."

And Nico is mine, definitely not Hawaiian Shirt Sam.

Nico's house is in Naples, an upscale neighborhood not far from Chrysalis, but even closer to the beach. We drive past it multiple times as we circle around looking for parking, and I stare out the window at the dark ocean, hoping it will calm my nerves.

The houses in this area cost millions—I remember from when Mom and I drove down to Long Beach one weekend to explore the city and check out the neighborhoods before the big move. We could never afford a house in Naples, but Mom pulled me into an open house anyway, saying it would be fun. That place was tiny and so close to the neighbor that you could probably borrow a cup of sugar through the window, and it was going for over two million. So when we pull up to Nico's house, my internal calculator starts spinning, because his place is four times the size of that one—with two freaking fountains in the front courtyard.

"Whoa."

"Yeah, the Luccheses got bank," Lenore says, tucking Sam's cookies under her arm. "Didn't you see that the fifth floor of the school is named after them?"

The first thing I notice when we walk inside is that the place is super white. Not, like, white people. Though there are a considerable number of those—just like Nico and the other founders' kids, I guess.

Everything in the house is white, I mean. White walls, white shag rugs over light hardwood floors, white leather couches, white fur pillows. The only color in the room is two fiddle-leaf fig trees in white tasseled baskets. It looks like a music-video set or a catalog or something. I wonder how they keep everything *so* white. Because in my house, everything would have a faint film of pizza grease, crumbs, and random dirt in less than twenty-four hours. Seeing people just walking around, touching things, and wearing their shoes makes me a little nervous for Nico. He's going to have a hard time cleaning all this up before his parents get home.

The second thing I notice, after the overwhelming whiteness, is Nico. First, in the pictures hanging on the walls. They look like photos that come already in the frames, a perfect family unit. Mother, father, daughter, and son—all attractive, all impeccably dressed. And then I see Nico in person. He's surrounded by a group of people, holding court with Poppy by his side. So, on-again, I guess. He must be saying something funny, because everyone around him starts laughing. A guy across from him laughs so much that something sloshes out of his red plastic cup, but Nico doesn't admonish him or make him clean it up—he just says something else that inspires another round of laughter.

Nico looks up just then and locks eyes with me from across the room, like he can feel my presence. He waves at me, a big smile on his face, and I struggle to catch my breath. Next to him, Poppy follows his gaze and then narrows her eyes at me—I can't tell if it's suspicion, though, or just disgust. I quickly look away, in case she can read on my face what I'm thinking.

"Ah, there's your boy," Lenore says, putting her arm around me. "But there's his girl . . . what's Caroline's plan for that?"

"I don't want to talk about that."

"You got it." Thankfully, she doesn't push the issue like Sam did . . . because I know it's murky. I'm just hoping it'll get less murky over time, before I actually have to deal with it. "You should let Theo take care of her. You know he wants to make that girl disappear, so she can't keep beating him out for the winter gala."

Lenore points to a couch, where Theodore, in a blue-striped button-up and tight shorts, is entwined with a dancer I've seen around campus before. The guy is tall with smooth copper skin and impressive muscles—and Theodore seems to be exploring every one of them as if they were completely alone.

"Um . . . they don't look very secret."

Lenore shakes her head. "He probably had a drink—he always gets all boo'd up when you get some vodka in him. Speaking of which . . . I'm thirsty. Let's go see what kind of bougie drinks they got in there."

She nods to the kitchen, pulling me after her, and I feel a little panic flutter in my chest. I've never had even a sip of alcohol before. The feeling of not being in control sounds awful, because I love being in control. I wish I could be even more in control than I am normally—why isn't there a drink for that? I didn't really think of a plan for what I would do if there was drinking at this party, but that was kind of stupid, because *of course* there's drinking at this party. Will Lenore think I'm some kind of little kid if I don't drink? Nico definitely will. And how is Lenore planning on driving? We didn't discuss that.

But then I see Nico walk away from Poppy, going into a back room, and my mind clears of everything but a chance to get some time with just him. I can figure this out later.

"Actually, I'm gonna go to the bathroom," I say to Lenore. "I'll catch up with you in a little bit."

"Okay!" She flits away, munching on another one of Sam's cookies.

Nico goes down a short hallway and I follow him, squeezing through a crowd of three musical theater girls falling over themselves and a guy I think is in my physics class. Nico turns into a back room that's a little less white—there's a buttery tan leather couch and a matching Eames chair, with a large abstract watercolor on the wall. And he slips out the door in that room into what I assume is the backyard. I'm about to follow him right out there too, after turning to make sure no one sees how stalker-y I'm being, but I stop myself. What did number four on Caroline's list say? Have a moment at a party? This could be the perfect time for that, but how will I explain why I suddenly appeared in his backyard? Needed some fresh air . . . but what if he's smoking? Would I still like him if he's a smoker? Probably.

Ready or not, moment, here I come. But then, through the large glass panel on the door, I see him hug a woman in a fitted black lace dress. *What the hell?* I dive behind the Eames chair. I can hear their voices through the open window.

"You heading out?" Nico asks.

"In a minute," she says. "But we need to chat about a few things first."

Does Nico have a secret older girlfriend? Does Poppy know about this? This is definitely going to screw up the happily ever after plan. . . .

"What's the rush?" a deep voice says. "You don't want your friends to see us? We're hip. We can hang."

Now, who's that?

I peek from behind the chair and see that there are two people outside with him. The lady—I notice her high heels with red bottoms and her giant geometric earrings—and an older man, wearing a black suit and wingtips. He looks just like Nico, has the same loose waves, but his have a distinguished amount of gray sprinkled at his temples. I recognize them from the pictures in the front of the house.

He's talking to his parents? That's strange. Right? I mean, I'm not a party expert or anything. My knowledge mostly comes from movies, but aren't these things supposed to happen when, like, the parents are out of town or something? I haven't actually been to a lot of high school parties, though . . . or actually any at all. So, what do I know? Maybe it's a white-kid thing. Or a rich-kid thing.

His mom looks upset. "We should have made you cancel this thing after what Ms. McKinney said at coffee this morning."

"Now, Nella, it wasn't negative," his dad chides her.

"Why do you get coffee with her, anyway?" Nico asks. "You don't even like her." His usual smile is replaced with a scowl.

"You never know when these connections will come in handy for you . . . for your future. Her most recent book just got optioned by Starz, though who even has Starz anymore?"

Nico definitely rolls his eyes that time. I duck back down, so I can just hear their voices.

"She said you shared in class yesterday, and it was underwhelming."

"She said that? Seriously?" Nico asks, his voice raised.

His dad cuts in. "She didn't say that, Nella."

"Well, I could tell by her tone. I just want to make sure

you're living up to your full potential, Nico. You don't want to get passed over for the gala again, and college applications are just a year away. Your sister was much further in the process at this point. Did you see the article I sent you about NYU? Jeffrey Eugenides is on their faculty, you know. . . ."

"I'm not talking about this right now!" Nico huffs, and then it's quiet, except for the shuffling of feet and the bass from the music at the front of the house.

"Well, we'll be home from the fundraiser by one," his mom finally says, her voice tight. "Make sure everyone is gone by then, and that includes Poppy."

"Drink responsibly!" his dad adds. "And absolutely no driving!"

"And don't forget to text Grace about coming in the morning to clean. I already saw that red Cheeto dust on the counters."

They seem to be wrapping up, so I take that as my opportunity to sprint across the room and back into the front of the house. I don't want him to catch me snooping like a creeper. And even if I could make it look perfectly normal, me just sitting there in that room, I don't think Nico would want anyone to have overheard that conversation. His parents were harsh on him—like, way harsh. I feel a lot of pressure to write now, but that's pressure I put on myself. I can't imagine how I would feel if my mom was meeting with my teacher and calling me underwhelming. How does he write anything like that?

There are a few dancers mingling in the hallway as I walk

through, and when I get back to the front of the house, I realize there's way more people here now. The kitchen is packed with Chrysalis students filling up their red cups with concoctions from various glass bottles and leaning against the marble countertops. And in the dim living room, a Kanye West song is blasting through the speakers (of course, since white guys love Kanye). I spot Grayson in a corner, scrolling through an iPhone hooked up to an aux cable. But I can't see Lenore . . . or anyone else I know. And I feel a familiar panic creep in as I think about facing this party without her. Maybe I should just go, get a Lyft. . . .

"Tessa!"

I hear my name from somewhere in the room, and with relief, I spot Theodore on the couch, all cuddled up with his secret boyfriend.

"Tessa! Oh, Tessa, you sweet thing!" His face is flushed red and he leans forward to kiss me on both cheeks. "And that dress! You look absolutely magnificent! An angel sent down from the cosmos to grace us with her beauty." He kisses my cheeks again. He is . . . unusually nice. Or drunk, I guess. But I officially like drunk Theodore.

"This is Lavon," he says, stroking the shoulder of the guy sitting next to him. Lavon is wearing a white tank top that shows off his arms, and he has freshly laid waves. He reaches out to shake my hand, a goofy smile on his face.

"Nice to meet you, Tessa. Theo has told me a lot about you."

So apparently *someone* gets to call him Theo.

Theodore leans forward, covers the side of his mouth, and says in a stage whisper, "He's my boyfriend." He turns and marvels at Lavon before leaning in to kiss him again. A second later, they're full-on making out, and then I'm just sitting there like a loser again.

I'm about to get up, but then someone plops down next to me.

"Hi. Tessa, right?" I have no idea who this white guy in a green flannel shirt is, but I search my memory because he seems to recognize me. And then it clicks. Fedora. Except instead of a fedora, he's wearing a man bun tonight. Maybe that's his fancy look.

"Hey, uh . . . you."

"We're in Art of the Novel together?"

"Yeah, yeah. I know you!" *Or your regular hat choice, at least.*

"That piece you shared last week. It was beautiful. You have a real unique voice."

I have no idea what he's talking about, because obviously I haven't shared a thing. Does Fedora have me confused with someone else? Is he trying to hit on me? Honestly, I'm kinda annoyed that Fedora is here at all. Did Nico just invite everyone?

"Mmm-hmm," I murmur, and Fedora starts going on about his work in progress, something about aliens, but I tune him out. I wish I knew where Lenore was. Or Sam . . . I wish Sam had come with us. I know if he was here, I would feel more calm. But I guess he would just have made things weird, considering how he feels about my plan.

Pushing those thoughts away, I spot Nico across the room again. He looks upset—and of course he is, after what I overhead. Poppy is next to him, though, in an oversized leopard-print top and short shorts, and she's kissing his neck, her hands wrapped around his hips. . . . God, what am I even doing here?

And then a Cardi B song I sorta recognize comes on, and *everyone* starts dancing. Dancing!

I hate dancing.

Everyone always expects me to be good at it, to perform their idea of what Blackness means, but I'm not. Like, not at all. I think it's because I can't let go in the way that you have to in order to dance. I try to always be measured and controlled, and dancing is none of that. I care too much about what I look like, how each movement looks to others, so moving my body like that would just be exhausting.

So I don't dance. Ever. Well, in public, at least.

I know there's an item on Caroline's list about a dance of romance, or whatever, but that's just not going to happen.

Fedora gets up and starts doing something that looks like a Peanuts character, all tiptoes and nose pointed to the sky. He beckons for me to join him, curving his two pointer fingers toward me and shimmying his hips.

Uh-uh. Nope.

I hop off the couch and scoot away, but then someone grabs me by the waist and pulls me into the middle of the crowd.

"I love this song! Don't you love this song?" Lenore squeals. Her breath smells sweet and her locs are down now, swirling around as she whips her head back and forth. Relief washes over me because I've found her, but it's replaced quickly by panic that I'm standing in the middle of a bunch of gyrating bodies.

I scan the room, making sure Nico can't see me standing here all awkward, but he's going up the stairs alone. Poppy and another girl are grinding on Rhys a few feet away, giggling as his face starts to match his hair.

This is my moment. Our moment. I can hear Caroline's voice whispering in my head. *Go!*

I stop Lenore in the middle of an enthusiastic twerk. "I have to go to the bathroom. I'll be right back."

She looks confused, and then leans in and whispers, "Girl, you got some poop problems?"

"Yep!"

I'm not so much fleeing as I am running to something.

CHAPTER TWENTY-TWO

I walk past more doors than there are people that live in this house. I have never lived in a house like that—not in Roseville and not in Long Beach. We've always had just enough rooms for our family, and most people I know are like that too. I wonder what it must be like to live in a house with such excess, to have rooms that people probably don't even go into every day. Does dust gather in those rooms? I guess that's what Grace must be for.

Most of the doors are shut, but there's a light on at the end of the hallway, and I slowly drift toward it, like a moth to a flame. And when I get there, I see Nico, back hunched over in a C, studying a large book. But squinting, I see that it's not something serious like the complete works of Leo Tolstoy or something. No, it's *Harry Potter and the Sorcerer's Stone*—the illustrated one. And I'm surprised. It doesn't fit this image of him I've created in my head.

I turn around to go back to the party, my neck feeling a little hot. But then I stop myself. *You can do this. Or at least—you*

will *do this, and you'll find out about your capability along the way.*
With a sudden pang of boldness, I knock on the doorframe, making Nico look up.

"Hi," I say, my voice a little strangled.

"Hey," he says, and smiles. Full-on cheeses. I take that as my invitation to walk in.

"What you reading?" I ask, even though I know.

He shows me the cover and then blushes, which throws me off. He's usually so confident. "I know it's kinda little kiddish."

"Not at all! I loved Harry Potter. Well, still love Harry Potter. They're my favorite books." I'm talking too much, trying to make him feel better, because they're definitely not my favorite books anymore. I almost even spill the beans about my Harry Potter fan fiction history, but luckily I have a little more self-preservation than that.

"Cool. Me too."

"Except . . ." Should I say it?

"Except what?"

"*Except*, I just wish there were more brown people in the books. It made my Halloween costumes in elementary school pretty difficult."

"Well, Hermione's Black in *Harry Potter and the Cursed Child*. I saw it on Broadway a couple years ago. And J. K. Rowling said Dumbledore is gay, right?"

I just give him the side-eye, and he laughs, loud and full, his head falling back to face the ceiling. It emboldens me further, and I close the space between me and the bed, sitting down at the end.

"The books," he continues, not acknowledging me sitting on his bed either way, "they're just . . . they're a comfort to me. I read them when I'm feeling kinda shitty. And these illustrated ones—have you seen them? They're dope."

He scoots closer to me and leans in to show me the page he was on. It's Hagrid, towering over Harry, their faces illuminated by the fireplace as Hagrid reveals something that will change Harry's life forever. The picture is beautiful, but I'm also distracted by the beautiful face of the guy presenting it to me. His lush lashes and full lips. His perfectly tousled hair. And this close, I can see a tiny scar above his eyebrow. I want to trace it with my fingers.

I start talking, to slow my heart rate down. "I remember the first time I read this book . . . it just blew my mind, you know, Harry being this special, important child and no one knew it for most of his life—he had this whole new identity just waiting for him. I mean, I know it's a trope, the chosen-one thing, but it was so thrilling for me at the time."

Nico nods, pulling the book back into his lap, but he doesn't scoot back to his original spot. "J. K. Rowling made me realize I wanted to be a writer. I wanted to write *like her*. But, like, don't go telling people in our classes that. I've got an image to uphold." I shake my head quickly, and he smiles. "She's just made such an impact on the world. I want to do that. And be famous! Be a celebrity author."

"But not *just* like her. Right?" I ask, searching his face for some recognition. He blinks at me.

"Because of, you know . . . what she's said," I continue. "It's ruined so much of the magic."

At that, he just shrugs. "She's still famous."

I consider saying something more. Caroline and I have discussed our anger and heartbreak over all this at length, but I also don't want to scare Nico off by getting too deep.

"Hey, what's your favorite book?" he asks.

So I guess my face isn't giving away everything going on in my mind. I decide to go with it.

"Prisoner of Azkaban."

"Solid choice," he says, nodding. I notice the book is closed now, and he's just focused on me. "My favorite is *Goblet of Fire*."

"Why?" I ask, and then add quickly, "Not that there's anything wrong with that. It's so good. I'm just curious."

"It's the book when things get dark, you know what I mean? And Harry realizes that he's not a kid anymore and this is all a part of something bigger."

"It gets dark way before that! The basilisk wasn't dark enough for you? And, um, Harry's parents getting killed?"

"But it wasn't in front of Harry! Voldemort straight-up murdered Cedric in front of Harry. That was some dark shit."

I laugh, and he joins in. "True, true."

I don't know if it's my imagination, but he seems to be even closer now—his knees are so close to my right hip that I can feel the heat coming off them.

"What house would you be in?" he asks.

"I don't know, I feel like there should be more overlap. Like, do you ever think it's strange, dividing people up by four strict personality types? I mean, what kind of world would it be if there were only four types of people?"

"Yeah, okay."

"But also I would totally be a Ravenclaw."

"Slytherin." He grins. And I'm not imagining it. He's definitely closer.

"So what's happening now?" I ask. "That you, um, need the comfort of Harry Potter?" I try to keep my tone steady, innocent, as if I wasn't just spying on the conversation he had with his parents.

His looks down and sucks in a sharp breath, and I'm worried I miscalculated this—that I ruined whatever ground we had gained from this conversation so far. I feel like I'm maneuvering across an obstacle course. But then he looks back up at me, eyes wide and vulnerable.

"My parents are big supporters of the arts. They actually helped to start Chrysalis, did you know that?"

I shake my head and try to sound surprised. "No. Wow." He doesn't need to know that I've heard all about the founders' kids.

"Yeah, well, you'd think that would be a good thing, because, like, most parents want their kids to be doctors or lawyers or whatever. Art school isn't on the table. My parents . . . they're all about it, yeah, but . . . they expect me to be the best. Like art is this competition. And it's a lot of pressure."

"I'm sorry, Nico," I say. "But you *are* so talented. I hope they see that. That piece you shared in class yesterday was really powerful. I can't wait to read more." .

"Really?" A smile spreads across his face, but then his eyes darken again, probably remembering what his mom said about it. "Anyway, it's not enough for them. I need to be chosen for the gala this year for my mom to be even mildly satisfied."

"You'll get it. No one else in that class is as good as you." He's blushing again, and it makes my whole body feel warm.

"Thank you, Tessa," he says, his voice small and sweet, and I'm all of a sudden aware that we're alone in his room. Alone in his room *on his one bed*. The lights are dim, and the sounds of the party are distant, like we're in our own little bubble. It's not a closet, but I think it's better. Nico Lucchese and I are having a moment, just like number four on the happily ever after list.

I get a blurry image in my mind of Tallulah and Thomas in the same place as us. Knee to knee on his bed, lips moving closer and closer like magnets, but then they slam together, all awkward noses and clinking teeth. And then—*poof!*—they disintegrate like all the good characters in that Avengers movie my dad made me watch. It makes my head hurt.

"My older sister, she was this dance prodigy," he continues, snapping me out of my almost inspiration. "Well . . . is. She's studying at Juilliard now. But when she went to Chrysalis, she was always chosen to solo at the winter gala. Even as a freshman. My mom expects me to be the same as her with my writing. I worry that I'll never be good enough. That I'll, um, I'll never measure up to everything she's already done. Does that make sense?"

"Mmm-hmm. That must be really tough, living in her shadow. I . . . I get it."

"Yeah? Do you have older siblings?"

"A brother—but it's not the same."

"Why?" he asks, his voice playful. "Is he a fuckup?"

"No. No, no. My brother has disabilities."

His face falls. "Oh, I'm sorry."

He takes my hand. And my body goes a little haywire, torn between those words that I hate so much and the fact that HE'S HOLDING MY HAND. Touching me, on purpose, not in my imagination.

"You don't have to be sorry," I manage to squeak out.

"I'm sure he's taught you so much," he continues, and now he's squeezing my hand. "That's probably why you're such a great listener."

And yeah, now he gave not just one but two of my most hated responses to people finding out about my brother. Plus there was that whole J. K. Rowling thing.

But . . . I push it out of my mind. It's easier to. I'm pretty sure it has to do with how his hand feels over mine, like he's not just holding on to my fingers, but to my whole heart, my whole *being*. All my insides feel like they're doing a dance, one with high kicks and twerking and shoulder shimmies.

And maybe I just need to get over it, the things that bother me. Maybe I'm being too sensitive.

I focus on memorizing every detail—his smooth palms, the bump on his middle finger from holding a pen—so I can share it with Caroline later. And use it all in the story, too, that I'll write at the end of this.

CHAPTER TWENTY-THREE

"And then what happened?" Caroline asks. I call her to download as soon as I get home.

"Well, we talked some more about the novel he's working on now. And he showed me some of his old notebooks from when he was younger. Get this—he used to write Avatar fan fiction when he was in elementary school!"

"*The Last Airbender* or those creepy blue things?"

"*The Last Airbender.*"

"Ah, phew! Did you tell him about your fan fiction?"

"Are you kidding me? Of course not!"

"Hey, he told you about his! He probably would have thought it was cool."

"I don't think so . . . but he did say I should eat lunch with them. That he wanted to get to know me better."

Caroline squeals so loud, I'm sure she's going to wake Lola up.

"Oh my god! Oh my god! I'm a genius!"

"Is this always going to come back to your genius?"

"Pretty much. You're welcome. So what else happened? Did he, like, throw you on his bed and ravish you?"

"No, we eventually just went downstairs, and then I found Lenore. She was leading this conga line through the living room? It was weird."

"She didn't drive, did she?"

"No . . . Lavon, that's Theodore's secret boyfriend—he wasn't drinking, so he drove us all home. She'll probably have to get her mom's car tomorrow. I hope she's not in trouble."

"Wow," Caroline says, her voice serious.

"What?"

"It's just . . . you survived your first high school party. I'm so proud. I literally look like the star-eye emoji right now."

"I didn't just survive. I thrived!" I laugh, imagining Caroline beaming at me like a parent on graduation day. "And hey, you've never been to a high school party."

Now she's laughing too, but her laugh sounds different from mine.

"Tessa, I've been to parties before."

"You have? When?"

"Well, I went to my first one when I went to stay with my ninang—"

"But that was in July! How come you didn't tell me?" My voice gets higher.

"It was right after you moved, and you were going through

a lot. I didn't want to make it about me." She must hear that I sound a bit hysterical, because her tone is softer now.

"I want to talk about you! I want you to tell me things." That's what best friends do, and if she's not telling me things as big as that, then the gap between us is growing even more than I thought. "Sorry, I was just surprised, that's all. Have there been any more?"

"Yeah, one with Brandon. Michael and Olivia went with us."

"Like, since school started?"

"Uh-huh."

"Oh my gosh, Caroline, it's like you're living a secret life! How did you get your dad to agree?"

She lowers her voice into barely a whisper, as if he can hear through the walls. "I told him we were studying for the AP Lit exam—trying to get a head start, you know? And I was home by ten."

"Did you have fun?"

"Yeah, we did."

I sigh. "Caroline, please keep telling me what's going on. I always want to know. And I'm sorry if—"

She cuts me off. "It's fine. I will."

Then there's this weird, long silence that feels really heavy—I don't like it. And I want to fill it, so I don't have to think about what it means. But Caroline must have the same idea, because we both start talking at the same time, and it comes out this garbled mess. We both laugh.

She says, "You go."

"I was just gonna ask, what's the next step in the plan? Like, I think I've done number two, number four . . . maybe even number three?"

She giggles, but it's quieter than before. She must be getting tired. "Well, it's fluid. You don't have to follow them in order. That's the brilliance of my plan. Let's strategize after you eat lunch with him on Monday."

"Okay, yeah, sounds good." I yawn, and then, a second later, she does too. I know it's silly, but it makes me feel connected with her, even though we're so far away.

"Tonight with Nico went so well. Do you . . . do you feel like writing?"

"Not yet." But I know it's only a matter of time.

CHAPTER TWENTY-FOUR

When I go outside Monday morning, Sam isn't outside by his car like usual, and after five minutes of waiting around, there's still no sign of him. Maybe he overslept? Or got caught up in some complicated recipe?

I mean, I don't want to bug, but I need to know soon if I have to find another ride. I wait a couple more minutes before walking up his steps and knocking on his door—quietly, just in case his mom is still sleeping. But to my surprise, it's her standing there as the door swings open, not Sam.

I've seen Audrey Weiner on TV. She has her own show on Food Network, and I'm pretty sure she was even a guest host on *The View* once, one day when I was home sick. So, like, I know what she looks like and all, but actually seeing her in person—here, just across the street—is still strange. Instead of the perfectly tailored fit-and-flare dresses she normally wears, she has on a burgundy-and-blush floral-print kimono over polka-dot pajamas, and her iconic curly auburn bob is pulled back with a thick headband. Familiar, but not. It's like catching Mickey off duty from Disneyland.

"Oh, Tessa!" she says, her eyes lighting up with recognition. "It's so good to finally meet you! I've heard so much about you from Sam and your lovely mother." We've lived here for months now, but Audrey Weiner and I have never actually met—even though I've shamelessly tried to catch sight of her ever since finding out that Sam's mom wasn't just *Sam's mom*. Which, by the way, I'm still very curious why she lives here in Long Beach, and not even in the biggest house on the street.

"Ms. Weiner, hi, yes—it's nice to meet you." I feel a little nervous, like because she's on TV, suddenly I'm on TV right now.

"Oh, call me Audrey!" Yeah, I don't think I can do that. "We need to have you over for dinner soon, one of these nights when I don't have to work late. I know Sam is just so fond of you." She reaches out to squeeze my shoulders, like we've known each other for years. "I'm so happy he's found such a good friend."

"Yes, dinner. I would love that. That's very kind of you." I shift awkwardly from one foot to the other. "Actually, I was coming here because, uh, where is Sam?"

Before she can answer, though, he appears at the door behind her. I almost gasp. Because he looks . . . different. Way different. Sometime since I saw him last, Sam got a haircut. It's short now, and polished, and it's transformed his whole face.

His jaw, which was pretty much hidden with his shaggy mop of hair before, is strong and prominent. He looks put together, more confident somehow. But also like Sam. It's weird.

"You cut your hair," I say, stating the obvious.

"Yeah, his biannual haircut," Ms. Weiner says with a snort, and I laugh. But then I stop immediately, seeing Sam's pink cheeks. That was maybe not a joke.

"You . . . I mean, it looks good."

"Thanks," he says, flashing a dimple. But then his face turns serious. "So, we're still driving together?" he asks. But it doesn't sound snarky. There's genuine concern and . . . something else there. Ms. Weiner looks between us, her brow wrinkled in confusion.

"Um . . . I thought so," I say slowly.

"Okay, yeah. Okay," he says, his eyes squinted like he's working out some complex math problem. "I just thought—I was worried, I don't know, that you were still mad at me or something. I was . . ."

"You were what?" I ask.

"I don't know. Just, uh, yeah . . . it's nothing. Never mind."

Sam's face burns red, and now Ms. Weiner is looking at us like she's trying to hide a smile.

He picks up his things. "Let's go."

We're in his car driving down Pacific Coast Highway when he brings it up again, his eyes looking straight ahead instead of at me.

"So, we're okay?"

"Yeah, we're good," I assure him. I didn't realize that it was this big of a deal—that he cared this much. I don't think I've ever had someone check in with me this many times, except maybe my mom.

"I'm sorry if I'm being annoying," he says, rubbing his cheek. He sneaks a quick glance at me. "I just wanted to check because . . . I like being friends with you."

My whole body feels warm.

"I like being friends with you too."

Sitting with Nico and his friends doesn't make me a bad friend to Sam. That's what I'm telling myself when I walk outside for lunch. What if he was drunk or something when he asked me to sit with him at lunch—or, like, joking? What if he woke up the next morning and immediately regretted being so nice to the social charity case? What if I imagined whatever that was between us?

I sit down in my designated rocker between Theodore and Lenore, happy just to be here with my friends and not having to stress out. But when I look up, Nico is shading his eyes against the sun and looking right at me. He starts to wave me over.

"Uh, Tessa?" Lenore says.

"You see that?"

"Mmm-hmm."

"So it's not a mirage?"

"Nah," she laughs. "I think he wants you to go over there."
Theodore actually looks up with vague interest. Luckily, Sam
isn't here yet.

"Okay . . . should I do that?"

"Yes! Go get him, sis!" She slaps my butt when I stand up,
like a coach sending me off to the big game.

As I walk across the lawn, I feel like all eyes are on me, even
though they obviously aren't. It's just lunch. Why am I making
this such a big deal?

But as I approach their spot, it feels like the biggest deal, my
heart beating about a million miles an hour as I try to imagine
every way this could go.

"Hey!" Nico says, giving me a sleepy smile. "Your friends
are welcome too."

I look back at Lenore and Theodore, just to catch the tail
end of their necks whipping around and the two of them all of
a sudden developing intense interest in Lenore's can of LaCroix.
I think them watching me up close would only make me more
nervous.

"No, they're good."

Rhys waves, and Grayson, leaning back on his elbows all
cool, sticks out his chin in my direction. "Sup."

Okay, this is going to be all right. Maybe I'm freaking out
for nothing. But then Poppy, not even hiding her disgust, looks
me up and down and turns to Nico. "What is she doing here?"

"She's my friend," Nico says, shrugging his shoulders.

"Since when?" Poppy asks. Her voice is ice, and her lip curls up.

Grayson calls out, "Oop!" and reels his head back, and Rhys starts to look at me with a little more interest. Nico doesn't look bothered at all, though. He grabs Poppy's hand and pulls her up. "One second, Tessa. We need to talk real quick."

They go off to the border of the lawn by the sidewalk, and Nico laces his fingers in Poppy's and pulls her into a tight hug. Her head fits perfectly under his chin. I look away.

"I remember you from the party now," Grayson says, nodding. "You and that other Black girl came together."

I guess technically nothing that he's saying is wrong, but it makes me bristle nonetheless.

"Her name is Lenore. And yeah, we were there."

Rhys snaps his fingers. "Hey, yeah, I remember seeing you too, coming down the stairs with Nico. What exactly were you two doing up there?" He waggles his eyebrows.

I shrug. "Talking about Harry Potter."

"Oh," he says, looking disappointed. "Well, that's good, I guess, that he found someone to talk about his nerd stuff with." He pulls his phone out of his pocket, and I'm pretty sure he's just looking at his own reflection in the camera from the way he's fluffing his hair and smoldering.

"Okay, well, I think I'm gonna go," I say, standing up. This isn't really what I thought it would be.

"Tessa!" Nico calls, making his way back to the group. His

smile is just as big as it was before, which is a stark contrast to Poppy, who's a few feet behind him. She gives me a death glare before heading toward the building.

"Sorry about that," he says, sitting down, and I can't help it. I follow. "She's just . . ." He gestures his hand like he's shooing something away. "She's upset about something, but she'll be over it when you're here tomorrow."

I can't help but notice the look that passes between Rhys and Grayson.

"Can I ask you something?" Nico's face is a little more serious now, even somber.

Will you actually not have lunch with us tomorrow? Because my very much on-again girlfriend knows what you're up to, and we both want no part in this desperate little ploy.

"Sure."

"What is Turkish delight, anyway?" Nico asks, easing himself down in a spot next to me. That definitely wasn't what I was expecting. "I've been thinking about this all morning. You've read the Chronicles of Narnia, right? Of course you have. They just talk about Turkish delight like it's something all kids are supposed to know or whatever. And it must be pretty fucking good to make Edmund act like such an asshole."

It's clear he's trying to lighten the mood, and it works.

I laugh. "I'm pretty sure we could Google that, but I always pictured it as, uh . . . fudgelike?"

"Maybe fudge with a little something extra," he says, miming taking a hit from a joint.

The lunch period takes a turn for the better from there, Nico and I falling into the same easy conversation that we had Saturday night. And Rhys and Grayson end up not being as douche-y as I thought. Rhys asks me all these questions about Northern California, still interested when I tell him there's a big difference between Roseville and San Francisco. And Grayson offers to throw out my trash at the end of lunch, which is pretty nice.

By the end I've almost forgotten the little exchange with Poppy. Or at least I've done my best to push it out of my brain, because she was definitely pissed—but that worked to my advantage.

Does it make me a terrible person if my love story can only exist by taking down someone else's love story?

Does it make me a terrible person if I want it anyway?

CHAPTER TWENTY-FIVE

"Are you going to sit with us today, or are you headed to your standing invitation with the Chrysalis bourgeoisie?" Theodore asks, scooting his chair toward my desk. We have US history together with Mr. Gaines, who went from the high-energy *Hamilton* rapping on the first day to just putting on movies vaguely related to American history while he sits at his desk. So we don't even have to be stealthy.

"Hey!" I whisper-yell.

Theodore's lips curve into the most subtle of smiles to let me know he's kidding. Sort of. "I just want to know if you'll be gracing us with your presence. Not that I care or anything."

"You say it like I never sit with you guys anymore!" That actually comes out as a real yell, earning a halfhearted stern look from Mr. Gaines. We both turn our attention back to the front, pretending to pay attention to the movie.

I've started sitting with Nico and his friends two days a

week. Maybe three, tops. Enough to fall into their rhythm and get a feeling for these people who I used to just watch from across the lawn. Like, Rhys's constant creation of "casual" videos for his Instagram stories and YouTube (I guess he's semi-famous there), even though he does at least four takes. And Grayson's speech, peppered with an embarrassing amount of slang (like, "Dead-ass, that dress is low-key dope, Tess!"), but somehow only to me.

And Nico. He drinks a green juice every day—the actually healthy kind that's all vegetables. He doesn't like to wear socks because they make his feet feel claustrophobic. Sometimes he likes to just be quiet, lying out in the afternoon sun like a lizard on a rock, his sleepy eyelids weighed down by his heavy lashes. And he's also constantly making sure I don't feel left out, always asking my opinion about things and making obscure Harry Potter references that only I will get. I find myself cataloging each piece of information like I'm studying a rare bird.

It's thrilling to be accepted into their inner circle, to be someone Nico searches for across the lawn. But Lenore cemented her status as a friend I want to keep forever the first day I met her, and Theodore and Sam have become equally indispensable. I have no interest in ditching them for a new group or throwing the gift of their friendship in their faces.

"I'm sorry if I've been over there too much," I say when Mr. Gaines is distracted again. "That's not cool."

"You're not," Theodore says quickly, letting out a snort

that's almost a laugh. "I'm just giving you a difficult time for my amusement. Maybe I'm just bitter because you're sitting with my nemesis."

"You know, I'm pretty sure Poppy is totally unaware that she's your nemesis," I say, and Theodore rolls his eyes. "And it's not like I'm sitting *with* her. She hates me probably as much as you hate her."

Even though I'd rather not, I'm getting to know Poppy too. How she brings a cup of nonfat Greek yogurt every day even though they all complain about the smell, and how, when it moves into October, she's the type of girl who layers on faux fur jackets and socks under her Birkenstocks even though it's still a million degrees. Also, her incredible skill at ignoring my presence—even when I'm just a few feet from her.

"Well, that's just because you're trying to steal her boyfriend," Theodore says matter-of-factly.

My eyes bulge and my mouth drops open.

Before my brain starts to spiral, though, he gives my arm a quick squeeze—a first—and looks me in the eye, another rare occurrence. "Hey, no judgment. There's no shame in going after what you want."

I smirk at him. "Well, now that we've thoroughly discussed my love life, let's dissect yours. You know, I talked to Lavon during—"

"Oh, shut up," he says, waving me away and scooting his chair back to his desk. "Why don't you go sit with my nemesis today? I'm sure you two will be very happy together."

★ ★ ★

So, I have Theodore's blessing, and Lenore is all about Plan Get Yo Man, as she's taken to calling it. She practically pushes me along to Nico at lunch and whenever we run into him in the hallway.

But Sam *never* bridges the gap. I usually don't even see him outside when I'm sitting on the lawn. When I asked him about it once, he says he's busy working in the class kitchen with Giancarlo. They've apparently resolved their mise en place drama.

Which is why I'm surprised when he comes striding over one afternoon, a determined look on his face. He is wearing a Hawaiian shirt, unsurprisingly, but he has on some black jeans that actually fit. I noticed them this morning as soon as we got out of the car. They make his usual dorky ensemble look almost okay.

"Weiner!" Grayson whoops when he sees Sam approaching, and it's almost imperceptible, but I notice Sam wince.

"Hey, Sam," I say extra cheerfully, trying to make up for Grayson.

"Sorry, I don't mean to bother you all—"

"You're not bothering," I cut him off, firm. "You want to sit down?"

"Join us, man!" Nico says, putting his arm out. I don't look around to see everyone else's faces, because if they do have a problem with it, I don't want to know.

"That's okay," Sam says, waving his hands. "I just wanted

to check with you, Tessa. Is it okay if we make a couple stops on our way home? It's for homework."

"Yeah, definitely."

"'On *our* way home,' hmmm?" Poppy asks after Sam walks away. "You and Weiner would make a cute couple, Tessa. You should go for it with him. I think you two would be *really* happy."

It's more than Poppy has said to me probably ever, and that throws me off for a second. But then Nico jumps in before I can even craft a response.

"They're just friends," he says, and maybe I'm reading into it a bit, but he sounds a little testy. He looks at me for confirmation, and his gaze lingers on me for a half second longer than necessary.

When I'm driving with Sam later after school, I want so badly to download the tiny—but *significant*—interaction with Nico, to dissect exactly what that look meant. But I can't call Caroline in front of Sam, and I don't want to send Lenore a wall of text. Luckily, though, Sam's stops provide an easy distraction.

"This is homework?" I ask when we pull up to the white and bubble-gum pink building on Atlantic, not too far from our houses. A spinning cupcake sign makes it clear what's waiting for us inside.

He grins, showing his signature dimple. "It is in my conservatory. How do you feel about tasting some desserts?"

"I mean, I *guess* I can help you. If I *have* to."

"You are a true saint."

Inside there are milk-glass cake stands filled with not just cupcakes but cake pops, tarts, and French macarons too. Sam orders an assortment of each, and then we sit at a tiny table, splitting each treat in half. It occurs to me when I'm cutting into a chocolate cupcake piled high with thick, sweet frosting, that this probably looks like a date to anyone watching us.

"What do you think of that one?" he asks, watching me after I take a bite.

"Can I marry a cupcake?"

He laughs. "Yeah, I think the peanut butter cream cheese frosting and salted caramel balance out the richness of the chocolate ganache."

He makes a few notes in his notebook, and I find myself watching him just like I did when he was baking at his house, a flutter in my chest. I don't know why, because it's just Sam—I guess maybe because it's, like, a privilege to see someone so passionate about their art. It makes me miss what I used to have.

I guess I was staring a little too intently, because his head pops up, and he arches an eyebrow in question.

"I was just thinking how you have the best homework ever. Maybe I need to switch conservatories."

"Yeah, and we're not even done yet."

Stop number two is an ice cream shop a few blocks over.

"Okay, I think we should order a flight here," he says once we're in line, rubbing his hands together as he studies the rainbow of flavors in the case. It's kinda cute how his jaw tightens and he looks all serious, like he's deciding on which color wire to cut on a ticking bomb instead of ice cream.

"Are there any nondairy flavors?"

"Oh, no," he says, looking panicked. "Are you allergic?"

I try to figure out the ladylike way to explain to a guy that ice cream, specifically, gives me crazy farts. But then I realize that it's just Sam, so I tell him exactly that. He falls over forward laughing, totally unaware of the white-haired woman in front of us who turns around to give us the death stare and shake her head.

When we reach the front, the freckled girl behind the case offers us little spoons with tastes of each flavor, Sam carefully considering each one like wine at a fancy restaurant.

"Oh, and you *have* to get this one," the girl gushes, offering us each another spoon. "It's our most popular flavor: Long Beach Crack."

Sam takes it gladly, but I wrinkle my nose and wave it away.

"Oh, Tessa, c'mon! You gotta try this one. It's freaking amazing."

"It has these toffee pieces in it, um, made with Ritz crackers," the girl explains. "It's sooooo addictive, right? Hence the name. Get it?" She lets out a high-pitched laugh like a tinkling bell.

"No, thank you," I say with a strained smile, and when Sam shoots me a questioning look, I nod toward the door.

When Sam finally decides on six flavors for our flight—three regular ice cream and three sorbet (our noses will be thankful)—we sit outside and he brings it up right away.

"You looked uncomfortable . . . about trying that ice cream? I know you didn't want too much of the dairy flavors because, uh . . ." He makes a fart noise, which is so much worse than just saying it. But it makes us both giggle. "You tried the other ones, though, so I don't know, was there something about that . . . ?"

"I just kinda hate when people—okay, *white* people—make light of stuff and say this or that is like crack. Does that make sense? Like, just because you can't stop eating chocolate or whatever doesn't mean you should compare your issues with an epidemic that destroyed people's lives. It's insensitive."

His brow furrows as he nods his head and considers that. He always seems like he's concentrating so hard on everything I say, actually—like every word I say is important. It's nice.

"It's probably kind of silly to be bothered by that, because they're just words, but—"

"Not at all." He stands up, a determined look on his face. "You know, we should say something to them."

I grab his hand, pulling him down, my neck burning hot. "No! No, no. We definitely should not."

Thankfully, he sits back down. And he also squeezes my hand once before letting it go. Probably a reflex. His cheeks turn pink.

After a somewhat awkward silence, he clears his throat. "So, uh, how is your plan working?" he asks. Now it's my turn to blush.

"Should we talk about that?" I'm worried we'll have a repeat of the blowup from before, even if we did eventually work things out.

"Yeah . . . probably not." He sighs. "I'm just curious if you're writing again."

"No," I admit. "But maybe soon . . . at least I hope so." I think again about what he looked like, writing in his notebook at the last stop. "I miss it, you know? Growing up, I used to always carry a notebook around, so I could make full use of any downtime. And I would wake up in the middle of the night with words floating in my head and jump up and start writing. It was, like, my constant. I loved writing. Or love, I guess, present tense—at least I hope so. It made me really happy." To my surprise, my eyes feel a little wet. I hope he doesn't notice.

"Well, then it will come back. You don't just lose something that you love like that," he says softly. I don't know how he can sound so sure about something that definitely isn't.

"Just because I love something doesn't mean I'm any good at it. Maybe it's good I'm learning this now."

He shakes his head. "But we're not talking about you being good at it. We're just talking about you *doing* it. Writing, I mean. They're two different things."

"Not at Chrysalis. I have to be good to stay at this school . . . and not just good, actually, great! There's no point in even writing if my writing isn't great."

He looks like he's going to say something, but my phone rings, interrupting him. My mom is frantic when I answer.

"Where are you, Tessa? I have to leave in five minutes for Book Club, and remember your dad has a client dinner that's going to go late tonight."

Her book club. I totally forgot. In an effort to get out more, she joined a book club with other moms of teens with disabilities. I actually think it's more of a drinking club, because she always comes home late in a Lyft in a pretty happy mood. I offered to hang out with Miles so she wouldn't miss it tonight. And I could tell she felt a little guilty, asking that of me.

"Oh my god!" I feel terrible. "I'm so sorry, Mom. I'll be there in a sec."

I look up at Sam. I don't know if it's the sugar high or whatever, but I'm not ready for this afternoon—now evening—to end.

"Hey, do you want to hang out with me and Miles?"

When we get there, Mom and Miles are waiting in the living room. She grabs her bag, kisses Miles on top of the head, and starts giving me directions. "So Dad won't be home until nine probably, and I'll be back right after that. If you're okay with this—are you sure you're still okay with this?"

I nod my head. "Of course, Mom."

She still looks unsure. Things have been good between us lately, and I can tell she's been hesitant to ask too much, to tip the scale in the wrong direction. But I don't want my parents to think I see helping with Miles as a burden—because I don't. So I give her a hug and try to say in my most reassuring voice,

"Mom, go. Have fun."

"Okay." I see her shoulders loosen a little as she takes a deep breath. "You don't have to help him with a bath. Dad gave him one yesterday, and for dinner, I left cash on the kitchen counter. You guys can just order pizza—"

She stops, and her head jerks around to Sam, her eyes popping out all cartoonlike. But then Miles's laugh rattles around the room, and it's infectious like it always is. Pretty soon we're all joining in.

"Can we just do half pepperoni this time, though, Miles? No offense, but I'm not really a fan," Sam says. And that just sets Miles off even more, coughing out, "That was a good one, right?" in between hysterical giggles.

Sam and Miles end up getting along great, trading jokes over our dinner of pizza (half pepperoni, half mushrooms and olives). I think a big part of it is that Sam talks to Miles normal, not in the loud and slow way that most people do—like Miles is a baby or hard of hearing. I mean, he does have trouble hearing, but that's what the hearing aids are for. He can hear just fine with those and doesn't need people to shout each extended syllable. Sam gets that without me having to tell him.

Also, he doesn't wait to follow my lead with Miles. Even Caroline does that sometimes, and she's known Miles forever. Sam, though—he laughs at Miles's jokes without looking at me for confirmation first, and if he doesn't understand something Miles says, he asks him and not me. They're little things, yeah, but they mean something.

And when Miles jumps on his computer after dinner to watch Dream Zone videos on YouTube, Sam doesn't even bat an eye at Miles's high-pitched, warbly voice singing along to "Baby I'll Give You (All of Me)." Instead he pulls up a chair next to him and peers closely at the screen.

"Hey, I remember this group. Are they still around?"

"Dream Zone. They're the best band ever. They don't perform anymore, but they will always be around," Miles says excitedly. "They're going to reunite soon, right, Tessie?"

"That's pretty unlikely, bud."

"It could happen," he says, eyes locked on this video he's seen a million times. The reflection glows on his glasses.

"Yeah, never say never," Sam agrees. "This group my mom liked way back in the nineties reunited and formed this . . . I don't know—supergroup or something with another boy band? Anyway, they toured all these county fairs last summer. So it could definitely happen, Miles."

"See?" Miles says, a bright smile taking up his whole face.

The video he's watching ends and another one starts from his playlist: "Together Tonight."

"Oh, this is Tessie's favorite song!" Miles shouts, jumping up in his seat.

I roll my eyes. "No, it's not."

"Yes, it is," Miles insists. "Tessie, you looooove this song. She really does, Sam. She knows all the words and can even do the dance."

It's true. Caroline and I once spent an entire summer

225

studying the music video and perfecting every jump, snap, and hip thrust.

Sam looks at me, smirking. "Oh yeah?"

I consider lying. I mean, I probably would with anyone else. But something makes me decide against it. Maybe it's knowing that Sam won't judge me. And even if he does, well, who cares? I'm not trying to impress him or anything.

"Guilty as charged," I admit with a shrug.

"Oh my god," he laughs. "I need to see that."

And that's how I end up belting out "Together Tonight" and doing the corresponding dance moves with Miles, while Sam looks on, alternating between falling over in laughter and looking mildly impressed.

The words and the movements come back to me easily, like they're permanently ingrained in my brain. And they probably are, with how often I used to listen to this song.

Oh, I've been dreaming of a night like this.
Girl, I can see forever i-i-in your kiss.
Let's not fight, let's turn out the light
And be together tonight.

Sometime after the second chorus, Sam jumps up and starts trying to do the dance with us—three snaps while you jump to the right, thrust, and then a spin and big step forward. He keeps tripping and he doesn't know what to do with his long arms and he can't stay on the beat no matter how hard he tries—and I know he's trying hard because his face gets all scrunchy in concentration, and he's biting his bottom lip. He looks so ridiculous, but he doesn't care. And I know I look ridiculous too, but *I* don't care. Which is weird because I *always* care. But there're no flaming-red neck hives. I don't worry if I'm being too loud or how he must see me. I don't feel embarrassed at all. Even when I get a little too into the moves and accidentally bump my hip into his, and he reaches out to grab my waist, steadying me—I'm *fine*. Perfectly fine.

When the song ends, and we finally sit down, giggling and breathing heavy, Miles looks Sam up and down. "He looks like Thad. Sam really looks like Thad. Don't you think, Tessie?"

With the tight pants and the new haircut, I guess I can kinda see what Miles means, but not really. Thad had blond hair and piercing green eyes, and he was, like, heartthrob status—the Dream Zone equivalent of Justin Timberlake. But while Sam has those same elements going on and is good-looking—*objectively*—he isn't that.

"Yeah, he definitely does!" Miles insists, getting louder. "Is that why you like him, huh? Is that why you like Sam?"

Okay, maybe I'm just a *little* embarrassed now.

"As a friend, Miles. I like him as a friend."

Sam looks at me—his eyes half-moons and his lips curved into a small smile—and it does something weird to my stomach. I look away.

I wake up with the faint flicker of . . . something gnawing at the edge of my brain. I haven't had this feeling in a while, but I recognize it. It's as familiar to me as breathing.

I see Tallulah and Thomas standing there; his hands are in her hair, her arms are wrapped around his strong shoulders, and her lips are open, poised to maybe give Thomas a response to his declarations outside the coffee shop.

But when I finally grab my laptop from under my bed (almost falling headfirst onto the floor in the process), Tallulah is still silent, her mouth gaping like Ariel in *The Little Mermaid* when her voice is stolen by Ursula. And then Thomas disappears entirely. And Tallulah starts to fade away too.

I stay up awhile, hoping the scene will float back into my brain, but eventually I fall back asleep with nothing.

CHAPTER TWENTY-SIX

Caroline's been on me to take things up a notch.

"I mean, I get that eating lunch with Nico is very thrilling and all, but that's not the point here," she lectures me on the phone one night. "Like, not going to lie, you're trying to write about love here, and chatting with him over a PB&J while his girlfriend looks on isn't even close to that."

I almost tell her about the close calls I've had, but then again, what is there to tell her? "I almost wrote?" "I got an idea about my two characters . . . standing and staring at each other?" That would only prove her point.

"It's building, though! I can feel it building. The way he looks at me . . . it's like we have a . . . I don't know, secret or something. Like there's all these people on the lawn at lunch, but I'm the only one he wants to talk to sometimes—"

She cuts me off. "You're sitting with him, yeah, but we need to get you sitting *on* him, do you know what I mean?" I can almost hear her eyebrows waggling over the phone.

"Caroline!" I yell.

"His face, preferably."

"Caroline!!!" She probably can't hear me over her giggles. Her laugh is contagious, and I can't help but join in—even though I feel equal parts mortified and . . . fluttery.

"How long were you planning that one?" I ask when we finally settle down.

"Awhile."

I roll my eyes and lie back on my bed, squeezed between my fuzzy reading pillow and my laptop. I still keep it there even though I'm not writing, because that's where it's always been, ready to take in all of my middle-of-the-night ideas. It doesn't feel right to put it somewhere else.

"What about Halloween? It's on a Saturday this year, and that's basically the universe throwing you a bone, because you know your parents will let you stay out late. Has he invited you to anything?"

"I don't know. . . . I think I might just hang out with Lenore, Sam, and Theodore. We were talking about going out to eat and then watching movies at Sam's house maybe—"

"Boring!"

I feel defensive all of a sudden. "His house is actually pretty cool. . . ."

"Okay, yeah, but hanging out with Hawaiian Shirt Sam isn't going to get you any closer to your happily ever after."

"He doesn't just wear Hawaiian shirts, you know."

"*Regardless*, you are not just wasting the magic of a holiday by hanging out with Sam."

"Is Halloween magical? I think all the Lifetime movies are about Christmas."

"Whatever. Okay. I got some options for you." I can hear the sound of her fingers feverishly clicking across her keys. "It looks like there's something called Pa's Pumpkin Patch going on in Long Beach, and they might have a Ferris wheel. Do you know where that is? Can you do a drive-by with Sam to look for the Ferris wheel, or should I call them and leave a message?"

"Caroline. Do not leave anyone a message."

"If that's out," she continues, ignoring me, "then there's also a Ferris wheel at some place called the Pike. Could you get him there—"

"What, like, lure him to a Ferris wheel? Whatever he's doing, it's going to be with Poppy. The chances of us being alone are pretty much zero."

"Oh yeah." Her voice sounds slightly deflated, and I feel it too. It's a necessary dose of reality, though. Perfect, beautiful Poppy will be wherever Nico is. Because she's his person.

"Have you thought about what you're going to dress up as yet?" she asks, changing the subject.

"Not really. I don't have my partner in crime!" Caroline and I have always been pretty big on costumes, even if our plans were nothing more than watching *Hocus Pocus* and passing out candy with Miles at home (she didn't think it was so boring then). Last year was our best yet: Cher and Dionne from that old movie *Clueless*. I was Cher and she was Dionne because those are our favorite characters, and no one got it because I wasn't the Black character, but whatever.

"Brandon and I can't decide what to be. First we were thinking Archie and Veronica, but that's probably going to be every couple at the party we're going to. So we're thinking maybe more obscure, like, maybe the kids from *E.T.* or that skinny guy with the sweatband and Elliot Page from *Juno*, but my dad will probably have a fit if I walk out of the house looking pregnant. . . ."

I kind of start to tune out as she starts to go through her list of ideas.

"Any of those sound good! You two are going to be so cute. Hey—have your parents okayed that weekend next month yet? The flight from Sacramento to Long Beach is pretty cheap, and my parents said they would pay for half of it."

"Uh . . . yeah. It took a while, but we're good to go."

"Oh, awesome!" I can't stop myself from doing a little dance in my bed. "It will be so good to see you in real life again. I'm beginning to forget that there's a whole body attached to your voice."

"Yep, still have arms and legs and a whole actual life going on over here."

"Maybe you can even meet Nico. Should we start planning something now to make that happen?"

"Sure."

Her voice sounds . . . weird. Like, she's not as excited as me about the trip. I start to feel anxious, but I tell myself that I'm probably just imagining it.

As if conjured by Caroline herself, the Halloween conversation comes up the next day at school.

"Yo, Tessa!" Grayson calls as I walk up. "You coming with us to Munchkin Town on Halloween?"

"What?" I ask. "Like *The Wizard of Oz*?"

"Oh, cut the PC crap, Grayson!" Poppy laughs. "Just call it what everyone used to before they got scared of hurting precious feelings. Midget Town."

My eyes bug out, momentarily stunned.

Nico must read my face, because he holds up his hands. "Yeah, that's not okay to say, is it, Tessa?"

"Why are you asking her? Is she some kind of woke expert?" Poppy asks, as if I can't hear her. She tightens her grip on his arm.

"Because Tessa is in tune with stuff like that. She knows what's up," he says, grinning at me. I notice that he pulls his arm away from her to scratch his back but then doesn't put it back in Poppy's reach. "That word's offensive, right, Tessa?"

I'm not sure if I know all the "stuff like that," but this one, at least, seems straightforward. "I think, uh, 'little person' is the accepted term? Definitely not . . . *that*. Or munchkin either." Nico nods emphatically, like I just said something wise. "What does that mean anyway? You guys are going to . . . this town?"

Poppy shakes her head and gives me a tight smile. "There's nothing wrong with saying it."

"Actually, Tessa, you might know where it is!" Rhys says, sitting up from his spot on the grass. "You live in the Virginia Country Club, right? I remember Weiner lives somewhere over there."

"I live in Bixby Knolls, not the country club." It's just a couple miles, but it's a huge difference.

"Ah dammit, I was hoping you could get us in!"

"But what is *it* exactly?"

They all turn to gape at me, as if I just asked something stupidly obvious.

"You don't know what Midget Town is?" Poppy asks.

"Don't call it that," Nico says, his lips curled up in annoyance, and Poppy scowls so hard it looks like she's going to break her face. I don't want to get my hopes up, but it seems like they're moving toward one of their off-again moments. "And I always forget you're not *from* Long Beach, Tessa, because you, like, fit in so well here. Little Person Town—yeah . . . that's going to take some getting used to. Well, anyway, whatever we call it—it's this Long Beach urban legend. I think I first heard it when I was in fifth grade, maybe?"

"Yeah, definitely," Poppy agrees. "Or maybe even earlier. Remember that one girl, Lily Mueller? She used to tell everyone that her aunt lived there and she would see all the . . . whatever—*munchkins* when she went to visit on Thanksgiving."

I fight the urge to correct her use of the word. "Okay, but what is it?"

"A town of munchkins, obviously," she says with an eye roll.

"Little people," I mutter. I can't help it. "Or you, know, just people. We can call them that if it isn't, uh, essential to this story. Because that's what they are."

"Oh, but it kinda is," Grayson says.

Rhys nods his head in agreement. "Yeah, like, that's the whole point. Okay, so, Tessa, the story is this: Way back like two hundred years ago when they were filming *The Wizard of Oz* . . ."

"It wasn't that long ago, man," Nico laughs. "Don't you, like, study this in your film classes?"

"Whatever," he continues on, standing up and pacing now, excited to tell a story. "The deal is this: When they were filming *The Wizard of Oz*, they needed special housing, or some shit, for the people who played the Munchkins. Because there were a whole lot of them, and they couldn't just live in the normal places for the rest of the cast, right? So they built this whole community in Long Beach, where there was more land. And it still exists, passed down from generation to generation, and there are little doorways and little windows. But see, they're real secretive and don't want people bugging them, so there's this fence around it, blocking all of it from public view."

All of this sounds very improbable, but I decide to focus in on the obvious issue here. "If they don't want people to bother them, then why would you guys go there?"

"For the experience!" Poppy says, leaving out a "duh," but it's still very much present in her tone.

"Yeah, and I'm going to film it for my channel," Rhys says. "It'll get allllllll the views!"

"We just thought it would be fun, you know, to find this place finally. After hearing about it for all these years. We can just hop the fence real quick and take a look around—maybe take a few drinks and hang out on Signal Hill after?" Nico says. "And the only semigood party going on is at Brett Kwan's, and it'll mostly just be music and theater kids being their normal pretentious selves and showing off their esoteric costumes. No offense, Grayson."

"None taken."

"Anyway, will you come with us, Tessa?" Nico asks.

"I don't know. . . ." I can hear Caroline screaming in my head because this isn't a Ferris wheel or anything, but it's definitely happily-ever-after-plan adjacent. I should be taking any opportunity to hang out with Nico, yeah—except trespassing and searching for some offensive urban legend with Nico and *his girlfriend* isn't exactly what I had pictured for the next act in our love story.

"Come on," Nico insists, tapping my foot with his across the grass. "I really want you to come. It'll be fun."

I, not we. *I really want you to come.* The words warm up my whole body, and I can feel a big ol' dopey smile spread across my face. I purposely don't look at Poppy, because I have a feeling she's giving me a massive stink face, and I don't want that to ruin how good I feel about the "I" and the "really."

"Yeah, okay."

"Wooo!" Nico cheers, and actually pumps his fist in the air. I for real almost faint.

Poppy must not be too mad, though, because she comes up and grabs my arm after we've all split up and are heading our separate ways for conservatory. And not in a *bitch, you better stop trying to steal my kinda boyfriend* way, but an affectionate squeeze, like we've been friends for years.

"I'm really glad you're coming, Tessa. You know, it's really nice to have another girl around here to break up this whole sausage fest." She sounds so genuine that I wonder if maybe I've been reading her wrong this whole time. Like, maybe I'm trying to make her a villain because that makes all of this easier in my brain and keeps me from looking at my own actions too closely.

"It'll be fun." I smile. "I'm excited."

"And don't forget your costume. We're really big on costumes," she says with a laugh. "I don't want you to feel left out."

I almost feel bad for what I'm trying to do.

CHAPTER TWENTY-SEVEN

I start Halloween night off squeezed into a booth with Sam, Lenore, Theodore, and Lavon at a place on Atlantic called Bake-N-Broil. It's the kind of diner that's probably been around forever and is mostly popular with the over-sixty-five, card-carrying AARP members set. We definitely stand out. But the burgers and French fries are good, and for dessert we order giant slices of pie, accompanied by scoops of vanilla ice cream. I watch as Sam takes small, thoughtful bites, and I can almost feel his hands itching for his notebook to write down all the intricacies of the flavor profile.

Lenore insists she doesn't want any pie but then sneaks bites of everyone else's. And Theodore and Lavon take turns feeding each other the French silk pie they ordered, sharing one fork. It's adorable.

"Oh, you two are so cute, and it's making me feel like my godmama Arlene, who lives alone in Torrance with her five cats," Lenore says. "No one told me this was going to be a date night!" Theodore smirks and snuggles in closer to Lavon. "Okay, since Tessa is ditching me for her soon-to-be boyfriend, Sam, you're gonna have to be my bae tonight. What do you say, boo boo?" She scoots in close to him, fitting her shoulder under his arm and rubbing his cheeks. Sam blushes and awkwardly pats her arm. I roll my eyes involuntarily.

"You good?" Lenore asks me, arching her eyebrow.

"Yeah. Just nervous about tonight, is all."

She nods but still looks at me curiously.

"You could always skip all that and stay with us," Sam suggests, pushing his clean plate away from him. I want to say yes. It would be so much easier to go to his house. All the tightness in my body would release, and I could just have fun—like we did dancing with Miles. Like we *always* do. But I think about the happily ever after plan and how I feel like the sun is warming my whole body when Nico looks at me with his sleepy smile. That will be fun too.

"That does sound tempting, but I want to go. The semester is halfway over, and you know, I need to do anything that may jump-start my writing—"

"I still don't get this rationale," Lavon cuts in. They were all happy to fill him in on the plan before we even got our waters. "Listen, if you would like to explore the very enticing specimen that is Nico Lucchese, just admit that. No need for pretenses."

"Enticing specimen, huh?" Theodore says, whipping his neck round and giving Lavon a look of mock outrage.

239

My neck flames. "That's not it!"

"Girl, it's *partially* it, and that's okay," Lenore says. "Most artists have used their own sexual awakenings as inspiration for their creations. I mean, there's the rococo art movement. And, like, Frank Ocean. Own it!"

"Why does everyone keep trying to make this a sex thing?" I shout, barely audible over Lenore, Theodore, and Lavon's laughter. All the white-hairs are starting to turn around and stare.

"What's Miles doing tonight?" Sam asks, rubbing the side of his pink face. I want to kiss him in gratitude for changing the subject. Well, not actually kiss him.

"He loves passing out candy, so probably that." I grin, remembering last year. "Actually, last Halloween he got obsessed with toilet papering someone's house after he saw it in a movie, but he didn't get more than a few sheets up before my parents caught him. Maybe he's going to try that again."

Sam laughs. "We could help him out with that. Steer him in Mrs. Hutchinson's direction."

"Oh my god. Please do not do that."

He shrugs his shoulders dramatically, as if to say, *We'll see,* and then gives me a big one-dimple smile. "But seriously, does he like scary movies? Maybe he can join our marathon."

I'm about to shoot him down, because, yeah, Sam is a nice guy and may be down with that, but that doesn't mean the rest of them want to spend their Saturday night hanging out with Miles. But before I can say anything, Lenore jumps up in her seat. "For sure! Miles is the best. Actually, he can be my bae tonight."

That doesn't cause me to roll my eyes, but it does make them a little watery.

I meet up with Nico and everyone outside the golf course at ten. The tall lights on the green aren't turned on, and at first I don't see them. I start to second-guess showing up here alone. But then their four figures appear out of the fog that hangs over the damp, dark grass.

The first thing I notice is that none of them have on costumes.

"*What* are you wearing?" Rhys asks.

I'm wearing Ravenclaw robes that I haven't put on since sixth grade, but they somehow made it through the move. I ran home to get them after leaving the diner. It's not my best costume, but I thought it would do. And it would be a little nod to Nico and the conversation we had on his bed. Now all it is is a glaring reminder of how juvenile and uncool I am.

"You come straight from trick-or-treating?" Grayson asks. "You and Weiner?"

What the hell? I want to ask Poppy, but when I see her satisfied smirk, I know exactly what's going on. But I mean, can I blame her?

"I thought we were wearing costumes," I say quietly, looking Poppy right in the eye.

"I love it," Nico says with a smile. He tugs on the kelly-green rolled-up beanie perched on the top of his head. "Green for Slytherin," he adds with a wink.

There—so much for your sneaky shit, Poppy. And I'm glad I'm wearing the robe anyway, because it's actually cold tonight. The dry heat that's been hanging over Long Beach since we moved here suddenly dropped as if instructed to by the holiday. It feels like a real fall night, with puffs of hot air escaping out of our mouths when we speak. Poppy snuggles under Nico's fleece-lined bomber jacket, and I look away.

"All right, let's go find Munchkin Town!" Rhys announces, and I realize he's talking into his phone, taking on his vlogger persona.

It's not just that he's yelling it (which probably isn't best for this supposedly covert operation), but it's the word he used. Again. Yeah, it's not as bad as the other M-word Poppy was throwing around before, but it's still offensive and insensitive— like the R-word and how people just drop that like it's nothing. It irritates me how they say it so easily, urban legend or not. I wonder if they say other words as freely too . . . when I'm not there.

"We decided that we're going to keep calling it that," Poppy says matter-of-factly. "Sorry, Tessa."

The words fall out of my mouth before I can think about them too much. "Well, you'll just sound like assholes then."

Grayson laughs, and Rhys jumps and calls out, "Oh!" (Probably for the enjoyment of his followers.)

Maybe I should have gone to Sam's instead.

"Hey, let's just agree to disagree?" Nico says, standing in between us. Even though it's dark, I can see Poppy's face is beet red. And it's not from embarrassment. No, she's just pissed. "We don't have to call it anything really," Nico goes on. "The mission is to locate it, not label it, right?"

"Whatever," Poppy spits out, pushing past both of us and walking ahead with Grayson. She pushes Rhys's phone out of her face when he tries to capture her on video.

I wonder if their status has changed since we last talked, because Nico doesn't chase after her or try to smooth things over. Instead, he stays next to me.

"Don't worry about her," he says, waving her off. He leans in close, so only I can hear. "And for the record, I agree with you." And then he winks. Again. The winks are like freaking breadcrumbs, stringing me along a path that I know I should probably turn back from. But the winks . . . and just *everything*—they aren't only in my head. Girlfriend or not.

The tension surprisingly diffuses from there, Grayson and Poppy walking ahead and me, Rhys, and Nico following behind. I realize Rhys has two phones—one for his IG stories and one for his vlog—and he alternates between them seamlessly, sometimes even using both at the same time.

After skirting the golf course for a bit, we finally come upon a wrought iron and brick gate surrounding a neighborhood of huge houses, and Rhys crouches down and explains to his followers that we've finally found it.

But Nico interrupts his celebratory dance. "Nah, man, that's just a normal gated community. My dad's golfing buddy lives in there." He looks at me sheepishly and then hurriedly adds, "A community for people of average height."

"Well, then where are we going exactly?" Poppy asks, annoyed, as Rhys quickly types an explanation on his stories. "How many gated neighborhoods can there be back here?"

I can't help but agree with her, as much as it pains me. "Did anyone check a map?"

"It wouldn't be on a map," Grayson says, shaking his head. "If they're trying to stay on the DL, why would they put their place on a map?"

"There must be something else back here," Nico says, and starts to look around. The golf course is on one side, and the gate is on the other, with only a dark paved road ahead. There's no sidewalk or streetlights on it anymore, and it's hard to tell how long it goes on . . . or what could be back there.

"We need to just keep walking," Grayson insists. "And don't turn your flashlight on, Rhys, because that's just going to give us away. I don't care about your video quality."

I'm pretty sure this is how horror movies start. And you know who dies first in those.

Suddenly a pair of headlights swings into the darkness, as if turning a corner. And we don't talk about it—we all just scatter across the road. Poppy, Nico, and I end up barely behind a bush next to the gate, and Rhys and Grayson are standing at the edge of the course. With our ineffective hiding spots, it's no wonder that the car slows and then idles. It's a black BMW with dark tinted windows. But the driver's-side window lowers, and a thirty-something man with cornrows and an orange pumpkin

T-shirt leans out, his elbow gripping the door.

He looks right at me, Nico, and Poppy and asks, his voice deep and gravelly, "You kids looking for Munchkin Town?"

"Oh, shit!" Rhys yelps, and runs over to the door, both his phones out and recording.

"Yes, we are, sir," Nico says, eyes wide.

"Well, you're on the right track, but you still got a ways to go. Walk down this road some more." He points to where he just came from. "And eventually you'll see an unmarked road leading to another fence. You're gonna have to jump it, because there's no way their security guy is going to let you through. As soon as you see it, go down the side—the, uh . . . right side, and you should be out of his view. And that's how you get to Munchkin Town."

He scratches his face and nods his head once, his duty done.

"Do you mind if I ask how you know this?" I say, and he looks me up and down, eyes narrowing on my robes.

"'Cause I seen it! That's why," he explains with a snort. "Me and my friends did just that back in high school, jumped the fence, and we went around and rang all the doorbells. And all those little people came running with all their little children, waving their hands in the air and carrying on or whatever. They never found us."

That makes Rhys and Grayson laugh, which honestly, just kind of makes me mad . . . and embarrassed. What am I doing here with these people looking for this stupid and offensive legend?

I guess it's not the big reaction that the man expected from his audience, because he looks irritated now too.

"Go see it for yourselves or not. I don't care." He rolls up his window then and peels off. One of the porch lights in the gated community next to us flicks on, and we all scurry over closer to the golf course and the darkness.

"That was awesome!" Rhys declares in a whisper-yell, and Nico high-fives him.

I shake my head. "I don't know . . . he's probably just a resident messing with us or something. That story sounded . . . far-fetched."

"That guy doesn't live here!" Grayson laughs.

"And why not?" I ask, my voice sharp.

He shrugs. "You can just tell."

I know exactly what he's getting at, and I'm ready to give him a lecture and call someone an asshole again. But I know that won't go over well, yelling at Nico's best friend. And it makes me feel sick, letting his ignorant comment slide, but I clench my fists and force myself to stay quiet again. I don't like who I'm starting to be with this group, swallowing down his microagressions. And it's made even worse by the fact that I'm standing here in Ravenclaw robes. They feel overwhelmingly itchy all of a sudden. I don't want to think about what it means that I have to be a dialed-down version of myself around them.

We debate it a bit, but it's clear that it's four against one. And before I know it, we're following the guy's directions down the almost pitch-black road. We reach the turnoff he described in about ten minutes, and just like he said, there's a second gate there, made of layered rocks.

"Who's going to go first?" Grayson whispers as we creep around to the side that's lined with tall oak trees. But Rhys is already scrambling up the wall, one arm dangerously out-stretched with a phone, so he can get his footage.

"Well, okay then," Grayson says, following after him.

This is one of those moments when I'm very much aware that I'm surrounded by white people. Like when we spend Thanksgiving with my mom's family and there's orange juice in the yams and crushed saltine crackers on top of the mac and cheese. Or anytime "Sweet Caroline" is played.

Because they all see absolutely nothing wrong with jump-ing over this fence in the middle of the night. They completely ignore the no trespassing and security system signs. They don't worry about what could happen if we're caught, if someone sees a figure and gets nervous in the dark, if that someone has a gun.

"You guys . . . I'm not sure—"

"Let me guess: you think we should all go home and sit in a circle and talk about some social justice warrior shit." Poppy cuts me off, scowling. "Well, go ahead. No one's begging you to stay, Miss Goody Two-shoes."

"Hey, Poppy . . . ," Nico says with his hand up.

"Hey nothing," she snaps back at him. "You better wake up, Nico, and remember who the fuck you're really with."

My mouth falls open as those words hit me in the gut, and that makes Poppy's face twist into a grin, satisfied. With that, she starts climbing up the rocks after the other two with surprising speed.

Nico turns to me, eyes wide and mouth twitching like he's about to say something, but then he just looks at the ground and shakes his head.

"I think I'm just gonna go home."

His head pops up. "No. Please don't do that," he says, taking a step toward me. "I want you to—"

I don't get to hear the end of that beautiful sentence, because it's interrupted by a blaring alarm that pierces through the quiet night.

"Fuck!" Nico shouts, and I can hear the sound of leaves rustling as he sprints away, but my legs are cemented to the ground. I can't run. I can't do anything. Because this is exactly what I was worried about, and my heart is making my whole body shake as I race through the possibilities of what could happen next.

"Tessa, over here," Nico whispers, making me jump. He pulls me by the waist back behind a dark hedge, and I whip around fast, startled. And then we're facing each other, so tight that our hipbones are pressed together. His are definitely bonier than mine, but I don't even care—like, I forget to be embarrassed. Because I'm close enough to count every last one of his eyelashes and his arm is on mine and it's sensory overload. My heart continues to pound in my chest, but it's a different feeling now—no longer fear. I feel like fireworks are going off in my stomach and exploding all around my body. He's looking right into my eyes and his lips pull into a small smile.

And then it starts raining. Seriously! Raining! For real water falling down from the sky, and this must be a miracle or something, because it never rains here. This is just for us. This is the universe reading my list and granting me a wish. Number six.

"Tessa . . . ," he murmurs, filling the small space between us. I've never heard my name sound so perfect. I want to record it, so I can play it for others and say, "There, that is my name." "Your hair . . . it looks like there's, uh, diamonds in it. With the raindrops? It's . . . *you're* so beautiful."

If there were fireworks before, there's freaking space shuttles being launched now.

But I can't help but ask. "What about Poppy?"

He shakes his head, keeping his dark brown eyes on mine. "Poppy and I . . . we haven't been great lately. Like I said, we aren't, um, exclusive . . . you know?"

What does that mean? my head screams. Because yeah—I've formulated this whole plan in disregard of Poppy. Girls like Poppy already have their own love stories. Is it really the end of the world if I get this, just this one time? I felt like it was okay. But . . . I don't know. It was really a lot easier to rationalize this happening when it wasn't actually happening.

And then his hand reaches up to my cheek and his head begins to lower down to mine. And all of those thoughts are gone, because now my head is full with shouts of *It's happening! It's really happening!*

Before our lips touch, though, bright red lights flash across our faces, followed by the *whoop whoop* of a siren. We both jump apart when a portly man in a white-and-black uniform appears next to the bushes.

"You two are gonna have to come with me."

CHAPTER TWENTY-EIGHT

It was a security guard, not a cop. And the same company patrols Nico's neighborhood too, so his dad is able to make a quick phone call, and all of a sudden their stern talks with references to laws broken turn into a *kids will be kids, just don't do it again* warning.

No arrests, no permanent records, no real consequences even. Just a silly youthful indiscretion. The kind rich white kids get to have.

But I can tell when I see my parents' faces at the door that they don't see it that way.

All the lamps in the house are on, but Dad's steely gaze sucks all the light out of the kitchen, where we go to talk. Mom is already pacing.

"Listen, I didn't actually jump the fence," I say, trying to get ahead of the conversation. But when Dad's face hardens even more, I can see it's the wrong choice.

"Can you imagine what that was like for us, seeing a cop car drive up here? Can you imagine what was going through our heads?" His voice cracks on the last word, and it makes my stomach fall down to the ground. It makes me feel like the lowest of all people. I want to do anything, say anything, to make these feelings—his and mine—go away.

"They weren't actually cops . . . ," I start, but again I got it wrong, because now Dad is shaking his head and looking at me like he doesn't even know who I am.

"I'm just so disappointed," he says, his voice quiet but piercing, and I sink even lower.

"I don't understand," Mom takes over, ramping up. "Who are these people? Why were you with them?"

"They're my friends from school. . . ."

"Friends from school?" She's stopped pacing, and her face is red now, matching the nightgown she's wearing. "As far as I know, your friends from school were having a nice wholesome night across the street, which they were kind enough to invite your brother to. Seems to me like those are the friends from school you should be hanging out with."

I stare down at my ballet flats, muddy from the rain, because she's right and I don't know what to say to that. How can I explain that I did it for love—the possible romantic kind, but more importantly, the all-encompassing, life-affirming kind I have, *had*, for my writing. That I'm trying to get myself back by not acting like myself anymore.

I can't say that, though, because it would make them even more worried.

"Are you acting out for attention?" Mom asks, her voice creeping up to a shrill volume. "I think we need to take you to see a therapist. You know we've talked about this before. . . ."

"No!" I shout, making her jump back, and one of Dad's eyebrows goes down real low. All of a sudden my shame disappears and I'm mad, something bitter and hot bubbling up from my chest into my throat. Because of course she's going to try and diagnose me and make this into something bigger than it needs to be. And I was feeling so good just an hour ago, things with Nico finally going the way they were supposed to. I just reached such a high after so many lows, and I want to enjoy it. I want to bask in it. But now the memories of tonight are all getting written over, tarnished.

Why do they have to take this away from me? Why can't they understand that this night was everything I wanted?

"I'm just doing what normal teenagers do." The words feel ugly coming out of my mouth, and I immediately regret them. I'm so glad Miles is asleep in his room and can't hear what a shitty person his sister is.

I look at Mom's cold face and Dad's lowered head, and I know the damage is done.

"I'm sorry. I didn't—"

"You're grounded!" Mom yells, and it feels like the walls shake.

"Go to your room. I can't even look at you," Dad whispers, and somehow that shakes me even more.

I run down the hallway and quietly shut my door. I want to cry—I *should* cry—but nothing comes out. Instead, my throat burns and my chest feels hollow, like someone came and scraped it out with an ice cream scoop. I can hear the faint edges of their voices in the kitchen, as they continue to talk about me, how much I screwed up. I wish there was some way to rewind, to go back and do that conversation over and be honest with them instead of defensive and spiteful. Instead of lashing out and saying something terrible I didn't mean, I could tell them how I'm not writing, and how it's the scariest thing ever because it's always been the hugest part of my identity and now what do I have? I could tell them how good it feels to have a boy who looks like he walked out of my stories pay attention to me this one time—to be of interest, to be wanted.

But somehow I know they wouldn't understand.

My phone pings, cutting through my thoughts. That shows how inexperienced my parents are at grounding me—this isn't a skill I've given them a chance to develop. They didn't even take away my phone.

The text is from Sam.

Are you okay? I saw a police car outside??

It wasn't a police car, I think, feeling irritated again. But it's sweet of him to care. Everything Sam does is sweet . . . thoughtful. I have the strongest urge to call him right now and find out everything that happened tonight with Miles. I'm sure

Miles will be talking about it all morning and for the foreseeable future.

Before I can even respond, though, another text comes in. A picture. From Nico.

I click on it quickly, and his face fills my screen. He's lying on his bed, his hair still damp and tousled from the rain, making a frowny face and holding a finger up to his eye to mimic a tear drop.

Sorry for that fail of a night!

Normally I would agonize over what to respond, rallying input from Caroline on multiple drafts. But I can still feel his hips pressed against mine, and the warmth of his pinkie finger brushing against my own in the back seat of the security guard's car. It makes me bold.

It's okay, I type out quickly. It wasn't all bad

Can you hang out tomorrow? So we can talk about . . . everything. In person.

God, I want nothing more, but . . .

I can't. Grounded.

He sends 👎 👎 👎 👎 👎

Can we talk at school on Monday? I send.

The three dots appear, showing me he's typing a response, but then they're gone. I wait five minutes, twenty, an hour . . . and nothing. I finally drift off to sleep.

CHAPTER TWENTY-NINE

"Tess!" Caroline yells, running through the gates of the tiny Long Beach airport.

I was worried we were going to have to cancel the reunion we planned for the long weekend in November, but I get time off for good behavior: coming straight home after school, helping with Miles, sitting quietly in my room. Which, you know, is what I do anyway. But whatever.

My parents and I talked about everything that happened . . . well, kinda. As much as we usually do, skirting around any big issues. I apologized for what I said, and they both said they forgave me. But Mom and Dad still keep looking at me like I'm some troubled teen straight out of an episode of *Dr. Phil*. I hope that goes away soon.

"Come here, you perfect, gorgeous ray of sunshine!" She drops her bag and jumps on me, and we twirl around like a couple reuniting after a long war.

I half expected her to walk out with Brandon attached to her. Because, like, all the pictures I've seen of her lately have had him pressed against her, cheek to cheek, their smiles basically conjoined.

But it's the same Caroline. *My* Caroline. With silky black hair that goes down past her armpits and always smells like coconut. Skinny wrists jingling with gold bracelets, including one she's had since her baptism that has her full name inscribed on it—Caroline Frances Fermin Tibayan. And that half-moon scar on her knee from when she was chasing Jonathan Solomon after school in third grade and fell on the asphalt. I remember that Lola made us turon when we got home that day and let us watch her shows with her on TFC all afternoon.

"Your hair is so long!" she says, ruffling her hands through my curls. She's the only person I'd let do that.

"Does it look okay like this?" I say, touching it self-consciously. I tried doing a twist-out again after watching a YouTube video last night.

"You look like freakin' Yara Shahidi."

I blush, because my hair looks good but not that good. "Okay now, let's at least be realistic with the compliments."

"I am, you crazy!" She squeezes me again. "I missed you so much. I didn't realize how much until now."

"Same." And it's true. We've talked on the phone constantly since I moved, but it doesn't make up for this, being here in the same place at the same time. I feel like my shoulders fall down a little lower, like I've been unknowingly hunching them, tense, all this time. And now that we're together I can finally relax.

We walk out to the curb, where Sam's Honda Civic is idling. As soon as he sees us, he pops the trunk and jumps out of the car, grabbing Caroline's suitcase.

"Hi, Caroline," he says, sounding nervous. "Nice to meet you."

"Sam! My man!" she says, clapping him on the back. "I feel like I know you already!"

"There are cheesecakes in the back seat for you. I made them this morning, so hopefully they've cooled enough by now."

She looks at me like, *Is this guy for real?* And I laugh. "This is just what he does."

"Well, thank you, Sam. For the cheesecakes and the ride," she says, climbing into the car. "But maybe I should advise you to pump the brakes on being all nice and stuff, or Tessa is going to change her best friend allegiances. Not going to lie, I never baked her anything."

"I'm pretty sure your spot is secure."

I slide into the back with Caroline, where she's inspecting one of the tiny circular cheesecakes. They're bright purple with a buttery crumble on the top, and their sweet smell fills the whole car.

"Are these what I think they are?" she asks.

"Ube cheesecakes," Sam says, looking proud in the rear-view mirror. "I was trying a new recipe. I hope they're okay. Let me know if I got the texture right, because it's kinda tricky."

Caroline gets a mischievous look on her face, but her tone is all cool. "Oh, you made me these because I'm Filipina. Do you think all Filipinos like ube?"

"No . . . I . . . it's just . . ." Sam rubs the side of his face, which is rapidly turning pink. "Tessa, uh—"

"Ha!" she says, waving him away. "Just playing. I was being a jerk. Ube is literally my favorite thing in the world."

"Yeah," Sam mumbles, recovering. "Tessa told me."

"Girl, be nice," I say, swatting her hand.

She shrugs me off, shoving almost an entire cheesecake into her mouth, and I can see the exact moment when the taste hits her tongue and then shoots a signal up to her brain. Pure bliss.

"Oh my god. OH MY GOD!" she says, falling back into her seat. "Sam, I can see why she likes you."

"It's not the *only* reason." I smile at him, making eye contact in the mirror. "But it's a pretty decent perk."

We end up going to Sam's house first, because I can see both my parents' cars in the driveway. And although I know they'll be excited to see Caroline too, I'm not quite ready to deal with them right now. I got my get-out-of-jail-free card, and I'm going to use it.

"Whoa, so you basically live on a TV set," Caroline says as we walk into Sam's huge and perfectly decorated kitchen. I'm worried he's going to be bothered by that or something, but he just laughs.

"Actually, the set of Mom's show is modeled after *this* kitchen. She insisted on it."

Caroline looks impressed, and I can see her hands itching

to whip out her phone and take a picture for IG. Thank god she doesn't. Sam talks about his mom so . . . normally that I forget sometimes that there's anything remarkable about her. Because he's just Sam, and she's just Sam's mom.

"I hope you guys don't mind if I work a little bit. There's something I want to try out today. Got the idea last night. . . ." He's already turning to the cabinets, ready to sort out his ingredients, as if drawn by a magnet.

"No worries. We've got some Nico business to handle," Caroline says. "I heard you know about the happily ever after plan."

"Yep," Sam says, but he doesn't turn around.

"Have you texted him yet, Tessa? See what he's doing tonight!"

"I don't know. . . ."

"What do you mean you don't know?" Caroline yelps, nudging me with her elbow. "I am here, and I'm pretty much your fairy godmother. You've got to give me a chance to see you two together and work my magic!"

"I just feel like . . . I don't know. Maybe it's time to call it."

On the Monday after Halloween, I went back to school certain that Nico and Poppy would be done, and we would skip off happily into our new life of coupledom together. Or that we would *at least* talk about what happened, or almost happened, that night in the rain. But at lunch, Poppy gave me an even more aggressive silent treatment than usual. And Nico acted like nothing had ever happened. It's been almost two weeks, with no signs that anything will change.

"We are not calling anything!" Caroline insists, slamming her hands on the counter. She's dramatic like that, and I've missed it. "Have you tried talking to him at all?"

"No."

"And why not?"

"Because I don't need him to tell me that he regrets what happened. Maybe he wasn't thinking—"

"Wait. What are you talking about?" Sam's busy hands are now still as he stares at us.

"It's nothing. Can we just— What are you making, Sam?"

"NICO AND HER WERE CAUGHT IN THE RAIN AND HE TOLD HER IT LOOKED LIKE THERE WERE DIAMONDS IN HER HAIR AND THEN HE TRIED TO KISS HER!"

"Caroline!" I snap, swatting her with my hand.

"Hey, he's your friend and therefore fellow endorser of Tessa's Happily Ever After. He deserves to know."

Sam is my friend, but he's definitely not that second part. Which is why, outside of a brief explanation of the security car, I haven't told him anything about what happened on Halloween. Mostly because I knew that he would look at me just like he is now. Cold and judgy.

"Poppy and Nico are still together," Sam says.

"I know."

"He told her they're not exclusive," Caroline chimes in.

"And he said your hair looks like there are diamonds in it?"

Sam scoffs, scrunching his nose. "Sounds like a stupid line to me."

"Yeah, well, who cares? Maybe I want to be someone who guys say lines to. Is there anything wrong with that?" It comes out harsher than I intend.

Sam just presses his lips together and doesn't say anything more, even though I can see him itching to.

"Oooo-kay," Caroline says, making a face like Chrissy Teigen in that one meme. Then she says, quieter, to me, "Just text him. We're not throwing the towel in yet, girlfriend."

I pull out my phone, and type out:

Hey, are you around this weekend?

I send it before I can think about it too much, and Caroline gives me an approving nod.

"So what you making, Sam? Anything as good as this?" She takes a big bite of one of the mini ube cheesecakes, and adds with a mouthful, "It looks like you're setting up a science experiment."

"I mean, baking is a science," Sam says, unwrapping a stick of butter. "I'm trying out this new recipe for a pâte à choux, and I have to get it just right. If there's even a drop too much water or not enough butter or the eggs are the wrong temperature, then the whole thing will be destroyed. I'll have to throw it all out and start again."

His eyes get wide and serious, like he's talking about throwing out a baby.

"Is this recipe particularly dire for any reason?" I ask.

"The gala," he says, turning around to preheat the oven. "I'm making éclairs for the final judging, to, uh . . . decide if I get to do the pastries for it. Or whatever."

"Sam, that's awesome!" I say. He just shrugs his shoulders like it's nothing, but there's a little smile on his face, his dimple showing itself. "I had no idea you were in the running. That's a huge deal, especially for a first-year student."

"It's no big deal."

"Oh, man, yes it is!"

Thanks to Theodore's rants, I'm well aware that the winter gala is *the* big event at Chrysalis Academy, where the school gets a chance to show off its talented students and raise a bunch of money from the loaded parents and alumni. I mean, it's black tie and the tickets start at a hundred bucks—that kind of big deal. The creative writing teachers have been talking up the gala and the final selection of students who are going to read too, but I've mostly just tuned them out. It's not like I'm going to be one of them.

"What is a gala anyway?" Caroline asks. "That's one of those fancy words that I know but don't really *know*."

"It's like a big party that our school has, a fundraiser basically," Sam explains, taking a roll of parchment paper out of a drawer. "I've been going to them every year with my mom. She was, um, a donor before she joined the board. But this will be the first time that . . . well, that I'll be there for me, you know?"

I get the strongest urge to jump up and give him a hug.

"Will there be dancing?" Caroline asks, her eyebrows

waggling. "That's on the list," she mimes whispering to me, but she is anything but discreet.

Sam looks between us, confused, but then I see his face change when he puts it together. Why does she keep bringing this up in front of him? And why does it bother him anyway?

"I don't dance," I say quickly, hoping to stop this train of thought.

"Girl, that's just what you think now, but when Nico takes you in his arms at this gala, you—"

"You dance, Tessa." Sam cuts her off.

"Oh yeah?" Caroline asks. "What have you seen our girl do, Sam? Fill me in, stat!"

"He hasn't seen anything—"

"You know, just a little . . ." He snaps as he does three jumps to the right and then thrusts. Caroline explodes with laughter.

"You. Showed. Him. TOGETHER! TONIGHT!" Caroline chokes out between her giggles.

"Come on, Tessa," Sam says, adding a spin and then jumping forward, a mischievous smile on his face. "You gotta, like, join me with this. These dances aren't meant to be done alone."

"No way." And I mean it. But then Sam comes around the counter, snap-jumping some more and doing this little arm-wave thing that I definitely did not teach him. And then Caroline plays the song on her phone, waving it in the air like she's at a concert. And somehow, for the second time, I'm dancing to Dream Zone with Sam—who, for the record, has gotten

much better at the dance than me. Almost as if he's been prac-
ticing.

When we finish, I'm practically hyperventilating with
laughter, and Sam is standing with his arms crossed, looking all
pleased with himself. Caroline has this big smile on her face as
she studies both of us, and it feels full of meaning—I'm just not
sure exactly what.

"Okay, you guys have to do that again, but I'm gonna film
it this time."

"Nope!" Sam says, returning to his place in the kitchen.
He starts to heat something in a saucepan like nothing even
happened.

My phone pings, and I grab for it. It's Nico.

Sorry, it's poppy's birthday and she has the whole weekend planned. See you at school?

I can feel Caroline looking over my shoulder, but I don't
even look to see if her face is as disappointed as my own. Or
even worse—if there's pity there.

Okay. So that's that.

I fill the rest of the weekend showing Caroline what have
become my favorite Long Beach things: potato tacos from Holé
Molé and marscapone-stuffed French toast from Starling Diner,
piled high with berries. People watching and exploring the
cute boutiques on Atlantic. And because the weather is back to
seventy-five even though it's November, we spend most of Sunday at the beach, reading (Christina Lauren for her, *On Writing*

for me . . . until I give up on that and take her backup Christina Lauren). The warm sun bakes our brown skin a few shades browner.

I'm surprised by how much it feels like old times, how quickly we fall into our rhythm—the buzzy staccato of our conversations, our footsteps always at exactly the same beat.

But as much as we are who we used to be, there are also hints of how we've changed. Like when she's trying to tell me about something funny that happened at a party, and I get confused by all the unfamiliar names. And when I'm responding to a few texts from Lenore, and Caroline makes a joke about putting away my phone that doesn't really sound like a joke.

On Sunday night, though, when we're lying in my room ready to go to sleep, it's almost like a merging of the old and the new. Lying there in the dark, squeezed into my twin bed even though my mom put out the blow-up mattress, I'm reminded of the countless sleepovers we had growing up—eating Swedish Fish until our stomachs were sick and pretending not to be scared by the creaks we would hear in the hallway. But our voices going back and forth in my pitch-black room also reminds me of all the conversations we've had late into the night on our phones, ever since I moved away and everything changed.

"Okay, Tess, can I tell you something without you getting mad?" Caroline asks, her voice raspy like it always gets when she's tired.

"Sure."

"Actually, it's more of a question, I guess."

"Just tell me already."

"What if . . ." She starts slowly, and I feel a little bit nervous. Usually she's a straight shooter. "Have you ever thought . . ." She tries again. "Have you thought about maybe having the wrong leading man?"

"What?"

"For your happily ever after, your love story—what if the love interest is all wrong? And that's why it's not working? Like in that movie you told me to watch, *Pretty in Pink*? The whole time you're rooting for Duckie and you just know they'd be perfect together, but then Andie ends up with that bland Blaine instead. And, like, that's cute or whatever, but it doesn't have the intended emotional impact, because you know it'll never work out between them, not like it would *obviously* work out with Duckie." She huffs as if she just got something big off her chest.

"I don't get it."

"Nico is Blaine."

"Okay."

"And Sam . . . is Duckie."

"*Oh.*"

"Do you get what I'm trying to say?"

I know exactly what she's trying to say. She feels sorry for me. It's so clear. Because this weekend showed her I have absolutely no chance with Nico, and now she's trying to lead me in a more reasonable direction. So I don't get all caught up in something that's never going to happen.

"But I . . . I like Nico." It sounds so feeble and silly coming out of my mouth.

"I know. *I know*, Tess. And you could have any guy you wanted." I wonder if she thinks that sounds believable. "But you and Sam—I saw something with him. Something real, and I don't want you to ignore that because you're zeroed in on someone else. Sam is a really good guy."

"I know."

"And he's not as much of a goober as I thought he'd be! You didn't give him credit! Have you paid attention to those cheekbones? And he wasn't even wearing a Hawaiian shirt."

"I told you he doesn't every day!"

"Okay, okay, but main point here: I think that Sam could be the one. *Your* one. I really think there could be something special between you two, and we should just . . . change the focus of the plan!"

She sounds so excited and eager, just as convincing as she was when she first came up with the list. And it would be so easy to go along with her, except:

"Me and Sam . . . we're not like that."

"Yeah, I know you think that now, but maybe you just need to open your eyes a little. I see it so much more with him than Nico, and—"

"Except you don't really know either of them. You've been

here for, what, two days, and this is my life. I think I know better what's right for me." The words come out all sharp and cold, and I can't see Caroline's face in the dark, but I feel her recoil. I don't want to be mad, but just because she has a boyfriend doesn't mean she's the expert on all this stuff. She doesn't know what things are like between me and Nico—the spark that has been there since the very first day. And she doesn't know Sam. He's an amazing friend, but he's not *that*.

"Okay," Caroline says, sounding weary. "It's just, I thought that . . . I'm sorry if—"

"You don't have to be sorry. I'm . . . Can we just not talk about it anymore? I appreciate all you're doing for me, really I do. And as we've thoroughly established, you're a genius." I reach for her hand and squeeze it. "But that's just . . . not what I want."

"Yeah, right. Of course."

The silence that fills the room is big and oppressive. I can feel it sitting heavy on my chest, and I know she feels it too by her slow, purposeful breathing. I want to say something to bridge the gap that's growing between us, anything to keep this conversation from spreading like a stain and tinting our entire happy weekend. But I don't know what to say. And that's unsettling because I always know what to say to Caroline.

Finally she breaks the silence though.

"So . . . I have something else to tell you. I've been waiting for this trip to talk about it because it just felt like too much over the phone. It's about me. If that's okay."

"What do you mean? I always want to hear about you."

"Well, sometimes . . . it— Never mind." She takes a deep breath. "Okay, so Brandon and I have been together for a few months now."

"Okay . . ."

"And I really like him. I love him, actually. We said it to each other last week."

"Caroline, that's huge! Why didn't you tell me?"

"I was planning on telling you. I'm telling you now."

"Who said it first?"

"He did. But that's not what I was going to tell you."

"Oh?"

"With just, with everything . . . with how good it's been between us. We've been talking about taking the next step. You know . . . going a little further in our relationship."

"Like, you want him to meet your parents?" Except I know that's not it. If that was it, she wouldn't be nervously playing with her hair—I can feel her next to me. If that was it, she wouldn't be dancing around the point instead of getting straight to it.

"No, Tess, we . . . Brandon and I, we're thinking about, um, doing it. Having sex."

"Oh."

There's a few beats while she waits for me to finish a sentence that's not coming.

"That's all you have to say?"

"No, it's just . . . I . . ." All the things I want to say run through my head.

I feel like I might not know you anymore.

I felt like we were okay, but now this is completely blindsiding me and making me realize how much else I'm missing.

I'm worried that you'll change so much that I'll get left behind.

"I don't know what to say."

"Well, what do you think I should do?"

I'm still reeling from what she's already told me, how Sam is my Duckie and Nico is Blaine, and now she drops this. This big thing. This *really* big thing that I didn't even really think of as a possible thing, but of course it is. Of course she's thinking about that when she has a perfect boyfriend who loves her. All I have is a crush that's so unrealistic even my best friend isn't encouraging it anymore. What advice could I possibly give her?

"You should do whatever you want. What makes you happy."

It feels like the thread that's between us, unconscious but constant until now, snaps.

"That's it?"

I yawn. I hope she can't hear how fake it is. "I'm sorry. I just . . . I'm tired."

There's a long pause, and I want to turn the light on to see what her face looks like. But I also like that it's dark. That I can hide.

"Yeah, right, right . . . we've had a long day. We can talk about it later." I feel relieved, even though I can hear the strain in her voice. "We should go to sleep. My flight's early."

"Okay."

I slow my breath, pretending to be asleep, until eventually it's real.

CHAPTER THIRTY

The next morning we wake up and act like everything's normal, and I almost convince myself that it is. But when we hug and say goodbye, it feels like something more.

I push it out of my mind and convince myself that Caroline and I just need some time. Once she gets home, things will go back to the way they were.

I end up not seeing Nico all week. But it's not like I go looking for him or anything. In fact, I make a point of not sitting with him and his friends at lunch, so I don't have to torture myself by seeing him and Poppy together.

And maybe it's just because my brain isn't consumed with overanalyzing every interaction with Nico, but what Caroline said about Sam keeps circling back in my mind. I know it was just a pity suggestion and all, but I can't help but start to see him that way. As a love interest. I mean, not *my* love interest, of course, but some girl's. With his sharp jaw that looks like it was chiseled by some sculptor. And his arms, covered with a fine layer of light blond hair, that always look so strong and capable as he's carrying a tower of Tupperware or securing an attachment on his stand mixer. And he always smells like butter and sugar, which is probably why when I'm around him I feel like I just crawled under a big pile of blankets on a cold night. And his lips . . . well, yeah, I could see how it would all work.

For another girl.

Not me.

We're planted firmly in the friend zone, no matter what Caroline says.

I usually dread going to Art of the Novel, as it's a reminder of my big failure. But when Friday comes along, I'm looking forward to it. Mostly because I know I'll see Nico without Poppy, and there's always a small chance that I'll get some answers, whatever they will be. But also because I hope it'll shake these other weird thoughts about Sam out of my head, which are probably just popping up because of the doubt Caroline filled me with.

I get there a little early and take a seat on a beanbag in the corner. I pull out my laptop and pretend to stare thoughtfully at a draft on my screen, but really it's just the happily ever after plan. Maybe if I study it enough, my next steps will become clear.

Ms. McKinney nods at me silently from the front of the room as the rest of the class begins to file in, and I avert my eyes quickly, worried that she'll want to talk to me again. I've been sending her "new" work, as that was the deal during our awkward conversation after class back in September. And by "new" work, I don't really mean new work, of course—just chapters from Colette's story now, instead of Tallulah's. Hopefully that's doing the trick. I don't know for sure, though, because I still haven't gotten the courage to dive into her comments again. I'm still paralyzed from the last ones.

But she hasn't asked me to share again. She even skipped over my name when it came up the second time around, maybe assuming that I'll fulfill my requirement at the very end of the semester. I don't know if I should feel grateful or embarrassed. I guess I feel a little bit of both.

"What's that you're working on?" Nico asks, tapping my foot with his. I fight the urge to slam my computer shut.

"I'm not sure yet."

"I've, uh, missed you this week," he says, sitting down next to me. I, not we. "You not going to eat lunch with us anymore?"

I shrug. "I don't know. It's just, you know, weird?" I don't need to elaborate beyond that, right? I mean, surely he's not oblivious to the fact that it's weird.

He gives me this look that makes my skin feel prickly, eyes smoldering under his dark lashes and full lips pursed. This is not the kind of look you give someone when you're letting them down easy. It's the opposite. It's an *I want you* look. So my whole body tenses in anticipation when he starts. "Tessa, I—"

Ms. McKinney claps her hands together at the front of

the room. "All right, I know you all are getting started. I just wanted to let you know that we're going to skip our workshop at the end of today—sorry, Lizbeth, next week—because I have a special announcement for you at the end."

Nico wrinkles his nose at me and smiles, mouthing, "Talk later." He takes out his Moleskine and a pen, and I close my mouth real quick, realizing it was hanging open. I am already fantasizing about a million possibilities that could have come after "Tessa, I—"

. . . *finally ended things with Poppy at lunch because I realized that it's you. It's always been you.*

. . . *really need you to stop looking at me all creeperlike. Also I saw what's on your computer screen. I'm going to alert the authorities.*

. . . *want you to follow me upstairs right now, so we can finish what we started on Halloween.*

I start typing all of these on my computer, hoping that maybe it'll jump-start some writing. I'll take anything at this point. At least I look like I'm busy.

I feel something soft and warm brush up against my thigh, and I see it's his pinkie finger, tentative at first and then followed by his whole hand. I don't think about Poppy or Sam or Ms. McKinney or even Fedora, who is definitely sneaking glances at us from his stool a few feet over—I just slide my hand under his and squeeze. This is not in my head. This is real and definitely happening. It's all the answer I need right now.

When class is almost over, Ms. McKinney calls us back to the circle, and she is beaming with whatever special news she has to share. Other people seem to be anticipating something too. The girl who always wears cat-print dresses—Angelica, I think her name is—is nervously biting her nails, and Fedora is tapping his foot so rapidly next to me, it's shaking my chair.

"So, as you know, the winter gala is approaching, and it is time for me to select who will be our honored writer from this course."

Oh, so that's what's going on.

I should feel embarrassed by how out of touch I am. I mean, if I was a real writer, I would feel just as nervous as they are. There might actually be a chance of her calling my name. But instead I'm thinking about what I'll say to Nico when class is over . . . what we'll do.

"As you know, this was an incredibly hard decision because this class is filled with such immense talent. It is truly an honor to be your instructor. Just because you are not selected to read at the gala does not mean that you should doubt your ability in any way." *Except for you, Tessa. None of what I'm saying applies to you.* "Anyway, I suppose I'll just get on with it already. The honored student for the gala will be . . ." Everyone in the room takes a collective breath. "Nico Lucchese!"

All of the confidence that he usually has seems to melt away, and he looks shocked, leaning back in his chair with his mouth moving but no sounds coming out. I wish it was socially acceptable for me to jump into his lap and give him a giant kiss right now, because that's exactly what I want to do, I'm so proud of him. I just give him a big smile instead. And when everyone swarms him with congratulations and handshakes and pats on the back, I just pack up my stuff and head out—because that's really all he needs or expects from me, right? I feel weird just hanging around, especially when I'm already dodging meaningful looks from Ms. McKinney, because, I mean, what am I waiting for even? No matter what hand-holding just took place, we're still friends and that's all.

As I reach the top of the basement stairs, though, I hear him calling my name, and when I turn, he's right there.

"Tessa, hey! I didn't want you to leave," he says, his cheeks adorably flushing pink. "We still need to talk. And I, uh— yeah, I'm not really sure what to say . . . it's just . . ."

He's trying to let me down easy. I know it. It's the only thing that could be coming. He's this talented, celebrated writer who already has a hot girlfriend, and I'm just me. I decide to make it easy for him.

"Don't worry about it," I say, waving it off like it's no big deal and I'm just incredibly casual. "And congratulations, Nico. Though I'm not surprised she picked you at all. Your parents are going to be so proud."

I turn to leave, but then he grabs my hand and pulls me into a hug. One arm is around my shoulders and the other envelops my lower back and his breath is warm in my ear and I think I might faint. And yeah, I know I sound like someone from a Disney Channel original movie going on about something as G-rated as a hug, but it feels special. Important. And I think I could just stay like this forever, but we're interrupted *(Again! I*

278

mean, come on, universe!) by someone clearing their throat.

We move apart to see Poppy standing there, arms crossed and looking pissed.

I don't wait to see what that could mean. "Well, congratulations again. It's really, really awesome!" And I speed past her without making eye contact, to find Sam and my ride home.

While we're driving home, I compose at least ten texts to Caroline about the hug, but I delete them all. It doesn't feel right to send her anything. What is she going to think about a silly hug, when she's considering something so much more important?

Anyway, drafting the texts that will never be sent is a good distraction from Sam and all of my confusing feelings about his jaw and arms and lips and perpetually sweet Bath & Body Works candle scent. Which is even more apparent as he reaches over me to grab his phone charger from the glove box at a red light, his whole body leaning over my thighs. My stomach does strange flip-floppy things. When we pull into his driveway, I jump out of the car before he's even turned the engine off and sprint to my house.

"Uh, bye?" he calls after me, and I wave quickly, anxious to escape to the quiet of my house and have some time to figure out whatever's going on in my brain.

Except when I get there, Mom is waiting for me in the kitchen. And she's not pacing or cleaning or full of the frenetic, busy movement she usually is. Instead she's eerily quiet and still, facing the doorway like she was waiting for me.

"Is there anything you want to tell me about school, Tessa?" she asks, her voice low and measured.

What could this be about? Did Poppy call my mom to tell on me or something?

"I don't know . . . no?" I can see from her eyes narrowing and her arms crossing that that was the wrong answer.

"I was looking up your grades online . . ."

Oh no.

"And I saw that you're failing your Art of the Novel class. According to Ms. McKinney's grade book, you're missing several assignments and have only gotten partial credit for the rest."

I don't say anything. I don't know what to say.

Of course I wasn't fooling Ms. McKinney after all. My heart sinks.

"Tessa, what is going on?"

I stare at her face, her jaw tight and her blue eyes watery. There's anger there, but more than that . . . disappointment. It's the same way she and my dad have been looking at me for weeks.

Seeing her looking at me that way makes me break, and before I know it, I'm crying. And not just a few drops—the for-real kind, dripping snot and all.

"I couldn't—I couldn't—write!" I choke out between sobs. "I tried! I'm trying! But the words—don't come! I'm stuck! And Ms. McKinney knows . . . and I don't know if I'm supposed to be at Chrys— I think it's all a mistake!"

I'm not sure if I'm making sense, but it feels good to get it out. Cathartic. Like maybe now everything is manageable because I've told my mom, and it'll be just like when I was little and she fixed everything—when she would listen to my worries while braiding my hair and tell me it's all right. But when I look up at Mom finally, face swollen with tears, I'm surprised to see her expression hasn't changed. If anything, it's even more alarmed.

"Why didn't you tell me any of this? How long has this been going on?" She shakes her head. "Sometimes . . . I just . . . I . . . I feel like I don't even know you anymore."

I don't even know myself, I want to say, but I can't tell her that. Maybe I shouldn't have told her anything.

Instead, I find myself saying the only thing that might change her face around, make her look at me with pride instead of constant disappointment and worry.

It's not true, but maybe that's not as important right now.

"But things are better now. Sorry, I forgot to say that." I mime hitting myself on the head. Silly me. I wipe away my tears quickly with the sleeve of my sweater. "Ms. McKinney probably just hasn't updated the grade book. Sometimes she's slow with that."

Mom runs both of her hands back through her blond hair. "Why . . . I'm confused. How do you know that? What happened?"

"I turned in a whole bunch of makeup work to her. Like,

ten chapters! And she loved it so much she chose me for the winter gala."

"What?"

"Yeah, sorry, maybe I should have led with that." I laugh and it sounds so fake, but she doesn't seem to notice. "I'm going to read at it. In December. It's kind of a big deal at our school."

"Yes, I've heard about it. In the parent newsletter." Her face starts to brighten, and a weight on my chest lifts too. "Tessa, that's incredible. Oh my goodness. You scared me for a second there!"

"Sorry," I mumble, and I start to inch toward my room, to escape what I just created. But she wraps me up into a hug, jumping up and down. "Woo-hoo! Our writer girl!"

I really have to get away now before I'm sick.

"Okay, I have homework to do," I say, pulling away.

"Yes, yes, go do your work! I'm going to call your dad! Oh, we need to buy tickets!"

I try not to think about how expensive they are.

CHAPTER THIRTY-ONE

The rest of the weekend is torture, with Mom calling all the relatives to brag and gushing about it at family dinner. Dad keeps kissing me on the top of my head and calling me his shining star. I don't recognize the girl they're describing, but then again, there's a lot I don't recognize lately. If I was asked to describe myself before, I would have called myself a writer, or at least someone who writes. I would have said I was a good person. But look at me now: no words for months, and permanently operating in the morally gray. Maybe not recognizing myself is just part of growing up, the storm before the rainbow. But I don't know. It doesn't feel right.

I feel like I've swallowed a golf ball, and it just hangs there in my throat all weekend. I almost come clean just to make it all stop, but I know it'll feel even worse to see their faces—heartbroken if I'm lucky, pissed if I'm not. The gala isn't until the week before winter break, and I'll figure out a way to tell them soon. I mean, I'll have to. But it's easier to put that off for future Tessa to deal with.

The bad feelings continue when I see Nico again in Art of the Novel on Monday. He didn't text all weekend, and I could rationalize that away. But in class . . . I can't ignore that. He doesn't ignore me or anything. He sits next to me while he writes and I "write," and he's perfectly cordial and friendly like we're just that: friends. Which is *fine*. Except, I thought Friday we were moving toward something more than that. I don't hold hands with my friends or hug them like that. Maybe Poppy changed his mind—again.

It makes me sad and anxious, but there's also a new feeling there . . . anger. There's a small part of me that's pissed off he's continuing to string me along like this. As if I don't have any say in the matter.

My face must be stormy, because Sam nudges me with his elbow on the drive home. "What's going on?"

"Nothing. I'm fine." I study a bus stop ad out the window like it holds the meaning of life.

"Sure . . . yeah." And I think he's dropped it. But a minute later: "It's just that . . . I don't know. You don't exactly look fine. You're really not good at hiding your feelings, you know? They're always all over your face. Is it, uh . . . anything you want to talk about?"

It would be nice to talk to someone, but that someone is definitely not Sam. The topic of Nico is off-limits with him. I can feel that.

"Nope."

"Okay."

The car starts moving again, and I keep staring out the window hard so I can continue to hide whatever my face is giving away . . . and also maybe avoid looking at Sam in the navy Members Only jacket he's wearing. I don't know who got him to trade the corduroy blazer he usually prefers for that, but it's working. And again, it's confusing.

While I'm looking out the window, though, I notice that it's not the usual landmarks I always see on our way home every day: the donut shop with the giant sprinkle donut fixed on top, the mural of sunset-colored kids playing, or the bright pink vintage clothing store with a rainbow flag flying outside.

"Um, where are we going?"

He looks at me like I just asked him why the ocean is blue. "To the spice store . . . I asked you if we could stop there real quick when we first got in the car? You nodded?"

"I did?" I guess I've been more present in my thoughts.

"I'm sorry," Sam says, suddenly looking alarmed and rubbing the side of his face. "I thought it was . . . We can go home." He flips on his signal immediately and starts trying to merge to the right.

"No, no, slow your roll." I laugh, putting my hands up. "It's cool. Sorry, I'm so spacey."

"Okay, thanks. I'll be fast. I promise. I just need to get a few things for a recipe I want to start tonight, and I need this specific kind of cinnamon stick."

"Working on anything special?"

"Not really. Well, I guess kinda. I found out on Friday that I was chosen to present at the gala and—"

"What! Sam! That's amazing!" I slap his shoulder. "How come you didn't say anything?"

Now he's the one avoiding my eyes, but I can see his pink cheeks. "I don't know. It's not that big of a deal."

"Uh-uh. Of course it is. It's huge! I'm so proud of you." I almost tell him that I'll be reading at the gala too, but then I have to remind myself that, no, that's a lie. It's easy to forget when I've spent the whole weekend submerged in it.

We pull up to a tiny shop squeezed between a bulk party supply store and a Laundromat in the Zaferia neighborhood. Sam rubs his hands together as we get out of the car, his face as excited as a little kid's on Christmas morning.

"My mom and I have been going to this place for as long as I can remember. Mr. and Mrs. Chen—they're the owners—they have the best selection of anyone in Long Beach. Everything from saffron to, like . . . borage. It's really something special!"

It's . . . cute, how he gets all worked up about spices. It reminds me of the time he let it slip that his stand mixer was named Ethel.

"I could stay here for hours. But of course I won't stay long! We can be in and out, promise."

My phone pings, and I'm surprised to see Nico's name.

"Why don't you go ahead and get started?" I say, waving Sam away. "I'll be in in a sec."

I don't look up to see him walk away because I'm too trans-fixed with the texts popping up on my screen.

Sorry if I was weird today

Not if. I know I was

I just dont know what to do

I can feel my heart beating fast, and I send a response before I can think about it.

I can't make that decision for you, Nico. But I'm here when you do.

Before my brain can spiral too much, I shove my phone into the pocket of my brown teddy coat and follow Sam into the store. I don't need to be wearing a coat—it's more for cuteness than to protect me from the pretty much nonexistent cold—and that's even further apparent when I walk into the warm store, a bell ringing above the doorway when I enter. It's bigger than it looks from the outside, with rows and rows of powders and seeds and dried plants in bags and jars. At the front is a tiny East Asian woman with white streaks in her black bob, standing in front of a cash register.

"Can I help you?" she asks.

"No, I'm okay," I say, trying to catch sight of Sam down one of the aisles. "But thank you."

My phone goes off again in my pocket, but I fight the urge to pull it out. Instead I force myself to look at the different products on the shelves. There's dried lavender in tall plastic baggies. Something especially fragrant called ras el hanout in glass jars. Next to that are tubs of something that looks like a mix of a beautiful flower and a terrifying bug the color of midnight. I sort of feel like I'm walking through a magical shop in a fantasy novel, and I can get why Sam likes this place so much. I want to reach out and touch everything, hold the containers to my nose, but I stick to the way I normally am in stores—hands out where they can be seen, standing at least a foot back.

I know it's a little silly, because it's not like I've ever stolen anything, but I always feel anxious in stores (well, more anxious than usual). I'm not oblivious to the way salespeople look at me, and I have had too many panicked nightmares about something accidentally falling into my bag and proving them right.

And it seems like I'm not wrong to worry, yet again, because I get that familiar prickly feeling of being watched. I look up to see that the woman has moved from her spot behind the counter and just happens to be rearranging something on the same aisle I'm in.

She smiles at me, but I catch her eyes flicking to my hands. I feel my neck burn red, even though I have no reason to feel embarrassed. I give her a polite smile back and then move on to another aisle.

Where is Sam? If I'm with him, maybe this lady will accept that I have a right to be here and stop giving me her suspicious looks. I go up and down two more rows looking for him, but he's nowhere in sight. I don't want to yell for him and make myself even more conspicuous, so I take out my phone and send him a text: **Where are you?** (I can't help but notice there's only a text from my mom asking when I'll be home. Nothing from Nico.)

I cross my arms and stand in the middle of an aisle, waiting for a text back. Maybe I should just go outside?

"This aisle is for our rarest spices," the woman says, appearing out of thin air just a few feet away from me again.

"Oh, wow," I say, slapping on the plastic smile again. I want to yell, *I don't steal! I don't even know what this stupid stuff is to want to steal it!* Instead I mumble, "Uh, have you seen anyone else in the store? A guy?"

Her dark eyes flicker around us nervously, and then she leans in close, like she's going to tell me a secret. Her breath smells like stale minty gum. "Everything here is very expensive. You sure you're in the right place?"

Rage shoots through me like a shaken-up Coke bottle exploding, but I grind my teeth together, take a deep breath, and walk past her out of the store. The bell clangs so violently that I think it might fall off. I hope it does.

When Sam comes out five minutes later, I'm still steaming.

"You decided not to come in?" he asks with a dimpled smile, but then his face changes. "Hey, you okay?"

"Mm-hmm. Fine." I just want to go home.

"No, you're not," he huffs. "We don't need to keep doing this. I can tell."

"Oh yeah? How?"

"I already told you, your face gives everything away. Like,

289

right now . . . you always do this thing when you're upset—like a wince? And you clutch your hands together," he says, imitating me. If I wasn't so pissed, I would laugh.

"It's just . . . the lady in there . . . ," I say slowly. I want to just drop it, because maybe it was just in my head. Maybe I was just being too sensitive. But no—I know that's not it. "She, um, she kept following me around. Like I was going to steal something. And she made sure to tell me how expensive everything was."

"What?" Sam asks, looking appropriately outraged. It somehow makes me feel better. "That's bullshit, treating you like some criminal. I mean, you have a right to be there just like everyone else!"

"Thanks, yeah . . ." I shrug. "It happens."

"I'm going to go talk to her!" He throws his bag down next to the car and storms off toward the store.

I grab his arm. "Please, Sam, no! It's not worth it." A scene is the last thing I want.

"Of course it's worth it!" he yells, shaking me off, but then he puts his hand on my shoulder more gently. "You're worth it," he says, his eyes locked on mine. The spot on my shoulder feels warm, and it spreads to my stomach and my toes.

Before I know it, we're both in the store again, standing in front of the woman. She's smiling at first, but then she starts blinking too fast, trying to put us together in her mind.

"Mrs. Chen, my friend Tessa here told me that you treated her in a disrespectful manner and made her feel uncomfortable,"

Sam says. He sounds all polite and perfect, like a Boy Scout. But still, my heart is beating too fast, and I have to fight the urge to run away from this confrontation.

"Sorry, Mr. Weiner," she says, her voice different than it was with me, all syrupy and sweet now. "I didn't know she was with you."

Sam's voice drops an octave. "It shouldn't matter if she was with me."

"We just have to be careful, you understand, we have our regulars and she isn't the typical customer—"

"What's a typical customer, huh? What do you mean by that? Let's at least be forthright about this." He's not yelling, but his words have the same effect.

"Mr. Weiner, I didn't mean anything by it," she says, shaken. "You know, we're a small business and it affects us when we lose inventory. . . . In the past, well, we've had shoplifters that look like . . . We have our policies, you see—"

"Well, fuck your polices." I gasp. Who is this Sam? He keeps going, his voice icy and strong: "I will never shop in your store with these racist polices again. And I will tell my mom and all her associates to do the same."

He turns to leave, but then stops and adds, "And fuck you too!"

With that, he's out the door, and I don't know what comes over me. Maybe it's just built-up anger at all the sales associates and shop owners who have made me feel like I didn't belong, like I had something to apologize for just for taking up space.

"Yeah, fuck you!" I yell. It feels good.

We strut to the car and slam the doors shut, and when I turn to Sam, I find myself blinking a few times. And then a few times more, like you do when you first wake up and the world is still coming into focus. Because something's different. He's different. Or maybe he's just who he's been all along, and the different one is me.

"That was . . . ," I start. "You didn't have to do that."

He hits his steering wheel once and then half laughs, half yelps, shaking his head. "Hey, sometimes you just have to say fuck you." He rests his arm on the back of my seat. "I'm just sorry you had to put up with that in the first place."

His hand falls to my shoulder, one finger stroking—slowly, tentatively. Our eyes meet, and I see the question there. A question that both thrills me and terrifies me.

I hear my phone ping, and without thinking about it, I take it out of my pocket. Sam quickly pulls his arm away and turns his key in the ignition. There's just a one-word response from Nico.

Okay

And looking at Sam again, I'm starting to realize that I'll be just that, regardless of what Nico decides.

CHAPTER THIRTY-TWO

I spend all week trying to nail down exactly what these new feelings for Sam are.

On Tuesday, I wake up thinking about the sturdiness of his voice when he was defending me and how it made every molecule in my body vibrate.

On Wednesday, he has a dentist appointment, and I realize just how off-kilter I feel without our early morning talks and Tupperware filled with his latest sweet creation just for me. Did I ever really appreciate it before?

And on Thursday, I almost miss Theodore's announcement that he was chosen by the visual arts department for the winter gala because I'm so distracted by this new desire I have to run my fingers through Sam's golden hair, glowing in the lunchtime light.

But I keep it all to myself. My go-to would be to call Caroline and analyze everything, and maybe, *just maybe*, if this is what I think it is, we'd come up with a new, extensive plan to make things happen. That doesn't feel right, though. I don't want to share this, whatever it is, with anyone just yet. Plus, Caroline saw it before I did, and instead of listening, I assumed the worst and messed things up between us. We've been strained ever since. My phone call to her about this is also going to need to come with a big apology.

"What's your family doing for Thanksgiving?" Sam asks as we pull up to Chrysalis. It's the Friday before fall break, and I'm looking forward to having some time off from putting on a show in my writing classes—though I guess I'll just be switching to putting on a show with my parents at home.

"Staying at home, just the four of us this year. Miles loves watching the parade with the balloons. My dad's going to try and re-create my granny's mac and cheese and her sweet potato pie. Mom already knows to not even try." I feel a little self-conscious. Another new weird development with Sam—I've never felt this way around him before. "It's probably nothing fancy compared to what you have planned. . . ."

"Oh, our standing dinner date with Rachael Ray, Ina Garten, and Gordon Ramsay?" He laughs. "Thanksgiving is actually pretty low-key for us. It's usually me and Mom, and sometimes my bubbe. But her new boyfriend got tickets to some big show on Broadway, so she politely declined our invite."

"Oh, Bubbe is savage!" I smile.

He shrugs. "Her and Mom usually just passive-aggressively take digs at each other the whole meal anyway, so this is better.

Mom handles the mains and the sides, and then I'm in charge of the desserts. We usually make enough for leftovers until Hanukkah, or even Christmas."

"You celebrate both?"

"Yeah. It's kind of strange, I know," he says as we both get out of the car and start to walk through the parking lot. I remember how I couldn't wait to get away from him on the first day, and now I wish this walk would last forever.

"Not at all."

"So, if it's just the four of you . . . then you're staying in town? You're not going back to Roseville?"

"No, most of my dad's family is in the South, and my mom's family . . . well, we don't see them much."

"Why not?"

"Well, they weren't very supportive when my parents got married. Dad wasn't what they envisioned for my mom, if you know what I mean. They skipped the wedding and everything. Things are better now, but not spending-holidays-together better."

"Wow." He shakes his head. "I thought that kinda thing was in the past. But I guess that's a . . . privileged way to think."

I playfully punch his shoulder. "What, are you going for white ally of the year?"

He pokes me back. "Can you put in a good word for me with the judges?"

"We'll see." I laugh and shake my head. "Anyway, yeah, I'll be here all week."

"Good, so . . . I don't know, maybe we could hang out? Because we won't, you know, have our daily drive . . . If you're not busy." He's looking straight ahead instead of at me, but I can hear something in his voice. "I make really good pie. I can save you one."

"I'd like that." My cheeks hurt with how big my smile is. "And you don't have to bribe me with treats. I'd hang out with you anyway."

"Aww, shucks," he says, nudging me with his shoulder. My whole body vibrates.

Yeah, I don't need to consult Caroline. There's definitely something there.

As we weave between the cars in the lot and walk into the shadow of the tall building that makes up half of Chrysalis, I see Nico standing there alone, head swiveling like he's looking for someone. And I'm stricken with how much I've barely thought about him all week because my mind has been crowded with Sam. It's such a dramatic change, especially when I was so sure so recently that Nico was it. That if I just found my happily ever after with him, then everything else would fall into place. But what if my happily ever after isn't what I thought it was after all?

Sam's not just a love interest for some other girl. He could be a love interest for *this* girl. Me.

Nico stops looking around, and he locks eyes on me. He starts to walk toward us, and he's looking at me strangely. I kind of don't want him to talk to me, which I wouldn't have believed if someone had told me a week ago. But I don't want to make

Sam uncomfortable. In fact, I'm trying to think of a way to hint at how I'm feeling . . . to see if maybe he feels the same way too. Nico will just muddle all of that.

But then Lenore appears in front of me, before Nico can reach us anyway. She's wearing all shades of pink: shiny rose-gold pants, a blush tank, and a slouchy magenta cardigan, all topped with a black, wide-brimmed Beyoncé Lemonade-era hat. I want to tell her how much I love her outfit, but I'm stopped by the serious, very un-Lenore-like look on her face.

She grabs my shoulder. "Has someone told you yet?"

Only then do I notice the stack of wrinkled papers in her other hand.

"Told me what?"

"Here. Just look." She hands me the stack, and the first thing I see is that my name is at the top of each page. Why is my name at the top of each page? I can't seem to make that fact make sense in my mind. But then I recognize some poems I wrote in ninth grade—the embarrassing kind with rhyming and too many similes. And then I see—*no no NO*—Dream Zone fan fiction. I mean, loose Dream Zone fan fiction, with just Thad, set before he joined the band. But still. Most of the stack, though, is pages and pages of the unfinished Tallulah and Thomas novel. Tallulah, who's a lot like me, and Thomas, who looks a lot like . . .

Nico is next to us now. "Uh, Tessa, can we talk?" His hands are filled with the papers too.

I don't think. I just run. Someone—maybe Nico, maybe

Sam—calls after me, but I keep going until I'm inside the building, pushing past people who are talking about me. I can feel their looks and their whispers tickling my skin. I hoped to find relief inside, but the hallway of the first floor is practically wallpapered with my work. I stop in shock. I'm scared to keep running, scared to find that all five floors look the same.

Is this actually happening? *How* can this be happening? This is like one of those things that happen in teen movies, not real life.

I rip one of the pages off the wall next to my US history class and see that it's even worse than I thought, as if that was possible. It's a page from one of my Tallulah and Thomas chapters, the one where she sees him for the very first time, and it's marked up, like someone was studying it for a test. Highlighted in blinding yellow are "dark hair" and "moody eyes" and "long eyelashes" and "skinny frame" and "tight black jeans" and "mysterious artist" and all the other things that make Thomas just like Nico. Written at the bottom in all caps is: SHE'S OBSESSED. The page next to it: STALKER MUCH?

No! That's not it! I want to scream to the two ballet dancers standing behind me smirking and murmuring something to each other. I wish I could go over the PA and explain that I wrote these stories before I met Nico. That it's not my fault he ended up looking like he walked out of my story. But at the same time, I want to just disappear, because how will anyone believe that I'm not the crazy stalker this is making me out to be?

I can feel my neck start to burn, and my breaths get too fast, each one providing both not enough and too much oxygen until I start to get light-headed. I think I see Sam, coming through the crowd—when did a crowd develop? But no, I don't want to see him right now. I want him far away from here, in a sensory-deprivation tank somewhere. What will this make him think about me?

And the bigger question: who would do this?

I get my answer to that, though, when Poppy appears next to me, her arms full of copies. She looks perfect in an oversized sweatshirt dress and bright red lipstick.

"I have some extras, if you want these," she says. Her lip curls in disgust, as if she's scraping something gross off one of her Chelsea boots. "God, how desperate can you be?"

Someone laughs. I don't know who it is because I can't see anyone's face anymore; everyone is blurred together. And my neck is prickly now on top of the burning, and I reach up to feel hives are starting to form there, covering my neck and spreading down my chest. I hate when this happens. It's my body's white flag. The final shut-down message letting me know that this is too much. That I can't process any more.

I am standing in the middle of my worst nightmare, and I'm completely frozen. I would probably stand there forever, until I stopped breathing altogether or my body became one giant hive or I just sank into the ground like I was begging the universe to make happen, but someone grabs my arm and gently pulls me outside. I know only from the familiar butter-and-sugar scent that it's Sam, but I can't look at his face. I can't look at anyone.

He leads me to his car, opening the passenger door and nudging me inside. We sit inside together, the only sound my quickening breath. I want to explain everything to him. I want to scream. I want to take off from the car and tackle Poppy to the ground. I want to run through the halls removing every last page. But instead I just sit, listening to my breath, blinking away tears, as the parking lot slowly clears and we're the only ones still there. In the distance, I can hear the bell ring.

After who knows how long, Sam reaches over and tentatively places his hand on my shoulder. It feels solid, tethering me to the seat, when my head is taking off in so many places.

"Breathe," he says, and then he models a long, deep one for me. I should be annoyed, but the reminder is everything I need. We do a few of them together, breathing slowly in unison until I feel my heart rate slow down and I'm taking in air steadily instead of in frantic gulps.

Sam reaches down with his other hand and squeezes mine. It's unexpected but not unwanted. It feels good.

"You know what?" he asks.

"What?"

"We should . . . Let's get out of here."

"Okay."

CHAPTER THIRTY-THREE

We drive down Second Street until it hits PCH, and I try not to think about what my parents would do if they knew I was skipping school. It would probably just add to the narrative they're building in their heads about what a messed-up teenager I'm becoming. But today was traumatic, and I can't imagine going back into that school and dealing with the whispers and stares for the rest of the day. I'm just glad Sam was there to save me. And hold my hand. I wish I could reach over and take his hand again.

"Uh . . . it's just . . . I—ugh!" I choke out, trying to make sense of the garbled mess in my head. My voice is scratchy and hoarse like I've been screaming for hours.

Sam doesn't push. He drives down a long street with cute shops and cafés and then pulls into a parking lot facing a beach I haven't been to yet. Seal Beach. When he finally clicks the car off, though, he turns to face me, a sympathetic smile on his face.

"It's just what?"

I take one more deep breath. "It's just that I think I can get over what she's trying to say about Nico and me . . . being obsessed or whatever."

He makes a face that I can't decipher. "Yeah?"

"Yeah, I wrote that story before I ever met him. I know that. And he can know that if we ever talk again. . . . I don't care if we do," I say, even though I'm not sure if that's true. "And maybe I deserve it."

"You didn't deserve that."

I wave that thought away. "The part I can't get over, what's making me so upset, is that it was all the worst of my writing. That everyone is going to see that and realize what a terrible writer I am."

"That won't happen," he says, smiling at me. His hand goes to my shoulder again. It feels like it's full of electricity, charging my whole body. "How do you think she even got it?"

"It was probably in my portfolio. And I mean, who knows how she got her hands on that? I guess her parents are on the board, so she has access—and of course she chose the worst stuff! But who am I kidding . . . it was probably all crap. I made this easy for her—"

"Tessa," he cuts me off. His voice is stern, so out of character it makes me look up, and I see that his face matches. "I really need you to stop talking shit about my friend."

"Since when is Poppy your friend?"

"No, you!" He laughs, the face breaking. He leans in closer to me. "You're always so down on yourself and your writing. But let's look at the straight facts. Those were the writing samples that were sent in. And the creative writing department read them and accepted you into the school, so I think we can conclude that the writing was, *is* good."

"Yeah, but—"

"I don't want your buts!" He blushes and says quickly, "You know what I mean. It's just . . . you need to get out of this mindset that you don't deserve to be here. You're here for a reason. As a writer, an artist, you *belong* here. And nothing, not some mean girl, or even your own inner critic, can take that away from you."

His words envelop me, warming up my entire body. How can he feel this way when . . .

"You've never even read my writing."

"I haven't. But I want to, and I hope you'll let me someday." I'm not sure how it happened, but we're only inches away from each other. I can see every one of the freckles below his eyes. "I do know that you're incredible, though, so your writing must be too. If you'll believe in yourself as much as I believe in you."

Something unlocks between us with those words, and then he's closing the remaining space, brushing his nose against mine. There's that question in his eyes again, and I nod. I want this. He brings his hands to the sides of my face, holding me delicately like I'm something precious and important, and my eyes flutter closed as our lips press together.

And I realize I've been describing kissing all wrong. In all my years of writing—kisses with Harry and Edward and Thad and Thomas—I never got it right. That was mechanics, logistics . . . and this, this is completely different. This is intuitive, this is urgent. This involves everything, my whole body, even though the only parts of us touching are our lips and his hands on the back of my neck, fingers woven in my curls. My heart has left my chest and is beating in my ears and my stomach is doing triple backflips. I think I've reached my limit. That I can't possibly feel any more. But then his hand trails down the side of my body, his lips move to my cheek, my neck, the side of my mouth, and it all gets dialed up to a hundred.

This is what kissing is.

And I get the urge to take out my laptop, write down every last detail. I could write entire novels just about kissing Sam.

He pulls away and stares at me, eyes wide.

I can't find any words, except: "Whoa."

Redness is creeping up his neck and to his cheeks. "I don't know what I . . . I know you like Nico—"

I grab his face and kiss him again.

And we keep kissing.

Eventually, after our lips are swollen and the car windows are starting to fog, Sam suggests, sheepishly, that maybe we get out of the car before someone calls a security guard or something. And I laugh way too much at the idea of that happening and the phone call my parents could get because now I'm ditching school AND making out in a car with a boy. It's hilarious what a turn my PG life has taken.

We walk down Main Street to a tiny bakery and order cinnamon rolls as big as our heads, taking them down to the beach. As we walk barefoot in the cold sand to the murky blue water, my hand brushes against his, and he takes it, confidently, like this is the way it always has been.

The beach is pretty empty, most people scared away by the cloudy sky, so it still feels like we're in our own little bubble. Just me and him, and all the other worries—like my words floating around the hallways or whether or not the school will call my mom or what everyone at school will think about me and Sam—they all just float away.

We sit and watch the waves, taking gooey, sweet bites of the pastries, our legs outstretched on a blanket he had in the back of his car. And I keep catching him out of the corner of my eye, staring at me instead of the water in front of us, like I'm more deserving of his attention than the Pacific Ocean. It makes me feel like the biggest treasure.

"What?" I finally ask, grinning and nudging him with my shoulder.

"I just can't believe that we're here. Like this. You and me." He laces his fingers through mine.

"I know," I say quickly. "It probably seems like it came out of nowhere—"

"It didn't for me," he says solemnly. "I've thought you were the most beautiful girl in the world from the first day I saw you."

"Oh yeah? Even when you were paying for my brother's pizza?"

"That wasn't the first time," he says, and I look up at him, confused. "I saw you when your family was moving in—you were carrying in a big box of books, and your dad kept trying to help you, but you just pushed him away, even though it took you twice as long . . . sorry, this probably sounds kind of stalker-y, doesn't it? Me watching you without you knowing?"

"I know aaalllll about being stalker-y."

He rolls his eyes. "Anyway, when your brother sent that pizza to the wrong house, I was actually pretty grateful. Because it gave me a chance to meet you. Ever since then I've just been waiting . . . well, desperately hoping that you'd catch up."

I go through the past few months in my head: all the treats he brought me every morning and what a jerk I was to him in the beginning—so worried about what other people would think, when that shouldn't have been my focus at all.

I trace the center of Sam's rough palm with my thumb. "I don't know," I say. "Sounds like just a line to me."

He reels back for a second but then smiles when he sees my smirking face and realizes I'm quoting him from that day with Caroline in his kitchen. "I've got all the lines for you, as many lines as you could possibly dream of, because you are deserving of lines from here to eternity."

He kisses my forehead. "Are you tired? Because you've been running through my mind all day." He kisses me on one cheek and then the other. "Did it hurt? When you fell from heaven?" He tugs on my shirt and then kisses me on the nose. "You know what this shirt is made of? Girlfriend material."

"I don't think that's how that one's supposed to g—"

He kisses my chin. "There must be something wrong with my eyes because I can't take them off you."

"Okay, stop," I say, cutting him off with a kiss on the lips. I lean into it, knocking him down on the sand, and he wraps his arms around me, pulling me close to him. The kisses start slow and tentative, but then his left arm goes down to my lower back and I run my hand through his hair and we both open our mouths, taken by this frantic energy, and the kisses become more urgent, quick, and—

Someone clears their throat, and we both spring up to see a mom in a one-piece, holding a beach chair and diaper bag in one arm and a dark-haired toddler in the other, giving us the death glare.

"Um, uh, sorry, ma'am!" Sam calls, waving at her. She does not look amused.

After she stomps off down the beach, Sam and I both just stare at each other, and it's like neither of us can stop grinning.

"Do you want to, uh, cool off?" he asks, gesturing toward the water.

I nod quickly, my heart beating too fast.

We stand up, and I realize he's wearing the khaki cargo

pants with the zippers at the knees. I used to think they were so embarrassingly dorky before, but I don't care now.

Now I just see him. This kind, funny, cute boy who I want to make out with a lot more, preferably somewhere in private. He leans down—I think to roll up his pants—but instead he zips off the bottoms, converting them into shorts. So people *do* do that.

I laugh so much, I snort a little bit, and when he looks up at me, self-conscious, I meet him with a kiss. We grab hands and run off into the waves.

CHAPTER THIRTY-FOUR

We spend the weekend together, eating all his test recipes for the gala and sneaking kisses around our families and watching *Enter the Dream Zone* with Miles. My mom finally won an auction for it on eBay, so we show it to Sam in its full glory, and he's appropriately impressed.

Lenore, and even Theodore, text me a few times, checking in to make sure I'm okay. I calm their worries and ask about their Thanksgiving plans, but I don't tell them about Sam. I want to keep this, whatever this is, between just us for now.

On Monday night, Sam asks if I'm free, because he has something special planned.

"Like a date?"

"Uh . . . I don't know, yeah? If that's what you want it to be. I know we've been spending a lot of time together, and it's okay if you need some time off—"

"I want it to be a date."

"Okay." He nods and then pulls me close, whispering in my ear. "Then that's what it is."

He picks me up at seven and, successfully ignoring the questioning looks from Mom (Dad, thank god, is working late), we drive over to Signal Hill. Signal Hill is a city within a city, a little island of a town right in the middle of Long Beach, marked by cookie-cutter new houses, incongruous oil-well pumps, and—that's right—a giant hill. Sam drives up a road that zigzags to the top of the hill and then pulls over at a deserted park.

My phone pings, and when I take it out, I see Nico's name. I quickly shove it back into my purse before I can read whatever he's sent. I don't need to know.

"What's this?" I ask Sam brightly, hoping he didn't notice. "Did you bring me up here for some necking and heavy petting in your car? Is this, like, Long Beach's make-out point?"

His cheeks immediately flush red. "No—not at all! I'm not expecting anything."

"Relax," I say, reaching over and squeezing his hand. "I'm just kidding."

"Sorry," he says, shaking his head. "It's just . . . I'm so worried I'm going to mess things up. Now that you're here with me, that I know you feel the same way . . ." He meets my eyes and laces our fingers together. "Well, I don't know if I could handle going back to before. I really like you, Tessa."

"I really like you too." I reach forward and kiss him, and then linger there, our noses touching. "And for the record, I wouldn't mind doing some necking and heavy petting with you. You know, if that *was* what you had in mind. But . . . what even is necking anyway?"

"Maybe like this," he murmurs. He leans in to gently kiss my neck, starting from right below my ear and then trailing lower, hesitant and then bold. My whole body burns up.

"Oh, I like necking." I meet his lips, and we explore each other some more, until the car windows are opaque with fog.

"Okay, I hate to end this," he says, pulling back finally, his hands still tangled in my hair, "But I'm worried what I brought you is going to melt."

"So you really planned more than this?"

"Of course I did!" he says, faking offense. "This is a date."

"Okay, okay," I say, holding my hands up. "Impress me."

He gives me a quick kiss and then reaches into the back seat to pull out a cooler. Inside is a carton of ice cream and two spoons.

"What's this?"

"I—uh, I made you your own ice cream."

"What?"

He looks down sheepishly. "Yeah, it's called Tessa's Happily Ever After. The base is rose flavored because . . . well, that's what your hair always smells like. Is that weird? I hope that's not weird." I laugh and shake my head. "And there's brown-butter shortbread cookies mixed in, and chocolate-covered raspberries. It's all supposed to represent—"

"Our first car ride." I remember those brown-butter raspberry muffins and how he helped me work in the conditioner on the back of my head. I also remember, with shame, what a jerk I was to him that day.

"Yeah . . . so you get it." His dimple has appeared.

"Of course I do! You win. I'm impressed."

"And it's dairy free . . . for your, uh, stomach problems."

"Completely and totally impressed." I kiss him and then take a bite of the ice cream, my ice cream, both things equally delicious.

"You like it?"

"I love it!" The word makes both of us look away quickly. I quickly change the subject.

"So this is ísbíltúr?" I ask him, hoping I'm getting the pronunciation right. "Like the restaurant you want to make one day—ice cream dates in cars?"

His eyebrows rise. "You remember that?"

"Yeah! Why wouldn't I?"

"I don't know. I guess I just . . . I'm just happy." He reaches up and wipes something off the side of my mouth—a smudge of chocolate. He licks it off his thumb.

"I'm happy too."

After we devour the rest of the carton together, we get out of the fogged-up car and walk to the edge of the park, our ankles getting wet from the dewy grass.

"This is why I brought you to this park in particular," he says, holding my hand with one hand and signaling out at the view with the other. "I came here all the time when I was a kid, and as soon as I got my license, I started coming here alone a lot. It's a good place to think. I've come up with some of my best recipes here."

From the top of the tall hill, we can see all of Long Beach, illuminated with the orange glow of streetlamps and the red and white of car lights. Beyond that, there's the ocean, the port in San Pedro, and even the twinkling lights of LA far in the distance. It makes me feel both tiny and huge at the same time.

"This is . . . beautiful."

"You're beautiful."

I turn and he's looking at me all starry-eyed like I'm the amazing view. Until Sam, I've never been looked at this way before, only described it in my stories. And just like our first kiss, it's better than any words I've ever put on a page.

He hooks his finger into the top of my high-waisted skirt and pulls me toward him, hip to hip, his hands settling on my waist. It's so damn sexy that my lower stomach aches and I can feel it all the way down to my toes.

It feels different being pressed up against Sam. His soft belly is nothing like Nico's sharp hip bones. I know I shouldn't compare the two, but I can't help it after imagining this with Nico for so long.

Sam feels good, though. So good. He's something I didn't even know I wanted, but now I can't imagine being without—like my own ice cream.

How has this Sam been here all along? And how did it take me so long to see him?

★ ★ ★

Sam and I convince our families to combine our two tiny Thanksgivings into one, which simultaneously thrills and terrifies my mom. I walk in on her Tuesday night crowd-sourcing hosting etiquette from her book club on speakerphone, as if we're having the president over instead of just Sam and his mom. Luckily she's too nervous to question why Sam and I are all of a sudden so close.

I spend the evening before in Sam's kitchen, watching him methodically press pie dough into dishes and lay out complicated lattices. Watching him work makes who he is and why I like him sharp and clear, like a camera coming into focus. He's precise in ways that matter to him and haphazard in the ways I thought mattered but realize now maybe don't. He's unapologetically soft, yet strong when he needs to be—when I need him to be. I don't know how I missed it for so long.

Thanksgiving goes better than I expect it to. Audrey is too modest to mention Sam's selection for the gala, and my mom's too starstruck to mention mine, or rather "mine" . . . which I've forced myself to put out of my mind for now, because it makes me too anxious to think about. Dinner conversation, instead, sticks to safe topics, like politics (that is a safe topic in liberal Long Beach) and whether it's puh-KAHN or PEE-can (that got a little more heated).

Sam brings four pies and a cake to share but spends the evening praising Dad's sweet potato pie, which makes Dad proudly strut around the kitchen. And when Miles bursts into his favorite Dream Zone song before everyone's even finished filling their plates, no one misses a beat. Instead, Sam joins in on background vocals flawlessly, making my parents clap in delight. And Audrey, inspired by their performance, gives us a rendition of some ancient boy band from the nineties' greatest hit, using Mom's fancy serving spoon as a makeshift mic. It's all so easy and fun that I can't help but imagine what next Thanksgiving might be like.

On Saturday night, Sam's mom has an in-store appearance at some kitchen supply place in the Grove, so we have his house to ourselves. I can think of a lot of things I want to do with that alone time, but we somehow end up cuddling on his couch and watching a Twilight marathon on Freeform. And we have time.

"But, like, he's a little possessive of her, right? In a sorta creepy way."

"That's how he shows that he loves her," I say, leaning in to him.

"Oh yeah?" he laughs. "He's basically using her scent to follow her around. I'm pretty sure guys get arrested for things like that."

"But he saved her! It's a little problematic, yeah, but there are literally thousands of fan fictions dedicated to just this attribute of his. It's romantic . . . kind of."

He gives me a playful side-eye. "I don't even want to know how you know that."

"At least it was way romantic when I was in middle school."

Another commercial break comes on, and he scoops my

legs into his lap. I always thought I would feel self-conscious about my body, having someone touch me like this, but all I want is more of it.

"Are your love stories like this?" he asks. "Guys who have all the control?"

"No! I try to give the girls more agency, I guess . . . they make their own choices and they pursue just as much as they're pursued. That's really the point of romance as a genre, I think: girls—*women*—asking for what they want, without apology."

The answer falls off my tongue so easily, it makes me wonder why I've never talked about romance this way before. I'm always worried that my stories aren't important like what my classmates write. But a good love story is smart. Empowering. It's why I've been drawn to the genre for as long as I can remember.

I also can't help but wonder: Do I live my life like the women in my favorite stories? Probably not, but maybe I'm moving in the right direction.

"So have you written yet? I'm not trying to check up on you or anything. But I mean, that was the point of your plan with Caroline, right? Making your own love story so you could write one again?"

His face suddenly turns an alarming shade of scarlet. "Not that this is a love story!"

I look straight at him. "I haven't yet, but I'm getting lots of inspiration."

I cup the side of his face, kissing him deeply, and soon

we're a little more horizontal on the couch—closer to where I thought this night would go instead of a Twilight marathon. His hand travels up the back of my shirt, hesitant at first, to make sure it's okay, and I press into him more and do the same to show my enthusiasm. His skin is soft, and the fine hairs on his back stand up, responding to my touch.

My phone pings, alerting me to a text. I plan to ignore it, but then it goes off again three more times.

"I better check that . . . in case it's my parents," I murmur. The last thing I need them doing is coming over here to check up on me.

I reluctantly pull myself away from him, grab my phone, and then settle back in his arms. And false alarm, they're all from Lenore, not my parents.

Why you been so MIA? Do I need to send a search party to Bixby Knolls?

My only companions this week have been my APUSH textbook and my irritating sibs NOT THAT YOU CARE

Have you talked to Nico????? Because I've been hearing some things

Your "happily ever after" just may be coming in the new year

Then there's a gif of Beyoncé whipping her ponytail around on a stage.

I consider pulling away so Sam can't see the texts. I can tell by his face, though, that he's already read them.

"You haven't told her about us?"

I can only be honest. "No. But I was going to! When we got back."

I can feel his body stiffen. "I haven't really talked to anyone but you this break," I rush to explain. "I've just been enjoying this . . . us."

I kiss him again, and he's happy to pick up where we left off. Thankfully that's enough of an explanation for now. Because the truth is, I haven't even let my mind wander to next week. I wish we could stay in this week forever, where it's just me and Sam and everything feels so easy and right between us— uncomplicated by what everyone else at school might think.

CHAPTER THIRTY-FIVE

But of course Monday comes. Before I can think of a plan or why I even feel the need for a plan, we're walking across the parking lot again. Hand in hand—because even in a week, that's become natural. Sam is going on about some new pie place downtown he wants to try when all of a sudden he stops and his body gets tense. And when I look up, I realize why. It's Nico, alone in front of us, looking at our faces, then at our interlocked hands, then back at our faces, trying to put it together.

I don't really think about it. I just let go of Sam's hand.

He looks at me, and the hurt I see in his eyes makes my chest feel tight.

What am I doing?

Nico closes the distance between us, and he gives us his best toothpaste-commercial smile, seemingly unfazed. And why shouldn't he be? He has Poppy. I'm just glad she's not here with him now.

"Hey, Weiner," he says, nodding at Sam. Then he turns to me. "Tessa, can we talk?"

"My name is Sam." His jaw is set, and his voice is deeper than usual.

Nico just waves his hand. "Yeah, sure. Sorry, Sam." He takes a step closer to me, as if Sam is no longer there. "Tessa, is that okay? You, uh—you didn't respond to my texts all break. Did you get them?"

I steal a glance at Sam, and his eyes are dark.

"Yes, I did. Sorry, I was busy," I say quickly to Nico. *I just want to get out of here.* "Look, this isn't really the best time. I have to go to class."

"Okay, yeah. But maybe at lunch?" Why isn't he letting this go? What would Poppy—*his girlfriend*, who obviously, probably justifiably, hates me very much—think about this?

"I'm going to sit with Sam today," I say. "And, you know, Lenore and Theodore."

Why did I add that? Sam and I are together, something that made me so happy—*makes* me so happy. So why aren't I making that clear to Nico?

"Sure, okay. Tomorrow then," Nico says with another perfect smile. He leaves before I can say anything else.

"All right, I'm not trying to act like a controlling vampire here, Tessa, but he texted you over break? Why didn't you tell me that?" Sam's trying to make this light, but I can tell from his face that he's upset. And I can't blame him.

"Just a few texts. They were nothing. Just him asking to talk. I didn't want things to be weird, and I *never* responded." I slip my hand into his again, and he looks at it meaningfully but says nothing.

"Listen, I'm sorry. I should have told you. But I didn't text him back."

"Yes, but . . . I don't know. Why didn't you tell him we're together now?"

"Was I supposed to announce it?" I poke his shoulder, playfully. I desperately want this fog that's falling over us to go away, to go back to the easiness of just a few minutes ago. I poke him again, and he's smiling now but still looks uneasy.

"I just . . . I think he should know."

I kiss him quick. "I'll tell him next time I see him."

"Ooooh!" I hear Lenore before I see her. But then her squeal makes its way through the crowd, and she appears in a gold-pleated wrap dress, Theodore sauntering slowly behind her.

"This!" she says, motioning rapidly between us. "I'm all about THIS!"

Sam blushes, but he looks happier now. I hold our hands up. "The secret's out!"

"EEEEEEEEEEEEE!" Lenore lets out a scream one pitch away from that kind that only dogs can hear. "I knew it! I knew it! Right, Theo, I called this, right?"

"Well, I mean, it wasn't rocket science." Theodore laughs, which sets her off even more.

I squeeze Sam's hand. "See, the whole school will know before first period now."

Nico is waiting for me outside at the end of my American lit class.

I see him, take a deep breath, and then start walking in the other direction.

"Tessa?"

"Nico, that story wasn't about you."

"Well, regardless, we need to talk about it."

"I really can't—"

"Can you just listen for a second? I need to tell you something." He's following after me, and even though I'm horrified that this is happening, I also can't help but feel a little thrill that Nico seems so into me all of a sudden. I keep moving.

"There's nothing for us to talk about."

"I want you to know that I broke up with Poppy!" he shouts. That stops me, and he takes the opportunity. "Like, for good this time. Things weren't working with us. They haven't for a while. We almost broke up after Halloween because she was all suspicious or whatever about how we went off alone. And then when she broke into the creative writing office and leaked your stories . . . well, I don't want to be with someone like that."

"That story wasn't about you," I repeat. I need him to know

this. "I wrote that before I started at Chrysalis. It's just a co-incidence that he—the character looked like you."

"Okay, yeah, sure." He smiles, like he's humoring me. It's irritating, but I think it'll be even less believable if I keep insisting. "You can't deny that there's something between us, though. I've felt it since the party, maybe even before that. And I think you have too. I'm sorry I've been so stupid and didn't end things with Poppy sooner. I want to be with you, Tessa."

The hallways are empty now, everyone else heading outside for lunch. His words feel loud, like they're echoing across the halls. And I'm thrown off. This is everything I wanted just a few weeks ago, and I can't believe it's actually happening, because I don't know if I ever *really* thought it would.

But now that it is happening, I feel frozen. Because I've found someone else I want, someone I didn't know I wanted until he was right in front of my face. And this whole week with Sam has been so perfect—the conversations and the desserts and the kisses. He gets along so well with Miles, treating him how I wish people always would. And, like, he made me my own ice cream—who even does that? In just one week, Sam has gone beyond any of my expectations of what a boyfriend could be. We haven't really talked about it, but I think that's what he's becoming, my boyfriend.

So why am I just standing here and not saying anything to Nico?

"Tessa, did you hear me? I want to be with you, and only you." It's the declaration of love, just like Caroline predicted in her happily ever after plan. All he needs is a construction paper sign held over his head.

"Say something, please? I'm starting to feel a little . . . I mean, don't leave me hanging like this." He reaches forward and lightly touches my arms. The touch flips a switch, jolting me awake.

"I'm with Sam," I finally manage to croak out.

"Weiner?" His head reels back like I just told him something crazy. "I thought you guys were just friends."

"We were . . . but we're not anymore. Now we're more than that."

He blinks a few times, taking that in, but then he shakes the thought away. "Ooh-kay . . . but there's something special between us. We can't just, like . . . ignore that."

Nico takes a step toward me, and his hands move to the sides of my face. His touch feels different from Sam's—Sam can be so tentative at times, but Nico feels sure.

It would be easy to go along with this. It would make sense to choose Nico. He's who I've wanted all along. But now that he's right here in front of me, is he *really* who I want?

It's like I'm watching a scene in one of my stories instead of real life. I feel like my legs are glued to the ground . . . until his face starts moving toward mine, and I realize what he's going to do. I turn my head just in time.

"I can't . . . I just . . ."

He looks flustered. It's clear this doesn't happen to him often.

"Will you just think about it?" His voice is soft. "Maybe we could even go out this weekend?"

I shake my head. "Nico . . ."

"Don't answer me now then. We don't have to make a decision yet. But I'll be waiting for you. You know it's right." Before I can stop him, he kisses my forehead real quick and walks past me down the hallway.

Only then do I notice Sam standing there, his entire face broken apart.

CHAPTER THIRTY-SIX

"Sam."

"I was . . . I wanted to walk you to lunch." He's shaking his head. His face is like someone punched him in the stomach. "I don't know why I'm surprised. I shouldn't be surprised."

I rush over to him. "There's nothing going on with Nico. He just—he wants there to be, but I told him I was with you."

"Is that why you didn't want to be seen holding my hand this morning? You're still holding out hope for him?"

"That wasn't it." But what was it then?

"So you didn't drop my hand and spring away from me as soon as you saw him walking up? That was just in my head?" His face is heavy with the challenge, and when I don't say anything—because I can't really deny that, can I?—his eyes darken even further.

"I guess I can only be mad at myself for being so stupid, for believing that last week . . . what we had . . . was anything real.

Was I just a nice little break for you? You know, before you got back to reality and the person you really wanted?"

"Of course not!" I grab his hand, and I can feel him wanting to pull away, but he doesn't. I touch the side of his face. "Last week was real life, and it was more than I ever could have imagined. You are perfect, Sam, and you have been so good to me, and I'm telling you now that I didn't let anything happen with Nico. I am with you and not him, and I would never do that to you."

"I don't want to be anyone's second choice, Tessa," he says, "some sort of consolation prize. You've always been my first choice, and I deserve that back. Can you tell me that I'm your first choice?"

I want to explain to Sam that he wasn't my first choice, but he is now. Or at least I think he is. Or at least he *will* be when I get a second to catch my breath. But this moment between us is so tenuous that I'm scared to say anything, do anything, that will scare him away.

Apparently my silence is enough of an answer, though, and his face shutters. The vulnerable, soft side is tucked away to be protected—to be protected from me.

"Forget I asked, Tessa."

He starts off down the hallway, moving fast, and pushes the button for the elevator, which opens immediately as if it was waiting for him. He gets in, but before the doors can close, I jump in after him.

"Are you sure you want to be seen with me?" He scoffs. I

327

flinch at his tone. He's never talked to me like this before.

"I just . . . I need you to let me get my thoughts together. It's a lot to process today."

"Why bother processing anything? Because if you're putting me and Nico up against each other in your mind, we both already know who's going to win. I don't need to wait around for the results."

"I'm not saying these things! Stop acting like you know what I'm thinking!" We're getting dangerously close to the first floor, and I can feel whatever is left between us slipping away. Once we get to the bottom, I know I'll lose him. So I do the only thing I can think of—I pull up the glass protective cover and slam the emergency button. The elevator car screeches to a stop.

"Sam, please, can we slow this down? You're assuming you know what I want, what I'm thinking, and I'm not even sure yet. I just know that I like me and you, and this isn't supposed to end. Not like this."

"Why delay the inevitable?" he says, not looking me in the eye. "And wait—" His gaze whips from the bright red emergency button that I pushed and back to my face. "Are you seriously trying to use something off that stupid happily ever after list right now? You know I've seen it, right?"

"I mean, that wasn't . . . It *is*, but I wasn't thinking about—I just want us to talk."

"This isn't a game to me, Tessa." His voice is small, and I can't stand the look of hurt on his face.

I know this is my chance to convince him—to explain away everything with Nico. To make him understand how I really feel. But all I can manage is, "I like you, Sam." I hate that my voice cracks when I say it. I hate that it doesn't feel like enough.

He looks at me, and his green eyes are shiny. There's pain there, but also resolution. "I like you too. But I'm done."

He brushes past me to pull the red button. The door springs open, and a crowd of students and staff members is waiting for us. He walks away without turning back.

CHAPTER THIRTY-SEVEN

I convince Mom that I'm sick and need to be picked up, so I can avoid the rest of lunch and conservatory. And really, I am sick—I feel nauseous and have a pounding headache—but it's all self-inflicted.

When I get home, I actually text Lenore first, but she quickly declares:

> I love you girl, but I'm Switzerland. I'm John Legend whenever Kanye shows his ass on Twitter.
> NOT THAT YOURE KANYE!!
> Don't be mad?

Of course not. I text back. I get it.

So I call Caroline. We haven't been talking much, not like we used to, since she came to stay earlier this month. But I also know she's always there when I need her, and I really need her now.

She picks up after the first ring, like she always does, and I tell her everything—all the details about my dreamy week with Sam and the hand-holding mishap this morning and Nico's declaration and the big blowup in the elevator.

"And that's how," I finish, "I had the makings of a happily ever after with not one but two guys. But because I couldn't figure out which of those endings I wanted, I'm left with none."

I take a deep breath. It feels good to get it all out.

But Caroline is unusually quiet.

"Tessa, I . . . I can't do this anymore."

"What do you mean?" I ask.

"I don't know if it's always been this way, or if it's just worse since you moved, but you . . . expect me to be this permanent sounding board for you, with just this unending patience and interest in your life, and I can't be that today."

"Caroline, I—"

"You know, I'm a human too, with her own life and her own shit going on. I'm not just some best friend sidekick who only exists when you need her. This isn't a movie."

"Do you think I think that? Because I don't think that."

"Well, you have a weird way of showing it," she mutters under her breath.

For the second time today, I feel both completely misunderstood and also horrifyingly seen, like I'm being examined under a microscope or caught in a spotlight. How can these two people I trust so much think so poorly of me? And what does that say about me?

I race to figure out where this is coming from. "Is this about what you were saying when you were here . . . about you and Brandon?"

"About how we were going to have sex! About how I was going to make one of the biggest decisions of my life! I wasn't sure if you even heard me, with how quickly you changed the subject. And here I was hoping that my best friend would pay attention to me for once, for something so freaking huge! But no, you went to sleep, and then we just pretend like it never happened . . . until you need me again."

There's a fierceness, an edge, in her voice that I don't recognize. Or I do recognize, but never when she's talking to me, only when we're talking about other people. People we don't like.

"I'm really sorry if I wasn't the best listener. I mean, I *know* I wasn't the best listener then. I just didn't know what to say."

"But that wasn't the first time, Tessa. It's just the time that hurt me the most. And listen, I put up with how self-absorbed you can be, because I love you. But I just . . . I just need a little break, I think. Because I want to keep loving you."

I can feel tears on my cheeks even though I don't recall starting to cry. I just feel so defeated. That I've screwed up so badly and been clueless about the whole thing. That I've made my best friend in the whole world feel so frustrated and unheard because of how self-absorbed I've been.

Did I do the same to Sam?

"I'm really sorry, Caroline," I repeat. But it rings hollow. It's not enough.

"I'm sorry too . . . for what happened to you today. And I'm sorry I can't be more there for you. Right now."

"No, no. You don't have to—"

"For what it's worth, you were happy when I saw you with Sam, and now you're not. I think if you're honest with yourself, you can figure out the right next steps."

"Thank you." It's all I can say. Even with that, she's giving me more than I deserve.

"Okay, I'm going to go now . . . but it's not forever. I just need some time, Tessa."

When we hang up, I want to call her back immediately, beg for her forgiveness, ask her all the questions about Brandon I should have been asking all along, and make up for all the ways I've been a terrible friend to her. But I know it won't be that easy. And even more than the desire to call her, I just want to curl up in my bed and hide under the covers from the mess I've made.

I feel like I've been shattered into a million pieces.

I need someone to pick me up, to help me gather the shards. But there's no one, and it isn't anyone's fault but mine.

This time, I'll have to do it myself.

CHAPTER THIRTY-EIGHT

Mom lets me stay home Tuesday, no questions asked, but by Wednesday she's suspicious.

"Do you think you have the flu?" she asks, sitting on the edge of my bed. She feels my forehead for what feels like the millionth time. "You don't have a fever. How are you feeling today?"

"I don't know," I grunt, pulling the blanket over my head and rolling away from her.

"Some fresh air might help. You haven't been out of here in days. . . ."

"I'm not leaving my room." I can't see her face, but that seems to do the trick, her weight lifting off the bed. I hear the front door open and close.

Some time later, though, there are footsteps in my room, and before I have a chance to be scared, the blankets whip off my head, and Mom is standing over me with a determined look on her face.

"I think we need a mental health day."

Our first mental health day was in sixth grade, after I had to give an oral presentation on Egypt and sneezed in the middle of it, getting slimy green snot all over my face and hands. I was rightfully mortified, and Mom let me stay home from school the next day, declaring it a mental health day—our own personal take-as-you-need Johnson girl holiday.

We ate giant pretzels in the food court of the Westfield Galleria, and when I couldn't decide between three dresses at Forever 21, she bought me all of them, capping the day off with a celebratory car dance to her favorite song, "As" by Stevie Wonder, in the parking lot. And when I say car dance, I mean she actually made the car dance, by jerkily pressing the brakes and annoying all the cars stuck behind us. That mental health day was followed by many more: staying in our pajamas all day and eating bowls full of Cheez-Its and M&M's and watching all four Twilight movies after Daniel texted me to say he had a new girlfriend. Two days in a row when I got my braces in middle school, claiming it was for the pain when we both really knew I was so anxious about people seeing them or getting food stuck in them that my neck was covered in hives.

There were so many good memories, but sometimes they get overshadowed by the not so good. And they slowed down over the years as she started working full-time, when a day off, unless it was for one of Miles's important appointments, became impossible. I wonder how she can afford to miss today with her new job.

"What do you say?" she asks, her blue eyes big with hope.

"Okay."

Mom lays out clothes for me on my bed like I'm a toddler and then instructs me to brush my teeth, take off my satin cap, and be ready in twenty minutes. It's easy to do what she says.

We walk to a little coffee shop in the neighborhood, and Mom leads me to a table outside under a black-and-white umbrella and then goes in to order. A few minutes later, she comes out with two steaming mugs of rose-milk tea, dried petals decorating the frothy surface, and a giant cinnamon roll with two forks. The rose and the pastry feel like signs from the universe, and they make my chest feel heavy.

"So, are you nervous about reading at the gala?" Mom asks, sipping her tea. When I don't immediately answer, she keeps probing delicately. "It's coming up soon. And that would be totally understandable. It's a lot for anyone. I just want you to remember that me and Dad and Miles are so proud of you."

Something inside me breaks with that—maybe it's because I don't deserve that pride, maybe it's because I've already disappointed two people and I want to shoot for that third strike. But before I know it, I'm sobbing—swollen eyes, snotty face sobbing—and Mom scoots closer to scoop me into a tight hug.

"Oh, Tessa baby, what is it?"

And so I tell her. How I started to tell her the truth that

day but then got scared and lied about the gala. How I was definitely not selected and actually had no chance in the world of being selected because I really haven't written a word since I started attending Chrysalis. How all I do is sit in my classes and pretend to write and just waste everyone's time because the words stopped coming and I'm so worried they'll never come again. How I've been so worried about disappointing her and Dad . . . and most of all, how I've disappointed myself.

When I'm finished, I peer up at her through my blurry eyes, and I'm expecting to see horror on her face. Or disgust. At least the dreaded disappointment. But to my surprise, there's none of that.

Her face is warm and open. She hugs me tighter.

"You need to cut yourself some slack, because you're learning," she says, her voice calm and steady. "And part of learning is making mistakes. Sometimes really big ones."

"You're not mad?" I ask.

Her eyebrows press together, and I get a hint of the anger that I deserve. "Of course I'm mad! Do you know how expensive those tickets were?" Her face softens again. "But I also love you. And I understand. I'm worried less about the gala than about you not writing."

"I don't know how to explain it other than I just felt . . . paralyzed. I was scared to write anything because it's not what they want. It's not good enough. I felt—*I still feel*—like I don't deserve to be there. That the admissions people made a terrible

337

mistake by letting me in, and any moment they're going to realize it and kick me out. I mean, that's probably already in motion, if Ms. McKinney has anything to do with it."

It feels so good to get it all out, like I'm purging my body of something toxic. And I guess I am—of all the bad feelings and lies. I stop short of telling her about Caroline's plan because I know how stupid it will sound, and it didn't even work anyway. I had Sam, I lost Sam (and maybe Caroline), and it didn't affect my writing either way.

"Oh, my girl, you've been carrying such a heavy load," she says, stroking my hair. "I'm so sorry I wasn't paying attention enough to help relieve some of that."

"Mom, that wasn't your job."

"Well, of course it's my job!" she shouts, letting out something that sounds like a cross between a cry and a laugh. "You know, you've been like this since you were small, always hesitant to join in with other kids, watching and observing before taking any action. And I know part of it was you looking different from the other kids—which I know I can't even begin to understand. Dad and I were never sure what would be the best environment for you two, but I know it probably wasn't Roseville. I'm so sorry for that."

She pulls back to look at me. Her face is a teary, booger-y mess just like my own. We look so different, and yet so much alike.

"And I understand your anxiety. So, so much. You probably get it from me." She takes a deep breath. "I've actually started going to therapy, you know, during my lunch breaks on Fridays. And, well . . . I know you've been hesitant in the past, but I really think it might do you some good. Therapy, I mean. It's helped me."

"Hesitant" is putting it very lightly. Outright refused is more accurate. It's come up many times over the years, when she's noticed me getting myself "into a tizzy," or letting my worries take control. But I've shot down Mom's suggestion that I try therapy each time.

Because, like I tell her now, "I didn't want to be a problem for you and Dad. Not that Miles is a problem. Just . . . I didn't want to be responsible for another appointment you had to keep track of when I could manage it on my own all right. But then . . . I guess I haven't been doing that too well, have I?"

"I'm sorry," she says, a new round of tears falling. "I'm so sorry. For whatever we've done to make you feel that way. Your dad and I have done our best, but . . . I know it's never been perfect."

I can almost physically feel her attempting to lift this off my shoulders onto her own, as I constantly see her doing for Miles—for our whole family, really. And it feels good, to let go of that burden, to place it on someone else. But I also know that I created this mess for myself, and this is no one's problem other than my own.

"You don't have to apologize for anything, Mom, really. I wish you'd stop that. I'm the one who lied to you."

She waves that away. "My point is, I should have noticed

what was going on. I should have been here for you more. I feel so sad that I wasn't."

We hug each other tightly. A hipster couple in matching plaid walks by and gives us strange looks, but I don't even care. I feel just right being here with my mom, whatever we may look like.

"Still . . . ," I finally venture, after we catch our breath and wipe our faces. "I can't get over the fact that maybe my anxiety was right in this case. Maybe I don't deserve to be at Chrysalis. My writing . . . when I was writing, at least . . . it's not the kind of thing that wins awards or gets read at galas."

"But does it make you happy?" she asks.

"Well, yeah. When I did it. But what does that matter?"

"Tessa, why wouldn't it matter? It's the only thing that does matter. Listen, I'm no expert. I'm just your mom. But I think there's something to be said for making art just to make you happy. Not to win awards or impress others or get the attention of your parents who can be a little clueless at times. But art for art's sake. Art for yourself."

I find myself nodding along. Creating something for no one other than myself. That's the way it used to be, when I first started writing down stories for just my eyes. When did I lose that?

"And let me tell you something I am an expert in," Mom continues.

"What's that?"

"You. I'm your biggest fan. I have been, ever since they

pulled you out of me and called you mine." She mimes this, and I can't help but roll my eyes.

"Ew, Mom, gross!"

She playfully swats me away. "And I know that you are a writer. You've always been, ever since you first learned how to spell and put words together . . . or even before that! You used to fill up notebooks with scribbles and spend hours 'reading' them to Miles. You've always been a storyteller, and this is not the end. It's just a blip in your career."

I fight the urge to roll my eyes at that too. "My career?"

"Yes, this is just the beginning. Because you were made to do this. You deserve to be there just as much as every last person at Chrysalis. You deserve that seat at the table, Tessa."

She strokes my hair back and kisses my cheek, something she hasn't done since I was really small. Any other day I would wipe it off and push her off me, but I'm relishing this closeness with her. It's a comfort I didn't know I was craving. But now that it's here, it fits into my heart like a missing puzzle piece. She knows me, and she loves me anyway. Or she loves me *because* she knows me. What would happen if I saw myself the way she sees me?

We finish our tea and cinnamon roll and end up ordering three cookies and a guava-and-cheese danish from the pastry case. That's another thing Mom and I have in common—our love of carbs. We talk about Sam and Caroline and how I'm not talking to either right now. I even tell her about my stories being spread around the school and how I'm embarrassed to look anyone in the eye after that.

"But did you die?" she asks, stacking the empty plates in front of us.

I giggle at first, but then I realize she's serious. "No?"

"That's right, you made it through. And now that you've faced the worst, nothing can touch you. You're free, my girl!" She points at me, accentuating each syllable. "And you can take that freedom and do whatever the fuck you want with it now."

"Mom!" I can't help but laugh.

"I can say whatever I want," she says, throwing her hands out. "Just like you can do whatever you want. And I can't wait to cheer you on—whatever you decide to do."

There's peace in knowing that she believes in me. That she'll support my next steps, and that she sees me as a writer, even though I've lost my vision for that part of my identity myself.

There's peace in the realization that she's right: my worst nightmares have happened, but I'm still here. I've survived. And I know if it happened again, I would still survive.

But even with all of that, what will I choose?

There's no guidebook, no eleven-step plan. No best friend or boyfriends leading the way. Just freedom to make the choices I want. I only need to figure out first what I want those choices to be.

CHAPTER THIRTY-NINE

I made my choice. Or I guess in the end, it was kinda made for me, because Sam is avoiding my texts and calls like he'd avoid a gluten-free, dairy-free chocolate chip cookie, and Nico has been relentless in his declarations that he wants to be with me.

We walk into the winter gala together, hand in hand. I can't help but search the room to see if I can find Sam.

The thing is, real life is not a romance novel. It's not always logical. It's not always linear. So even though my mom helped me see things differently, it's not like everything just fell into place perfectly. Sometimes the heroine (who is, I guess, me) doesn't run into the sunset with the man of her dreams.

Being with Nico feels more like the absence of making choices. Just going with the flow, which is all I want to do after screwing up so badly before. And it all happened so quickly, which I suppose is how things go when you don't have a best friend to agonize over pro and con lists with you or talk you through what to wear on the first date. I try not to think about what Caroline would think of this, because she probably wouldn't approve, and that doesn't make me feel great.

But *no*, I'm not going there. I made the decision myself, and I decided to let myself have what I always wanted. Even if I'm not completely sure it's what I want anymore, it's okay for now.

"Come here," Nico murmurs, wrapping his arms around my waist and pulling me into a dark corner of the crowded room. He kisses me on the cheek, clearly wanting something more, but I scan around us to make sure my family isn't anywhere nearby, because Dad would probably kill Nico, then kill me, and then kill Nico again. They decided to come to the gala anyway, even when they found out I wasn't presenting . . . because, like Mom said, "Then we'll know our way around when you're reading next year." I'm trying to believe her.

I turn back to Nico, and he's looking at me like he always does now—in a way that makes me want to check behind me and make sure Zoë Kravitz isn't standing there. It doesn't feel real, but it's nice enough.

Chrysalis's winter gala is held in a loft in downtown Long Beach. It's beautiful—brick walls and exposed industrial ceilings. There are twinkly lights everywhere, and they reflect off the huge windows that offer a panoramic view of the city—the Queen Mary, the aquarium, and the tall art deco buildings. I gasped when I saw it all, even as Mrs. Lucchese, the gala chair, walked around with her nose up, critiquing each petal in the all-white flower arrangements.

Nico was the first to read (probably also arranged by Mrs. Lucchese), and then he sat by my side while our fellow class-mates displayed their talents—a monologue from *The Importance of Being Earnest*, a black-and-white short film, three ballerinas dancing en pointe to Tchaikovsky, and a rendition of "And I Am Telling You I'm Not Going" that covered my whole body in goose bumps.

Afterward, we floated around the reception together, Nico's hand permanently on the small of my back as he led me between the galleries of students' sculptures, photographs, and paintings. At one point, I caught the eye of a girl from our Art of the Novel class, Angelica, looking at us like I used to look at him and Poppy. And I was overcome with a feeling that's become familiar over the past couple weeks—a rush that it's me he chose, me he wants.

Am I making the right choice? I don't want to think about it too much. And it's easy not to think when Nico is stroking my shoulders, like he is now, and planting light kisses on my neck.

"You'll be the star of the gala next year," Nico whispers in my ear, his arms tight around my waist. His breath feels too warm, his hold almost oppressive. But I shake away those feel-ings and remind myself, *This is what you wanted.*

"You think so?"

"I know so, Tessa."

He doesn't know, of course, that I still haven't written yet. I guess I have inspiration now . . . or something. But the words are still locked away behind big, heavy doors, impossible for me to reach.

We hear his name called and both look up to see his mom standing across the room, nodding her head in the direction of two important-looking men in tuxedos next to her.

"Ugh, sorry. Those are the admissions directors for the creative writing program at UC Irvine. She thinks because Michael Chabon went there for grad school, it should be in my top picks, but I'm not convinced." He rolls his eyes like it's some nuisance. I try to imagine being him, the possibilities so endless I can afford to take them so lightly. "Excuse me for a sec?" he asks, kissing my cheek.

"Yeah, sure."

Instead of waiting here alone, I decide to go check out Theodore's gallery again. It was the first place I went when I got here earlier, but he wasn't there. Still, I almost cried seeing the full scale of his creations. Giant color versions of all the sketches I'd seen him laboring over this year. A girl in a dress of flowers, long locs made out of blooms, and the star of the gallery: Lavon in a simple white tank top, with a crown of peonies on his head, each of his features so perfectly realized that I had to fight back the urge to reach out and touch the piece.

"Theodore." And the tears definitely come now, as I see him standing there in the middle of his art with a navy floral suit and rosy cheeks. He's flanked by two people who must be his parents. The man has the same lanky build as Theodore, and the woman is beaming proudly like only a mother could.

He says something to them in Khmer and then makes his way over to me.

"Oh, don't you dare," he says. "You know I'm not fond of excessive displays of emotion." Despite his words, there's an air of uncertainty about him that seems so foreign coming from the almost obnoxiously confident guy I know.

"It's just . . . ," I croak out, trying to suck my tears back in. "You did it."

"Of course I did it. I've always been doing it. Consistently. It's just that now other people are taking notice." He shrugs. "But I guess it does feel quite good."

We look around at all of the people crowded into his gallery, and one of these people catches my eye, in a tight hot-pink gown, and—my heart stops—gray hair. Of course Poppy chooses that moment to turn around and look me straight in the eye. She's walking in our direction before my brain catches up and I can run away.

"Theodore," she says when she reaches us. "This is so impressive. Really. Congratulations."

"Thank you," he says simply. Much more precise and to the point than all the rants I've heard about Poppy this semester.

"I don't know why you haven't gotten an exhibit before," she continues. "You've always been the most talented in our class. I've been so jealous of you since freshman year."

She turns to me before Theodore can respond—his mouth practically hanging open.

"Tessa, uh, can we talk?"

After what she did, I know I should say no. I know I should find the closest drink and throw it in her face like a Real Housewife. I know she most likely hates me and this might be the beginning of her next public act of revenge. But also . . . I'm curious.

"Sure."

I let her lead me to a quiet corner of the room.

"So . . . uh, you and Nico," she says finally. "That's what you've wanted this whole year, right?"

I just shrug. What am I supposed to say to that? I don't have the energy to lie.

She arches an eyebrow. "I bet you see me as the villain in your story."

"Poppy . . ."

"Whatever, I get it," she says, waving her hand to the side. "I know what I did wasn't great . . . even if you sort of deserved it. But also, it wasn't all on you." She's looking around the room, at the floor—everywhere but at me. "Anyway, let's just say I've been where you are, so . . . be careful, okay? His attention span doesn't last long. I know that more than anyone." She pauses and looks at me. "Maybe you—and I—deserve better than that."

With that, she reaches forward and squeezes my shoulder, and then she disappears back into the party, leaving me standing there alone. As if summoned by his name, though, Nico is back at my side.

"What was that? What did she say to you?"

I consider telling him, but how would that go? I'm still processing that conversation myself.

"Nothing," I say. And that seems to be enough for Nico, who lets his fingers find their way to my lower back again and puts his lips on mine. I don't need to think. I don't need to worry. I let myself get lost again.

And I would probably be lost for another twenty minutes, but someone coughs next to us, making me spring away. I'm expecting the stern face of Dad, but luckily it's just Lenore.

She's wearing a lavender wide-legged pantsuit with a knee-length faux fur coat and glittery gold pumps. Her locs are pulled into an impressive bun on the top of her head, tall and intricate like a birdcage. She wasn't chosen to present at the gala, but she's presenting her look anyway.

"Oh my god, girl, how do you look so good?" I mime taking a picture of her with my hands, and she expertly motions into poses before pulling me into a hug.

"I'm surprised you can see me at all, seeing as how you're otherwise occupied," she says, giving me and Nico the side-eye.

"I mean, can you blame me?" Nico says, holding his hands out to me.

"Yes, she's a catch, and you better not ever forget that," Lenore says, going all hard for a second and needling a finger in his chest. But then her face switches back into a bright smile, and she holds up a plate full of sweets. "Have you tried this shit yet? Sam is a straight-up wizard of sugar!"

On the plate there are round, buttery cream puffs; mini

pies (that look a whole lot like sweet potato); layers of chocolate ganache, cake, and cream in a shiny flute; a cupcake piled high with frosting; and light pink macarons.

The sight of all Sam's creations makes my throat catch. It's unexpected—the tight, sharp feeling, so different from the way I normally feel when I see any kind of treat. When Lenore passes the plate under my nose again, doing a silly fake-seductive dance, I wave her away.

"Are you sure?" she asks, confused.

"Yeah, I'm surprised," Nico laughs. "You never turn down dessert!"

Lenore arches her eyebrow at him, and he adds quickly, "Not that that's a bad thing!" He puts his arm around my waist again and kisses my cheek. "Poppy treated sugar and carbs like they were Voldemort or something. Dessert which must not be named. I like that you don't care."

I sigh and try to smile. He does that a lot, I realize, comparing me and Poppy, almost like he's trying to justify this to himself. But it's still early, I tell myself, and he'll get over it soon enough. Lenore looks between us, her face so open that I can almost read her mind. But I push those vibes away.

"Oh-kay, well, I'll leave you two lovebirds to it!" she says, hugging me again. "And girl, you have to at least try this thing. It tastes like a flower, but, like, without making my mouth feel like it's full of Grandma Lenore's perfume? Fucking hea-ven-ly!"

She shoves a macaron wrapped in a napkin into the hand

Nico isn't holding as she walks away. It's baked just right, so it has little feet (Sam taught me about that), metallic gold brushed across the shiny blush surface, and perfectly piped white butter-cream in the center. It's a tiny work of art.

"Miles! My man!" I hear Lenore exclaim from across the room, and when I look up, she's squeezing my brother into a big hug. Mom catches my eye, waving excitedly, and when they're done greeting Lenore, my family makes their way over to me.

Here goes nothing.

Dad holds himself stiffly in his gray suit as he walks over, clearly putting on airs to start psyching out Nico. It's equal parts hilarious and nerve-racking. And Mom looks beautiful in her teal sheath dress. It's nothing like Mrs. Lucchese's floor-length sequined midnight-blue number—I know my mom got it for fifty percent off at Kohl's. But her smile beams off her like a bright, illuminated orb. I run up to her and give her a hug.

And there's no way around this. "You guys, this is Nico," I say, holding my hands out. "And Nico, this is my family."

"Nico, so nice to finally meet you!" Mom exclaims, over-compensating for Dad's curt nod.

"Yes, hello, Mr. and Mrs. Johnson." Nico reaches out to shake their hands. Luckily my dad takes his and even gives him a small smile, patting him on the back.

"And hi, Miles." Nico's voice changes dramatically, going all high and slow when he waves at Miles. I hate it.

"You're Tessa's boyfriend!" Miles calls. "Do you guys K-I-S-S?"

I laugh it off, mostly to diminish the effect of his comment on my dad, who may still be in the danger zone of murdering Nico. But when I glance at Nico, he suddenly looks different than I've ever seen him. His body is tense, and his eyes are shifty, going back and forth between Miles and the groups of people surrounding us.

I follow his gaze to Miles and try to see what he sees. Miles is excited about his joke, so his arms are pulsing back, tight in the suit Mom went out to Men's Wearhouse to buy him. His head is twisting around in circles, making his hearing aids ring. And there's a big smile on his face. I can feel my face stretching into a matching one. When I look at Miles, I just see his pure, infectious joy, but it clearly bothers Nico. He's not standing as close to me as he was before.

"Nico, that was a wonderful piece you read," Mom says. "You're a very talented writer. Don't you think so, James?" She nudges my dad, who nods in agreement. I don't know if she's picking up on the weirdness like I am, but regardless, she's trying to make this conversation easier.

"Thank you, Mrs. Johnson," Nico says, but he barely looks at her. His eyes are still shifting around the room, and he takes a step back like he's looking for an escape route.

"Have you been writing for a while?" she asks, smiling at him.

"Yeah," he says. Just one word. Cold and quick. Where's the charm he's always trotting out for everyone else? Does he not think they're deserving of it?

My stomach feels sick.

"Well, anyway, we'll leave you two alone. I know you probably don't want to hang out with your parents!" There's nothing sharp in the way she says it, no guilt or judgment. But I still feel shame creeping over me like a cold breeze. Shame at the way that Nico is acting . . . and the fact that I'm with him. That he is the one I chose.

What am I doing?

"Yeah, well, nice to meet you all," Nico says, and I hug each of them and we say our goodbyes. Mom makes some half-hearted comments about wanting to see an embroidery exhibit, as if that's the reason they're leaving in a hurry. It's so awkward I want to scream. Because I know, and I think they must know, what's going on.

Nico is embarrassed. He doesn't want to be seen with my family. Miles, being his happy, normal self. My mom, going out of her way to be kind. My dad, just being my dad. And I can't help but wonder . . . maybe those feelings even extend to me? It's not like he called me over to talk with his mom and the admissions people from UCI, even though I'm a writer too.

Now that my family is gone, Nico looks visibly relieved. "Your family is nice," he says, but the way he says it, it sounds like the four-letter word it is.

This is wrong. The realization snaps into place, finally clear, like a pair of glasses being put over my face. *I got this completely and totally wrong.*

It's crazy how quickly things can shift.

"Why did you act like that?" I ask.

He feigns confusion. "Like what? I was polite."

"You were looking around and, like, checking who was watching. Weren't you?" I ask the question, but I already know the answer.

"I mean . . . yeah?" I'm shocked, but at least he doesn't deny it. "But is that so wrong? Your brother was all—"

He imitates Miles's jerky movements, and a rage surges through me, hot and blinding.

"You grew up with him, so I guess you're okay with that," he continues. "But it's just . . . a lot." His lip curls as he says those last two words.

There it is. I can't ignore it like before.

"Oh, I'm so sorry that my brother's disabilities are *a lot* for you!" My voice rises as I step back from him. "I really should have thought about the inconvenience his disabilities would cause you!"

"Tessa, you're taking this the wrong way," he says, speaking lower in an effort to get me to temper my volume.

"I'm really not. I see exactly what's going on. And exactly who you are." I shake my head as all the red flags I've been letting myself explain away flood in. "All of the dog-whistle crap that you just let slide with your friends. What kinds of things do you all say when I'm not there, huh? And you strung me along for so long, keeping me on the back burner just in case things with Poppy got, what, boring? And I let you! I let you!" I feel so much shame realizing all that I turned the other cheek to, just so I could have the perfect story I thought I wanted. "Plus you act like you know what kind of writer I am, but have you ever even asked me about it? Like, do you even know what kind of stories I write? And now this, with my family . . . fuck, I've been so stupid!"

People are turning, but it doesn't make me want to shrink. I don't feel that familiar urge to quiet down. I feel powerful. I like it. "Nico, this isn't going to work out between us."

Now he looks shocked. "What are you talking about? Tessa, you need to calm down."

"I actually don't." I laugh, filled with conviction. "You . . . you are *not* who I want to be with."

He looks around again, self-conscious, and for a second it's like a curtain has been pulled back, and I can see that he's not so special. He's just as worried and aware of what other people think as I am—as I used to be. Maybe even more so.

Is that what I was like with Sam? Did I look this shallow, this simple?

But then, just as quickly, the curtain comes back down, and Nico has his shield of confidence, that swagger that made me swoon before.

"Yeah, all right, Tessa," he scoffs. "If that's what you want to do."

"It really is."

I turn and walk away.

Unbothered by the stares we're getting from the people in fancy dresses and tuxedos around us. Not worried about

Angelica from our Art of the Novel class, who's gawking and shaking her head now, like I'm some fool.

I know that in the past I've cared too much about what others think of me, and of my writing. And maybe we all care about those things.

But what I know now is that I'm done taking up less space than I deserve. I'm done staying quiet just so I can be someone others might like. I want to like—no, *love*—myself.

Like I love Caroline, Lenore, and Theodore. Like I love my parents and Miles.

And Sam.

I love Sam too, I realize. *I LOVE SAM TOO.*

Sam, who has been accepting of me since the very first time I met him. Sam, who never made me feel like I wasn't good enough, like I needed to change.

So why didn't I do the same for him?

CHAPTER FORTY

I want to storm out of the whole gala, make that big dramatic exit, but instead I need to think of logistics, like how I'm going to get a ride home without Nico. I have to find my family.

Luckily, that's not difficult. Miles's tinkling-keys, car-crash laugh carries across the wide room, and I follow it until I find him standing near the entrance to the kitchen. Right next to Sam.

Sam looks handsome in a white chef's coat over slim black pants. His face is lit up, laughing over something my brother is telling him, but it shifts as soon as he sees me. I expect my newfound realization of love to be written all over my face, but his guarded expression reminds me that things are still the same between us.

"Tessie!" Miles calls when I walk over. I can't help but pull him into a tight hug. He is exactly right just the way he is, no matter what anyone thinks, and he is mine.

"I love you, Miles."

"I love you too," he says, and then he gives a sly smile, signaling that he's gearing up for some sort of snark. "You know I'm not your boyfriend, right?"

"Oh, be quiet!" I snort, and he smiles wider, satisfied. I grab him tight around the shoulders, giving him a noogie, and his giggles bounce around the room. I don't care who looks.

"Are you going to eat that?" Sam's voice cuts through our fun. When I look at him, confused, he just motions to the macaron, which I didn't realize was still in my hand from earlier, a little crushed in the napkin now.

I give Miles one last squeeze, and then I take a big bite of it, the crackly shell melting into the gooey insides. It's just as perfect as it looks. And it tastes like rose. My mind starts to spiral, wondering if that means something.

"You've really . . . this is just amazing, Sam. All of it."

"Did you see the dessert table, Tessie? He said he put cookies-and-cream donuts on it just for me!" Miles is practically vibrating, he's so excited (and probably hopped up on the sugar he's already had). I follow his pointing fingers to a three-yard-long table, covered in tiered cakes of various heights, a chocolate fountain, and countless trays of sugary creations. It's the most popular spot in the gala, more crowded than any gallery set up in the room.

"I'm getting some right now! Bye!" Miles moves over there at a speed I've never witnessed from him. I'm about to chase after him, but then I see my parents waving from the crowd. Mom winks at me.

I turn to Sam, and he's already turning to go back to the kitchen. I need to say something to keep him here. I need to somehow repair what I've broken.

"So . . ."

I didn't say it had to be genius.

"So, where's Nico?" he asks, his voice full of scorn.

"Not here."

"You two look good together."

"Well, we're not together anymore."

"Sure didn't look like that."

I sigh. This isn't going to be easy. And it shouldn't be—I don't deserve that. But right now I would give anything for the closeness we used to have. Maybe it just starts with being honest.

"How about a congratulations? Can we talk about that? Because what you've created tonight is really impressive, Sam. I mean, I'm not surprised. I always knew the greatness you were capable of. But I'm glad everyone else can see it now too."

He rubs the side of his face. "I don't know . . . I guess it's going okay."

"Hey, stop talking shit about my friend!" I say, and that makes him crack a smile. "Look at all these people. Look how *happy* everyone is. And it's all because of your creations— your art that you're sharing with them." I point to Miles, who is bouncing and giving a thumbs-up from across the room, crumbs all over his suit. "I mean, if that's not an honest review . . ."

"Thanks, Tessa." His voice has softened a bit now. "It's been . . . well, it's been a hard week, getting ready for this. Food prep, and I don't know. Mentally."

"Yeah?"

"I kept getting struck with this panic, this fear, you know? And I'd think I was forgetting something, so I'd check my prep list, and everything would be right on track. But the feeling wouldn't go away. I finally realized it was just all the pressure of tonight getting to me . . . proving the people right who only think I was chosen because of my mom, *disappointing* my mom, having people laugh at me. Now that it's here and almost done . . . I finally feel like I can breathe."

He looks up at me with a start, just as surprised as I am that he's shared this much with me.

"I thought you were never nervous," I say. "Not about your food, at least."

That makes him laugh. "Of course I am! I'm fucking terri-fied. I'd be crazy not to be, doing all this." He waves around the room. "But I have to push past the fear. I'll never know unless I put myself out there."

. . . and you won't either. It's unspoken, but his heavy look says it all.

"You say it as if it's easy."

"It's not," he says. "But it's necessary."

Sam is so unapologetically himself. Someone who knows his worth—even when it came to me.

"Excuse me, can I have your attention please?" Dr. Hoffman, the principal of Chrysalis, is standing on the stage at the front of the room. I recognize his face from the website and pamphlets I pored over before starting the school. "Hey, is this thing on?" A polite chuckle comes from some of the adults, and then a silence falls over the room. I don't know what, but something important is about to happen.

"Every year at our winter gala, we review the unique and impressive accomplishments of our featured artists and choose one student to receive our Metamorphosis award. The Metamorphosis award is given to a student who demonstrates talent, innovation, and a remarkable commitment to their art. They are the butterfly coming out of the chrysalis, so to speak." He chuckles again at his cheesiness before continuing. "And as you can probably gather from what you've seen tonight, it's an extremely tough decision."

People applaud, but next to me, Sam stiffens. I can feel the nervous energy pulsing off him.

"All right, well, without further ado"—Dr. Hoffman's voice booms from the stage—"the recipient of this year's Metamorphosis award has been a pioneer in Chrysalis Academy's brand-new Culinary Arts conservatory. He has demonstrated through both his hard work and his beautiful, and really quite tasty, works of art that he is on his way to becoming a leader in the field. Ladies and gentleman, please congratulate with me our Metamorphosis award winner, Sam Weiner!"

Sam's mouth drops open, and I scream and pull him into a tight hug. It feels good, familiar, but I come back to myself and jump back, self-conscious.

Sam smiles at me, a real smile with his dimple showing, and then he begins to make his way through the crowd. People pat his back and shake his hand. Lenore grabs his hand and twirls him around, and then passes him to Theodore, who dips him right in front of the stage.

As he climbs the stairs, I think, *He deserves this*. Putting his heart and joy on a plate for others, being his authentic self, taking the risk that so many of us are afraid to—pushing past the fear that I let paralyze me and force me into letting go of something I love so much.

And that is the greatest risk, presenting something that you love and asking others to love it too.

But I can see—looking at Sam's beaming face, his mom with tears pouring down her cheeks in the audience—that the risk is worth the reward. And maybe now I'm finally ready to take that risk too.

CHAPTER FORTY-ONE

When I get home, I pull my computer out from under my bed, open up Google Docs, and write.

It's like my body is taken over by an outside force. I don't even realize what I'm doing until I'm on the sixth page and a story is forming like magic. Names and places, sentences and paragraphs, relationships and conflict and the connecting thread of love.

I write like I used to, not worrying about what other people think. Not worrying about what it all means, just what it means to me.

I write until my hands cramp up and my back aches. I keep going.

I write through my mom's insistence that I come out for breakfast, then lunch, then dinner. I write until she finally brings me a tray of grapes and pretzels and cubes of cheese—things I can eat one-handed, the other hand consumed with the tap-tap-tapping of words. She smiles and kisses my head, leaving me to it.

The anxiety comes in waves, and I don't ignore it. I acknowledge it, examine it, and then let it go. I don't let it stop me.

Writing again feels like reuniting with an old friend. Except no—that's not right. Because it's a part of me, it always has been, even through these lost months. It's more like reattaching a limb. Or my hair growing back after the Big Chop, different but wholly mine.

I almost lost sight of what the whole purpose of the happily ever after plan was. Not just finding the happily ever after of love, but finding my words. Seeking out my voice again. And it's easy now, because it's loud—screaming. Not the hushed whisper it was before, but booming, all caps, thunderous and self-assured.

And when Sunday night comes and I have pages that I'm proud of—maybe not perfect, but perfect to me—I finally share my words again, attached to a long email that ends with "I love you, I miss you, I'm sorry."

CHAPTER FORTY-TWO

I was worried she wouldn't even open the attachment, but my phone rings in less than an hour, her smiling photo flashing on the screen.

"This is amazing," Caroline says. Her voice sounds happy. Normal. I'm surprised but grateful. "Better than anything you've ever written. And I didn't think that was possible!"

I love it, and that's what matters. But it feels good to have her approval too.

"I was so bummed it wasn't finished! You know I'm going to start bugging you for chapters again, right?"

"I don't know how it will end yet."

A heavy silence creeps between us, full of all the feelings we haven't talked about yet, the moments we haven't shared from these past few weeks. It would be easy, maybe, to slip into the way we used to be, but it would be just hiding the larger problem. Like when you try to cover up major BO with a few more heavy-handed swipes of deodorant, but it doesn't really fix the problem—what you need is a shower. And that may not be the prettiest simile, but it's real.

"I meant everything I wrote. I'm so sorry."

She doesn't miss a beat, like she was waiting for the chance. "I am too. I was really short with you on the phone."

"But I deserved it. I was so focused on myself that I was a bad friend to you . . . when you had so much going on."

"You were. And I do."

I thought it would hurt to admit what I did wrong, but it feels cleansing, freeing. The tension between us is melting away. "I was just scared that you were moving so far past me. I wanted to hurry up and catch up to you, so I wouldn't get left behind. But in doing that, I was making myself the center of everything and pushing you out. I was a terrible friend."

"Oh, Tessa! I will never leave you behind. Even if we're going through different things in our lives, we will always be side by side." Her voice switches to its familiar playful tone. "And now that you're writing again, not gonna lie: I'm gonna need a new story with me in it—or Colette, I mean. Can you write up a love interest who looks like Brandon?"

"Of course!" The ideas are already brewing, and even though my hands are sore, they're twitching to start typing again. But I need to be honest with her about one more thing. "You know, that's one of the things that scared me the most about not writing," I say meekly. "That it could lead to losing you . . . because I know that's, like, the big reason why you still like me . . . now that I'm not there."

"Are you kidding me?" she shrieks, so loud I'm surprised her parents don't come to check on her. "I like you because of way more things than just your stories! I like that I can say anything to you because you won't judge or think it's shallow. I like that you're skinnier than me, so Lola can be distracted with fattening someone else up." She giggles. "And for real, for real, I like your heart. How you have this delicate baby one that registers every last change of mood and tone, tears apart every comment that someone makes. How you just . . . *feel* everything so much and so fully. I like your stories, of course! But that's because I like seeing the world through your eyes, where it's possible for everyone to have a happy ending."

I laugh. I can't help it.

"You're laughing because you realize how silly you were, right? Because obviously I like you. Love you! You're my best friend, Tessa, and some stupid distance and a boyfriend isn't going to change that."

The words make my whole body hum. I shake my head, even though she can't see me. "I'm laughing because that sounded like one of those declaration-of-love speeches at the end of a romance novel. You know, when the hot guy shows up to, like, a church or the airport, or whatever, and lists all the reasons why he's in love with the girl?"

"Hah! Well, I love the way you always order sauce on the

side, and then end up using all of it anyway."

I join in. "I love how you always sigh at the end of *The Notebook* and say, 'Well isn't that nice,' even though they freakin' die!"

"I love how you started wearing knee socks after watching *To All the Boys I've Loved Before* but still refused to admit you'd become a Lara Jean stan."

"I love how instead of blowing your nose, you wrap the tissue around your finger, like some kind of booger glove."

"I love how you always fart after you eat ice cream but think no one can hear you."

"I love that you told your dad it was Lola's copy of *Fifty Shades of Grey* when it was really yours."

"Shh! They might hear you!"

We explode into giggles, just like we always do. And I wish we were together right now, so I could wrap her up in a hug. How could I have doubted her, my best friend? I should have known all that she—all that both of us are capable of. I should have given her the chance to be fully herself instead of letting my own insecurities and jealousy take over.

We spend over an hour catching up on our weeks apart, the longest we've gone since she assaulted Jesse Fitzgerald for me in first grade. "I know the love story plan is over and everything," she finally says. "But at least you got your big happily ever after credits-rolling scene after all. Next time I'm down there to visit, I'll bring signs to the airport, do it up right."

"The love story plan isn't over." It's been floating around in my head all weekend, but saying it out loud, it's like I'm making it real for myself.

"What?" she yelps. "But you broke up with Nico. You're not still hung up on him. . . ."

"No, no. Definitely no. I hope, though, that my chance for a happily ever after isn't lost with the one who should have been at the center of my love story all along." I see his messy sandy hair. His deep dimple on his right cheek. His faded red Hawaiian shirt.

"Well, besides myself," I add quickly. "Because, I think . . . that accepting myself should have come before trying to find the perfect guy. It's no wonder it didn't work out with anyone. I needed to love myself first. And I do. I really do."

"That's right, girl! I'm pumping my fist in the air. I wish you could see it," Caroline shouts, as if she hadn't given me the advice that led me in all kinds of crazy ways this semester. But I took it. And in the end, maybe there isn't anything wrong with chasing after a happily ever after. As long as it's the happily ever after that's full and nuanced and really right for me.

"But . . . I don't get it. What does that mean you're going to do?"

"I'm going number eleven. Actually, this conversation was good practice."

"Is that the Ferris wheel?"

"No."

"Oh!"

★ ★ ★

On Monday morning, I pull my rainbow dress out of the back of my closet and pick out my hair as big as it will go. I'll stand out, and I want to. It doesn't scare me anymore.

I get to school early. Mom has been driving me to school since I stopped riding with Sam, and she rearranged her schedule so I could be dropped off one hour before the bell today. That's already cutting it close for how much work has to be done. I slip into the creative writing copy room and scan my pages, making more copies than I can count. And when I've used up all the paper I can find, I start to make my way around campus, taping page after page on classroom doors, lockers, throughout the stairwell. It's exhausting work. Poppy must have *really* hated me to do what she did. I think again about this whole story from her perspective . . . maybe I'll try writing that next.

When the stares come during passing periods, I'm ready. I welcome them. At lunch, I walk up to our normal spot on the porch of the Bungalow to find Theodore, Lavon, and Lenore waiting for me. They put their food down and start applauding. It takes everything in me not to cry.

"Now this is art, baby girl!" Lenore shouts, snapping her fingers and then pulling me into a tight hug.

And I don't deflect or laugh or explain away my achievement. I just say, "Thank you."

I get to Art of the Novel fifteen minutes early, armed with another stack of copies.

"Ms. McKinney?" I say, and she looks up at me and then looks around quickly, as if I might be talking to another Ms. McKinney.

"Yes?"

I hand her one of the packets I created, selected chapters of an unfinished novella, stapled and perfectly formatted, with one exception: my name is in bold at the top.

"I'm ready to read today. If that's okay . . . if it fits in the schedule. I know it's late in the semester, and it probably won't do much for my grade because, well, as you know . . . I haven't been submitting anything new. But I need to do this. For myself."

"I got a preview earlier," she says, and her face is hard to read. "I look forward to listening."

The class starts to fill in shortly after, and Ms. McKinney directs them all to sit down. We will be going straight into workshop. I thought it would help with the anxiety, jumping right in. But I still have to push down the fear that's burning in the back of my throat, the familiar scratchy feeling prickling on my chest and my neck.

I can do this. It will be hard. It will be scary. But I can do this.

As my packets are passed around the circle, I take one more opportunity to look around the room, scanning past the faces of the people who have intimidated me all semester in search of the one I hope to see. Nico is here, his face a mask of indifference, but he's not who I'm looking for.

This morning, I taped my final pages on the door to the culinary arts studio, accompanied by a note.

Dear Sam,
    This is for me, but it's also for you. Can you meet me in the Bungalow's basement for conservatory?
                            Love, Tessa

He's not here, I see, but I guess I already knew that. I would have felt it if he had entered the room, the tug of his energy on mine. His butter-and-sugar scent. I'm disappointed. I want him to be here, but I also know I will be okay in this moment if he's not. This is the big finale of two love stories that became intertwined, but when I separate them, really parse them out, the one for myself comes first. I can stand here on my own.

I take a deep breath, look down at my paper, and begin to read.

My body and voice feel huge, like I'm taking up all the space in the room. I imagine if I could see myself, I would look like Alice after she ate that cake in Wonderland, limbs sticking out of windows and chimneys. But it doesn't terrify me like it always has. For how little I've shared this year, I deserve all this space. I deserve the whole room.

I read my love story, what I've labored over all weekend. It's a story of an insecure girl and a dorky boy, though only one had something to overcome. Of dances of romance to Dream Zone, dairy-free ice cream, zip-off cargos, and Hawaiian shirts. Of a sparkly night high above everyone else, toes in the Pacific Ocean, and so many conversations over dessert in a warm car. Of fear and mistakes and risk. Of sugar and brown butter and flour.

It's fluffy and it has too many adjectives and it veers into the territory of purple prose, but it also makes Angelica swoon next to me. I can hear it in her sigh, feel it in the energy of her fidgety fingers.

I'm intoxicated with the magic of it all, being able to share my words with others. And I wouldn't have been able to experience this joy, this rush, without first taking the risk of sharing myself. Without saying, *Here. This is something I love, please love it too.*

I thought I needed a real-life love story of my own to start writing again. And I did find love with Sam—I know that now. But what I really needed, to find my words and my voice again, was to love myself. And I do.

I just have to trust that like I found my way back to myself, I'll get back to Sam too. And if I don't, well, I'll also be okay.

By the time I get to the last page, my voice is hoarse and my face is wet. I'm not sure when that happened. I should feel embarrassed, but instead I feel a tremendous release, like every cell in my body has been traded out for new ones. In this crowded basement, my voice and my words as the catalyst, I have been transformed.

I finally look up, ready—and shockingly—*excited* to take the criticism of the group. I can't wait to hear what they think, good or bad, because I know that whatever is said won't shake me down to nothing. I have a secure foundation holding me up now.

I scan the faces in the room one more time, but my eyes are drawn like magnets to the basement stairs. A flutter in my chest, a catch in my throat. I see him standing there.

ACKNOWLEDGMENTS

First to Danielle Parker: You are responsible for putting the ridiculous idea in my head that I could do this. Thank you for that spark and for your friendship.

Kristin Botello, your mentorship transformed me as a person. Thank you for always cheering me on, calling me out, and pushing me to be better. I'm sorry that I left, but I hope I've made you proud.

To all my former students: Kierra, Kayla, Kyla, Maaliyah, DJ, Jose, Terence, Jorge, Kevin, Edward, Misael, Israel, Miguel, Alexis, Melissa, Alex, Leslie, Andy, all the Anthonys, Bryan, Omar, Shadia, Victor, Hannalene, Tywayne, Eddie, and so many more. Thank you for showing me what it looks like to do hard things with grace, humor, and tenacity. You brought so much joy to my life as I wrote the first draft of this book (and the one before that), and I am so grateful for the little part I've played in your stories. I love you all.

Taylor Haggerty, thank you for believing in me so much that I had no choice but to believe in myself. Thank you for matching all my exclamation points and smiley faces in emails and for effortlessly calming all my worries. You are my superhero, and I'm so grateful for our partnership. Many thanks, also, to everyone at Root Literary, especially Melanie Castillo. Heather Baror-Shapiro and Debbie Deuble Hill, thank you for helping me to bring Tessa's story to an even wider audience.

Alessandra Balzer, thank you for your sharp eye, kind delivery, and patience (so much patience!) while I learned on the go. You sifted through all my overwritten drafts and shined up my book until it was something I could be proud of. Working with you is a dream that I hope I never wake up from.

Thank you to everyone at Balzer + Bray/HarperCollins, especially Caitlin Johnson, Valerie Wong, Ebony LaDelle, Jane Lee, Aubrey Churchward, Renée Cafiero, Alison Donalty, Andrea Pappenheimer, Kerry Moynagh, Kathy Faber, Patty Rosati, Mimi Rankin, Katie Dutton, and anyone else who helped this book along the way. Jessie Gang, thank you for the perfect cover design. Michelle D'Urbano, your cover art still makes me cry on a weekly basis and probably will forever. Thank you for getting it so right.

To the first ones to read this story: Sarah Lavelle, thank you for giving me the encouragement I needed to be brave and keep going at the very beginning. And Katherine Locke, thank you for your spot-on feedback and for your patience and support while I learned what to do with it.

Thank you to Ellen Rozek, Danielle Seybold, Kathrene Faith Binag, and others for reading so carefully and thoughtfully, and for challenging me to make each character the best they could be.

Susan Lee and Tracy Deonn, thank you for being my first writing friends, even before I dared to call myself a writer. Your support and advice along the way has been invaluable. Natalie Parker, Tessa Gratton, Zoraida Cordova, and Justina Ireland, thank you for building the wonderful community that is Madcap. My first retreat was the perfect environment to begin writing this story, and I hope I'll be lucky enough to attend many more. Leah Koch, thank you for reading my book and for writing a blurb that would have made teenage Elise pass out (thirty-something Elise got pretty close). And two of my writing heroes: Becky Albertalli and Brandy Colbert. The fact that you two even know who I am still blows my mind because I've cherished your words for so many years. Thank you for your kindness and for making me feel like I belong.

So much love and gratitude go to the women who have made it possible for me to do this, by filling in the gaps, supporting me and my family, and/or helping me feel well. Thank you to: Sonia Ramirez, Dr. Mireya Hernandez, Shannon Kennedy, Dr. Noreen Hussaini, Alexa King, and so many others.

Mom and Dad, you raised me to believe that I could do anything if I worked hard enough. Thank you for giving me the strong and secure foundation that made that possible, and for being such consistent examples of selflessness and persistence.

(Mom, you always said I would write a book, and just because I know you love to hear it: You were right. You're always right.) (Dad, I'm sorry about all the kissing.)

Bryan, being your sister is one of my greatest joys. You are my compass for what is right and what is funny. We are going to visit this book in Barnes & Noble together and I am going to cry and you're going to make fun of me and then wander over to the *National Geographic* section. I can't wait. And Rachal, my little sister, though you functioned more like my big sister as I decided to try writing again. Thank you for believing in me, for encouraging me, and convincing me I wasn't wasting my time. I promise you'll be in another one.

Joe, my love, thank you for reading everything, making dinner every night, telling me to take a nap, and meeting all my increasingly bonkers what-ifs with enthusiasm. I'm so grateful to be partners in our happily ever after with you.

And to Tallulah and Coretta: I hope that seeing me achieve my impossible dream shows you that you can claim the space you deserve and chase what you want, without apology. I'll be here cheering you on, always. I love you, my brilliant, beautiful girls.

Turn the page for a sneak peek at Elise Bryant's new novel,
ONE TRUE LOVES.

CHAPTER ONE

My life is not a romance novel.

That's what I'm trying to explain to my best friend, Tessa, as she's going all heart-eyed and swoony over my summer vacation plans. But the girl is having none of it.

"Lenore, you don't understand," she says, throwing herself on her bed like it's a goddamn fainting couch. "I literally begged my parents for this scenario for years. Years! Or it was *at least* in the top five."

I arch my eyebrow at her in the mirror as I add another layer of mascara. I want my eyelashes to be thick and spidery, like Diana Ross's in the seventies. "Top five? That sounds very official. Was it, like, written down?"

"Yes, in fact, but I can recite it from memory." She nods her head all serious and straightens her spine, oblivious that I'm messing with her. "Number one"—she starts pressing a pink-manicured finger into her palm—"summer camp that's conveniently popular with boy band members just trying to live a normal life. Number two, small town that's inexplicably having a monthlong Christmas festival. Number three—"

I throw my hands up. "Okay, I got it, sis. You really don't have to continue—"

"Number three," she cuts me off, narrowing her big brown eyes at me. "European vacation. And on a cruise ship too! The Mediterranean! The summer after graduation! It's like you've hit the romance jackpot! Except instead of money pouring out of the slot machine, it's hearts and cute boys and sunshine and gelato and romantic historic buildings, and, I don't know, maybe even condoms."

A mischievous smile spreads across her face, and I think back to the Tessa I first met last year—mousy and anxious and likely to fall into a conniption if anyone even spoke the word "condom" in her presence. I know this is positive growth or whatever, but man, she can be irritating.

I turn around, rolling my eyes at her. "You've conveniently left out my parents and my sister and my brother, who, oh yeah, I'm sharing a tiny little room with. Ain't no condoms happening anywhere near me this summer."

"Not with that attitude," she snorts. She holds her hands out wide, and her eyes go all unfocused, like my grandma Lenore (yes, we have the same name) when she's talking about what she got on a T.J. Maxx run. "I can see it now. You're in a floppy striped hat and that red high-waisted bathing suit you bought at Target last week—"

"How do you remember that? You weren't even with—"

"Lying outstretched on the pool deck, your skin glowing in the sun. And a handsome stranger with a, like, ten-pack walks by, and is mesmerized by your beauty, and notices you're having trouble reaching the very middle of your back with your sunscreen . . . well, maybe not sunscreen because we don't wear that—"

"Hold up," I say, and she's jerked out of her heart-eyed daze. "What you mean, 'we don't wear that'?"

"I mean, we don't need to wear sunscreen. You know"— she waves vaguely—"melanin."

I blink at her, but no *I'm just fucking with you* smile appears. This girl is serious. "Of course we need to wear sunscreen! Tessa, are you really out here just walking around in the sun unprotected? You know, my uncle Vernel—well, he was Grandma Lenore's next-door neighbor when she still lived in Jacksonville, so basically my uncle. He got a weirdo-looking mole on his back, and when he finally went to the dermatologist, they told him it was cancer. He had to get it removed. It was a whole thing!"

She shrugs and heads for her bookshelf. "Anyway, that's not important right now."

"Uh, skin cancer is important. Actually, I wonder what happened to him—"

"This is a love emergency, Lenore! *Love* is important. Honestly, you need to take this seriously," she scoffs, and now I don't know if she's messing with me. *Love emergency?* Ma'am, I'm going on a family vacation.

"We really don't need to be doing this right now," I say, but she's ignoring me, hands on her hips as she stands in front of her huge bookshelf with the spines arranged in a perfect rainbow. "Research," she mutters to herself, tapping her chin. "She needs to do research."

I shake my head and return my attention to the mirror, putting on a coat of bright coral lipstick that pops against my skin. Mom braided my locs into an intricate updo earlier today, and I tuck a few wayward strands in.

This is how Tessa is. Well, it's a little extra, even for her. Probably just nerves for tonight. And lord knows, I've got them too. Jay still hasn't texted. Maybe I should check one more time. Tessa's too busy to notice and try and stop me, after all . . .

A loud crash stops me from grabbing my phone that I *definitely should not* check one more time. Tessa was, judging by the chaos of fallen books around her, standing on something to reach a book on the top shelf. That wouldn't be too difficult normally, except it is right now considering she's wearing a fluffy, pale pink, tulle ball gown. Because, oh yeah, back up: we are about to leave for prom. Which means we actually really, *really* don't need to be doing this right now.

"Are you okay?!" I jump up, gathering the skirt of my teal lace mermaid dress, and rush to where she's flat on her back, lost in her fluttery confection of an outfit. The only body part I can find is an arm outstretched in the air, holding tight to a paperback book.

"I'm fine!" she insists, batting away fabric so I can see her

4

face. "Fine, fine! This is what I was looking for!"

She smiles slowly, and then presents the book to me, cradling it like it's some sort of holy text. *Anna and the French Kiss*. It's hot pink with a heart and a picture of the Eiffel Tower, i.e., something I wouldn't read if you paid me. Well, okay, maybe if you paid me. But it would have to be enough to buy a Pyer Moss dress straight off the runway or something, and I know that's not what's happening here.

"I need you to read this before you leave, and then"—she chuckles with a knowing smirk—"and then, well, you'll see."

I shake my head. "Get out of here with that. You know I don't have time to read this. What with finals and grad night and graduation. And the kinda big thing happening in, uh"—I check my phone for the time, and also to see if Jay has texted (he hasn't)—"two hours! Here, let me fix your hair. The back is flat now." I gently put the book that I'm no-way-in-hell reading on her nightstand and grab a pick to fluff up her curls. But her arms are crossed and I can feel the scheming energy just wafting off her. "Plus," I add, hoping it'll get her to let that book go, "I'm not even going to Paris."

She dives for her desk, almost losing a fistful of curls in the process, and picks up a piece of paper. "Oh yeah, you're right. This says Marseille. But they're both in France, so how different can they be?"

Is that? I move in for a closer look. *It is.* Our cruise's itinerary. I don't remember giving her that, but okay.

"It's online," she says, reading my mind. "Public knowledge.

Anyone could find it. Not weird at all. Here, let me send you something . . . it's gonna take me a minute to find it though."

Her eyebrows press together as she types and scrolls on her phone, and I use this break in the nonsense to gather the rest of my outfit: gold starburst earrings, metallic pumps with embroidered block heels, a beaded purse that I picked up at an estate sale last week, and my leather jacket draped over my arm in case it gets cold later. I take it all in through Tessa's mirror, confirming what I already know: this look is guh-ood. Two syllables good. I hope it goes well with whatever Jay picked out. We didn't coordinate or anything because it's not like that. Like, not at all. But it would be cool if it worked out anyway.

My phone pings, and I feel this irritating flutter in my chest. Is that him finally? But Tessa chases that stupid thought away.

"Okay, I'm going to preface this by saying this is really old and way cheesy, but if you don't have time to read a book—" She pauses to give me a look that makes it clear what she thinks of my excuse. "—this is the next best thing. It's the first thing I thought of, honestly."

I open up her message to see a YouTube link. The preview shows a movie poster with a blond girl holding a suitcase and standing on her tiptoes for no damn reason.

"What is this? Did it come out before we were born?"

"Yeah, but it's still good. See, this girl goes on a class trip to Rome—which *is* on your itinerary—and there's this pop star that looks just like her, but she's missing—"

"Was she murdered?"

"No, it's not that type of movie. But then she meets this guy named Paolo—"

"Did he murder her?"

"No . . . you know, actually, now that I'm remembering it, she doesn't end up with the Italian guy in the end because he's evil or something. Here, wait, let me send you something else."

My phone pings a few seconds later, with a link to another old-ass movie. A badly photoshopped picture of two more blond girls posing in front of the Italian flag.

"See, this is some white girl shit," I say, before Tessa can even tell me the ridiculous plot of this one. I take a deep breath and toss my phone on the bed. "Nobody's gonna be checking for me when I'm on some boring tour with my family. No European boy is gonna go all ooh-la-la and drive me away on his moped to get baguettes and gelato. Not everyone gets some happy ending all wrapped up in a bow. That stuff is for your movies and your books, but not for real life, Tessa. At least not for me."

All I get is secret prom dates and unanswered texts, I add to myself, swallowing down something tight and sharp in my throat.

Tessa maneuvers around the piles of books, her dress *swish-swish*ing. Her eyebrows press together, and she grabs both of my hands in hers. "That's not true. *Everyone* deserves a happy ending. Especially you, Lenore. You are the kindest, coolest person I know, and the right guy is gonna be drawn to that like a magnet."

This type of Hallmark-movie speak is Tessa's brand. She's

earnest. I'm talking Taylor Swift before she discovered snakes earnest. Like, two a.m., kissing in the rain, alllllll that shit. But she actually *believes* what she's saying, so you can't even hate her for it. And at least she usually uses it for good: these beautiful love stories starring Black girls like us that have earned her a fairly large fan base online—oh, and admission into UCI's creative writing program this fall.

"Whoa, what is going on here?" Our friend Theo is standing in the doorway, an expression of concern on his face as he surveys the mess. His black hair is slicked back, and he looks all debonair in a pinstriped suit, baby-blue button-up, and floral bow tie. "Did you finally snap, Tessa?"

"No, we're planning how Lenore's going to have an epic love affair with an Italian boy named something sexy like Enzo on her cruise this summer," she says matter-of-factly.

Theo looks me up and down, barely holding in his smirk. "Love that for you."

"See?" she says, widening her eyes in her signature *I told you so* face. "Now, can you stop being difficult and just agree to watch this stuff already? We need to get ready!"

As if I'm the one who's been holding us up. Honestly, I'd want to punch her if I didn't love her so much.

I shake my head. "Yeah, whatever."

I want life to be the way Tessa sees it. Really, I do. I want an epic kiss while the credits roll, happily ever after. And having that happen in Italy or Greece or France or Spain—all the stops on this cruise my parents planned—would be magical. I'm not too jaded to imagine myself sipping espresso at a café with a handsome boy. Or long walks hand in hand through mazes of blindingly white buildings, while the sun goes down over the bright blue sea. I mean, come on. My heart isn't completely shriveled up.

But also, what if I don't need all that? What if I've already found my love story, and it just doesn't look all mushy gushy like the stuff of Tessa's love stories? That doesn't mean it's wrong.

I can't say this out loud to her, of course. I can already see their reactions now, the usual ones when I bring up Jay. Tessa's judge-y look, masquerading as concern, and Theo raising his top lip like he's smelled something funky. I don't want to deal with all that right now. And anyway, Theo has moved on from my love woes to his own.

"—and I wasn't sure if I should buy it because the rules are unclear, you know? Who buys the boutonnieres? If both of us do, they might not match. And that could be interesting . . . but then what if he'd rather have a corsage?"

It's weird seeing him like this. Usually he talks like a cross between a robot and a butler from a PBS show, all proper and shit. But right now his tan skin is turning pink, and he's all twitchy and nervous. It's really cute, but he would totally roll his eyes if I said that out loud.

"Why didn't you ask him what he wanted?" Tessa asked, switching her laser focus to him. This kinda stuff is her jam, and I'm glad Theo is taking the spotlight off me.

"Because I didn't want to stress him out about it," Theo

says, adjusting his bow tie for the tenth time. "With . . . everything already going on with his parents? I just want it to be a good night for him. A happy memory."

I feel a pang in my chest, seeing the hurt on Theo's face. Theo's been out to his parents since middle school, and they're all about it. Like, marching in the Pride parade downtown in matching rainbow tutus all about it. But Lavon, his boyfriend, just came out to his parents this year, and it didn't go well. They've pretty much pretended that it didn't happen at all. And when he told them he was going to prom with his serious, long-term boyfriend, they told him he could do what he liked, but they didn't want to hear about it any further.

"Oh, Theo, it will be," I say, pulling him into a tight hug. "Because he'll be with you."

"Theodore," he growls, but he lets me hug him.

"It's almost graduation," I coo as I pat his head. "I think it's about time for you to give that up and accept my nickname, love."

"Never."

The door squeaks, and I look up to see Miles, Tessa's brother, standing there, a lopsided smile taking up his whole face.

"Group hug!" he shouts, crashing into us, as his infectious laugh makes his whole body shake.

"Yes, group hug," Tessa says, and I can hear her sniffling. "I love you all."

"You better suck those tears back in!" I say, pulling her in close. "We got pictures to take."

"Yeah, right now! Mom sent me in here to get you because everyone's here," Miles says, jerking back. "Tessa, you better fix your hair because it's so flat and you don't want to look like a flat head in all these pictures because then Sam might dump you. He's outside, and he told me he's looking for a new girl-friend anyway!"

"These are valid concerns, Miles," I add with a snort. "I was just telling her the same thing about her flat head."

"You jerks!" Tessa says, pushing out of the hug and smacking Miles's shoulder. He runs out of the room in a burst of giggles, and she *swish-swish*es after him, stopping in front of the mirror to fluff up the back of her fro.

Before she makes it outside, though, she collides with Sam, her cinnamon roll of a boyfriend. His blond hair is freshly cut, and he's wearing a black suit and a tie that perfectly matches the blush pink of her dress—a step up from his typical uniform of Hawaiian shirts.

He cradles her cheek, pulls her in close at the waist, and stares at her all wide-eyed and reverently, like she's a treasure.

"You look . . . beautiful," he whispers. "I mean. Wow. Just . . . wow."

Her eyes sparkle and a smile stretches across her face as she moves in for a deep kiss.

Of course she sees the world the way she does. I might believe this one true love, happily ever after bullshit, too, if some guy looked at me like that.

Jay doesn't. But maybe he will? Maybe tonight.

"God, get a room," I snort, sounding a little more harsh than I intend.

"No one better be getting any rooms!" Tessa's dad booms, appearing out of nowhere. Sam's cheeks flame and he takes two giant steps back. "Now come on, y'all," he continues. "Carol is about to have a fit if she doesn't get some pictures for her Facebook soon. I'm warning you, she's got poses planned and everything."

When we get outside, all the families are standing outside like some sort of paparazzi line. Miles, Mr. and Mrs. Johnson (I can never call them Carol and James no matter how much they insist I do that casual shit), Mr. and Mrs. Lim (they prefer those names like normal parents). And then Mom, Dad, and my little sister, Etta, who begged Mom and Dad to come but is sitting on Tessa's porch now with her nose buried in a textbook like the freaky prodigy kid she is.

"That's good, now get together," Mrs. Johnson calls, crouching down low for some reason, getting a good shot of our nostrils. "Do you guys know the Charlie's Angels? That could be fun!"

It goes by in a blur, my brain rushing to catch up with the fact that this big high school tradition is actually happening, right now. I've been feeling this a lot lately, with every simultaneous first and last that pops up with more frequency as graduation day looms closer. You look forward to and dream about all the moments and then, hey, it's here, it's happening, and then, bam, it's over and it will never happen again. The end.

It makes me want to be present and intentional, to reach out and capture these moments so I can store them and save them for later. For when we're all spread out at different colleges and everything I know and love is never the way it is again, just right now.

For about a year when I was little, I used to carry around a gigantic pink Polaroid camera, and whenever I saw anything interesting—a family of ants, a lunch box abandoned on the school lawn, skies that looked like watercolor—I would disappear behind it and *click.* I went through so much film, basically wallpapering my room with the photos, that my mom put me on a weekly limit. Like some old man with a cigarette habit.

"Why do you take so many pictures?" I remember my older brother, Wally, asking me. "They're not even good."

"I'm just memorizing," I said, and he rolled his eyes at me. But really, I still think that's the best word for what I was doing. How else can you make sure the little moments aren't forgotten?

I don't know what happened to that pink camera, and I don't have my own camera now. Only my phone, and it won't do any of this justice.

So, I use my mind to memorize how Theo throws his arms around me and hugs me tighter than he ever has in the four years I've known him. I memorize my mom stepping in for Lavon and straightening out his bow tie, the same way she did when my brother went to his first dance with his boyfriend. I memorize Sam pulling Miles into his picture with Tessa, right in the middle, like it's no big deal. I memorize Dad's sparkling white smile, so big you can see the pink of his gums.

I wish I could know for sure that I've gotten all of it, that I would never forget. I wish I could guarantee that this was not the end of the good, that I could ensure that there's just as much good waiting for me at NYU next year.

And I wish . . . I wish Jay was here for it all. I finally let myself admit it. In my head, of course, because there's no need to bring drama to the buzzy, giddy vibes in the limo when we're finally on our way. I know he's being irritating and not texting me back right now, but that doesn't erase the fluttery feeling I get in my chest when he whispers "Hey, lady" late at night on the phone or the ache in my stomach when we sneak away to the fourth-floor stairwell during conservatory.

I wish Jay was here to hold my hand and let my head rest on his shoulder, like my friends are all doing with their people right now.

But of course, he can't be.